MIRROR
IMAGE

Danielle Steel

Mirror
Image

Delacorte ▤ Press

LARGE PRINT EDITION

This Large Print Edition, prepared especially for Doubleday Direct, Inc., contains the complete unabridged text of the original Publisher's Edition.

Published by
Delacorte Press
Bantam Doubleday Dell Publishing Group, Inc.
1540 Broadway, New York, New York 10036

ISBN 0-7394-0086-X

Manufactured in the United States of America
Published simultaneously in Canada

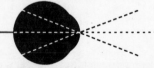

This Large Print Book carries the
Seal of Approval of N.A.V.H.

To the people we love,
The dreams we dream,
The people we become
in loving hands, if we dare.
To courage, to wisdom,
the pursuit of dreams,
and those who help us across the bridge,
beyond our fears, from hope to love.
To great loves lost,
and small ones mourned,
and good times won,
albeit so hard earned.
To my daughters, Beatrix, Samantha, Victoria,
Vanessa, and Zara, may your dreams
be fulfilled swiftly and easily, and your choices wise.
To my sons: Maxx, may you be blessed
and brave, and wise, and kind;
And Nick, who was brave and giving,
and so very, very loved.
May all your dreams come true one day,
and with luck, someday mine.
May you all be greatly loved by those you love.
I love you with all my heart.
Mom.

Chapter 1

The sound of the birds outside was muffled by the heavy brocade curtains of Henderson Manor, as Olivia Henderson pushed aside a lock of long dark hair, and continued her careful inventory of her father's china. It was a warm summer day and, as usual, her sister had gone off somewhere. Her father, Edward Henderson, was expecting a visit from his lawyers. Nestled as they were in Croton-on-Hudson, nearly a three-hour drive from New York, his attorneys came to see him fairly often. Edward Henderson ran all his investments from here, as well as overseeing the steel mills which still bore his name, but which he no longer ran himself. He had retired from business entirely, two years before, in 1911, maintaining all his holdings, but trusting entirely in his attorneys and the men who ran the mills for him. With no sons, he no longer had the interest in business that he once did. His daughters would never run his steel mills. He was only sixty-five, but his health had begun to fail over the past few years, and he preferred viewing the world from his peaceful perch in Croton-on-Hudson. Here, he could observe the world quietly, and it was a healthy, wholesome life for his two daughters. It was not exciting, admittedly, but they were never bored, and they had friends among all the grand families up and down the Hudson.

The Van Cortlandt manor was nearby, as were the Shepards on the old Lyndhurst estate. Helen Shepard's father had been Jay Gould, and he had died twenty years before, and left the extraordinary property to his daughter. She and her husband, Finley Shepard, ran it beautifully, and gave frequent parties for the young people nearby. The Rockefellers had finished building Kykuit in Tarrytown that year, with its splendid gardens and magnificent grounds, and a house which rivaled Edward Henderson's just north of them at Croton-on-Hudson.

Henderson Manor was a handsome home, and one which people came from miles to see, peering through the gates into the lovely gardens. They could barely see the house from where they stood, shielded as it was by tall trees, and little turns in the road which led to the formal driveway. The house itself sat high on a cliff, looking over the Hudson River. And Edward liked to sit in his study for hours, watching the world drift by, remembering times past, old friends, and the days when his life had moved a great deal more quickly . . . taking over his father's mills in the 1870's . . . being instrumental in the many industrial changes at the end of the last century. His life had been so busy then. When he was younger, his life had been so different. Edward Henderson had married when he was young, and lost a wife and a young son to diphtheria. After that he had been alone for many years, until Elizabeth came along. She had been everything any man could ever dream of, a bright shining streak of light, a comet in a summer sky, so ephemeral, so dazzling, so beautiful, and so much too quickly gone. They were married within the year they met. She was nineteen, and he was in his early forties. By twenty-one, she was gone. Much to Edward's horror, she had died in childbed. After her death, he had worked even harder than usual, driving himself until he was numb. He had left his daughters to the care of his housekeeper and their nurses, but finally, he realized that he had a responsibility to them. It was then that he began building Henderson Manor. He wanted them to have healthy, wholesome lives, out of the city. New York was no place for children in 1903. They had been ten when he'd actually moved them, and now they were twenty. He kept the house in the city and worked there, but he came up to see them as often as he could. At first only on weekends and then, as he fell in love with it, he began spending more time on the Hudson, rather than in New York, or Pittsburgh, or Europe. His heart was there in Croton with his daughters, as he watched them grow, and little by little his own life began moving more slowly. He loved being with them, and now he never left them anymore. For the past two years, he had gone absolutely nowhere. His health had begun to fail three or four years before. His heart was a problem, but only when he worked too hard, or let things upset him, or got terribly angry, which he seldom did now. He was happy in Croton with his daughters.

It had been twenty years since their mother had died in the spring of 1893, on a warm balmy day that had appeared to him to be God's ultimate betrayal. He had been waiting outside, filled with such pride, and so much excitement. He had never dreamed it could happen to him again. His first wife and infant son had died in an epidemic of diphtheria more than a dozen years before. But this time, losing Elizabeth had almost killed him. At forty-five, it was a near mortal blow to him, and he almost couldn't bear going on without her. She had died in their home in New York, and at first he felt her presence there. But after a while, he came to hate the emptiness of it, and he had hated being there. He had traveled off and on for months after that, but avoiding the house meant avoiding the two little girls Elizabeth had left him. And he couldn't bring himself to sell the house his father had built, and that he had grown up in. A traditionalist to the core, he felt an obligation to maintain it for his children. He had closed it eventually, and it had been two years since he'd been there. Now that he lived in Croton full-time, he never missed it. Neither the house, nor New York, nor the social life he'd left there.

And as the summer sounds droned on, Olivia continued her painstaking inventory of the china. She had long sheets of paper on which she wrote in her meticulous hand, making note of what they needed to replace, and what had to be ordered. Sometimes she sent one of the servants to the house in town to bring something up to them, but for the most part, the city house was closed, and they never went there. She knew her father didn't like it. Her father's health was frail, and, like him, she was happy here in their quiet life in Croton-on-Hudson. She had actually spent very little time in New York since she was a child, except for the brief time two years before, when her father had taken them to New York, to present them to society and all his friends. She had found it interesting, but truly exhausting. She was overwhelmed by the parties, the theater, the constant social demands made on them. She had felt as though she were onstage the entire time, and she hated the attention. It was Victoria who had thrived on it, and who had been in a state of total gloom when they returned to Croton at Christmas. Olivia had been relieved to return to her books, their home, her horses, her peaceful walks high on the cliff which led her sometimes to neighboring farms. She loved riding here, and listening to the sounds of spring, watching winter melt slowly away from them, seeing the splendor of the turning leaves in October. She loved taking care of her father's house for him, and had since she was a very young girl, with the help of Alberta Peabody, the woman who had raised them. She was "Bertie" to them, and the closest to a mother the Henderson girls had ever known. Her eyes were poor, but her mind was sharp, and she could have told the two young women apart in the dark, with her eyes closed.

She came to check on Olivia now, and asked her how far she had gotten. She didn't have the patience, or the eyes, to do this kind of minute work anymore, and she was always grateful when Olivia did it for her. Olivia carefully checked the embroidery, the crystal, the linens. She kept an eye on everything, and she loved doing it, unlike Victoria, who detested all things domestic. Victoria was, in every possible way, different from her sister.

"Well, have they broken all our plates, or will we still be able to manage Christmas dinner?" Bertie smiled as she held up a glass of ice-cold lemonade and a plate of gingersnaps fresh out of the oven. Alberta Peabody had spent twenty years caring for the two girls she had come to think of as "her children." They had become hers at birth, and she had never left them for a day, not since their mother had died, and she had first looked into Olivia's eyes and realized instantly how much she loved her.

She was a short, round woman, with white hair in a small bun at the back of her head. She had an ample bosom where Olivia had rested her head through most of her childhood. She had comforted them whenever they needed it, and whenever their father wasn't there, which had been often when they were young. For years, he had grieved silently for their mother and kept his distance. But he had warmed toward them in recent years, and softened considerably since his health had begun to fail and he had retired from business. He had a weak heart, which he attributed to the shock and grief of losing two young wives, and the aggravations of modern business. He was far happier now that he was running things from here, and everything could be filtered for him through his attorneys.

"We need soup plates, Bertie," Olivia reported solemnly, brushing the long dark hair back again, totally unaware of her startling beauty. She had creamy white skin, huge dark blue eyes, and thick shining black hair the color of a raven. "We need fish plates too. I'll order them from Tiffany next week. We must tell the girls in the kitchen to be more careful." Bertie nodded, smiling up at her. Olivia could have been married by now, she could have had her own soup plates to inventory, instead she was still here, and perfectly at ease, taking care of her father and his house, and all his people. Olivia had no desire to go anywhere. She never even thought of it. She was happy right here at Henderson Manor. Unlike Victoria, who talked constantly about places halfway around the world, or at the very least in Europe. She glowered every time she thought of the house they were wasting in New York, and the fun they might have had there.

Olivia looked down at Bertie then with a childlike grin. She was wearing a pale blue silk dress, which reached almost to her ankles, and it looked like a piece of summer sky wrapped around her as she stood there. She had had the dress copied from a magazine, and made by a local seamstress. It was a Poiret design, and it looked lovely on her. It was Olivia who always selected and designed their dresses. Victoria didn't really care. She let Olivia choose them, particularly, as she put it, since Olivia was her older sister.

"The cookies are awfully good today, aren't they? Father will love them." Olivia had ordered them especially for him, and John Watson, his principal attorney. "I suppose I should organize a tray for them, or have you

9

already done it?" The two women exchanged a smile, born of years of sharing responsibilities and duties. And slowly, over the past few years, Olivia had grown from child to girl, to young woman, and mistress of her father's home. Olivia was very much in control of her surroundings, and Bertie knew it. She respected that, and most of the time deferred now to Olivia's opinions, although she thought nothing of opposing her, or scolding her, when she went out in the pouring rain, or did something childishly foolish, which she was still sometimes wont to do even at twenty. But nowadays Bertie found that less worrisome than refreshing. Olivia was so serious and responsible, that it did her good sometimes to forget all that she was supposed to be doing.

"I've set the tray up for you, but I told Cook you'll want to order it yourself at the last minute," Bertie told her.

"Thank you." Olivia came down the ladder gracefully, and kissed the old woman's cheek as she wrapped her long, elegant arms around her. Olivia lay her head on Bertie's shoulder for an instant, like a child, and then, after kissing her cheek affectionately again, she hurried off to the kitchen to see to the tray for her father and his lawyer.

She ordered a pitcher of lemonade, a large plate of cookies for both of them, and small watercress and cucumber sandwiches, with paper-thin slices of tomatoes from their garden. There was sherry for them as well, and stronger spirits if they preferred them. Having grown up in her father's company, Olivia was not a girl who shrank from the thought of men drinking whiskey, or smoking cigars, in fact she liked the smell of them, as did her sister.

When she'd approved the linens and the silver tray Bertie had set out, she left the kitchen, and found her father in the library. The curtains were drawn to keep the room cool, they were deep red brocade with heavy fringe, and Olivia adjusted them instinctively as she glanced at her father over her shoulder.

"How are you feeling today, Father? It's terribly hot, isn't it?"

"I rather like it." He smiled proudly at her, well aware of her outstanding domestic talents. He often said that if it weren't for Olivia, he couldn't have run his home, or certainly not as smoothly. He had even jokingly said that he was afraid one of the Rockefellers might try and marry her, just so she could run Kykuit. He had been over to see it recently, and it was a spectacular home that John D. Rockefeller had built. It had every possible modern amenity, including telephones, central heating, and a generator in the carriage barn, and Olivia's father had teased that it made their home look like a bumpkin's cottage, which was hardly the case, but Kykuit was certainly their grandest neighbor.

"This heat is good for my old bones," he said comfortably, lighting a cigar, as he waited for his lawyer. "Where's your sister?" he asked casually. It was always easy to find Olivia somewhere in the house, making lists, writing notes to the staff, checking on something that needed to be fixed, or arranging flowers for her father's table. Victoria was a great deal more difficult to keep track of.

"I think she went to play tennis at the Astors'," Olivia said vaguely, with no clear idea of where she was, but only a vague suspicion.

"Typical of her," he said with a rueful grin at his older daughter. "I believe the Astors are in Maine for the summer," as were most of their neighbors. The Hendersons had gone to Maine in previous summers too, and Newport, Rhode Island, but Edward Henderson no longer liked leaving Croton, even in the hottest of summers.

"I'm sorry, Father." Olivia blushed in embarrassment at the lie she'd told on behalf of her sister. "I thought perhaps they were back from Bal Harbor."

"I'm sure you did." He looked amused. "And God only knows where your sister is, or what mischief she's been up to." But they both knew that her vagaries were fairly harmless. She was an individual, a person on her own, and full of spirit and determination. She was as independent as their late mother had been, and in some ways, Edward Henderson had always suspected that his younger daughter was faintly eccentric. But as long as she didn't indulge it too excessively, it was something he could tolerate, and she could come to no great harm here. The worst she could do was fall out of a tree, get heat prostration walking miles to her nearest friend's, or swim a little too far down the river. The pleasures were all quite genteel here. Victoria had no romances in the neighborhood, no young men in hot pursuit, although several of the young Rockefellers and Van Cortlandts had certainly shown considerable interest in her. But everyone was well behaved, and even her father knew that Victoria was actually far more intellectual than romantic.

"I'll look for her after I leave you," Olivia

said quietly, but neither of them were particularly concerned, as the tray from the kitchen was brought in, and she told the kitchen boy where to put it.

"You'll need another glass, my dear," her father instructed her as he relit his cigar and thanked the boy whose name he never remembered.

Olivia knew all of the people who worked for them, she knew their names, their histories, their parents, their sisters, their children. She knew their foibles and their strengths, and whatever mischief they occasionally got into. She was indeed the Mistress of Henderson Manor, perhaps even more than her own mother would have been, had she lived. In some ways, Olivia suspected that their mother had been far more like her sister.

"Is John bringing someone with him?" Olivia looked surprised. Her father's attorney usually came alone, except when there was some problem at the mill, and she had heard nothing about it this time if there was. Usually, their father shared that kind of information with them. All of that would be theirs one day, although more than likely, the girls would sell the mills, unless they married men who were capable of running them, but Edward considered that less than likely.

Her father sighed over his cigar in answer to her question. "Unfortunately, my dear, John is bringing someone today. I'm afraid I've come too far in this world. I've outlived two wives, a son, my doctor last year, most of my friends in the last decade, and now John Watson tells me he's thinking of retiring. He's bringing along a man who's recently joined his firm, and whom he seems to think quite a lot of."

"But John's not that old," Olivia looked surprised, and almost as disturbed as her father, "and neither are you, so stop talking like that." She knew he had begun to feel ancient since he'd been unwell, and even more so since he'd retired.

"I am ancient. You have no idea what it's like when everyone around you starts disappearing," he said, scowling and thinking of the new attorney he didn't want to meet that afternoon.

"No one is going anywhere, and neither is John for the moment, I'm sure," she said reassuringly, as she poured him a small glass of sherry and handed it to him, with the plate of fresh ginger cookies. He took one, and looked extremely pleased as he looked at her.

"Perhaps he won't go after all, after he tastes these cookies. I must say, Olivia, you get them to make miracles in that kitchen."

"Thank you." She leaned over and kissed him, and he looked up at her with all the pleasure he felt each time he saw her. She looked remarkably comfortable and cool on such a hot day, and she took one of the gingersnaps herself and sat down next to him as they waited for John Watson. "So who's the new man?" she asked curiously after a few minutes. She knew that Watson was a year or two younger than her father, but it still seemed young to retire, to her, and he had always seemed very youthful. But perhaps he was wise, bringing someone new into their affairs sooner rather than later. "Have you met him before?"

"Not yet. This will be the first time. John says he's extremely good at what he does, mostly business affairs, and he's done some estate matters for some of the Astors. He came to John's office from an excellent firm, with a very good recommendation."

"Why did he change?" she asked, intrigued. She liked hearing about her father's business. Victoria did too, but she was far more hotheaded in her opinions. Sometimes the three of them had rare go-arounds about some issues of politics or point of business, but all three of them thoroughly enjoyed it. Perhaps because he had no son, Edward Henderson loved discussing intelligent matters with his daughters.

"According to John, the new man, Dawson, had a hard blow last year. Actually, it made me feel sorry for him, and I think that's why I let John bring him . . . it's the sort of thing I'm afraid I understand rather too well." He smiled sadly at her. "He lost his wife last year on the *Titanic*. She was a daughter of Lord Arnsborough's, and I think she'd gone home to visit her sister. Damn shame she came back on the *Titanic*. Nearly lost his boy too. Apparently, they got him off in one of the last lifeboats. It was already too full, and she put another child in her place, and said she'd come on the next one. There was no next one, and she didn't get in the last of the lifeboats. I gather he left the firm he was with, took the boy, and spent the year in Europe. It only happened sixteen months ago, and I think he's only been with Watson since May or June. Poor devil. John says he's very good, but a bit gloomy. He'll come out of it, we all do. He'll have to, for the boy's sake." It reminded him all too much of when he'd lost Elizabeth, although his loss had been due to complications of childbirth and not a disaster of the magnitude of the *Titanic*. But still, it had been disastrous to him, and he knew only too well how the man felt. Edward Henderson sat lost in thought for a moment, as did Olivia, digesting what her father had said, and both of them looked startled when they looked up and suddenly saw John Watson standing in the doorway.

"Well, how did you get in unannounced? Have you taken to climbing in the windows?" Edward Henderson laughed at his old friend, as he stood to greet him, and crossed the room looking extremely healthy. He was in good form these days, thanks to Olivia's constant care, and in spite of his complaints about how badly he was aging.

"No one pays any attention to me at all," John Watson laughed. He was tall, and had a shock of white hair, much like Olivia's father, who was also tall and aristocratic, and had once had the same shining black hair as his daughters. The blue eyes were the same too, and they came alive now as he chatted animatedly with John Watson. The two men had known each other since school. Edward had actually been the closest friend of John's slightly older brother. He had been dead for years, and Edward and John had long since become fast friends, and associates in all of the Henderson legal matters.

Seeing them engaged in earnest conversation almost at once, Olivia glanced at the tray again, to see that all was in order, and prepared to leave the room, and then she turned and was startled to almost walk into the arms of Charles Dawson. It was odd seeing him there, after they had just talked about him, and embarrassing to know so much of his loss, and his grief, without ever having met him. As she looked at him, he seemed very handsome and somewhat austere, and she thought she had never seen sadder eyes on anyone. They were like dark pools of green, almost the color of seawater. But he managed a small smile when her father introduced them. And as they spoke, she saw something more than just tragedy about him. There was great kindness in his eyes, and gentleness, it almost made her want to reach out and console him.

"How do you do," he said politely, shaking her hand, and seeming to take every inch of her in with interest. He didn't look her over improperly, although he was certainly aware of how beautiful she was, but he seemed mostly curious about her.

"May I offer you some lemonade?" she asked, feeling suddenly shy, and hiding behind her comfortable duties. "Or would you prefer sherry? I'm afraid Father prefers sherry, even on days as hot as this one."

"Lemonade would be fine." He smiled at her again, and the two older men went back to their conversation.

She gave John Watson a glass of lemonade as well, and all three men gladly accepted the gingersnap cookies. And then, having fulfilled her responsibilities to them, Olivia quietly withdrew and closed the doors behind her. But as she left the room, something about the look in Charles Dawson's eyes haunted her, or maybe it was just because she knew his story from her father. She wondered how old his little boy was, and how Charles managed without a wife, or perhaps he had someone in his life by now. She tried to shake off her thoughts of him, it was ridiculous to be worrying about one of her father's attorneys, and quite inappropriate in fact, she scolded herself, as she turned quickly to go back to the kitchen, and nearly collided with her father's under-chauffeur. He was a boy of sixteen who had worked in the stables for years, but knew a great deal more about cars than he did about horses. And since

her father had a great love for the modern ma-
chines, and had bought one of the earliest cars
while they still lived in New York, Petrie, the
stable boy, had made a rapid and pleasing tran-
sition.

"What is it, Petrie? What's wrong?" she
asked matter-of-factly. He looked totally di-
sheveled, and completely flustered.

"I have to see your father right away,
miss," he said, obviously near tears, as she tried
to lead him away from the library before he
disturbed her father in his meeting.

"I'm afraid you can't. He's busy. Is there
something I can help you with?" she said gently
but firmly.

He hesitated, and then looked around, as
though afraid someone would hear him. "It's
the Ford." He looked terrified as he told her.
"It's been stolen." His eyes were round with
tears, he knew what would happen to him when
word got out. He would lose the best job he
could ever have, and he couldn't understand
how it had happened.

"Stolen?" She looked as startled as he did.
"How is that possible? How could someone
come on the property and just take it, and no
one notice?"

"I don't know, miss. And I seen it just this

morning. I was cleaning it. It was all bright and shiny like the day your father bought it. I just left the garage door open for a little while, to air the place out, because it gets so hot, you know, with the sun directly on it, and half an hour later, it was gone. Just gone." His eyes filled with tears again, and Olivia put a gentle hand on his shoulder. There was something about his story which had struck her.

"What time would that have been, Petrie? Do you remember?" Her voice and her manner were extremely calm, most unusually so for a girl of twenty, but she was used to handling minor crises on the estate daily. And this one had a particular ring to it.

"It was eleven-thirty, miss. I know it exactly." Olivia had last seen her sister at eleven. And the Ford he was so distraught over was the car her father had bought the year before for staff purposes, errands into town, missions to be carried out in something other than the Cadillac Tourer he was driven in whenever he left Henderson Manor.

"You know, Petrie," Olivia said quietly, "I think you ought to let the dust settle for a moment. It's entirely possible that some member of the staff might have borrowed it for an errand, without thinking to mention it to you.

Perhaps the gardener, I asked him to look at some rosebushes for me over at the Shepards', perhaps he forgot to tell you." She was suddenly certain that the car hadn't been stolen, and she needed to stall him. If he told her father, then the police would be called, and that would be terribly embarrassing. She couldn't let that happen.

"But Kittering can't drive, miss. He wouldn't have taken the Ford to go look at your roses. He'd take one of the horses, or his bicycle, not the Ford, miss."

"Well, perhaps someone else is driving it, but I don't think we should tell my father just yet. Besides, he's busy anyway, we'll wait until dinnertime, shall we? And we'll see if anyone brings it back. I feel sure they will. Now, would you like some lemonade and cookies in the kitchen?" She had led him slowly in that direction, and he seemed slightly mollified, though still very nervous. He was terrified he'd lose his job when her father found out that he'd let the car get stolen right out of the garage. But Olivia continued to reassure him as she poured him a glass of lemonade, and handed him a plate of the irresistible cookies, as the cook watched them.

She promised to check in with Petrie later

in the day, and made him promise not to whisper a word of it to her father in the meantime, and then with a wink at the cook, she hurried out of the kitchen, hoping to avoid Bertie, whom she saw advancing on her from the distance. But Olivia was faster than all of them. She slipped out a pair of long French doors into the side garden, and sighed as she felt the crushing heat of the NORTHERN New York summer. This was why people went to Newport and Maine. It was unbearable here in the summer and no one stayed, if they could possibly help it. By fall, it would be lovely again. And in spring, when the endless winter finally came to a close, it was always idyllic. But winters were brutal, and summers were more so. Most people went to the city in winter, and the seashore in summer, but not her father anymore. They stayed here in Croton-on-Hudson all year round now.

Olivia wished she had time to go swimming that afternoon, as she walked absentmindedly down one of her favorite paths toward the back of the property, where there was a beautiful, hidden garden. She loved to come riding here, and there was a narrow gate to their neighbor's property which she would often slip through in order to enjoy her ride on his property as well, but no one minded. They all shared these hills like one happy family, and the good friends they were who had built here.

In spite of the heat, she walked a long way that afternoon, no longer thinking of the lost car, but oddly enough, she found herself thinking of Charles Dawson, and the story her father had told her. How awful to lose your wife so tragically, and so dramatically. He must have been sick with worry when he first heard. She could just imagine it, and she sat down on a log finally, still thinking of him, and as she did, she heard the rumble of a motorcar in the distance. She sat very still for a minute then, listening, and looked up to see the missing Ford scraping through the narrow wooden gate at the back of their property, with a sudden grating noise, as the driver took the rubber and the paint off the side of the running boards just to get through it. But despite the obviously tight fit, the car didn't slow for a moment. Olivia watched in astonishment as the car chugged into full view, and her sister grinned at her from behind the wheel, and waved. And in the hand that Victoria waved at her was a cigarette. She was smoking.

Olivia didn't move from where she sat, she just stared at her and shook her head, as

Victoria stopped the car and continued to smile at her, and blew a cloud of smoke in her direction.

"Do you realize that Petrie wanted to tell Father that the car was stolen, and he would have called the police if I'd let him?"

Olivia was not surprised to see her there, but she wasn't happy either. She was all too familiar with her younger sister's exploits, and the two women sat looking at each other, the one perfectly calm, and obviously not pleased, the other greatly amused at her own indiscretion. But the most remarkable thing of all was that except for the difference of expression, and the fact that Victoria's hair seemed looser and more windblown than Olivia's, the two women were totally identical. For each of them, it was like looking in the mirror. The same eyes, the same mouths, the same cheekbones and hair, right down to the same gestures. There were infinitesimal differences about each of them, and there was an aura of easygoing good nature about Victoria that more than bordered on mischief, and yet one would have been hard-pressed to tell them apart if one had to. Their father often made mistakes when coming upon one of them alone in a room or on the property somewhere, and the servants mistook them constantly. Their friends in school, when they'd gone and hadn't been tutored at home, had absolutely never been able to tell them apart, and their father had eventually decided to have them taught at home, because they caused so much consternation at school and attracted so much attention. They switched places whenever they chose, tormented their teachers mercilessly, or at least Victoria did, or so Olivia claimed. They had a wonderful time, but their father seriously doubted that they were getting an education. But being tutored at home had left them isolated, and with only each other's friendship. They had both missed going to school, but their father was emphatic about it. He was not going to have them behaving like circus freaks, and if the school couldn't control them, Mrs. Peabody and their tutors could. In fact, Mrs. Peabody was the only living person who unfailingly knew exactly who was who. She could tell them apart anywhere, back, front, even before they spoke. And she also knew the single secret from which one could distinguish them, one small freckle which Olivia had at the top of her right palm, and Victoria had identically and equally minutely on her left one. Their father knew about it too, of course, although none of their friends did, but it was too much trouble to remember to look for it. It was easier to just question them, and hope they were telling the truth about their identities, which they usually did, now that they were older. They were totally identical, mirror twins, and had caused a furor all around them since birth, right up till the present.

It had turned their presentation to society in New York into a total uproar two years before, and it was why their father had insisted on bringing them home that year even before Christmas. It was just too difficult having that much attention everywhere they went. He felt they were being treated as curiosities and it was far too exhausting. Victoria was crushed to have to come home, although Olivia didn't mind it. She had been ready to come back to Croton. But Victoria had been chafing at their life ever since, and all she ever seemed to talk about anymore was how incredibly boring life was on the Hudson. She wondered how any of them could bear it.

The only other subject that truly inspired Victoria was that of women's suffrage. It was the fire with which she burned, the passion which lit her every moment. And Olivia was sick to death of hearing about it. All Victoria seemed to talk about anymore was Alice Paul, who had organized the march in Washington that April, where dozens of women were arrested, forty were injured, and it took a cavalry troop to restore order. Olivia had also heard far too much about Emily Davison, who had been killed two months before, when she ran in front of the King's horse at the derby, in England; and then there were the Pankhursts, *mère et filles*, who were busy wreaking havoc in the name of women's rights in England. Just talking about them made Victoria's eyes dance, and Olivia roll hers in boredom. But now Olivia sat waiting for her sister's excuses and explanations.

"So did they call the police?" Victoria asked, looking amused, and not in the least apologetic.

"No, they did not call the police," Olivia said sternly. "I bribed Petrie with lemonade and cookies and told him to wait till dinner. But they should have. I should have let them. I knew it was you." She tried to look angry, but something in her eyes said she wasn't, and Victoria knew it.

"How did you know it was me?" Victoria looked delighted, and not contrite for a single instant.

"I felt it, you wretch. One of these days they will call the police on you over something, and I'll let them."

"No, you won't," Victoria said confidently, with a glint in her eyes that would have reminded their father of their mother. Physically Victoria was the portrait of Olivia, right down to the blue silk dress she was wearing.

Olivia laid her sister's clothes out for her every morning, and Victoria always put them on without question. She loved being a twin, always had, they both did. It suited them perfectly. And it had gotten Victoria out of every scrape in her life. Olivia was always either willing to make excuses for her, or even to trade places with her, either to get her out of a jam, or when they were children, just because sometimes it was fun to do it. Their father had often lectured them about being responsible, and not taking advantage of their unusual circumstances, but sometimes it was hard not to. Everything about them seemed unusual. They were closer than two people could ever have been. And sometimes, to each of them, it almost seemed as though they were the same person. And yet, in so many ways, deep inside, they each knew they were very different. Victoria was bolder, and both far more mischievous and more adventuresome. She had always been the one who'd gotten into trouble. She was so fascinated by a broader world than Olivia was. Olivia was happier to stay at home, and let her boundaries be those set by family, home, and tradition. Victoria wanted to fight for women's rights, she wanted to demonstrate and speak. She thought marriage was barbaric, and unnecessary for truly independent women. Olivia thought all of that was quite crazy, but she also thought it was only a passing fancy of her sister's. There had been others, political movements that had fascinated her, religious ideals, intellectual concepts she had read about. Olivia was far more down to earth, and much less willing to ride into battle for obscure causes. Her world was a great deal smaller. And yet, to the naked eye, and the uninitiated, they appeared to be one and the same, even to those who knew them.

"So when did you learn to drive?" Olivia asked, tapping her foot, as Victoria laughed from the car. She had just tossed the last of her cigarette into the dirt near where her sister was sitting. Olivia always played the role of the stern older sister. She was eleven minutes older than Victoria, but it was those eleven minutes that had made all the difference. And in sadder moments, when they bared their souls, Victoria had long since confessed to her twin that she felt she was the one who had killed their mother.

"You didn't kill her," Olivia had said firmly, when they were only children. "God did."

"He did *not!*" Victoria had defended Him, in outrage. And Mrs. Peabody had been appalled when she discovered what the argument was about, and later on she had explained that childbirth can be very difficult at best, and having twins is something superhuman that only angels should attempt. And clearly, their mother had been an angel, had deposited them on earth with their father who loved them so much, and had returned to Heaven. It settled the question of blame, at the time, but Victoria had always secretly felt that she had in fact killed their mother, and Olivia knew it, and nothing she had ever said in all their twenty years had ever changed that.

Neither of them were thinking of that now, as Olivia questioned Victoria about her driving. "I taught myself last winter." Victoria shrugged in amusement.

"Taught *yourself*? How?"

"I just took the keys and tried it. I banged

the car up a little the first few times, but Petrie never figured it out, he kept thinking that other people had run into him when he'd been in town and left it parked." She looked pleased with herself and Olivia forced herself to scowl at her, in order not to laugh, but Victoria knew her better. "Stop looking at me like that. It's a damn useful thing to know. I can run you into town anytime you like now."

"Or into a tree more likely." Olivia refused to be mollified. Her sister could have killed herself tooling around the countryside in a car she really didn't know how to drive. It was crazy. "And your smoking is disgusting." But at least that she'd known about it for a while. She had found a package of Fatimas in their dresser that winter, and been horrified. But when she mentioned it, Victoria only laughed and shrugged, and refused to comment.

"Don't be so old-fashioned," Victoria said amiably. "If we lived in London or Paris, you'd be smoking too, just to be fashionable, and you know it."

"I know nothing of the sort, Victoria Henderson. It's a revolting habit for a lady, and *you* know it. So where were you?"

Victoria hesitated for a long moment, while Olivia waited. She was expecting an answer, and Victoria always told her the truth. The two had no secrets, and the few times they did, the other always instinctively knew the truth. It was as though they each always knew what the other was thinking.

"Confess," Olivia said sternly, and Victoria suddenly looked much younger than twenty.

"All right. I went to a meeting of the National American Women's Suffrage Association in Tarrytown. Alice Paul was there, she came especially to organize the meeting, and see about setting up a group right here on the Hudson. The president of NAWSA herself, Anna Howard Shaw, was supposed to be there, but she couldn't make it."

"Oh for God's sake, Victoria, what are you doing? Father will be calling the police if you get yourself into demonstrations or anything of the sort. More than likely, you'll be arrested, and Father will have to bail you out," she said in sudden outrage, but Victoria did not look discouraged by the prospect, on the contrary, she seemed to like it.

"It would be worth it, Ollie. She was absolutely inspirational. You should come next time."

"Next time, I'm tying you to the bedpost. And if you steal the car again for nonsense like that, I'll let Petrie call the police, and I'll tell them who did it."

"No, you won't. Come on, hop in. I'll drive you back to the garage."

"Great. Now you'll get us both in trouble. Thank you very much, my darling sister."

"Don't be such a stiff. This way, no one will know which one of us it is." As always, their being so totally identical was an excellent cover. No one ever knew which one did anything, which served Victoria's purposes better than her sister's, who rarely needed a scapegoat.

"They'd know, if they had any brains," Olivia grumbled as she got in cautiously, and Victoria roared off across the bumpy back road, while Olivia complained loudly about her driving. Victoria offered her a cigarette then, and as Olivia was about to read her the riot act again, she suddenly started to laugh instead at the absurdity of the situation. It was hopeless to try and control Victoria, and Olivia knew it, as Victoria drove the car right into the garage and almost ran over Petrie. He stared at them with his mouth open, as they both got out in unison, both thanked him solemnly and Victoria apologized for the minor damage.

"But I thought . . . I . . . . when did you

. . . I mean . . . yes, Miss . . . thank you . . . Miss Olivia . . . Miss Victoria . . . Miss . . .” He had no idea which was which, who had done what, and had no intention of trying to find out either. All he had to do was replace the rubber on the running board and touch up the paint now. At least the car hadn’t been stolen after all. And looking very dignified, the two young women walked back to the house arm in arm, and up the front steps, as they began to giggle.

“You really are awful, you know,” Olivia scolded her. “The poor thing thought Dad was going to kill him over it. You’re going to end up in jail one day, I’m sure of it.”

“So am I,” said Victoria with total unconcern, as she gave her sister a squeeze. “But maybe you’ll switch with me for a month or two and I can go out and get some air, and go to some meetings. How does that sound?”

“Disgusting. My days of covering for you are over,” Olivia said, wagging a finger at her, but loving her more than ever. She loved being with her. Her twin was her best friend, and like the other side of her own soul. They knew each other better than any two people could ever know anyone, and Olivia was at her happiest, they both were, when they were together. Although Victoria certainly seemed to spend enough time going off on her own and getting into mischief.

The two girls were just walking through the main hall, talking and laughing, as the library door opened and the three men walked into the hall, still talking about their own plans and decisions. And as they saw them, the two girls fell silent, and Olivia immediately saw Charles again, and watched him, as he stared at both of them, totally startled and confused by what he was seeing. He looked from one to the other repeatedly, as though trying to derive an explanation in his own mind for two women so totally identical, and so beautiful, and yet it was as though he sensed a difference between them. His eyes were riveted on Victoria, with her hair slightly more windblown than Olivia's, her dress identical, yet somehow more easily worn, there was something irreverent and shocking about her. And yet, to the naked eye, one couldn't see how outrageous she was, but one could sense it.

"Oh my," Edward Henderson said, smiling as he watched Charles' reaction. "Did I forget to warn you?"

"I'm afraid you did, sir," Charles Dawson said, blushing, peeling his eyes off of Victoria, and glancing at Olivia again in confusion, and then back at their father. They were used to it, and were amused, but he obviously wasn't.

"Merely an optical illusion, don't worry about it," Edward Henderson teased him. He liked Charles. He seemed to be a good man. And they had had a very good session, full of bright new ideas, and ways to improve his businesses, and protect his investments. "It must have been the sherry." He grinned at the younger man, and Charles Dawson laughed, suddenly looking boyish. He was thirty-six years old, but in the past year, he had come to look so serious that his friends said he looked suddenly much older. And now, he looked like a boy again as he stared in confused disbelief at the two beauties before him. And even more confusingly, they moved toward him in unison, unconscious of how totally their movements mirrored each other. They each shook hands with him, and Edward introduced Olivia again, and Victoria for the first time, and they both laughed, and pointed out to their father that he had gotten it wrong, which made Charles laugh even more.

"Does he do that often?" he asked, feeling more at ease with them than he had a moment before, though still quite dazzled. It would be impossible not to.

"All the time, though we don't always tell him," Victoria answered, meeting his eyes squarely. Charles seemed fascinated by her, as though he could sense something unusual about her. In the subtlest of ways, she was more sensual than her sister, yet the clothes, the look, the hair were the same, but the inner workings weren't.

"When they were very young," Edward explained, "we used to put different-colored hair ribbons in their hair, to identify them. It worked perfectly, and then one day, we discovered that the little monsters had learned to take off their hair ribbons and tie them again, very carefully, to confuse us. They would trade places that way, and it went on for months before we discovered it. They were quite dreadful as children," he said, with obvious pride and affection. Despite his dislike for the public stir they caused whenever he took them out, he adored them. They had been the final gift of a woman he had loved with his entire soul, and he had never loved anyone again after her, except her daughters.

"Are they better behaved now?" Charles asked, still amused by them, and the shock they had caused him. He had had absolutely no warning that there even were twins, neither from Edward Henderson, nor John Watson.

"They're only slightly better now," Edward said grudgingly, and they all laughed, and then he scowled at both of them, as though issuing a warning. "But you'd better behave yourselves, you two. These two gentlemen tell me that it's necessary to go to New York for a month or so, in order to take care of some of my business, and if you can manage not to turn the town on its ear this time, I'll take you with me. But any nonsense from either of you," he said, wishing he could tell which one of them was Victoria, but he couldn't, "and I'll pack you right back here with Bertie."

"Yes, sir," Olivia said quietly with a smile, knowing that the warning was not meant for her, but for her sister. Suspecting that he wasn't quite sure at the moment which of them he was addressing, Olivia could always tell when he wasn't certain.

But Victoria wasn't making any promises: her eyes were dancing at the prospect of a month in the city. "Are you serious?" she asked, wide-eyed with delight.

"About sending you back?" he blustered. "Absolutely."

"No, about New York, I mean." She looked from her father to the lawyers, and they were all smiling.

"Apparently," her father answered. "It could even be two months, if they don't do their jobs right, and dally around once we get there."

"Oh please, Daddy," Victoria said, clapping her hands and doing a little pirouette on one heel and then grabbing her sister by the shoulders. "Think of it! New York, Ollie! New York!" She was beside herself with joy and excitement, and it made her father feel guilty when he thought of how isolated they were here. They were of an age where they belonged in the city now, meeting people, and finding husbands. But he hated the thought of them leaving him forever, particularly Olivia. She was so helpful to him, she did so much for him. What would he ever do without her? But he was worrying prematurely. They hadn't even packed their bags and gone to the city yet, and he already imagined them married, and himself abandoned.

"I hope we'll see more of you, Charles, when we come to the city," Edward said as he shook his hand finally in the doorway. Victoria was still talking about New York to Olivia, paying no attention at all to the two men who had come to visit. And Olivia was quietly watching Charles as he said good-bye to their father. He assured Mr. Henderson that he would see a great deal of him at the office, as long as John Watson was willing to let him handle his business. John assured him that he would, and Edward urged Charles to come to see them at the house as well, as Charles thanked him politely for the invitation. And as he left, Charles glanced over the older man's shoulder and looked into Victoria's eyes again. He wasn't sure which one she was, but he felt the oddest pull whenever he looked at her. He couldn't have explained it if someone had asked him to, it was a kind of electricity he felt from her, and not from her sister. It was the oddest feeling not knowing which was which, and yet he was fascinated by both of them. He had never met anyone like them.

Edward Henderson walked the men to their car, and as they drove away Olivia stood watching them at the window. And despite her wild excitement over New York, Victoria noticed.

"What's that all about?" She had seen Olivia's intense look at the car driving slowly down their driveway.

"What do you mean?" Olivia asked, turning away to go and check on the library, and make sure the tray had been removed directly after the meeting.

"You're looking awfully serious, Ollie," Victoria accused. They knew each other far too well. It was dangerous sometimes, and at others merely annoying.

"His wife died on the *Titanic* last year. Father says he has a little boy."

"I'm sorry to hear about his wife," Victoria said, sounding unmoved. "But he looks terribly boring, doesn't he?" she said, dismissing him, in favor of countless unnamed delights soon to be discovered in New York, among them political rallies and suffragists' meetings, none of which interested her sister. "I think he looks incredibly dreary."

Olivia nodded, and made no comment as she walked into the library to escape her sister. And when she emerged again, satisfied that the tray was gone, Victoria had gone upstairs to change for dinner. Olivia had laid her clothes out for her earlier that afternoon. They were both going to wear a white silk dress, each with an aquamarine pin, a pair that was their mother's.

And a few minutes later, Olivia went to

the kitchen to find Bertie. She knew instantly that she was Olivia, and not her sister.

"Are you all right?" she asked Olivia, looking worried for a moment. It had been a terribly hot day and she knew Olivia had been out walking. And the young woman looked suddenly very pale now.

"I'm fine. Father has just told me we're going to New York at the beginning of September. We're going to stay for a month or two, while he does some business." The two women exchanged a smile. They both knew what that meant. An incredible amount of work and planning to open the house in New York. "I thought you and I could get together tomorrow morning to start making plans," she said quietly. She had a great deal to think about, a lot to do for him, most of which her father was entirely unaware of.

"You're a good girl," Bertie said softly to her, touching the pale cheek, as she looked at the huge blue eyes, wondering if something had upset her. Olivia was feeling something she had never felt before, and she was finding it unnerving and confusing. Even more so, worrying that Victoria was going to march right into her thoughts and expose them. "You work so hard for your father," Bertie praised her. She knew them both so well, and loved them both with all their similarities and differences. They were both good girls, as different as they were, beneath the surface.

"I'll meet with you tomorrow morning then," Olivia said quietly, and then left the kitchen to go upstairs to change. She went up the back stairs this time, trying to clear her thoughts, so Victoria wouldn't look right into them like a body of clear, translucent water. It was impossible to keep secrets from her, impossible for either of them. They had never even tried to.

But as she tried to think of other things, as she approached their huge room where they shared the same canopied bed they'd slept in all their lives, Olivia found she couldn't get her mind off of him. All she could think of were those green eyes, those deep dark pools that led straight to the soul of the man who had lost his wife to the Atlantic. She closed her eyes for a moment then as she turned the knob, and forced herself to think of more mundane things, like the new sheets she would probably need to order for New York, and the pillowcases she needed to bring for her father. She filled her head with banalities, and then she walked briskly across the room to her sister.

Chapter 2

On the first Wednesday afternoon in September, Olivia and Victoria Henderson were driven to New York by their father's chauffeur, Donovan, in the Cadillac Tourer, with Petrie driving Mrs. Peabody in the Ford just behind them. They brought endless supplies with them, and two other cars had been sent down the day before, carrying trunks of linens and clothes, and everything that Olivia and Bertie had decided were dire necessities that they absolutely had to have with them to run a decent household. Victoria didn't care what they took. She packed two trunks of books, a case full of papers she wanted to read, and she let Olivia pick all their clothing. She really didn't care what she wore, she had always deferred to Olivia's taste, which seemed excellent to her twin sister. Olivia read all the magazines from Paris. Victoria preferred political journals, and underground papers put out by members of the women's party.

But Olivia was seriously concerned with the state of the house on lower Fifth Avenue, which had been uninhabited for two years, and seldom visited for several years before that. It had been comfortable once upon a time, and much loved long before that, but that had been twenty years before, and Olivia was sure that it wouldn't be easy giving it a welcoming feeling. It was, after all, the house where her mother had died, and she knew how painful her father's memories were of it. And yet it was also the house where she and Victoria had been born, and a place where, not long before that, Edward Henderson and his young bride had been immensely happy.

After seeing to the amenities, and setting Donovan loose in all the bathrooms with a wrench in each hand, to tighten and loosen whatever needed it, she had Petrie drive her to the flower market on Sixth Avenue and Twenty-eighth Street, and she returned two hours later with a carful of beautiful asters, and fragrant lilies. She was determined to fill the house with the flowers he loved for her father's arrival two days later.

Dustcovers were pulled off and put away, rooms were aired, beds were turned topsy-turvy, mattresses were flipped over, carpets were beaten. It took an army to do it, but by the following afternoon, Bertie and Olivia met in the kitchen for a cup of tea, and smiled at what they'd accomplished. The chandeliers were sparkling, some of the furniture had been rearranged until rooms were barely recogniz-able, and Olivia had pulled all of the heavy cur-tains back in order to let more light in.

"Your father will be very pleased," Bertie congratulated her as they poured a second cup of tea, and Olivia made a note to herself to see about getting tickets to the theater. There were several new plays opening, and she and Victo-ria had vowed to see all of them before they went back to Croton-on-Hudson. But thinking of that made her wonder where her sister was. She hadn't seen her since early that morning, when Victoria had said she was going to the Low Library at Columbia, and the Metropoli-tan Museum. It was a long way, and Olivia had offered to send Petrie with her, but Victoria had insisted on taking the streetcar. She pre-ferred the adventure. And after that, Olivia had completely forgotten her, until now when she began getting an uneasy feeling in the pit of her stomach.

"Do you suppose Father will mind all the furniture we moved?" Olivia asked distractedly, hoping that Bertie wouldn't detect her growing worry. Olivia's back was aching from all they had done in the past two days, but she didn't feel it now as she began to worry about her sister. She always had an instinctive sense about her, and knew without fail when Victoria was in trouble. It was something they each had, and had often talked about. It was a special kind of warning device that told each of them when the other was either sick or in trouble. And Olivia wasn't sure what it was telling her this time, but she knew that she was getting some kind of a signal.

"Your father is going to be so happy to see the house like this," Bertie reassured her again, seemingly unaware of Olivia's growing discomfort. "You must be exhausted."

"Actually, I am," Olivia confessed uncharacteristically, just so she could go to her room, and think for a moment. It was four o'clock in the afternoon, and Victoria had left the house shortly after nine o'clock that morning. Just thinking about it made Olivia panic, and berate herself for not insisting on sending someone with her. This was not Croton-on-Hudson. Her sister was young and well dressed, and obviously inexperienced in dealing with big cities. What if she'd been attacked, or kidnapped? The thought didn't even bear thinking. But as Olivia paced her room, worrying, she heard the phone ring, and knew instinctively it was her sister. She flew toward the only phone they had, in the upstairs hall, and grabbed it before anyone else could answer.

"Hello?" she said breathlessly, sure that it would be Victoria, and instantly disappointed when it was an unknown male voice. Olivia was sure it was a wrong number.

"Is this the Henderson residence?" the voice asked in an Irish brogue, as Olivia frowned. They didn't know anyone in New York, and Olivia couldn't imagine who was calling.

"It is. Who's calling?" she said firmly, feeling her hand tremble as she held the earpiece in one hand, and the speaker in the other.

"Is this Miss Henderson?" he asked in resounding tones, as Olivia nodded, and then answered.

"Yes, it is. Who is this?" she insisted.

"This is Sergeant O'Shaunessy at the Fifth Precinct," he said firmly, and Olivia held her breath and closed her eyes, knowing what was coming before he said it.

"I . . . is she all right? . . ." It was barely a whisper. What if she'd been injured? Kicked by a horse . . . stabbed by a petty criminal . . . thrown to the ground and run over by a carriage . . . or a runaway horse . . . hit by a motorcar . . . Olivia couldn't bear it.

"She's fine." He sounded exasperated, rather than sympathetic. "She's here with . . . er . . . a group of young ladies . . . and we . . . uh . . . the lieutenant determined from the look of her that she didn't . . . ah . . . quite belong here. The other . . . er . . . young ladies . . . are being detained overnight. To put it quite bluntly, Miss Henderson, they've all been arrested for demonstrating without a permit. And if you'll be good enough to come and get your sister immediately, we'll send her home without booking her, and no one will be the wiser. But I suggest you don't come down here alone, if there's someone you can bring with you." Her mind went completely blank. She didn't want Donovan or Petrie knowing that Victoria had just been picked up by the police and narrowly missed being arrested, and she certainly didn't want them telling her father.

"What exactly did she do?" Olivia asked, overwhelmed with gratitude that they were willing to let Victoria go and not arrest her.

"Demonstrate, like the others, but she's very young, and very foolish, and she tells me she only got to New York yesterday. I suggest the two of you go back where you came from as soon as possible, before she gets herself in more trouble with this damn fool Women's Suffrage Association she's gotten herself mixed up with. She's giving us quite a time. She didn't want us to call you. She wants us to arrest her." He said it with a tone of amusement, as Olivia closed her eyes in horror.

"Oh my God, please don't listen to her. I'll be right there."

"Bring someone with you," he said again sternly.

"Please don't arrest her," Olivia breathed into the phone in a whisper, begging him, but he had no intention of doing that and causing a scandal. It was easy to see from her shoes, and her clothes, and even the hat she wore, however "simple" she thought she appeared, that Victoria did not belong with the others. And he wasn't about to get kicked off the force for arresting some fancy aristocrat's daughter. He wanted her off his hands as soon as Olivia could get there.

But Olivia didn't even know where to begin, or who to talk to. Unlike her sister, she couldn't drive a car, and didn't want to alert the servants. She'd have to get a cab, it would take too long if she went by streetcar, and there was absolutely no one she could take with her, not even Bertie. She couldn't believe what had happened. Victoria actually *wanted* them to arrest her. She was completely crazy, and Olivia promised herself to be absolutely furious as soon as she had retrieved her from the Fifth Precinct. But first, she had to go get her. And as she tried on all the possibilities of how to get to her, how to get her out, and how to get there in a city she scarcely knew, and had no idea how to get around in, she realized the sergeant was right, and she had to bring someone with her. And as much as she hated to do it, she knew she had to. She had no choice, and she sat down quietly in the little closet they used for the telephone, and slowly lifted the receiver. As soon as the operator came on the line, she gave her the familiar number. It was the last thing she wanted to do, but there was simply no one else to call, not even John Watson, whom she had known all her life. But she had no doubt whatsoever that if she called him now, he would tell her father.

The receptionist answered immediately, and told her to wait while she went to get him. She was extremely attentive once Olivia said who she was, although she had hoped not to have to. It was four-thirty by then, and she was terrified he might have left early. But he hadn't, and Charles Dawson's deep, quiet voice came on the line a moment later.

"Miss Henderson?" He sounded surprised more than anything, and Olivia had to force herself not to whisper.

"I'm terribly sorry to bother you," she began apologetically.

"Not at all. I'm glad you called." But he could hear in her voice that something had happened, and he only hoped that nothing had happened to her father. "Is something wrong?" he asked very gently. He knew, himself, only too well how swiftly tragedy can strike, and he sounded incredibly kind as he asked her, and she didn't know how to answer. She had to fight back tears as she thought of what Victoria had done this time. She tried not to think of the disgrace to their father if Victoria had in fact been arrested, and she wanted to scream with mortification and fear every time she thought of her sister being held at the Fifth Precinct.

"I . . . I'm afraid . . . I need your help, Mr. Dawson . . . and your absolute discretion." She sounded so worried and he couldn't even begin to imagine what had happened. "I'm afraid my sister . . . I . . . could you possibly come here to see me?"

"Now?" He had come out of a meeting to speak to her, and he couldn't imagine what needed his immediate attention. "Is it urgent?"

"Very," she said, sounding desperate, and he glanced at his watch as he heard her.

"Shall I come at once?"

She nodded, as tears stung her eyes, momentarily unable to answer, and when she spoke again, he could hear that she was crying. "I'm terribly sorry . . . I need your help . . . Victoria has done something terribly foolish." All he could think of was that she had eloped. She couldn't be injured, or her sister would be calling a doctor and not an attorney. It was impossible to imagine what had happened. But he took a cab straight to her front door and was there less than fifteen minutes later. Petrie let him in, and Olivia was waiting for him, pacing in the downstairs salon. Bertie was occupied elsewhere in the house, and fortunately hadn't heard him.

And the moment he walked in, she saw those eyes again, the eyes that had so mesmerized her the first time she met him.

"Thank you for coming so quickly," she said, and it was easy to see how distraught she was, as she picked up her hat and put it on quickly, and grabbed her handbag. "We must leave immediately."

"But what's happened? Where is your sister, Miss Henderson? Has she run away?" He was baffled by the mysteries surrounding them, and anxious to do what he could, but he had no idea what she wanted of him.

For an instant, Olivia stood to her full height and looked up at him, her eyes filled with embarrassment and terror. She was a capable girl, but this was by far the most shocking experience of her sister's career, and she was beside herself over not wanting anyone else to know it. Surely they wouldn't understand how spirited she was, or how innocent some of her pranks were. And this was one instance where Olivia's trading places with her would solve nothing. For the first time in her life, she felt entirely helpless.

"She's at the Fifth Precinct, Mr. Dawson," Olivia said in a grief-stricken tone. "They just called me. They are holding her there, and they won't arrest her, if we come quickly." Unless of course Victoria talked them into it, and they arrested her before she and Charles could get there.

"Good heavens." He actually did look surprised this time, as he followed her out the front door, and down the front steps, and then hurried to hail a taxi. He helped Olivia into it, in her quiet gray work dress that she'd been wearing since that morning. She'd put on a very fashionable black hat with it, and realized that Victoria had worn the identical hat when she'd left that morning. Even when they didn't plan to wear the same things, they almost always did, just as she had done now. But she wasn't thinking about their hats, as she tried to explain to Charles Dawson what she thought must have happened.

"She's totally enamored with this stupid National American Women's Suffrage Association, and the people who run it." She told him all their names, explained about the demonstration in Washington five months before, and the arrests of the Pankhursts in England. "These people glorify arrests like some sort of an award, it's a medal of honor, and I suppose that Victoria went somewhere that they were having a demonstration this afternoon and got picked up with them. The sergeant who called said he had no intention of arresting her, but he said that Victoria *wanted* him to arrest her." Charles Dawson tried to repress a smile as he looked at her, and suddenly Olivia found herself smiling too. Listening to herself explain it to him made it sound utterly ridiculous, and Victoria even more so.

"She's quite a girl, this sister of yours. Does she always do things like this while you're keeping house for your father?" She had explained to him that she had been busy and wasn't paying attention to where Victoria had gone that day. She really took her role as older sister seriously, although there were barely more than ten minutes' difference between them.

"She stole one of my father's cars to go to one of these meetings the day you came to see us in Croton." She was suddenly laughing with him, although she still felt desperately worried.

"Well, at least she's not dull," he said calmly. "Think of the children she'll have. It makes one quake, doesn't it?" He was laughing again, but they both looked serious as they reached the Fifth Precinct. It was in a dismal neighborhood, with poor people in rags loitering in doorways, and terrible refuse in the streets all around them. And as Olivia got out of the cab with Charles, she saw a rat scurry across the street into the gutter. She drew instinctively closer to him, and as they walked into the police station, there were drunks, and two petty thieves who had just been brought in, in handcuffs, and three prostitutes were screaming at the desk sergeant from a holding cell, as Charles glanced at Olivia to see if she was ready to faint at their surroundings. But she looked quite stern, and seemed relatively unmoved by the comments of the drunks or the prostitutes, as she pretended to ignore them.

"Are you all right?" he asked in an undervoice, tucking her hand into his arm as she stood very straight beside him. He had to admire her for her good sportsmanship, and the poise with which she was enduring the abuse of the hookers who were shrieking at her in envy.

"I'm fine," she whispered back to Charles, barely raising her eyes to his, "but when we get her out of here, I'm going to kill her."

He had to repress a smile as he turned his attention to the desk sergeant then, and the sergeant led them both into a locked room where Victoria was sitting in a single chair, drinking a cup of tea, as a matron watched her. Victoria was looking irritated, and she put the cup down, and stood up when Charles and Olivia entered the room, but she did not look happy to see them.

"It's your fault, isn't it?" Victoria asked her without even acknowledging Charles Dawson. And for him, it was eerie seeing them, so totally identical, from their faces to their eyes, even to their hats, although Victoria's had shifted imperceptibly and she seemed to be wearing it at a rakish angle. Charles was watching both of them, mesmerized, and he sensed instantly the electricity between them.

"What is *my* fault?" Olivia asked, clearly furious at her sister.

"It's your fault they wouldn't arrest me." Victoria looked equally angry.

"You're deranged, Victoria Henderson," Olivia accused. "You deserve to be locked up, but not here. You belong in Bedlam. Do you realize the scandal it would make if you got arrested? Do you have any idea of the embarrassment you'd cause Father over this? Do you ever think about anyone but yourself, Victoria? Or is that just not on your agenda?" The sergeant and the matron exchanged a smile. There was very little they could add to all that, and Charles arranged quietly with them to simply remove her. No real harm had been done, she had been in the wrong place at the wrong time, and they were entirely willing to ignore it. The sergeant suggested they keep an eye on her in the future, and he asked Charles if the two girls were his younger sisters.

He was surprised by the idea, and flattered, now that he thought of it, that Olivia had called him. And she'd been right to do so, coming down here on her own would have been terrifying for her, and dangerous as well. He still had the cab waiting outside, and as the two sisters argued in the small room, he finally interrupted them and suggested they continue their conversation in the taxi. Olivia was absolutely fuming. For an instant, he thought that Victoria might refuse to leave, but there was nothing for her to do here. The police didn't want her there, and the excitement was over. But Olivia was still berating her as they left and got back in the cab, and Charles very quietly handed them both into the taxi, and then got in between them.

"Ladies, may I suggest we call it a day, and agree to forget this unfortunate incident. Nothing untoward happened here, and no one ever need be the wiser." He turned to Olivia then and suggested she forgive her sister for her foolishness, and then he turned to Victoria and asked her to stay away from demonstrations for the rest of her stay. Or if not, they might truly arrest her.

"That might have been a little more honest, don't you think? Than to pull class on them, and come running home to Daddy." She was still annoyed at having been "saved" by her sister and their father's lawyer. And she thought Charles was a complete fool to have come with her. She wanted to tell him to mind his own business in the future.

"Do you have any idea what it would do to Father if he knew?" Olivia asked her bluntly. "Why don't you think of him for a change instead of your stupid groups, and women getting the vote? Why don't you behave for once, instead of expecting me to get you out of it?" Olivia's hands were shaking as she carefully put her gloves on, and Charles watched them both with fascination. The one so restrained and so capable, the other so fiery and so totally without remorse. In some ways, Victoria reminded him of his late wife, Susan, always espousing unusual ideas and difficult causes. And yet there had been a tamer side to her as well, a docile side that he longed for on quiet nights as he lay alone, trying not to think of her. He had to think of Geoffrey now, and not the boy's mother. But try as he might, he could never bring himself to forget her, and in his heart of hearts, he knew he didn't really want to. But this wild, foolish girl, in the black straw hat, with the smoldering blue eyes, intrigued him, far more than her obviously tamer sister.

"I'd like to point out to you," Victoria said coldly as the cab pulled up in front of their house, "that I didn't call either of you, and I didn't ask to be rescued." She was being childish, and Charles couldn't help smiling as he looked at her. She was like a naughty girl who needed to be sent to her room, or scolded until she paid attention. But she was certainly not contrite or grateful that they had come to get her.

"Perhaps we should send you back then," Charles said, and Victoria glared at him as she got out of the cab, and let herself into the house ahead of her sister. She had her back to both of them as she took her hat off and threw it on the table.

"Thank you," Olivia said in embarrassment to Charles, furious at her sister. "I wouldn't have known what to do without you."

"Anytime," he smiled, and Olivia rolled her eyes at the thought.

"I hope not."

"Try and keep her on a leash until your father arrives," Charles said in a whisper. She was clearly an unrepentant rebel, and there was a certain charm to that, if one viewed it from a safe distance.

"Thank God Father will be here by to-morrow night," Olivia said, and then looked at Charles with worried eyes. She had trusted him and hoped he wouldn't betray her. "Please don't say anything to him, it would upset him terribly."

"I promise. Not a word." But now that it was over, what he had just done amused him. "One day you'll laugh about this, I promise, when you're both grandmothers, and remember how she *almost* got arrested." Olivia smiled at what he was saying, and Victoria muttered a curt thank-you at him, and then swept upstairs to change for dinner. They were only having dinner with Mrs. Peabody that night, but Olivia asked Charles if he would like to join them. It seemed the least she could do after the last two hours he'd spent, rescuing Victoria, in spite of herself, from the Fifth Precinct.

"I can't, but thank you very much." He

looked embarrassed at the invitation. "I try to dine with my son every night, or as much as possible at least."

"How old is he?" Olivia asked with interest.

"He's nine." That made him eight when his mother died . . . when he had seen her for the last time, before he left her on the *Titanic*. The thought of it almost made her shudder.

"I hope we meet him sometime," she said genuinely, and Charles looked hesitant and thankful.

"He's a good boy." And then, he surprised her with his honesty. But there was something about Olivia that made her easy to talk to, unlike her sister, who made him want to spank her. "We've both had a hard time without his mother," he said quietly.

"I can imagine." And then, "I never knew mine," she said softly. "But Victoria and I had each other." Her eyes seemed huge as they looked into his, and something about her made his heart ache.

"It must be extraordinary," he said thoughtfully. "I can't imagine having anyone that you're that close to. Except maybe a husband or a wife, but even then. You two almost seem like two halves of the same person."

"Sometimes I think we are," and then she looked toward the second floor, glowering expressively, "and at other times, I think we're strangers. We're very different in some ways, and completely alike in others." In looks certainly, despite their very different personalities, he still could not actually see a difference between them.

"Does it bother you that people confuse you all the time? I suppose that could be very annoying." He was fascinated by them, and he liked being able to ask Olivia these questions.

"You get used to it. We used to think it was funny. Now, it's just the way things are." It was so easy talking to him, and he seemed comfortable speaking to Olivia as well. She was the sort of woman he could be friends with. And yet it was Victoria he was mesmerized by, and tongue-tied with. He couldn't tell them apart, and yet some deep, inner part of him sensed when he was in Victoria's presence, and something about her turned him topsy-turvy. But Olivia with her gentle ways made him feel comfortable, and at ease, like a dear friend or an affectionate younger sister.

He left a few minutes after that, and she closed the door quietly behind him, and walked slowly upstairs to talk to her sister.

Victoria was sitting in her room, staring unhappily out the window, thinking of the afternoon, and how foolish she had felt when the sergeant had separated her from the others.

"How am I going to show my face to them again?" she asked unhappily as Olivia watched her.

"You shouldn't have been with them in the first place." Olivia sighed, and sat down on the bed, facing her sister. "You can't keep doing things like this, Victoria. You can't go off chasing some wild idea, without thinking of the consequences. People can get hurt by it, you can get hurt by it. I don't want that to happen."

Victoria looked slowly at her, and the light that Charles saw in her eyes burned very brightly. "What if more people are helped than hurt? What if one had to die for an idea, a cause, in order to make the right things happen? You know, I know it must sound crazy to you, but sometimes I think I'd be willing to do that." The worst of it was that Olivia knew in her heart of hearts that Victoria was being truthful. She had that kind of fire in her, that bright, burning thing at her core that would allow her to die for an ideal, or follow what she believed in all the way to the horizon.

"You frighten me when you say things like

that," Olivia said quietly, and Victoria reached out and took her hand and held it.

"I don't mean to. I think that's just who I am. I'm not you, Ollie. Even though we look so much alike, how could we be so different?"

"Different and the same," Olivia said, puzzling over the mystery that had followed them since they were born, so much the same in so many ways, so totally different in others.

"I'm sorry about this afternoon. I didn't mean to scare you." Contrite at last, not because of what she'd done, but because she had upset her sister. Victoria loved Olivia too much to hurt her.

"I knew something was wrong. I felt it here." She touched her stomach, and Victoria nodded. They were both familiar with that sensation.

"What time?" Victoria asked with interest. The telepathy between them had always intrigued her.

"Two o'clock," Olivia said, and Victoria nodded. They were both used to the phenomenon which always seemed to tell each of them when the other was in trouble.

"Just about right. I think that's when they picked us up, and tossed us in the wagon."

"That must have been charming," Olivia

said, looking disapproving again, but Victoria laughed, looking highly amused about it.

"Actually, I thought it was pretty funny. They were so determined to get everyone in, and no one wanted to be left out. They all *wanted* to be arrested." Victoria laughed more, and Olivia groaned, remembering the phone call from Sergeant O'Shaunessy at the Fifth Precinct.

"I'm glad they *didn't* arrest you," Olivia said firmly.

"Why did you call him?" Victoria asked her then, combing her eyes with her own, looking for unspoken answers. There were a myriad of things that always went unsaid, but were clearly understood, between them.

"I didn't know who else to call. And I didn't want to take Donovan or Petrie. I was afraid to come alone, and they told me not to when they called me."

"You could have though. You didn't need him. He's so insignificant." Victoria brushed Charles Dawson aside with a wave of her hand. To her, he was entirely unimportant. She didn't see any of the merit in him that Olivia did. Nor any of the interest.

"He's not insignificant," Olivia defended him. He was subdued, one could see easily that his fire had been dimmed, but he had been dealt a cruel blow by one of life's swift hands, and Olivia felt desperately sorry for him. It didn't make her pity him, but she liked him. She could see the merit in the man, the man he might have been before, and could be again, with a little kindness, and perhaps even the right woman. "He's wounded," Olivia explained.

"Spare me." Victoria grinned, easily unkind, and quick to dispense with the impaired or injured.

"That's not fair. He came here in ten minutes today in order to help you."

"Our father is probably one of his biggest clients."

"That's a disgusting thing to say. He could have told me he was busy."

"Perhaps he likes you," Victoria said mischievously, but without much interest.

"Or you," Olivia said fairly.

"Maybe he still can't tell the difference," Victoria said truthfully.

"That doesn't make him a bad person. Father can't always tell the difference between us either. Bertie is the only one who ever could."

"Maybe she's the only one who ever cared enough to," Victoria said cruelly.

"Why are you so unkind sometimes?" Olivia said unhappily. She hated it when her sister said things like that. Sometimes she could be so unfeeling.

"Maybe that's just the way I am." Victoria looked matter-of-fact, but not remorseful. "I'm hard on myself too. I expect a lot of everyone, Ollie. I expect to do more with my life than just sit here, and go to parties and balls and the theater." She sounded suddenly very grown-up and Olivia was surprised by what she was saying.

"I thought you wanted to come to New York. You're the one who always complains about being stuck in boring old Croton-on-Hudson."

"I know I do, and I love being here, but it's not just the social life I want. I want something important to happen in my life too. I want to make a difference in the world. I want to stand for something more than just being Edward Henderson's daughter." She looked so intense and alive as she said it.

"It sounds so noble when you talk about it that way." Olivia smiled at her twin. Victoria had such grandiose ideas sometimes, and yet Olivia knew she really meant them. But still, she was a child in a way, and sometimes a very spoiled one. She wanted everything, people and fun and parties and New York, and there was a serious side to her too, that wanted to fight all the battles, right all the injustices, and make a difference in the world. She didn't know exactly what she wanted yet, but Olivia sensed sometimes that Victoria would do a lot more with her life than just live in Croton.

"What about being someone's wife?" Olivia asked her quietly, it was something she thought about once in a while, although she couldn't really imagine ever leaving her father. He needed her too badly.

"That's not what I want," Victoria said firmly. "I don't want to belong to anyone, like a table or a chair, or a motorcar. 'This is my wife,' it's like saying this is my hat, or my over-coat, or my dog. I don't want to 'belong' to anyone, like an object."

"You've been spending too much time with those ridiculous suffragettes," Olivia growled at her. She disagreed with almost everything they said, except maybe about voting. But all their ideas about freedom and independence seemed to be at the expense of values that Olivia cherished more, like family and children, and being respectful of one's father or husband. She didn't believe in the kind of anarchy they were preaching, although Victoria said she did, but Olivia sometimes wondered. Victoria liked smoking and stealing her father's car, and going places by herself, and even risking arrest to stand up for something she believed in, but she loved their father as dearly as anyone, and Olivia had the feeling that if the right man came along, Victoria would fall for him as hard as any other woman would, possibly harder. She was filled with fire, and beliefs that she was almost willing to die for, and a kind of unbridled passion. How could she say she never wanted to "belong" to anyone, or be a man's wife? It just wasn't like her.

"I'm serious," Victoria said quietly. "I made up my mind a long time ago. I don't want to get married." She looked incredibly beautiful as she said it, and Olivia smiled, thinking that she didn't believe her.

"When was 'a long time ago'? At the suffragettes' meeting you went to today, or the one last week? I don't think you know what you're saying."

"Yes, I do. I'm never going to get married." She said it calmly and firmly, with total conviction. "Actually, I don't think marriage would suit me."

"How can you possibly know that? Are

you telling me that you're going to stay at home with Father and take care of him?" The idea of it was sounding more ridiculous by the moment. Olivia might stay home and take care of him in his last years, but not Victoria. They both knew she didn't have it in her. Or at least Olivia knew it, she wondered if Victoria hadn't figured that out yet. Could she really believe that she would be happy at home with him in Croton? Not likely.

"I didn't say that. But maybe I'll go to live in Europe one day, when we're older. Actually, I think I'd like living in England." The cause of women's freedom was a lot more developed there, though it was not any better received than in New York, or elsewhere in the United States. In the past few months alone, at least half a dozen major suffragettes had been arrested and sent to prison in England.

But Olivia was surprised by the things Victoria had said, particularly about never getting married, and living in Europe. It all sounded so foreign, and so strange, to Olivia, and it reminded her again of how different they were. In spite of the similar instincts they sometimes shared, and their apparent similarities, there were some enormous differences between them.

"Maybe you should marry Charles Dawson," Victoria was teasing her by then, as they both began dressing for dinner with Bertie. "Since you think he's so sweet. Maybe you'd like being married to him," Victoria said, as she did up the slide fastener on the back of Olivia's dress, and then turned around to have hers done in turn. It was a new invention that had just come into fashion that year, and it was incredibly easy, and a vast improvement over rows of tiny buttons that tangled one's fingers.

"Don't be stupid," Olivia said of her sister's comment about Charles Dawson. "I've only met him twice in my life," Olivia said quietly.

"But you like him. Don't lie to me. I can see it."

"All right, so I like him. So what? He's intelligent and pleasant to talk to, and terribly useful when my sister winds up in jail. Maybe I will have to marry him if you make a habit of becoming a jailbird. Either that, or go to law school myself."

"Now, that would be much better," Victoria said firmly.

The two sisters had made their peace with each other again by the time they were dressed, and Olivia had almost forgiven her for the exotic end to the afternoon, but she had forced Victoria to swear that she would stay away from demonstrations for the rest of their stay in New York. She didn't want to spend her time there getting Victoria out of trouble. Victoria promised reluctantly, and lit a cigarette in their bathroom while Olivia combed her hair and complained about how unattractive it looked for a lady to smoke cigarettes, but Victoria only laughed at her and told her she sounded like Bertie.

"If she ever knew you smoked, she'd kill you!" Olivia waved her hairbrush at her twin to emphasize her point, as Victoria laughed, looking terribly racy as she sat with her long legs crossed on the edge of their huge tub, in one of the dresses Olivia had just bought them. It was bright red and a little shorter than some of the dresses they wore, in fact it was extremely fashionable and suited them both to perfection.

"I like it by the way," Victoria complimented her as they walked downstairs to the dining room with their arms around each other. "I like all the dresses you pick for us. Maybe I'll just live with you for the rest of my life, and forget about Europe."

"I wouldn't mind that," Olivia said softly, feeling sad at the thought of a time when they might not be together. She had never let herself think of marriage because she couldn't bear the thought of leaving either of them, her father, or her twin sister. It would have been like leaving part of herself behind, and she felt at times that there would have been nothing left of her without them. "I can't imagine ever leaving you," Olivia said as she looked at the familiar face she had seen all her life, so totally identical to her own that it was like looking in the mirror. Each detail that the one had, the other had on the opposite side, so that it really was like looking in the mirror. "I couldn't leave you," Olivia said, looking at Victoria, who smiled and kissed her cheek gently.

"You won't ever have to, Ollie. I don't suppose I could bear to go anywhere without you. I'm all talk," she said, sensing that she had upset Olivia with her talk of Europe. "I'll just stay home with you and get arrested whenever I need a breather."

"You dare!" Olivia wagged a finger at her again, as Bertie joined them in the dining room in a black silk suit Olivia had had copied for her from a magazine from Paris. It looked surprisingly well on her, and she wore it whenever she had dinner with the family, which she considered an honor.

"And where were you all afternoon, Victoria?" Bertie asked as they took their seats, and both girls averted their gazes as they opened their napkins.

"At the museum actually. There was a splendid exhibit of Turners from the National Gallery in London."

"Really?" Bertie said, opening her wise old eyes wide, pretending to believe her. "I'll have to be sure and see it while we're here."

"You'll love it," Victoria said, smiling brightly, as Olivia looked up at the ceiling of the house her parents had once lived in. She wondered what it had been like when their mother was there, what she had been like, and who truly resembled her more spiritually, herself or her sister. It was a question they often pondered, but they both knew their father preferred not to discuss it. Even after all these years, it was still too painful for him.

"It'll be nice to see your father tomorrow, won't it, girls?" Bertie asked pleasantly as the meal drew to a close, and the kitchen girl served them coffee.

"Yes, it will," Olivia said, thinking of him, and the flowers she wanted to put in his bedroom, as Victoria wondered if Olivia would really kill her if she squeezed in just one more demonstration. She had heard about one that afternoon, on the way to jail, and she had promised to be there. But as she thought of it, Olivia glanced over at her and shook her head, as though she knew what she was thinking. They did that to each other sometimes, they never knew how it happened, but it did. It was almost as though they could hear each other's thoughts before the other said them.

"Don't you dare," Olivia whispered to her behind Bertie's back, as they left the table.

"I have no idea what you're talking about," Victoria said primly.

"Next time I'll leave you there, mark my words, and let you explain it to Father."

"I doubt that," Victoria said with a laugh as she tossed her long dark hair over her shoulder. There was almost nothing she was afraid of. Even being in jail that afternoon had made no impression on her whatsoever. She had found it interesting, but not daunting.

"You're incorrigible," Olivia said, and then they kissed Bertie good night and went upstairs to their bedroom. Olivia looked at fashion magazines while Victoria read a pamphlet by Emmeline Pankhurst about hunger strikes in prison. She was, according to Victoria, the most important suffragist in England.

Victoria dared to light a cigarette in their room, knowing that Bertie had already gone to bed, and she urged Olivia to try one, but she wouldn't. Instead, Olivia sat looking out the window, at the warm September night, and despite everything else she had tried to think of that night, her mind wandered back to Charles Dawson.

"Don't," Victoria said to her, as she lay on her bed and watched her sister.

"Don't what?" Olivia asked, as she turned to look at Victoria reclining elegantly and smoking.

"Don't think about him," Victoria said quietly, blowing a long, slow cloud of smoke toward the window.

"What do you mean?" Olivia looked startled. It was always eerie when either of them guessed what the other was thinking.

"You know exactly what I mean. Charles Dawson. You had that same look in your eyes when you talked to him. He's too boring for you. There are going to be lots of wonderful men here. I can feel it." She looked very worldly as she said it, but Olivia still looked startled.

"How do you know what I'm thinking?" It happened to them so often.

"The same way you do. I hear you in my head sometimes, like my own voice, thinking. Sometimes I can just see it when I look at you."

"It scares me sometimes," Olivia said honestly. "We're so close I don't know where you end, and I begin, or do we? Do we just blend into one sometimes?"

"Sometimes," Victoria smiled at her, "but not always. I like knowing what you think . . . and I like being able to surprise people, and change places, like we used to. Sometimes I miss it. We should do it again sometime, while we're here. Nobody would ever know the difference. And it would be great fun, wouldn't it?"

"It seems different to me now that we're older. It seems deceitful," Olivia said, looking thoughtful.

"Don't be so moralistic, Ollie. It's harmless. It doesn't hurt anyone. I'm sure all twins do it." But they had only met twins once or twice in their lives, and never of comparable ages or sexes, nor quite as identical as they were. "Let's do it soon," Victoria prodded her, always willing to cross the line and be daring, just as she had been in their childhood. But this time, when Olivia looked at her, she only smiled, and didn't answer, and Victoria knew she wouldn't do it. They were grown-up now. And Olivia thought switching was childish. "You'll turn into a dreary old crone if you're not careful," Victoria warned, and Olivia laughed at her with genuine amusement.

"At least if I do, maybe by then you'll have learned to behave yourself."

The two sisters exchanged a warm look, and Victoria chuckled. "Don't count on that, big sister. I'm not sure I ever will 'behave myself.'"

"Neither am I," Olivia whispered, and then left the room to get ready for bed, as Victoria looked longingly out the window.

Chapter 3

Their father arrived, on schedule, late Friday afternoon, from Croton-on-Hudson. Donovan had driven up to pick him up in the Cadillac, and Olivia had the house in perfect order for him. Everything was exactly as it should have been, everything had been dusted and shined and fluffed, and his bedroom was exactly the way he liked it. Olivia had flowers everywhere, and it smelled exquisite. Even the garden had been cleaned up for him so he could use it, although it was just a small patch of green after what he was used to in Croton. But when he arrived, he was extremely pleased with what he saw, and he had high praise for Bertie and both his daughters. He always included Victoria to be kind to her, although he knew that it was Olivia who ran his household.

He was happy to see them both and looked lovingly at both of them. And then he kissed Victoria, and thanked her for Olivia's hard work, which made them both giggle and he understood immediately what had happened. "I'm going to have Bertie make you wear colored ribbons in your hair again, except that you'll probably do what you did then, and switch them."

"We haven't switched in ages, Father," Victoria said plaintively, and Olivia looked pointedly at her.

"That's right, and who was trying to talk me into it just last night?" Olivia said, as Victoria pretended not to remember.

"She won't do it anymore, Papa. She's no fun anymore," Victoria complained and he laughed ruefully at her. "You two will make everyone miserable enough just by confusing them completely, without switching." He still shuddered when he thought of their presentation year two years before, they had both been so striking in their finery, that he hadn't been able to go anywhere with them without stopping traffic. In his opinion, it had truly been excessive. And he was hoping that this time people would be a little less excited each time they saw them. It remained to be seen. They were going out the next night to the theater.

On the night of his arrival, Olivia had planned one of his favorite dinners, with venison and asparagus and wild rice, and some clams that had been brought to them that morning from Long Island. There were vegetables from their garden in Croton that Donovan had brought down with them at her request, and a chocolate cake that her father swore would kill him, but of course he ate it. And after dinner, the three of them had coffee, while he talked about some of the treats he had planned for them, including the theater the following night, and several times in the ensuing weeks. There were people he wanted them to meet, two new restaurants he hoped to try with them, and he told Olivia that night that he wanted to give a party. It had been years since he'd entertained in New York, and he thought it might be interesting for them, particularly now with everyone home from New England and Long Island from the summer. This was the opening of the season. And it sounded intriguing to both of them as they listened.

"In fact," he said, smiling at both of them, and looking better than he had in years, "we've already been invited to a ball at the Astors', and the Whitneys are giving a huge party two weeks from now. I'm afraid you ladies will have to do some shopping." It all sounded exciting to both of them, but Olivia was even more excited about their party. Her father had said that he wanted to invite about fifty people. Just big enough to be lively, and small enough to get to talk to almost everyone at the dinner. He promised to give Olivia the guest list the next day. He had already written down all the names, and she and Bertie would have to get busy. He knew only too well that Victoria would be no help to them.

And the next morning, Olivia was already at her desk, poring over the names, and writing out invitations. The party was to be in two weeks, the same week as the ball at the Astors'. They were going to be very busy. Olivia was also pleased to realize that she recognized many of the names from two years before, although she couldn't always add faces. But she remembered meeting them, and thought it would be fun seeing them again, particularly here at the house. She loved entertaining for her father. She had already put together several menus in her head, and early that morning she'd been examining their linens. She was going to have to have more of them brought down from Croton. The crystal and the china were adequate here, and she knew exactly what she wanted in the way of flowers, and she hoped she could still get them by late September.

Olivia stayed at her desk most of that afternoon, working on her plans, and Victoria went out for a drive with their father. They drove uptown in the Cadillac, and eventually took a slow walk down Fifth Avenue, where Edward ran into several people he knew and was proud to introduce his daughter. They were both in high spirits when they got home, and so was Olivia. She had organized the entire party.

And that night, when they went to see *The Seven Keys to Baldpate* with Wallace Eddinger at the Astor Theater, their father seemed to know everyone in the theater. And as usual, when they were introduced, they created quite a stir. The girls were wearing matching black velvet evening suits with little ermine wraps and collars, and each of them wore a single long black beaded feather in her hair. Together, they were like a double vision straight out of a fashion magazine from Paris, and by the next morning, they were once again in the papers. But this time, Edward was calmer about it than he had been two years before, and the girls were less excited by it. They were two years older, and they were somewhat used to causing a sensation in public.

"That was wonderful," Victoria said, talking about the theater the night before. She had liked the play and had been so engrossed by it she scarcely noticed the attention being lavished on them by the people around them.

"It's a lot better than getting arrested," Olivia whispered to her with a grin, as she went to get their father another cup of coffee.

They went to church together later that morning, at St. Thomas, and everyone greeted them, and then the three of them got in the car behind Donovan, and came back to the house on Fifth Avenue to spend a quiet Sunday together. And the next morning, Olivia had work to do, running the house and ordering things for their party, and her father left to meet his attorneys, which was, after all, why they had come here. Both John Watson and Charles Dawson came back to the house with him later that afternoon, and Olivia had a little moment of terror when she first saw them come in. She was afraid Charles might slip and say something to her about the day he had taken her to the Fifth Precinct. But in fact, he said nothing at all to her. He nodded politely to her as they arrived, and said good-bye to her when they left, and showed no particular recognition, which was a great relief to her, although Victoria said she wouldn't have cared, when Olivia told her.

"Father would go right through the roof," Olivia warned her, bringing her back to earth rapidly, "and you know it. You'd be on the next train back to Croton."

"Maybe you're right." Victoria grinned at her. She was enjoying New York too much to take that chance again. She wanted to go to meetings of the National American Women's Suffrage Association, but she had promised to stay well away from all their demonstrations.

They went to the theater again that night, and to dinner with friends of her father's later that week, and Victoria had been amused to listen to them talking about some utterly scandalous man named Tobias Whitticomb, who had apparently made a vast fortune in somewhat speculative banking, and an even larger one by marrying an Astor. He was supposedly a very good-looking young man and had quite a reputation with the ladies. Everyone in town was said to be talking about him after some recent, scandalous liaison which no one would explain in any detail to either Victoria or her sister. And then their father shocked everyone by saying that he had recently done business with him, and found him both civilized and pleasant. In fact, they had concluded some very profitable dealings, and he had found him to be nothing but honest and very decent.

After that, everyone argued with him, and there was a great outcry and exchange of stories about Whitticomb, and the assembled company had to admit that in spite of his reputation, he was invited to all the best homes and parties. But that, they said, was because he was married to Evangeline Astor. And everyone in the group agreed that she was a sweet girl, and an absolute angel to put up with Toby. But she'd apparently been putting up with him for a while, since they'd been married for five years, and had three children.

And it was only on the way home that night that Olivia remembered the Whitticombs were invited to her father's party.

"Is he really as bad as they say?" Olivia asked with curiosity as they rode home in the comfortable Cadillac at the end of the evening. Victoria wasn't paying any attention to them, she had had a nice time talking to some woman about politics, and she had seemed to have a great deal to say on the subject.

But Edward Henderson smiled at the elder of the twins and shrugged in answer to her question. "One has to be careful of men like Tobias Whitticomb, my dear, he's very handsome and very young, and probably very appealing to most women. But in all fairness to him, I gather that most of his conquests are among married women, and they ought to be wise enough to know better. And if not, then more pity to them. I don't think he goes around ravishing young girls, or I wouldn't have had you invite him to our dinner."

"Who's this?" Victoria asked vaguely, as she turned her attention to their conversation. They were almost home by then, and she wasn't particularly intrigued, as she hadn't heard the earlier conversation.

"Apparently, Father has invited some terrible libertine to our party, and our hostess tonight was warning us about him."

"Does he murder women and young children?" Victoria asked, almost without interest.

"Apparently just the opposite," Olivia explained to her. "He's supposed to be very charming, and women drop at his feet, like little dogs, waiting for him to love them."

"How disgusting," Victoria said with un-
reserved disapproval, as Olivia and their father
laughed at her reaction. "Why are we inviting
him?"

"He has a charming wife as well."

"And does she wait for men to drop at
her feet too? They could create quite a problem at the party, with everyone dropping on the
floor around them all evening."

They were at the house by then, and the
three of them went in, tired, and well pleased
with their evening. And the subject of Tobias
Whitticomb was quickly forgotten.

But in spite of having invited the dubious
Whitticombs, who had actually accepted by
then, they were all looking forward to their
party. Almost everyone they had asked had accepted, and there were going to be forty-six
guests at four round tables in their dining
room, and dancing in their drawing room afterwards, and even a rather elaborate tent over
the garden so people could stroll there. Olivia
had gone to a great deal of trouble on behalf of
her father.

It seemed only moments before the big
day arrived, and for two days, Olivia did nothing but check flowers and linens and china. She
tasted food, and watched them set up the tent

over the garden. There were ice sculptures set up in the dining room, and the orchestra arrived and she put them in the drawing room. The preparations seemed to go on forever.

Mrs. Peabody did what she could, but even she seemed slightly overwhelmed, and of course Victoria could never be found in time to make herself useful. In the past weeks, she had begun to gather a circle of friends, most of them fairly intellectual, one or two of them writers, and several of them artists, all living in odd places. She had begun visiting them at their studios, and she found that they shared many of the same political views. She was making far more friends than Olivia, who always seemed to be busy taking care of either the house or their father.

Victoria had always told her that she needed to get out more than she did, and Olivia promised she would, as soon as she finished organizing the party. After that, she would be free to do whatever she wanted. In fact, they were going to the Astors' ball the next day, and she could hardly wait to enjoy someone else's evening. But tonight was her big moment as a hostess. This was the first New York party she'd ever given. And she was actually trembling with excitement when she and

Victoria came downstairs in the dark green satin gowns she'd had made by their seamstress in Croton. They had bustles in the back and small trains and the low-cut bodices were encrusted with jet beads. Their hair was piled high on their heads, and they were wearing high-heeled black velvet slippers. And they each wore the long strand of pearls they had gotten from their father when they turned eighteen, and identical diamond earrings. They were like a vision of symmetry, a perfect duet, and even the way they moved seemed in complete unison, as Olivia checked everything one last time, and Victoria followed her around the room looking happy and excited. The band had just begun to play, and the house looked extraordinary, almost completely lit with candles. All of the chandeliers had been lit, there were fragrant flowers everywhere, and the twins themselves looked incredible as they stood in the candlelit drawing room, next to their very handsome father. He took a step back for a moment, looking at them, and it was impossible not to be struck by how beautiful they were, how graceful, and how poised. One of them would have been dazzling, but two left one staring at them in mesmerized disbelief, which was exactly what happened when the guests began to arrive and saw the twins standing beside their father. Prepared as people may have been, suddenly seeing them there took one's breath away, and the guests stared at them constantly, unable to remember which was which, and in some ways, seeing them more as a unit. Neither seemed whole without the other just behind her.

They identified themselves quickly to their friends, and Edward introduced them to everyone, but most of the guests had no idea which twin was Olivia and which Victoria, and Charles Dawson didn't even try when he arrived. He simply greeted them both with a warm smile, and glanced with interest from one to the other. And it was only when he actually began speaking to them in the drawing room that he began to sense again which one was the wilder one, and in a lowered voice, he even dared to tease her about it.

"This is a long way from the Fifth Precinct, isn't it?" he asked with a spark in his own eye, and Victoria looked at him with unabashed defiance, as she grinned at him, not even embarrassed lest anyone might hear her.

"I told Olivia, you should have let them arrest me. I expected it. I was actually very disappointed when they didn't."

"I don't think your sister was," Charles said quietly, admiring her. She was the most beautiful woman he had seen in years, and so was her sister. "I think she was very relieved we got you out of there as fast as we did. I frankly thought we'd have a harder time of it," he said, sounding relieved himself. It had been an awkward moment.

"We can always try it again, I'll call you myself next time," she said, her voice a sensual hint of future naughtiness, and he wondered how Edward Henderson kept his sanity, with two daughters like this to worry about, except that Charles had understood that Olivia was far better behaved than her allegedly "younger" sister, and Edward had said as much to him. He had said that Olivia was his godsend.

"Let me know if you ever need any help. I'll be there," Charles said quietly, and then drifted away to speak to several other guests he knew, and of course, his associate John Dawson. They were under the tent covering the garden by then, admiring the ice sculptures when the last guests finally arrived, and Olivia was mingling with their guests freely. It was Victoria who was still standing near the door, when the Whitticombs arrived. She had no idea who they were, and had no recollection of the earlier conversation about them. She noticed only a very pretty woman in a silver coat and dress, with a silver turban which exposed a lock or two of pale blonde hair. And she was wearing an extremely impressive diamond necklace. And the man at her side was even better looking than she was. He almost took Victoria's breath away as she looked at him, and a moment later his wife drifted away, to meet up with friends she had seen going to the tent, inexorably drawn toward the champagne and the music. She was a very pretty girl, but he seemed not even to notice her, as he stared at Victoria in the dark green and extremely fashionable dress, put together by nimble fingers in Croton, and slightly redesigned by her even more talented twin sister.

"Hello there, I'm Tobias Whitticomb," he said, accepting a glass of champagne from a passing silver tray, and never taking his eyes off Victoria's spectacular figure. He looked into her eyes as he said his name, as though he expected her to know everything that it meant about his reputation. "And you are?" he prompted her, his eyes never leaving her face, wondering why he had never seen her before, and who she was. She was quite a rare beauty.

"I'm Victoria Henderson," she said modestly, suddenly embarrassed in the face of his obviously sophisticated manners.

"Oh dear," he said, clearly disappointed, "you're married to our host. What a lucky fellow." He smiled at her woefully, it was his wife who had responded to the invitation, and Victoria was laughing at him, not remembering anything she had heard about him from her father or her sister. She hadn't been paying close attention to them, and their gossip about one of their future guests had seemed singularly unimportant. And now, all Victoria could see was his shiny black hair, the laughing dark eyes, and the handsome figure. He had a face like an actor, and everything about him said that he was full of fun and mischief.

"I'm not married to the host," she corrected Whitticomb, laughing at his mistake, and wondering if he meant it. "I'm his daughter."

"Oh thank God. The evening has been saved. I couldn't have borne it if you'd been married to him, charming though he may be. In fact, we've done some rather pleasant business." He said it very smoothly as they walked into the drawing room, and without even asking her, he swept her into his arms and began dancing. It was as though they were magnetically drawn to each other, and there was no way to resist it. He told her he had studied in Europe for several years, at Oxford actually, he had played polo there, and two years later, had gone all the way to South America to play polo in Argentina. He told her a fair amount about himself, and all of it was intriguing. He was fascinating, and danced exquisitely, he whirled her around the floor, making her laugh, and being irreverent about almost everyone in the room. Eventually they left the dance floor and he told her funny stories about everyone he could think of, everyone except Evangeline and their children. He never mentioned them, and by their second glass of champagne, he and Victoria were fast friends, and he was vastly amused when he lit a cigarette, and she took a long drag of it when no one was looking.

"My, my, you're a racy one. What else do you do? Drink to excess, smoke cigars, stay up fascinatingly late? Are there other vices I should know about? Absinthe, perhaps? Some mysteries of the Orient?" He was constantly and totally playful, but beyond that he was handsome and sophisticated and standing diz-zyingly close to her. She knew she had never met anyone else like him. After their last dance, she excused herself, and said she had to check on dinner. But she promised to be right back. Then she did something she knew Olivia would be furious about, but she had to do it. In fact, she did it for her twin too, and was satisfied that she had assured the outcome of the rest of the evening.

As Victoria crossed the room to return to Toby, she saw him looking extremely confused. Olivia was talking to him, and he was actually blushing. He had whispered something in her ear, about slipping into the garden for a cigarette, and he was holding her around the waist, as he had done to Victoria while they were dancing, but Olivia did not look pleased, and realized instantly what had happened. And with that, Victoria appeared, and Toby Whitticomb found himself facing both of them, feeling as though he had double vision.

"Oh my God." He looked almost ill as he stared at them. "Did I drink that much champagne? What's happening?" He stared at them in disbelief, never having realized that there were Henderson twins, and for once he was completely stunned into silence.

"Did you behave very badly with my very proper older sister?" Victoria asked him with a wicked grin, as Olivia stared at both of them.

She had no idea yet who he was, or how her sister knew him.

"I'm afraid I did," he said, trying to recover from the embarrassment of having grabbed Olivia around the waist, when he didn't know her, though he scarcely knew Victoria better, but she seemed far more open to advances like his, and far more forgiving. "I offered her a cigarette in the garden, I do hope she smokes too. Perhaps we could all go, although I'm afraid I need another drink now." He gladly grabbed another glass of champagne, and took a long swig as he stared at both of them in continuing disbelief and amazement. "You know, you are absolutely extraordinary, both of you. I've never seen anything like it."

"It's a bit of a shock at first," Olivia said graciously to him although she didn't like his manners, or his air of familiarity with her sister. "But one gets used to it. Or at least, people seem to."

"I'm terribly sorry if I was rude," he said, sensing that she was not as easygoing as her sister. "You must be yet another Miss Henderson. I've outdone myself tonight, I thought your sister was Edward's wife," he laughed at himself this time, and they all did, "and I'm Toby Whitticomb." He held out a hand to her and Olivia immediately stopped laughing. She was extremely cool and prim when she shook his hand, and Victoria immediately saw her tightness.

"I've heard a great deal about you," she said, hoping to dampen his interest in her sister.

"In my case, that's usually not a compliment," he said, looking undisturbed by it, just as the butlers began announcing dinner.

Olivia was greatly relieved by that, knowing that she had chosen a good seat for her twin, between two attractive, wellborn young men, far, far from Tobias. Her own seat was somewhat more dutiful, next to one of her father's oldest friends, and a young man who was excruciatingly shy, and painfully unattractive. But she had thought to do a good deed for him, and had sat herself next to him, and her father's old friend, who had an acute hearing problem. For Olivia, it was going to be a very long dinner. And she had given her father two of their most honored guests on either side of him. She wanted him to have a perfectly delightful evening. He hadn't entertained in New York in years, and it was as much a rebirth for him as for them, and she wanted it to be absolutely perfect.

So far, the evening had been very good, the music was excellent, the food thus far had been tasty, and the champagne superb, chosen by her father. And as Olivia followed her guests slowly into the dining room, she kept an eye on them, seeing that people were finding their seats easily, and were comfortable where they sat. There were four large, ample, exquisitely set tables. The crystal and silver glimmered in the candlelight, almost as handsomely as the jewels on the ladies. And it was only when she saw Victoria sit down that Olivia realized what her sister had done. She gasped, fearing that she had wrought havoc with all her seating, but in fact, she had changed only her own seat with one other guest, to allow herself to sit next to Toby.

Olivia signaled angrily to her, but Victoria was wiser than that, and wouldn't come. Olivia was furious at what Victoria had done to her seating. But a quick glance around the room showed her that other people were sitting where they were supposed to, with the exception of the rather plain woman who had been intended for Victoria's seat. Olivia had done that on purpose. And that woman was now sitting with the two attractive young men meant for her twin, and she seemed very happy about it.

Resigned to her sister's outrageous behavior, but determined to deal with her for it later, the foolishness of letting herself be pursued by a married man, let alone one with his reputation, put Olivia in a dreadful humor as she went to her own seat, and then found someone else in it. And then she realized what other trick Victoria had played on her. She had improved Olivia's seat as well, and put her very kindly next to Charles Dawson. Olivia blushed as she realized it, and then quietly took her seat beside him.

"What an honor," he said politely, staring at her, obviously unsure which one she was, and he leaned close to her as he whispered, "Are you the jailbird or the rescuer? I'm ashamed to admit that I can't always tell the difference." She laughed at his optimism. She couldn't imagine that he could "ever" tell the difference, let alone "always." And he made her laugh just enough to free her somewhat from her earlier ill humor due to Victoria's appalling behavior.

"Do you think you could ever tell us apart, Mr. Dawson?" she asked, teasing him. For an instant, she was tempted not to let him know which one she was, and see if he could guess it, but she felt too guilty to play with him for very long, and it really wasn't like her to do that. He stared long and hard at her, wanting to know for certain who she was, but unable to tell her, and it seemed too cruel to keep it from him, though Olivia let the game go on for a few minutes longer.

"Your movements are even so incredibly similar. The looks in your eyes are different at times, but I'm still not sure which is which. One of you sometimes has something wild there," he said carefully, having observed it both in Croton and the Fifth Precinct. "It's something in your eyes that will probably allow you to go to lengths you will regret . . . but then which-ever one it is who is wild, the other sister will tame you. One of you has a quiet, peaceful soul, the other seems somewhat restless," he said, looking at her with interest, already begin-ning to sense which one she was, and relieved to be sitting next to Olivia, and not her sister. Victoria unsettled his soul, and was much too full of unbridled passion for him to be comfort-able near her.

But Olivia was intrigued by what he said, and had to admit he had observed them well. "You have identified us correctly, sir," she said, smiling softly at him, and he was almost sure now which one she was, though he didn't say it. "You're a very observant man," Olivia said quietly, and he nodded.

"I try to be. It's part of my profession," he said simply.

"And part of who you are as well," she said, having observed him carefully too.

"And will you tell me now who you are?" he asked, "or will you keep it a mystery all night?" He seemed willing to play if that was what she wanted. Victoria would have let him suffer, but Olivia couldn't.

"I don't suppose that would be fair. I'm Olivia." She smiled at him as she said it, and although she was still furious at her twin for her antics over the seating, and with Tobias Whitticomb for his behavior with her, she was suddenly grateful for her seat beside Charles Dawson.

"You are the rescuer, the one with the quiet soul," he said, and she felt somewhat less so than his description, though she certainly didn't look it. She was every bit as beautiful as her sister. "Are you truly both very different? It's hard to see at first, though I must admit I've noticed something unsatisfied in her, something searching. You seem much more at home in your own skin than she is."

"I don't know why that is. Perhaps because she thinks she killed our mother." It was an odd confession to make to him, but he seemed to be someone one could talk to and trust, and she knew she hadn't misjudged him. He had already proven himself trustworthy by not divulging their secret, after helping to pick up Victoria at the Fifth Precinct. "Our mother died giving birth to us, and Victoria is the younger twin. It was her birth that seemed to do it, although one can't help but wonder what difference eleven minutes would make. I'm afraid we did it together." She had felt the same guilt too, but not to the same degree that Victoria had suffered from it.

"One can't see things that way. There's no way to know why something like that happens. You were both a great gift for her, it's a shame she could not live to enjoy it. I'm sure your father has derived great joy from both of you over the years. I think being or having twins would be wonderful. You're very lucky."

She knew that they had touched on the death of his wife as well with what he had just said, he must have questioned often in the past year and a half why she had died, and there could be no real answers.

"Tell me about your son," she said very gently.

"Geoffrey?" He smiled at her. "He's nine years old, he is the light of my life, and I love him very much. We're alone," he said, not sure if she knew that. "We lost his mother a little over a year ago . . . on the *Titanic*." He seemed to choke on the word, and she barely touched his hand unconsciously with her own, and he looked at her and nodded. "It was very difficult for a long time. I went back to Europe with Geoff to stay with her family. It was a terrible shock for all of us, especially Geoff. He was with her."

"How awful for him," she said sincerely, deeply moved by the way he looked as he said it.

"He has some terrible memories, understandably. But he's better now." He smiled ruefully then, feeling as though he'd made a friend. She was surprisingly warm and easy to talk to. "Better than I am. I never go to evenings like this anymore, but John and your father insisted."

"That's not fair to you, is it? You can't keep to yourself forever."

"I suppose not," he said gently, looking at her, and admiring her. It had been easier talking to her than to anyone in the past year and a half, and it surprised him.

"You'll have to bring your son to visit. Children love coming to Croton. I loved it there when I was a child too. I was about his age when we moved there."

"And now?" He was curious about her, she seemed to have an unusual depth of understanding. "Do you still love living in Croton?"

"I do. It's my sister who doesn't. She'd rather be here, or in demonstrations somewhere, or in England with the suffragists, starving in prison."

"That's what I said," he smiled at her, "restless."

"Actually," she laughed, "I owe her an unexpected debt tonight. I am not directly responsible for our seating."

"I thought you were the one who handled everything like this for your father." Edward had raved about her, and her invaluable assistance in running all his households, and even putting together every detail of this party.

"I do, but Victoria changed her seat tonight, and mine. She didn't like where she was sitting."

"Well, I'm very grateful to her." He smiled at Olivia, clear on who she was now. "Perhaps you should let her do the seating more often." He asked her to dance then, and they moved circumspectly around the drawing room, with his hand barely upon her. And as soon as the dance was over, he brought her right back to the table. It was hardly a sensual experience, but it was pleasant being with him. He was intelligent and nice to talk to, and it was easy to understand now why he kept his distance. She sensed from what he'd said and the way he behaved that he had obviously been very much in love with his wife, and had no intention of getting close to anyone else at the moment. Olivia understood that, but it didn't stop her from feeling attracted to him, or thinking that if life had been different for all of them, he would have been everything she wanted. But there was no chance to think of that now. She couldn't have left her father anyway, and didn't think she ever would. And Charles Dawson had no intention of opening his heart to anyone, not even for the sake of his little boy, Geoffrey.

The ladies withdrew and went upstairs briefly at the end of the meal, and it was then that Olivia spoke to Victoria again and warned her not to continue pursuing Toby.

"I'm doing no such thing." Victoria looked highly annoyed by her sister's warnings about him. He was charming, intelligent, danced brilliantly, and was even more outrageous than Victoria had ever dreamed of being, and she saw no harm whatsoever in a little mild flirtation. What she didn't understand was that with Toby there was no such thing. And he always got what he wanted.

"I absolutely forbid you to spend the rest of the evening with him," Olivia said to her in an undervoice, just as his wife happened to walk by. But Victoria was not going to give in to her sister.

"You have no right to say that to me, Olivia," Victoria shot back at her. "You're not my mother, and he's not the man you think he is. He's kind and decent, and I enjoy talking to him. That's all this is, Olivia. It's a party, an evening, a conversation. I'm not running away with him. He's not having an affair with me. This is just a little talk and dancing. There's no harm in it. I think it's very sad if you are unable to understand that."

"I understand a great deal more than you think I do, or you seem able to discern yourself," she said, still in a furious whisper. "You're doing something very dangerous with him, Victoria. You're teasing a lion." But the phrase only made her laugh, and Victoria repeated it to him the moment they went downstairs again, where she had been quick to find him. No one seemed to have observed what was going on between them. And Victoria and Toby disappeared into the garden and even went beyond the tent. He stood with an arm around her in the warm September air, and shared a cigarette with her while he told her something he said he had never told anyone else before, outside his marriage. But as crazy as it sounded, after only one evening with her, he said he thought he loved her. He told her too that he had nothing more than an arrangement with Evangeline, that he had been so lonely for years, he thought it might kill him. Their families had forced them into it, and their marriage was hollow, meaningless, and meant nothing to him. It was a loveless union, and he had been starved for true love for so long that meeting Victoria tonight had changed everything for him. Had Olivia heard his speech, she might have killed him.

Victoria sat listening to him, outwardly sophisticated, but in fact incredibly naive, believing every word he said to her, as she looked up at him adoringly but innocently, and then he kissed her. He wanted to know when they could meet again. He doubted he could live without her another moment. He said he knew how strong her principles were, after all she'd said to him that night, how ardently she believed in the cause of feminism, and of suffrage, but he was a man who shared those views with her, and he would never take advantage of her in any way. He just wanted to be near her, and get to know her.

Victoria was dazzled by him, and believed every word he said to her. She wanted to believe him. She had never heard anything like it. And by the end of the evening, she felt as though she had become a part of Toby. They talked about the coincidence that they were both going to the Astors' ball the next day, and after that they would have to figure out some way to meet, he said. And for an odd moment, with a strange glint in his eye, he asked if Victoria would be more comfortable, when they met, if she brought her sister. But Victoria looked horrified. She already knew what Olivia thought of him, and that she'd do everything she could to prevent their meeting. Victoria told him that she would not bring Olivia with her, and he seemed to accept that. It had just been a rather amusing idea that he had clung to for only the briefest of moments. And then, having agreed to meet somehow, somewhere, the day after the Astors' ball, he took her back into the tent, and from there to the drawing room, and was then quite dismayed to discover that Evangeline had a dreadful headache and insisted on going home immediately, but by then the damage was done, the deal was made, the date was set, and Victoria was already head over heels with Toby.

Olivia was elsewhere in the house when the Whitticombs left, and she saw none of it, but Charles had, and he stood across the room afterwards watching Victoria with interest. There was something about the way she moved her head, the way she looked at men, her secretiveness, her seductiveness, her mysteriousness, that was entirely different from her sister. Olivia was completely open, willing to hold out her heart and her hand, he sensed easily how giving she was, how caring. And yet it was the tormented one who fascinated him, the one who didn't know yet what she wanted, and wanted all the wrong things thus far, that intrigued him. There was something so insanely perverse about it that it even annoyed him, and there was a part of him that wanted to stride across the room and grab Victoria and shake her for her foolishness, but of course he didn't.

There was yet another part of him that wanted to forget her entirely and concentrate on the far more sensible, infinitely decent Olivia, and yet she seemed so uncomplicated, so able to give and to receive that she frightened him. He was far too tortured and too bruised himself, after Susan's death, to accept all that Olivia offered. He had grown used to pain, to unbelief, to frustration and anger, and it was far easier for him to be near someone who didn't want him, had no expectations of him, than to be near all that Olivia had to give him. To even let her close to him, with her wide-open heart, would have been a betrayal of Susan. Victoria was something entirely different. And he watched her as the evening wound down, fascinated by her. She had something on her mind now, probably the infamous Tobias Whitticomb. And he couldn't help wondering what she was going to do about it. Would he be getting rescue calls again? Would Olivia dare to stop her? Did she even realize what was happening, or was Victoria clever enough to conceal it from her? Just watching her intrigued him.

And at last Charles went to speak to their father, and thank him for the evening. It had been a splendid party, the first he'd been to in more than a year. He had woken some old and new feelings that faintly unnerved him. Both the tenderness that Olivia had aroused, and the raw hunger and aching loneliness that Victoria caused him. None were emotions he could put up with. And he left with an odd feeling of emptiness that night, that neither the polite excess of alcohol he'd consumed could numb, nor his son sleeping peacefully at home could fill. He wanted one thing, one life, one person, and she was gone now. And neither of the Henderson twins, however lonely, were adequate substitutes for her.

Charles said good night to both twins when he left, and thanked them for the party. Victoria had said very little to him. She had looked somewhat heated, and distracted, and he realized that she'd been drinking too, although Olivia hadn't. She'd had a few sips of champagne while they talked, and she thanked him for coming. He said good-bye to her, trying not to look straight into her heart, but she made it all too easy for him. He wanted to warn her that life would be cruel to her, that a heart like hers was dangerous, and she would do well to hide it. But in truth, it was Victoria who was in real danger. And Olivia knew that. She had seen Toby with her, and after the last guest left, and they finally went to their room well after two o'clock in the morning, Olivia followed her there and watched her.

"You agreed to see him, didn't you?" She confronted her, the party was nearly ruined for her, from worrying about her sister.

"Of course not," Victoria lied, and Olivia knew that too. She knew everything. It was impossible not to. Victoria was far too transparent. It didn't even require their special bond to understand it. "Besides, it's none of your business."

"The man is a rotter," Olivia shouted at her, "everyone in New York knows that."

"He knows his reputation too. He told me so himself."

"How clever. But that does not absolve him. Victoria, you *cannot* see him."

"I can do anything I want to, and you can't stop me," Victoria hissed at her. Nothing would stop her. Toby's lure was far more powerful than her sister's caution. He was the devil, the serpent in the Garden of Eden.

"Please . . . listen to me . . ." There were tears in Olivia's eyes as she begged her.

"You'll get hurt. You're not sophisticated enough to handle a man like this. No one is, except maybe someone like him. Victoria, listen to me. Believe me. The stories about him are awful."

"He says they're lies," Victoria said, thoroughly convinced and manipulated by him in a single evening. The man was a genius at convincing people of whatever he wanted, particularly women. "Because people are jealous of him."

"Why?" Olivia tried to reason with her, to no avail. It was hopeless. "Why should they be?"

"His looks, his position, his money." He had told Victoria all that himself, and she believed him.

"His looks will be gone soon, his position is his wife's, and he was lucky with the money. So what's to be jealous of?" Olivia said coldly.

"Maybe you want him for yourself," Victoria suggested evilly, not sure whether or not she believed it, but determined to say it anyway. She was furious with Olivia for trying to keep her from seeing Toby. "Maybe you want him, and not that dreadful dullard attorney of Father's."

"Stop being so rude about him. He's a decent man, Victoria, and you know it."

"He bores me," she said, the champagne talking as much as her own heart now.

"Charles Dawson won't hurt you. Toby Whitticomb will. He'll use you, and then he'll throw you away, like paper to write on. And when it's all over, he'll go back to his wife and have another baby."

"You're disgusting," Victoria said to her, and Olivia felt the familiar pain in her stomach she always got when they argued. She hated fighting with her sister, and seldom did it. This was not like their innocent squabbles, or even their more serious ones, about Victoria's childish pranks and adventures. This was a death dance, and Olivia knew it.

"I won't speak to you about this again, but I want you to know that I'm here for you, always, and I love you. And I'm begging you not to see him. I know you'll do what you want, but he's dangerous, Victoria. And Father would be very upset if he knew you had spent the evening with him. He only invited him to be polite, and you were very foolish sitting yourself next to him. You're lucky Father had his back to you and never noticed. You're playing with a lion, Victoria. You're not big enough or strong enough to win. And eventually, the lion will eat you."

"I'm not worried," she said confidently, "we're just friends. That's all. He's married anyway." She was trying to get Olivia off the scent, so she could have some freedom. And she didn't bother to tell her how empty their marriage was. He had even hinted to her that they had been talking about divorcing recently. It would be a terrible scandal, of course, but he said he couldn't bear to go on in a loveless marriage like this for much longer. Victoria felt desperately sorry for him. But Olivia didn't, she hated him and wanted to send him away before he destroyed her sister.

When they went to bed that night, long after three o'clock, all Olivia could think of was the mess her sister was in, and all Victoria could think of was the Astors' ball the next night, when she knew she would see him.

Chapter 4

Olivia woke the next day to muffled sounds from downstairs, and as she lay in bed and listened to them, she remembered instantly the agonizing argument with her sister. But when she turned on her side to look at her, she saw that the other side of the bed was empty. Olivia got up quietly, combed her hair, and put her dressing gown on to see what the noises were, and then she remembered.

As soon as she got downstairs, she saw men everywhere, there were people in the garden taking down the tent, furniture being put back where it belonged, and flowers from their guests being delivered by the armful. It was total chaos. And Mrs. Peabody and the butler were standing in the midst of it, directing traffic.

"Did you sleep well?" Bertie smiled at her, and Olivia nodded, apologizing for not having gotten up early enough to help her.

"You did a lovely job last night, my dear. You deserved a little rest this morning. I'm glad you could sleep through all this racket." Though it was difficult to imagine how, as they were making a huge amount of noise taking down the tent in the garden. "Everyone says the evening was a great success. I'm sure that all of New York is talking about it today, they must be, judging by the amount of flowers we've received. I've put most of them in the dining room for the moment."

Olivia wandered into the dining room quietly, wondering where Victoria had gone, and almost the first bouquet she saw was a huge vase filled with two dozen long-stemmed red roses, but when Olivia read the card attached to it, it said only "Thank you for the most important evening of my life." It was unsigned, and then she saw that the envelope was addressed to her sister. It was far too easy to figure out who had sent it. The other arrangements all had signed cards, and were a great deal more circumspect, though possibly less pretty. There was a lovely arrangement though, she noticed, from Charles, addressed to all three of them, thanking them for a delightful evening. She knew that it was the first time he had gone out formally since his wife had died, and she was glad that he had had a pleasant evening. She certainly had, seated next to him, though she was still somewhat annoyed at Victoria for having changed the seating.

Olivia wandered into the kitchen then, and observed the activity there, and then she saw Victoria, sitting alone in the breakfast room, drinking a cup of coffee. Olivia stood looking at her for a moment, worrying about her again, and then she walked over and sat down beside her.

"Did you sleep well?" Olivia asked uncomfortably, still ill at ease after their argument of the night before. It had been far more serious than any they'd had in years. And this time was far more lethal than their childish fights. Olivia was convinced that her sister was in real danger.

"Very well, thank you," Victoria said formally, without looking at her. "I'm surprised you could sleep with all the noise down here," she said, glancing over her shoulder. Olivia thought she looked particularly beautiful, which was odd. She never thought of herself that way, and yet she could always see something different, and more exciting, in her younger sister. And there was something she had never seen before in Victoria's eyes that morning.

"I think I was exhausted." Olivia didn't mention the altercation of the night before, but after she had sat down and been served coffee by one of the kitchen maids, she asked Victoria if she had seen her flowers.

"Yes, I did," she answered after a moment's hesitation.

"I think I can figure out who sent them. I imagine you can too." Olivia said it cautiously, and there was a long silence. "I hope you'll think about what I said last night, Victoria. It's a very dangerous situation."

"They're only roses, Olivia. There's no need for you to get up in arms over them, or about anything that happened last night. He's a very interesting man, that's all. You don't need to make anything more of it," Victoria said, trying to make light of it in the morning sunshine, but Olivia could see something in her twin's eyes that frightened her, something very determined and powerful. And she knew instinctively that Victoria was not going to let go of Toby.

"I hope you don't spend time with him again tonight. It would make people talk, and the party is at his wife's cousins' house. You really have to be careful," Olivia warned her.

"Thank you, Olivia," Victoria said, and stood up, looking down at her sister. They were so identical without, and so different within, sometimes it was hard to believe they were even sisters, let alone twins. Olivia felt a shiver of fear at the chasm she suddenly felt between them.

"What are you doing today?" she asked innocently.

"I'm going to a lecture. Is that all right with you, Olivia dear, or do I need your permission?"

"I just asked. You needn't be so sensitive, or so rude," she said tartly, tired of the sparks and the sudden enmity that had come up between them because of Victoria's flirtation with Toby. "Since when do you ask my permission to do anything? You only expect me to cover up for you, you never bother to ask before you do whatever it is you wanted to do in the first place."

"You won't need to cover up for me today, thank you very much." It was times like this that made each of them wish they had other friends. But the exclusivity of their relationship, their unusual closeness, their isolation from school, and the remoteness of where they lived, had always deprived them of other people. They had always been closer to each other than to anyone else, and although they liked it most of the time, at times it left each of them feeling somewhat lonely. "What are you doing today?" Victoria asked. "Housework, I assume, as usual." She made Olivia sound incredibly dull, and Olivia felt it, as she looked at her sister. No one had sent her two dozen roses with an anonymous card. The man she admired had sent an impersonal card addressed not only to her, but to her father and sister, and for a fraction of a second, Olivia found herself wondering if Victoria was right, and she was jealous.

"I'm going to help Bertie put the house back in order again. It'll drive poor Father crazy to live with this mess for very long. I thought we could do it all today before the ball at the Astors' tonight."

"How entertaining."

Victoria swept upstairs then, and she left the house an hour later, in a dark blue silk suit and a fashionable hat, and had Petrie drive her to her meeting. It was in a very ordinary neighborhood, and after he dropped her off, he came back very quickly.

The rest of the day sped by for all of them, Victoria came back early in the afternoon, and Bertie put her to work too, ordering the men who were bringing back the furniture from where it had been stored in their carriage house around the corner. Olivia was working frantically, trying to help repair some of the damage that had been done in the garden, and by five o'clock, miraculously, the house looked as though no one had been there. Bertie congratulated both of them on their fine work, and almost as though on cue, their father walked in and told them how nice the house looked.

"You'd never know we had so much as a dinner guest, let alone fifty people dancing all over the place, and a tent damn near destroying the garden. How bad is it out there?" he asked, and Olivia reassured him. "Everyone in New York is talking about what delightful hostesses you are," he said to both girls, but Victoria looked uninterested in his praise, and a few minutes later she went upstairs to dress for the Astors' party. Olivia had already put their dresses out for them, they were pale pink gauzy dresses she had copied, as usual, from Poiret, and they were quite demure. She'd had a moment of doubt when she set them out, and then decided that perhaps it was what was needed at the moment, precisely not to entice Toby.

"It really was a lovely party, Olivia," her father complimented her again, and sat down in his favorite chair in his comfortable study. Everything had been replaced precisely as it had been, and Olivia poured him a glass of port and handed it to him, as he looked up at her with a warm smile. With each passing day, he seemed to enjoy her company more than ever. "You spoil me terribly, my dear. I'm not even sure your mother would have been as kind, if she were alive. She was a bit more like your sister, a bit fiery at times, and determined to remain independent." Being in this house always reminded him of her. It was painful for him at times, and yet he liked being there now with his daughters. He was happy with his business deals, and the time he was spending with his attorneys making plans, they were interesting, intelligent men, and it reminded him of the days before he'd retired, when he was running an empire, and not just a portfolio of investments. He had been thinking of selling his steel mills in Pittsburgh recently, and Charles thought he had located a serious, interested buyer. But it was not a simple decision to make, and he was thinking now that they might be in New York at least until the end of October, if not longer.

"Are you enjoying it here?" her father asked, happy to have a moment alone with her.

"Yes, Father, I like it," she said with a quiet smile. "I'm not sure I'd like living here all the time. I think I'd miss the country if we lived in the city permanently, but I like the museums, and the people, and the parties. There's always so much going on. It's fun being here." She smiled at him more warmly, and for a moment she looked like a child again, but she was still very much a woman, and there were times when he felt guilty for being so possessive of them. He knew they were of an age when they should be out in the world, as they were now, and finding husbands, and yet he knew he would be heartbroken when they finally left him.

"I suppose I should be making more of an effort to introduce you to eligible young men," he said halfheartedly, sipping his port, and they exchanged a smile. "You and Victoria should be getting married one of these days, though I hate thinking of it, I'll admit. I don't know what

I'd do without you. You most of all, I'm afraid. You'll have to stop taking such good care of me, my dear, so it won't be such a shock when you go. I absolutely dread it." His eyes were filled with fatherly love, as she took his hand in her own and kissed it.

"I'll never leave you. You know that. I couldn't." It was what she had said to him when she was five, and then ten, but now she really meant it. His health had weakened considerably over the years, his heart wasn't strong, and she couldn't imagine leaving him. Who would look after him if she did? Who would run his homes? Who would keep after everyone, or see when he was lying about his health and actually feeling ill, and really needed the doctor? She knew she could never trust anyone else to take care of him, certainly not Victoria who never even noticed when he was ill, until somebody, usually Olivia, told her. "I couldn't leave you, Father," she said firmly, and meant it.

"You can't stay an old maid, not as pretty as you both are," he said, admiring her, and knowing that it would have been wrong to let her do that. And yet, there was a part of him that wanted to let her have her way, even if it meant sacrificing herself. He needed her as much as she thought he did, and it was so easy having her take care of everything domestic. It was almost as though she was already married to his life, she took care of the most minute details. He would have been lost without her, but he also knew that not pushing her out of the nest eventually would have been incredibly selfish. And then, not even wanting to think of losing her, he carefully changed the subject. "Has Victoria met anyone exciting here? I haven't paid much attention to any prospective suitors." He had noticed that Charles Dawson seemed to be somewhat fascinated by her, but he was probably intrigued by both of them. Most people were, it was hard not to be overwhelmed by such doubly extraordinary beauty.

"I don't think so, Father," Olivia lied, as always, for her, even now, worried about the abominable Toby. "We haven't really met anyone yet. I mean . . . not really . . ." They had of course met everyone who was anyone in New York, at the theater when their father took them out, at dinner parties, at concerts they had gone to. But no one had specifically introduced them to any young men with the intention of marrying them off. In some ways, Olivia correctly guessed that some people were intimidated by them, or viewed them as freaks, or thought they would never agree to leave each other. Most people had no concept of how different they were, how divergent their tastes and interests. They just saw them as one very pretty girl, seen double.

"Victoria is behaving, isn't she?" her father asked with a look of amusement. He had finally heard, through indirect means, that his daughter had learned to drive and had actually stolen one of his cars, and had gone somewhere with it in Croton. He had never heard of her near arrest, fortunately, and the escapade with the Ford struck him as harmless and somewhat silly. Her mother might have done the same thing at her age, and driven right over his favorite flowerbeds in the process. She had actually walked her horse into their living room once, on a bet with a friend, and everyone had been horrified. But Edward had thought it was very funny. He was actually surprisingly tolerant for a man his age, and had never been particularly upset by Victoria's high spirits, in fact, he had indulged them, because she reminded him so much of her mother.

"Will you be all right down here?" Olivia asked when she left him to dress for the party at the Astors'. She poured him another glass of port, and left him sitting next to the fireplace, comfortably reading the evening paper. He said he was going upstairs in a few minutes himself to dress, and told her what time to be ready for the party.

And as she walked upstairs, she thought of the questions he had asked, about Victoria meeting any men in New York, and either of them finding husbands and getting married. And she thought too about what she'd said to him. She really couldn't imagine leaving him and getting married. What if his health failed? Or he became ill? Who would take care of him? It would have been different if her mother had been alive, they would have had the luxury of normal lives then. But now Olivia felt that at least one of them should stay and take care of him, and she was the obvious one to do it. But as she thought of it, she let her mind drift to Charles, and she suddenly asked herself what would happen if a man like him ever asked her to marry him. What would she do then? It made her heart beat faster just thinking of it. She couldn't imagine a man like Charles ever pursuing her . . . but if he did . . . if . . . she couldn't even allow herself to think of it. She had obligations here. And Charles had absolutely no interest in her. He was only being kind to her whenever he came to see her father.

When Olivia reached her bedroom, she could hear her sister dressing in the bathroom beyond. They had closets and mirrors there, and when she walked in to run a bath, she saw half a dozen dresses on the floor, among them the pink one she had selected for them to wear to the Astors'.

"What are you doing?" She looked at Victoria in surprise, and then quickly understood what had happened.

"I'm *not* wearing that *thing* you picked out for tonight," Victoria said viciously, throwing another reject on a chair. "We'll look like a couple of country bumpkins, although I suppose that was your intention."

"I think it's very pretty," Olivia said noncommittally, admitting nothing to her overwrought twin sister. "What else did you have in mind?" She had obviously already been through half their closet. And at the moment she was holding up a dress Olivia had never liked. She had tried copying a dress by Beer, in deep crimson velvet with tiny jet beads, and a long beaded train behind it. Olivia had always thought it was far too low cut for them, and other than at a Christmas party at their father's house in Croton-on-Hudson, they had never worn it. "I don't like that, and you know it," Olivia said to Victoria as soon as she saw what she was holding. It had a black satin beaded cape that went over it, lined in the crimson velvet. "It's too low cut, and too showy. We'll look vulgar."

"This is a ball, not a tea party in Croton, Olivia," Victoria said coldly.

"You're trying to show off for him, Victoria, and I won't help you do it. In that dress, in this town, we'll look like harlots. And I won't wear it."

"Fine," Victoria said, pirouetting on one heel, and Olivia didn't want to admit to her how sensational she looked. The dress was a lot better than she remembered, but it also seemed far too daring. "Then why don't you wear the pink, Ollie dear, and I'll wear this one." Much to Olivia's surprise, she sounded as though she meant it.

"Don't be stupid." They never went out in different outfits. All their lives, they had matched every single thing, right down to their underwear and their hairpins. It was simply what they did, and going out in something different than her twin would have made Olivia feel naked.

"Why not? We're grown-up. We don't have to wear the same thing anymore. Bertie always thought it was sweet when we were children. But we don't have to be sweet anymore, Olivia, in fact, I refuse to. That pink thing is 'sweet,' it's so 'sweet' it makes me sick to look at it. This is what I want to wear, what I'm *going* to wear to the Astors' tonight, and if you don't like it, feel free to wear something different."

"That's spiteful of you, Victoria, and I know precisely what you're doing and so do you. And let me tell you, last night was *not* the most important evening of his life, but it may have been of yours, if you choose to ruin it for Tobias Whitticomb. You're a damn fool if you do that." Olivia spat the words at her, yanking the identical red velvet dress out of her closet. "I *hate* this stupid dress, and I'm sorry I had it made, particularly if you're going to make fools of us, forcing me to wear it to the Astors'."

"I told you," Victoria said, having laid the dress aside again, while she brushed her hair. "You don't have to wear it." But this time, Olivia didn't answer.

The two never spoke to each other again, as they bathed and dressed, and powdered and perfumed. And Olivia looked surprised when she saw Victoria put on the merest hint of lip rouge. Neither of them had ever worn it before, and Olivia thought her sister suddenly looked very different. She looked not only beautiful, but more than a little racy.

"I'm not wearing that," Olivia said sullenly as she finished doing her hair, and watched Victoria put on the lip rouge in the mirror.

"No one said you had to."

"You're in over your head, Victoria," Olivia said darkly.

"Maybe I swim better than you do."

"He'll drown you," Olivia said sadly, as Victoria left the room, dragging the satin-and-velvet beaded cape behind her.

As the two girls came down the stairs a few minutes later, their father stared up at them in total silence. Everything about the way they looked that night told him they were no longer little girls. They looked like truly dazzling women. Victoria came down the stairs first, and even the way she moved spoke of worlds she knew nothing about, and yet was instinctively a part of. It was Olivia who looked considerably less at ease in the highly visible outfit. Their figures suited it, and the dress showed off their creamy skin and lithe young bodies. They both had tiny waists and high breasts, all of which were shown off to full advantage in the low-cut crimson velvet.

"Good Heavens, where did you get those dresses?" their father asked, surprised to see them in something so fashionable and almost exotic.

"Olivia had them made for us," Victoria said sweetly, "I think she designed them."

"I had them copied actually," Olivia said unhappily as the butler helped them put their capes on, "but they didn't come out the way I wanted."

"I'll be the envy of every man there," their father said generously and led them both outside to the waiting limousine. There was a chill in the air, and he looked at both girls as they stepped into the car ahead of him. He'd been right that afternoon, they were certainly no longer children. And it would be a miracle if every man there didn't propose to them that night. He was almost sorry to take them out looking like that, they were far too sensuous looking and too appealing. But he wasn't nearly as sorry as Olivia, sitting pressed into the corner of the car, hating the dress she'd been forced to wear, and furious with her sister.

When they arrived at the Astors' palatial

home on Fifth Avenue, it was ablaze with light, and inside and out, it looked like a palace. There were four hundred people there, and faces and names that the girls had only read about or heard of. The Goelets and the Gibsons were there, Prince Albert of Monaco, a French count, an English duke, and an assortment of minor nobles from other countries. All of the available New York aristocracy was there, some who hadn't been out in years, like the Ellsworths who had been in seclusion for two years, since the death of their eldest daughter. A handful of survivors from the *Titanic* disaster the year before were there, and some said it was literally the first time they had been out, which made Olivia think immediately of Charles Dawson. She nodded to Madeleine Astor, who had lost her husband John when the ship went down, and she was looking exceptionally pretty. The baby she'd had after his father died was almost a year old now, and it saddened Olivia to think that he would never know his father.

"You're looking exceptionally well tonight." She heard a familiar voice and turned to see who it was, and was surprised to see Charles Dawson. And then he laughed, "I know you're Miss Henderson, and I could pre-

Danielle Steel

tend to know which one you are, but I'm afraid I don't, so you'll have to help me."

"Olivia," she said with a slow smile, with a sudden mischievous temptation to pretend she was her sister, just to see if he would say anything different. "What are you doing here, Mr. Dawson?" she asked with a smile. He had told her the night before he never went to parties.

"I hope you're telling me the truth," he said, as though he knew what she had just been thinking about tricking him. "I shall just have to believe you. Actually, I was related to the Astors by marriage. My late wife was the niece of our hostess, and she was very kind and insisted that I come. I'm not sure I would have, if it hadn't been for last night. You broke the ice for me, but I'm afraid this is rather more serious than I expected. It's an absolute madhouse," not like their elegant little soirée of the night before, with a mere fifty people. But the Astors' home accommodated the glittering crowd easily, and in fact Victoria had vanished the moment they entered.

Charles stayed and talked to Olivia for quite a while, they chatted about his son, and the few people Olivia knew there, and some she recognized, and then he said something about Madeleine Astor having been on the ship

142

with his wife when it went down. He always looked so desperately sad when he talked about her, that it tore at Olivia's heart to see it. She had no idea what to say to him, and she suspected that it was a grief from which he might never recover. He seemed to be functioning, but there was a piece of him which was clearly so torn apart that it appeared as though it could never be mended.

"I assume your sister must be here to-night," he said pleasantly. "I haven't seen her."

"Neither have I. She disappeared as soon as we arrived. She's wearing the same awful dress," Olivia said woefully, but at least in this crowd it didn't stick out, there were others like it, or even far more daring. But Charles laughed at what she'd said.

"I take it you don't like it. It's very handsome though. Very," he looked slightly embarrassed as he said it, "is 'grown-up' the wrong word to use with a young woman your age?"

"Inappropriate might be better. I told Victoria I feel like a harlot. She chose it, but I had it made in the first place, so she can blame me, and has. Worse yet, my father thinks it was my choice."

"Did he object?" Charles asked, amused, and she watched his eyes as they spoke. They were so deep and so green and so intriguing. And without meaning to, the crowd pushed her gently against him.

"No, he liked it." She made a face, referring to her father liking the dress she detested.

"Men always like women in red velvet," Charles informed her. "I think it gives them the illusion of something wicked." Olivia nodded, hoping that in her sister's case it would be nothing more than an illusion.

Charles took her in to dinner eventually, and after a while he left her with a group of young ladies. He introduced Olivia to all of them, and hoped she was comfortable with them, when he went in search of his wife's cousins. He had already explained that his little boy was ill and he didn't want to stay late at the party. She was sorry to see him go, because the music had just started. And a few minutes later, she saw that her sister was one of the first on the floor, far too predictably in the arms of Toby. She watched them circle slowly around the floor in a slow, easy waltz, and then was shocked a little while later, to see them still there, and doing the brand-new fox-trot.

"Good lord, it's like seeing two of you," one of the girls said, staring at her, fascinated by how much she looked like her twin sister.

She said she'd never seen anything like it. "Are you totally, totally alike in every way?" she asked, consumed with curiosity while Olivia smiled. It was always like this for them, people wanted to know what it was like being identical twin sisters.

"Pretty much. We're mirror twins. Things I have on the right, she has on the left. My right eyebrow goes up a bit, her left one does. My left foot is bigger, her right one is."

"What fun it must have been growing up," another of the Astor cousins said. And two of the Rockefeller girls had joined them to listen. Olivia had met one of them on the old Gould estate, and she had seen the other at a tea the Rockefellers had given in the music room at Kykuit. All Olivia could remember about it was the incredible organ. Since the Rockefellers neither danced nor drank, they seldom gave grand parties the way the Vanderbilts and Astors did, but they often had small musical soirées, or lunches at Kykuit.

"Did you switch *all* the time?" one of the girls asked.

"No," Olivia laughed. "Only when we wanted to get into mischief, or out of it. My sister hated taking exams in school, so I always took all of them for her. When we were very little, she kept talking me into taking her medicine for her, and I'd get very sick taking it for both of us, until the lady who took care of us caught on to what we were doing. She usually knew, but sometimes she'd have one of the maids give us castor oil, or things we really hated. And we could always fool them."

"Why would you do that?" One of the girls made an awful face at the thought of a double dose of castor oil. It was a hideous prospect.

"Because I love her," Olivia said simply, always at a loss to explain the lengths to which she would have gone for her twin sister. The bond between them was beyond severing, beyond challenging, beyond explaining. "I did a lot of silly things for her, and she for me. Eventually, our father took us out of school because we caused so much trouble. We had a lot of fun though." Olivia smiled at them, and they marveled at her stories. But talking to them had distracted her, and an hour later, Olivia realized that Victoria was still dancing with Toby. They had never left the floor, and Victoria looked as though she were molded into his arms as they circled slowly around the floor, lost in each other's eyes, and oblivious to the hundreds of people around them.

Olivia excused herself from among the young ladies then, and went to look for Charles, and she was relieved when she found him nearly at the front door, with his coat on.

"Will you do me a favor?" she asked quietly, with pleading eyes that he found hard to resist. They matched the tone he'd heard in her voice the day she'd called him and asked him to come to the Fifth Precinct with her.

"Is something wrong?" he asked, concerned, and surprised at how comfortable he was with her. In some ways, she was like a little sister. It was nothing of what he felt when he was in the presence of her twin sister. And yet side by side, ignoring his instinctive feelings for them, he would have been unable to determine who was who. It was only when he talked to them, when he stood with them for a while, and felt a strange stirring in his soul, that he knew. He liked to think he could have told them apart instantly, if he'd known them better. "Is our friend up to some mischief again?" he asked, concerned. It always seemed to be Victoria who was in trouble, and Olivia who was rescuing her. He had long since understood that much about the relationship between them.

"I'm afraid so. Will you dance with me, Mr. Dawson?"

"Charles . . . please. I think we've gotten past 'Mr. Dawson.' " He took off his coat, handed it to the butler again, without a complaint to her that it had just taken him half an hour to get it, and he was anxious to get home to Geoff. He followed her dutifully through the next two rooms and onto the dance floor, and then he saw instantly what her problem was. Toby and Victoria were dancing closer still by then, and Olivia looked extremely unhappy when she saw them.

Charles led her onto the dance floor and danced as close to them as possible, but Toby was artful at avoiding them, and Victoria appeared to be oblivious to her sister's glances and pointedly disapproving faces. Finally, she turned her back on them, and whispered something to Toby, until at last they left the dance floor, and disappeared into the next room. And Olivia couldn't see them as soon as the crowd closed around them.

"Thank you," Olivia said, looking very grim, and Charles smiled down at her.

"That's not an easy job you've set yourself. She's a very headstrong girl." He still remembered how annoyed she had been not to be arrested, and how ungrateful for her sister's succor. "That was Tobias Whitticomb, wasn't it?" He knew all the stories too. All of New York did. But they had more meaning now, if he was planning to make Victoria his next victim. Charles hoped he would tire of her before he did any real damage. Or perhaps the Hendersons would step in before it went any further. Olivia certainly looked as though she meant to. And she thanked Charles again for his help in chasing her sister off the dance floor.

"She's been making a spectacle of herself for the past hour," Olivia said with eyes full of blue anger.

"Don't worry about it. She's pretty and young, there will be lots of roués running after her until she finds a husband. You can't worry about all of them," he tried to reassure her, but he had to admit Whitticomb's reputation was worth worrying about, and he couldn't tell Olivia she was wrong to watch them.

"Victoria says she is never marrying. She is going to live in Europe and fight for women's suffrage."

"Oh dear. She'll grow out of it, I'm sure. When the right man comes along, she'll forget all that. Just don't tell him she wants to get arrested," he teased, "and don't worry about her so much. You deserve to have some fun," he said, as he said good-bye to her finally and left a few minutes later.

Olivia went to the ladies' room then, and looked in the mirror as she smoothed down her hair. She had a terrible headache, the argument with Victoria had gotten the evening off to a bad start, and seeing her glued to Toby for the past hour hadn't helped it. But before Olivia could turn around, she saw Evangeline Whitticomb in the mirror, bearing down on her, and within an instant, she was standing directly behind her, as Olivia turned slowly to face her.

"May I suggest, Miss Henderson, that you play with children your own age, and at the very least confine yourself to bachelors, rather than married men, with three children." She looked Olivia right in the eye, without wavering, and Olivia felt a hot flush hit her cheeks, as she realized that she'd been mistaken for her twin. And Toby's wife was livid, and Olivia didn't blame her.

"I'm terribly sorry," Olivia said quietly, tacitly agreeing to be Victoria, and hoping to pour oil on troubled waters. It was a golden opportunity, and she hoped to convince his wife that it was nothing more than friendly conversation. "Your husband has had several business dealings with my father, ma'am, and it was purely a matter of discussing our families. He has done nothing but speak of you and the children while we were dancing."

"I doubt that," Toby's wife said angrily. "I'm surprised to hear he even remembers he has us. Just be sure that you do, or I can assure you," she looked pointedly at her and lowered her voice but not her venom, "you'll regret it. You mean nothing to him, you know. He'll play with you like a toy, for a while, and then he'll drop you, and wherever you fall, you'll lie broken. He'll come back to me in the end . . . he has to." And with that, she turned on her heel and left, and Olivia felt as though all the air had been squeezed out of her. Fortunately, there had been no one else in the room at the time, and she had to sit down after the other woman left, she was so dizzy. And she was right of course. Evangeline Whitticomb knew her husband well, she had seen his performance dozens of times, and he always came back to her, because of who she was, what she represented, and because he was far less foolish than the women he played with.

Most of them were young and inexperienced, many of them were virgins. They were dazzled by him, by his good looks and smooth ways, the breathtaking things he said to them, and their own girlish illusions, or even ambitious aspirations. But whatever they thought, and whatever he told them, in the end, it made no difference, he always left them. Just as Olivia had tried to warn her. She hoped that she had at least assured his wife of her respectability, or rather Victoria's, but she doubted it, and when Olivia left the powder room again, she saw Victoria back on the dance floor in Toby's arms, and this time they looked a great deal more intimate, their bodies pressed close, their lips almost touching. Olivia wanted to scream looking at them, but instead she did the only other thing she could think of. She went to tell her father that she had a terrible headache, and he was instantly solicitous, sent a maid to find her coat for her, and went to get Victoria himself. He found her dancing with young Whitticomb, and although he didn't seem pleased, he thought nothing serious of it. He knew they had met in his home, and he hadn't seen them together since then. He did make a comment though on the way home that he had been surprised, after all he'd said, that Olivia had seated Toby next to her sister. But he said rather pointedly that he was sure no harm had come of it, and Victoria was wise enough not to let him woo her. He hadn't seen Toby watching her as they left, or the look they exchanged that only confirmed everything they'd said that evening. Toby and Victoria had found a delicious little room in a little pavilion at the very back of the garden, and it was there that he had kissed her for the first time, and that they had spent all their time, in each other's arms, whenever they weren't dancing.

"I'm so sorry, my dear," her father apologized to Olivia for her headache all the way home. "It's been too much for you, after the party last night and the ball tonight, I don't know what I was thinking of when I accepted it. I thought it might be fun for you girls, but you must be exhausted." Victoria looked anything but, and she looked daggers at Olivia as soon as their father glanced out the window. She knew her sister far better than that, and found it hard to believe she had a headache. She had no idea how much she'd upset her.

"That was very clever of you," she said icily when they got upstairs to their bedroom.

"I don't know what you're talking about. I do have a headache," Olivia insisted, as she took the hated dress off. She wanted to burn it.

And after the way Victoria had behaved, she did indeed feel like a harlot.

"You know exactly what I mean. But your little ruse won't change anything. You have no idea what you're doing." She knew for a fact that Toby was totally sincere. He had fallen madly in love with her, and it did not shock her in the least that he wanted to divorce his wife. She didn't even care if he did. She was totally modern in her ideas. She didn't have to marry him. They could be lovers forever. He had even talked to her about leaving the country eventually, and living in Europe. Toby Whitticomb was everything she'd ever wanted. Daring, brave, bold, honest, willing to pay any price for what he believed. She saw him as a knight in shining armor, ready to rescue her from her mundane little life in their incredibly boring home on the Hudson. He had already lived in Paris and London and Argentina. It was all music to her ears, and every time she thought of him, her entire body trembled.

"His wife attacked me in the powder room tonight," Olivia said as she put on her dressing gown. "She thought I was you."

"How convenient. Did you tell her how sorry you were and that it was all a terrible mistake?"

"More or less." Victoria laughed when she heard it. But Olivia went on solemnly.

"She told me that Toby makes a habit of this, just as everyone says, and when it's all over, he drops the girls he flirts with like broken dolls. I don't want you to be one of them," Olivia said hoarsely. This was the first thing that had caused a serious rift with them, and it was making Olivia feel sick as it continued. And she couldn't see how anything would change until Victoria came out from under his spell. It made Olivia wish, more than anything, that they were back in Croton-on-Hudson. "Victoria, please, be sensible . . . don't get close to him . . . he's dangerous. I want you to promise me you won't try to see him."

"I promise," Victoria said without sincerity or expression.

"I mean it." Olivia had tears in her eyes when she spoke. She hated him even more now for making them argue. Nothing and no one had a right to come between them. As far as Olivia was concerned, their bond was sacred.

"You're jealous," Victoria said coolly.

"I'm not," Olivia said, desperate to convince her.

"You are. He's in love with me, and that frightens you. You're afraid he'll take me away from you," Victoria said with some truth in it, but not exactly the way she meant it.

"He's doing that already. But don't you see the risk you'd be taking if you let yourself fall in love with this man? I cannot say it often enough, Victoria, he's dangerous. You *have* to see that."

"I'll be careful. I swear," she said, softening a little. She hated fighting with Olivia, she loved her too much, and it scared her. But suddenly she knew she loved Toby too. She was falling head over heels in love with him, and it was too late to stop it. When he had kissed her that night, she thought her entire body would melt, and when he had reached into the bodice of her dress and touched her breast, she would have done anything he wanted. No one had ever done that to her before. No one had ever made her want them more than life itself, and how could she explain that to her sister?

"Promise me you won't see him," Olivia begged, now that she had her sister's ear. "Please."

"Don't ask me that. I promise I won't do anything foolish."

"Seeing him is foolish. Even his wife knows it."

"She's angry because he's divorcing her. Wouldn't you be?"

"Think of the scandal that will make. Especially for an Astor. Why don't you at least wait for that to happen, and for the noise to die down, and then he can come to see you openly, and you can explain it to Father." Now she could do nothing except see him on the sly, and get caught in the cross fire between him and his wife and a world which already condemned him for his past follies.

"Ollie, it will take forever."

"And when we go home again? Then what? Will he come to see you there? What will people say, Victoria? . . . and Father? . . ."

"I don't know. He says we can conquer anything if I love him. And I do, oh Ollie, I do love him." She closed her eyes and her heart nearly flew out of her chest as she thought of him, and then opened her eyes again and looked at her sister. "How can I tell you what it's like? I would die for him if he asked me." At least Victoria was being honest with her, but it didn't make Olivia feel any better.

"That's what I'm afraid of," Olivia said sadly. "I don't want anyone ever to hurt you."

"He won't. I swear. You must come to tea

with us one day. I want you to know him. I want you to love him too . . . Ollie, please . . . I can't do this without you." But that was too much for her. Silence was already too much to ask of her, but asking her complicity as well would be far too painful.

"Victoria, I can't help you this time," Olivia said quietly. "I think that what you're doing is dangerous and wrong, and I'm afraid you'll get hurt. Perhaps I can't stop you, but I won't help you do it. Not this time."

"Then swear you won't say anything . . . swear to me," Victoria begged her on her knees, her eyes filled with tears, as Olivia began to cry too, and took her in her arms and held her.

"How can you ask me to do this? How can I let him hurt you?"

"He won't . . . believe me, he won't . . . trust me . . ."

"You're not the one I distrust here," Olivia sighed, taking a deep breath and wiping away her tears finally. "I won't say anything for now . . . but if he hurts you, I don't know what I'd do to him. . . ."

"He won't. I know him better than anyone in this life, except you." She looked like a child as she rolled onto their bed, and lay there spread-eagled, grinning.

"In two days, Victoria Henderson? I doubt that. You're a dreamer. For someone so full of radical ideas, you certainly are a romantic fool. How can you trust the man so quickly?"

"Because I know who he is. I understand him completely. We are two completely independent people, with exactly the same ideas, who were lucky enough to find each other. It's a miracle, Ollie. Truly, it is. He says he's waited for me all his life, and now that I'm here he can't believe it."

"What about his wife and children? How do they fit into all this?" Olivia looked skeptical, and Victoria looked momentarily confused, not sure what to answer.

"He says she forced the children on him, he never would have had children in a loveless marriage. It's really all her fault, and her problem now what she does with them."

"That's a nice sensible attitude," Olivia said, and the sarcasm seemed to go over Victoria's head as she continued to rhapsodize about Toby.

They turned off the light a little while later, and Olivia lay with her arms around her twin. "Be careful, little sister . . . be wise . . . be wary . . ." she whispered, but Victoria was already half asleep as she nodded sleepily, and curled closer to her sister. Victoria's mind was whirling as she thought of him. They had made a date for the following day. They were meeting at the library at ten o'clock the next morning.

Chapter 5

Olivia was going over their lunch and dinner menus the next morning with the cook when Victoria slipped away. She had told Bertie she was going to the library, and meeting one of the Rockefeller girls, and she would be home late that afternoon. Bertie had had Donovan drop her off at the library, and nobody seemed to notice that she was wearing the new white suit with the matching hat, copied from Doeuillet, that Olivia hadn't even worn yet. She looked very fashionable as she walked up the library steps, holding her books to return, as Donovan drove away and went back to the house to drive Mr. Henderson to John Watson's office.

Victoria returned the books as soon as

she arrived, and as she glanced past the librarian, she saw him standing, watching her, just behind the polite spinster with glasses who had helped her. Victoria stood beaming at him as their eyes met, and a moment later they walked away, arm in arm. It was still early, and no one they knew ever went to the library at that hour, if ever. She had absolutely no idea what they were going to do, but she didn't really care, as long as they were together.

Toby had left his car outside, a Stutz that he had bought just that year, and he laughed when Victoria told him she would love to drive it.

"Don't tell me you know how to drive too," he said, sounding delighted and amazed. "You really are the modern girl you say you are. Most people pretend they are, but really aren't." He offered her a Milo cigarette as though to prove the point, and she took it, although it really was a little early, even for her. For a little while, they drove around the East Side in lazy circles, and then finally, he pulled the car over and looked at her, as though drinking in every detail of her face, her eyes, her soul. It was as though he wanted to engrave her on his heart forever. "I adore you, Victoria," he whispered into her hair. "I've never known anyone like you." His words were like an aphrodisiac to her, and when he kissed her, she felt her soul melt into his. There was nothing she wouldn't have done for him at that moment, and he was breathless as he kissed her. He sat back against the seat of the Stutz after a long moment, and looked at Victoria in total amazement. "You drive me mad, you know. You make me want to kidnap you to Canada or Mexico, or run away to Argentina, or the Azores . . . you're a woman who deserves to be in exotic places. I'd love to be on a hot beach with you somewhere, listening to music, and kissing you," he said as he leaned over to kiss her again, and this time she could hardly breathe as he held her. It was she who pulled away this time, unable to think straight as she looked into his dark eyes, and wished that they could run away forever. It was unbearable to think of ever leaving him again, of being apart even for a moment.

But as he looked at her longingly, he suddenly smiled, as though he'd thought of something. "I have an idea," he said, starting the car again, and heading north at the next corner. "I know exactly where we'll go today. I haven't been there in ages."

"And where's that?" she asked, looking

very relaxed as he handed her a small flask, and she took a tiny sip, not to be outdone by him. It was brandy, and it burned her throat as it went down, but the warmth it gave off afterwards was very pleasant.

"Where we're going is a secret," he said mysteriously, looking over at her adoringly. It was as though they had always been meant to be together, and they both knew it. She questioned him about where they were going as they drove uptown, but he refused to answer her questions, and pretended he was kidnapping her, but she didn't look worried for even a single moment. He stopped to kiss her again several times, and they shared the flask yet another time, but the third time he handed it to her, she declined it.

"Do you always drink brandy before lunch?" she asked casually. It didn't really bother her, she knew a lot of her father's friends drank fairly heavily, and even John Watson carried a flask in winter. But it wasn't cold today, it just seemed to add to the heady quality of their excitement.

"I was so nervous this morning," he confessed, "I thought I might need it. My knees were shaking when I came to meet you." He looked boyish as he glanced over at her, and seeing him look so vulnerable and so much in love with her made Victoria feel very worldly. He was thirty-two years old and she knew she had absolutely bowled him over. It was very flattering, and everything about him was exciting, even the fact that being with him was forbidden to her, and he supposedly had a terrible reputation. Suddenly even that was exciting too, because she knew none of it was true. The one thing she never let herself think about was the fact that he was married. It didn't matter to her, after all he had told Victoria that he was divorcing Evangeline, that he had made a terrible mistake, and that he had spent five years in a loveless marriage. The idea that an Astor divorce would be the scandal of the century never even occurred to her, although it had occurred immediately to her twin sister.

They were far, far uptown by then, and the houses around them were small, and simple, and square, and had begun to look almost rural. Twenty minutes after they had left the library, Toby stopped the car in front of a small, neat white house, with some overgrown hedges in front, and a half-painted picket fence all around it.

"What is this?" Victoria asked, looking

amused, wondering who they were going to visit.

"It's my dream house," he smiled at her, and walked around the car to help her out. She stood hesitating for a moment as he grabbed a picnic basket. She hadn't seen it before, but there was champagne in it, and caviar, and a small cake, and some other treats he had pilfered from his kitchen. Everything had been carefully arranged, and as she looked at him in amazement, he took a key out of his pocket.

"Whose house is this?" she asked, not feeling afraid, but only curious and uncertain. It was odd not knowing where she was, or who they were visiting, and she followed him cautiously to the door as he unlocked it. She could see a small neat living room beyond. The furniture seemed to be in good repair though plain. Nothing was fancy here, but it looked like a pleasant place to spend a quiet evening, and before she could step inside, Toby took her in his arms and kissed her, pushing the long dark hair back from her face, and feeling her body next to his, so close he barely dared to breathe for fear he'd lose her. And then he looked down smiling at her, and without a word, he picked her up and carried her over the threshold.

"You'll be my wife one day, Victoria Henderson," he said quietly. "You barely know me now, but you will one day, and you'll be the next Mrs. Whitticomb . . . if you'll have me . . ." He looked boyish and unsure, and totally humble as he looked at her in the small room, his broad shoulders suddenly seeming too big for it, his words almost more than she could cope with. She was the girl who had said she'd never marry anyone, that she wanted to be free, and one day live in Europe, and now here she was, alone with this man, and totally his slave, to do with whatever he wanted. She knew that she shouldn't be alone with him, and that in some ways what they were doing was wrong, and yet how could it be? How could this be anything but right? Anything but perfect? She knew in her heart of hearts just how much she loved him. She had been totally swept away by his heart, his charm, his guileless ways. She trusted him as much as she did her own father.

"I love you so much," she whispered softly, and he kissed her again, and a moment later they were lying on the couch, kissing passionately, and she could feel his body throbbing beside her. She had no idea what to do, or what he expected of her, and she knew she wouldn't do anything foolish, and yet all she could think of was being here with him, being his, being with him forever.

It was Toby who stopped finally, who played with her long hair with his gentle fingers, as her blouse lay open. They put the picnic basket in the kitchen, and he opened the champagne, and they sipped it as she buttoned her blouse again and they went outside to the garden. There were no neighbors nearby, there was no one anywhere, and as they walked around, he explained to her that he had rented this just so he could be alone, and get away from Evangeline, so he could think and dream and have some time to himself. He told Victoria that it was here that he had finally decided to divorce her.

"Will you miss the children terribly?" she asked sympathetically, as they walked slowly back to the house, holding hands and talking softly.

"I will. But I hope that she'll be reasonable and let me see them. It will be a shock to everyone of course, but I think she'll be relieved too. No one should have to live like this forever. It will be harder on our families than on us, because they won't understand it." Victoria nodded, as she began to realize with sudden seriousness that it would be a frightful scandal. And undoubtedly, their father would be deeply shocked, but perhaps in time, he'd listen. Victoria had no need to marry him immediately. She didn't care at all, as long as they could be together. And she realized it would be hard for both of them when she went back to Croton. But he could come to visit frequently, and perhaps while he was going through the divorce, it would be better for them, and much more private. It was amazing how one's life changed, she mused, in a matter of days or moments. Suddenly the course of her entire lifetime was set in a different direction from what she had expected.

He asked her about being a twin, and he laughed at some of her outrageous stories, and then suddenly they were in the doorway and he was kissing her again. She didn't even know what time it was, or care, all she knew was that she wanted to be with him.

They sat in the living room and talked again for a little while, and then he poured her more champagne and they kissed some more, and this time, without thinking or asking her, as they kissed, he slowly took her blouse off. She began to object, to say something, but he silenced her with able lips and nimble fingers, and the force of her own desire almost frightened her as he kissed her, and then slowly let his lips drift from her mouth to her neck, and then slowly down over her breasts to her nipples. She was moaning softly, and he was aching with desire for her, and suddenly she was looking at him, and she knew, as they both did, that their lives had been changed forever. The moment and the lifetime was theirs, the risks, the dangers, the griefs, the joys, she was willing to share them all with him. And slowly her clothes melted away in his hands, and he lifted her gently in his arms and took her into the bedroom.

The shades were drawn, the light was dim, there was a kind of mystical haze all around them it seemed, and with the greatest care and gentleness, the most infinite expertise, he took her. Her body sang and keened for him, her heart long since his, her mind a blur from all that he was doing. And it was hours later when she lay in his arms, startled, but no longer afraid, half asleep, filled with love for him, and completely trusting. She had given him everything she had to give, and she knew without a doubt that she was his forever.

It was five o'clock when he woke her at last, and the light had grown a little dimmer. He hated to wake her, but he knew they had to leave. The last thing he wanted for her, or himself, was to cause her any trouble. It was almost a physical pain to tear herself away from him and she dressed quietly as he watched her, totally enthralled with the long, graceful limbs, the beauty of her movements. It was as though he couldn't believe his good fortune in finding her, and she still couldn't quite believe all that had happened.

"I will never, ever let you be sorry that you love me," he said to her before they left, both of them somewhat shaken by the enormous steps they'd taken, and yet she had no regrets. She had cast her lot with his that day, and now they were bound to each other forever.

He let her drive part of the way home, and several times she frightened him, but he loved it. They laughed, they sang, they were like two children who had set sail in a tiny boat on a stormy sea, and all they could do now was trust the Fates to protect them.

"I love you, Toby Whitticomb," she said in a strong, clear voice when he dropped her three blocks from home, hating to leave her.

"Not as much as I love you. You'll see, you'll be mine one day," he said proudly, "though I don't deserve you."

"I already am yours," she whispered, and then kissed his cheek, before stepping back onto the sidewalk, still a little dazed by what she'd done for him, and the enormity of their commitment.

She waved as he drove away, her eyes riveted to him for as long as she could see him. They had promised to meet again the next day, at the library again, and they were going back to the little house that was theirs now.

Chapter 6

October was fraught with activity for all of them. Edward Henderson had all but concluded an enormous business deal, and he was actually enjoying it greatly. He went to John Watson's office every day, and spent hours at conference tables, surrounded by bankers and attorneys.

Olivia had made several friends, and was invited everywhere for luncheons and teas, and although Victoria was invited too, she seldom joined her. She told Olivia she was going to lectures and meetings of the National American Women's Suffrage Association, but Olivia suspected there was more to it than that. She knew instinctively that among the other things she did, she was secretly meeting Toby Whitticomb. Olivia no longer said anything, but she was constantly watching her sister. She saw the changes in her, knew how much in love she must have been, but knew just as well how little she could do to stop it.

The Hendersons continued to go to concerts and plays, and at her father's request, Olivia gave two more small dinners. Charles Dawson came to one of them, but he spent much of the evening discussing business with her father. And Olivia was less talkative than usual. She was far too worried about her sister. There seemed to be a silence between them these days, a block of something impenetrable that Olivia felt but could not see or reach through, and whenever she tried to question Victoria about it, she insisted that Olivia was imagining it, nothing between them was any different.

Olivia was beginning to long for the time when they would go home, and she could reclaim her sister from her infatuation with Toby. More than ever, she found that she missed her. But in late October, Edward Henderson was saying that he doubted they would go back to Croton until Thanksgiving. He was concluding the sale of the mill, and he thought that being in New York was good for them anyway, it gave

them a chance to make friends, and he sometimes winked at them, perhaps even meet husbands. In any case, it was obvious how much
they enjoyed it. Olivia was in many ways still
the same, but she had honed her social skills
and became the perfect hostess. But it was Victoria who seemed to have blossomed into wom-
anhood, and there suddenly seemed to be an
aura of something much more sophisticated
about her. It was something which no one discussed, but all of those who knew her well had
noticed. Olivia had seen it too, but never questioned it openly, she decided that it must have
been a style Victoria was affecting in order to
appeal to Toby. And Victoria said nothing at
all, to anyone, and least of all to her sister.
Olivia knew nothing of her twin's trysts with
him, and certainly not what was happening at
the little house far uptown, where they met
each morning, yet she sensed that Victoria's relationship with him had deepened. Olivia knew
also that Victoria was avoiding her, and
seemed far too busy, which Olivia thought was
suspicious.

"You haven't tired of our city yet?"
Charles Dawson asked Olivia one afternoon
when he came to see her father. She had come
to oversee the serving of the tea tray, and her

father had asked her to stay, since they had concluded their business.

"Perhaps a little," she smiled. "I like it here, but I miss the turning of the leaves in Croton."

"We'll be back soon." Her father smiled at her, grateful for all her help. For the past two months, she had had the house in New York running to perfection.

"You must bring Geoffrey to visit us," she said warmly to Charles, sorry that she still hadn't met him.

"He'd love it," Charles assured her.

"Does he ride?" Charles shook his head regretfully in answer. "Perhaps I could teach him."

"I'm sure he'd like that."

"Where's your sister this afternoon, by the way?" Her father interrupted them, curious about the whereabouts of his other daughter.

"Out with friends. The usual. The library. I'm really not sure. She should be back any minute."

"She's certainly out a lot these days," he smiled at her. He was happy that they had enjoyed New York so much, everyone was enamored with them, and fascinated by the totally identical sisters.

Charles left a little while after that, and Victoria was just coming up the front steps as he left. A car drove rapidly away, but no one noticed, and he chatted with her for a moment. There was something odd in her eyes this time, something vague and dreamy, and once again he was struck by how similar she was to her twin, and yet at some vague, mystical level, how different. And yet there were definitely times when he saw them together that he couldn't tell them apart for a single instant. He was still musing about it as he drove home to his son. Thanksgiving and Christmas would be upon them soon, and Charles was dreading them. The holidays had been an agony the year before, without Susan.

The Hendersons went to a concert at Carnegie Hall that night, and ran into several acquaintances, among them Tobias Whitticomb who was sharing a box with friends, but his wife was not among them. Someone said that they had heard she was ill, and someone else laughed and volunteered that they had heard she was expecting. Victoria only smiled to herself, knowing that she couldn't be, and that he was leaving her in the very near future. Perhaps they had decided that it was simpler if he went out alone. But whatever the reason, he and

Victoria spent most of the evening with their eyes riveted to each other.

Her father noticed it this time too, but he said nothing to her on the drive home, and silently hoped that young Whitticomb had not singled her out as the next object of his affections.

"Father saw what happened tonight," Olivia warned when they undressed, but Victoria brushed her off as she always did now. It pained Olivia constantly to feel the distance between them. It was a physical ache, a visceral pain she never seemed to be rid of.

"Father doesn't know anything," Victoria said with complete assurance.

"What exactly is there to know?" Olivia asked softly, suddenly terrified of how far it had gone, but Victoria didn't even deign to answer, and that night both girls had nightmares.

But in the morning, the nightmares came true. John Watson called, as he often did, and asked if he might come by to see Edward Henderson at home on his way to the office. The visit did not seem unusual, and Henderson was always glad to see him.

Bertie brought them coffee in the library, and there was a long pause as John sat and watched Edward. When they were alone John still didn't have any idea how to begin what he had to tell him. He thought of his old friend's weak heart, the health that had wavered somewhat in recent years, and yet he knew there was no other choice available to him. He had to tell him. He owed it to Edward.

"I'm afraid," he began slowly, "I have rather bad news." The two men exchanged a long look. It was like watching a door open to reveal an abyss into which neither of them wanted to leap now.

"The sale of the mill has fallen through?" He looked disappointed, but not devastated, but John shook his head in answer.

"No, fortunately, all's well there. In fact, we hope to have the entire matter complete by Christmas."

"I thought so," Edward said, they had worked hard on it, and there had been no suggestion of any problems.

"It's personal, I'm afraid. Something that grieves me deeply to tell you, and will grieve you. I talked to Martha about it at great length last night, and we both felt you should know. It's Victoria, Edward. I'm afraid," he could hardly bring himself to say the words, for fear it would kill his friend, or at best wound him deeply. "She's done a very foolish thing. She's

Danielle Steel

involved with young Whitticomb . . . seriously . . . I'm sorry." Their eyes met, awfully,
and said a thousand unspeakable things between the two men. "Apparently there's a little
house just north of town where they meet . . .
where they've been meeting. Someone's housekeeper has been seeing them there every day
for the past month. I'm afraid she . . . you
can imagine the rest. Oh God, Edward, I'm so
sorry," he said, watching his old friend's eyes
fill with tears, but for a moment Edward Henderson said nothing.

"Are you sure of this? Who is this
woman? Should I speak to her? Perhaps she's
lying. It could be blackmail."

"Possibly. But given the man's reputation,
I was inclined to believe the story. I wouldn't
have come to you unless I was fairly sure of it."
And then, "Do you want me to speak to him?
Perhaps we both should."

"I might kill him, if it's true," Edward said
grimly. "I just can't believe that of Victoria.
She's impulsive occasionally, and she's not
above driving my cars or stealing my favorite
horse from time to time for a nice fast ride over
the fields, or even through my best garden. But
not this, John . . . not this . . . I just can't
believe it of her."

"Neither can I. But she's very young, and naive. I believe he's quite adept at this. The woman says that he keeps the house just for that purpose."

"The man belongs in prison."

"And if it's true? What about your daughter? She can't marry him. He already is married, with a house full of children, an aristocratic wife, and I understand from Martha that she's expecting another baby. I'm afraid this is quite grim."

"Do you suppose anyone knows?" Edward's eyes met his squarely, though he hated asking the question. But for Watson, this was almost the worst part.

"He said something to Lionel Matheson at his club a few days ago. I didn't believe it when I heard it then. Someone in the office told me. The man is obviously a complete lout if he's willing to destroy a young girl's reputation. He told Matheson that he was having an affair with a sweet young thing who had no idea what time it was, and when he was through with her, there was an identical sister. He didn't mention any names, but given that comment, he doesn't have to." Edward Henderson went pale, and if John Watson hadn't been there, he would have gone straight upstairs to see his daughters. "You'll have to do something about this quickly," Watson said what was already clear to both of them, "if he's making comments like that, it'll be all over town in no time. What about sending her to Europe for a while, on a trip somewhere . . . anywhere . . . just to get her away from here, and from him. But after that, you'll have to think seriously about her future. You'll have to do something. You can't just leave this as it is, it'll ruin her. She'll never find a husband after this, or if she does, it won't be someone you'd want for her."

"I know that," Edward Henderson said miserably, grateful to his old friend for his honesty, yet agonized over what he'd been hearing. "I'll have to think this out. I'll send her back to Croton tomorrow. But after that, I'm not sure. Europe's not the answer . . . I don't know what to do with her. I'd force him to marry her if I could, but what the devil am I supposed to do with a married man with four children?"

"Shoot him," John Watson said, trying to inject a little humor where there was precious little, but Edward shot a wintry smile at him and nodded.

"Believe me, I'd like to. I think I should speak to him. I'd like to know what happened."

"I don't think you should do that, it's fairly obvious, and you'll upset yourself for nothing. I'd like to think that he's sincere, though I doubt it, but even if he is, what will that do for Victoria? He can't marry her. He can't possibly divorce Evangeline, certainly not if she's having another child. The scandal would be appalling. The best thing Victoria can do is forget him."

"Try telling her that if she's truly in love with him. I saw them dancing and even flirting once or twice, but I never imagined it would go this far. I should have seen all this. I don't know what I was thinking. No wonder she's out all the time." He was wringing his hands and blaming himself for all of it, and by the time John Watson left, Edward Henderson was thoroughly agitated. It was a nightmare. The two men had agreed finally that Watson would go and speak to Toby Whitticomb, and Edward would stay out of it completely. It seemed far more discreet this way, and Watson was afraid Edward's heart would give out if he went to confront Toby.

In fact, John went straight from the Henderson home to Toby Whitticomb's office, where Toby seldom went anyway, but by sheer chance, he happened to be in that morning.

Victoria had had a dentist's appointment, and he was hoping to meet her afterwards, once she got rid of her sister.

But the story John heard from him was even more dismaying than what they'd gathered so far. He was quite gentlemanly, if you could call it that, and assured John that he wouldn't see the girl again now that the affair had come to light. It was all in good fun, he said. He said she was quite wild, and that it was she who said she was accustomed to pursuing married men. There had never, ever, been any promises made, no hope of a future certainly, since he and Evangeline were quite happy, within reason, despite what one may have heard, and of course John knew, he assumed, that Evangeline was expecting again in April. And there had never been any mention of anything so scandalous as his leaving her. That was quite obviously out of the question. It was simply a matter of a young girl run wild, and he had been, according to him, her victim. He said she had literally seduced him. And he looked rather startled as he said it.

John Watson didn't believe a word of it, and he was sure now that the whole story he'd heard previously was true. Victoria had in fact had an affair with him, and he was equally sure that she had been the victim and not Toby. More than likely, he had made outrageous promises to her, lied to her, did God knows what else to her, and seduced her. She was young and naive and he was very glamorous, in his own disgusting way. It was all quite obvious to John, though sickening certainly, and the big question now was what to do with her future.

He was back at the Henderson house at noon and told Edward as much as he dared to. He softened most of it, but the final word was that she had been involved with Whitticomb, and Whitticomb in turn was more than happy to end it. He certainly didn't want any trouble. But what they could do for Victoria now, socially, remained a serious problem. If nothing was done at all, and Toby talked, she was ruined, no one decent would ever go near her.

Edward thanked John once more when he left the house again, and he looked gray by the time Victoria and Olivia returned from the dentist. It had been an incredibly painful morning for him, and he was filled with despair as he stood in the doorway of the library and spoke to his daughters.

"We're going home in the morning, Olivia," he boomed with a terrifying look, as he glared at both of them. He couldn't help wondering if Olivia had known and concealed her sister's dark secret, and blamed her silently for the deception. "Please pack and close the house at once. Do what you can today, and whatever you don't finish, we'll leave Petrie and some of the others to finish after we've left." He looked so stern that Olivia almost trembled.

"We're leaving now? So soon? But I thought . . . you said . . ." She looked totally stunned by his announcement.

"I said we're leaving," he shouted at her, which was very rare for him, but he was overwhelmed by the events of the morning. And then he turned to Victoria, and without a single word, beckoned her to him. She felt her legs dissolve under her as she looked at him, and then glanced at her sister. It was obvious to both of them that something terrible had happened.

"Is something wrong?" Olivia asked softly, and for a long moment, he didn't answer. He just stood there silently, waiting for Victoria to join him. And as soon as she walked into the library, he closed the door resoundingly behind her. Olivia stood in the hall, staring at it, with her hat still on, wondering what was going on, and suddenly afraid that he had found out that Victoria was sneaking out of the house to meet Toby. But she couldn't imagine who had told him. And Victoria had been foolish certainly, but she wasn't a criminal, though that was how he had looked at her. She had never seen her father so angry.

Olivia hurried into the kitchen then to tell Bertie what had happened, or what she knew of it, and that they were leaving in the morning. She was just as surprised as they were, and within moments, the two women were bustling everywhere, taking out boxes and suitcases and issuing orders and directions. It was going to be impossible to do everything, but her father had been quite clear. They were leaving in the morning, and she was to do what she could now. The rest would be done by servants.

As the two women worked frantically, with their aprons on, Victoria was sobbing in the library as her father watched her.

"You've ruined yourself, Victoria. That's the beginning and the end of it. You have absolutely no future. None. There isn't a decent man alive who would have you." Just saying the words to her sickened him, and listening to her sob made his heart ache. He didn't even want to know what had happened between them, yet he couldn't bear to believe that she had been callous or cheap about it. The man must have promised her the moon in order to take advantage of her.

She was sobbing miserably, but she looked up at him then bleakly. "I've never wanted to be married anyway," she said, as though that made a difference now. It was one thing to stupidly say you would never marry, it was another to be a pariah, and know that no one would have you.

"Is that why you did this? Because you didn't care? Did you want to ruin your future . . . perhaps even your sister's future? And our family reputation?" All she could do was shake her head and cry in answer. "Did he promise you anything? Did he promise to marry you, Victoria?" She wouldn't look at her father, her eyes just stared at her lap as she wrung her hands and cried, and nodded. "How could he? What was he thinking of? The man is a complete rotter. I never should have brought him into this house. It's all my fault." Her father then told her that Toby had begun making remarks about her, had told men in his club that he was sleeping with her. He had behaved like a complete cad, and had told John Watson that it was entirely her fault, that she had seduced him.

He was almost in tears as he spoke to her, and then finally she told him, as much as she dared, as much as she could now.

"He told me he'd never been in love with anyone but me, that he'd never felt this way about anyone. . . ." She sobbed miserably, but her father did not approach her. "He said they were getting divorced, that it was a loveless marriage, and he was going to leave her, and marry me." So the girl who hadn't wanted to marry had wanted to after all. For all her brave, new ideas, she was a complete child, and a romantic.

"And you believed him?" He looked horrified, and she nodded. "What were you doing alone with him in the first place?" That appalled him too and made him realize that he had to monitor them both much more closely, though Olivia certainly never went anywhere, or did anything she wasn't supposed to.

"I thought we'd just meet for the afternoon. I never intended . . . I never thought . . . I wouldn't have . . . oh Father . . ." It was a hideous wail, not so much even for the grief she had caused him, but for the horror of realizing that Toby had betrayed her. He had told John Watson that it was nothing more than a casual affair, and that she had seduced him

189

. . . not that he had told her he loved her more than life itself and promised to marry her. She could hardly believe how incredibly stupid she had been, and how totally he had betrayed her. He was every bit as bad as people said he was, and worse. He had lied to her from beginning to end, and she had believed him.

With a look of total despair, her father asked her one final question. "I don't suppose you'll tell me the truth about this, but I'm going to ask you anyway. Did your sister know about this, Victoria? Has she been aware of what you were doing?"

Victoria was almost unable to speak by then, but she shook her head and looked him squarely in the eye. "No, she didn't," she whispered. "She saw us dance at the Astors', at their ball, and we had a terrible argument. She said everything I should have known myself . . . but I didn't believe her. I never told her what was happening. I think she knew I had seen him once or twice, but not . . . not the rest . . ." She was so ashamed now that he knew, she could barely face him. And soon the entire town would know, if Toby made a laughingstock of her. She was glad suddenly that they were going back to Croton. She never wanted to see New York again, or any of the people in it. The story they were going to tell was that one of the twins had fallen ill, and they had had to return to Croton at once. It was in fact going to become a very long bout of influenza. In fact, like his daughter, Edward had absolutely no desire whatsoever to return to New York now. Nothing good ever happened to them there. His wife had died there, the girls' first presentation to society had been little more than a circus act for them, and this second go-around had led to complete disaster. Edward Henderson doubted very much that he would ever bring them down again from Croton. But as he looked at Victoria, he knew that for her, despite what she said, it was not yet over. And he knew he had to address her on the subject.

"I forbid you to ever see him again, Victoria, is that clear? The man doesn't care about you. He denied you, he ridiculed you, he betrayed you. If he had told John that you were the love of his life and he didn't know what to do now, it would have been a different story. I don't think it would have ended any differently, but you could have gone to your grave fifty years from now, hopefully, knowing that the man truly loved you. You could have clung to that in your darkest hours. You have nothing to cling to now except your own disgrace, the shreds of the reputation you've destroyed that can never be repaired again, and the fact that you were used by a complete cad who thought nothing of you. I want you to remember that. Perhaps there will be some way to redeem you one day. I want to think about that. But in the meantime, have no illusions about this man. And remember," he boomed at her and she trembled as she listened, "I forbid you to see him. Do you understand me?"

"Yes, sir." She nodded and blew her nose again, trying to stifle fresh sobs, but she just couldn't. He had said it all far too clearly. And there was no hiding from it now. It was a total nightmare.

"Now go to your room and stay there until we leave in the morning."

She slipped out of the library as quickly as she could, and ran straight upstairs, grateful that there was no one in the hallway. Bertie and Olivia were in the attic by then, opening trunks and collecting their valises, and by the time they came downstairs again, Victoria had run swiftly down the stairs and out the front door, wearing a black dress and a hat with a veil that concealed her face entirely. She had heard what her father had said, but she had to hear it for herself this time. It was impossible to believe. Maybe John Watson was lying.

She had taken a cab to his office, and had almost collided with him on the steps just as he was leaving. He looked as handsome as ever, but startled to see who it was, and not particularly pleased to see her.

"I have to speak to you," she said, fighting back tears, as Toby looked down at her with obvious irritation.

"Why didn't you just send another lawyer? What did you think you were going to do? Pressure me into leaving her this week? What's the hurry?"

"I had nothing to do with that. Someone told my father's attorney that you made a remark about me, that we were having an affair, and he told my father. And apparently, someone's seen us at the cottage."

"Oh so what, for God's sake. You're a big girl, Miss Modern I Never Want to Get Married. You knew what was going on. You just wanted to hear all the pretty words, but you knew exactly what it was all about, and don't tell me you didn't." She looked shocked at the harshness of what he was saying, and wished they could go somewhere to talk, but he clearly didn't want to. He made no move off the steps, and did not invite her to go back into the building, to his office.

"What was it all about? I don't know what to think now." She asked him fearfully, as she stood there trembling, the heavy veil concealing the tears that flowed down her cheeks in silence.

"It was about then, this is now. It was fun. It was great fun. I would do it all over again in a minute. But that's all it was, a good time for a short time. All you damn women are the same, you have to pretend you're going to get a gold ring at the end of it. Don't tell me how modern you are, you're just as dishonest as the rest of them. You don't want to go to bed with a man unless you get a wedding ring out of it. How real is that? Do you really think I'm going to be able to leave Evangeline and three kids . . . four now . . . do you really think she'd let me go? Or that this is the love of my life? How the hell would I know after two days? How do you? All you knew was what I knew, what was between your legs and what you wanted there, so don't tell me any pretty stories. That was it, baby, a good time, and we had it. And don't tell me you thought I was leaving her. The Astors would kill me, and you know it. So we were playing. We both played. And if you talk, so

will I. I'll tell everyone just how good you were
. . . and you were good, baby . . . you were
great." He tipped his hat to her, and bowed
low, and when he came up with a smirk on his
face, she slapped him hard and a woman walking past them looked startled.

"You're a bastard, Toby Whitticomb," she
said, as the tears flowed faster. She had never
heard anything as disgusting as what he'd just
said to her. He had only used her, and he didn't
even have the grace to admit it. He tried to
blame it on her too, to cheapen her, and make
her think that she'd never loved him. The sad
thing was that she had, far too much. She had
been incredibly stupid.

"I've been called that before," he smiled,
"by people who really know too, not just by
babies." She had been a complete innocent,
easy prey for him, and he knew it. He had
taken every advantage of her, and didn't give a
damn what it did to her now, or what even happened.

"We're leaving tomorrow," she said miserably, as though she still expected him to stop
her, but of course he wouldn't.

"I think that's a good thing to do. Am I to
expect a visit from your father now too?" he

asked unpleasantly. "Or does he only send his minions?"

"You don't deserve more than that," she said, wanting to hate him, but not there yet. He had broken her heart, and yet a part of her still loved him.

"You know better than that," he said, looking incredibly seductive again, as he walked her slowly to a taxi. "We had a good time, Victoria . . . let it go at that . . . don't ask more of it than there was. . . ." It was just a game to him. It always had been.

"You said you loved me." Tears rolled down her face as she said it. "You said you'd never loved anyone like this . . . you said . . ." He had said he would leave his wife, that he wanted to spend the rest of his life with her, and wanted her babies. They were going to run away and live in Paris. She was sobbing as she watched him.

"I know what I said, I lied," he told her as he put her in a cab. "It doesn't matter now." He looked at her, almost sorry for her this time. She was such a kid. It wasn't even a fair game this way, but it was too late now anyway. The game was over. "Go home and forget me. You'll marry someone nice one day, but I'll bet you'll remember this as the most fun you ever had." He grinned at her evilly, and she wanted to slap him again, but there was no point. It was over. He didn't even begin to understand what she had felt for him. He was so empty he would never know, and her heart ached as she looked at him, and slowly, finally began to hate him. "I know," he whispered, as he looked at her for a last time, drinking in the way she looked. She was even pretty when she cried. It was almost too bad she wasn't older. But he'd had enough fun for a while. It was time to move on now. "I'm a bad one," he whispered to her. "That's just the way it is sometimes." He gave the driver her address and got out of the cab, and then he turned and walked down the street without ever looking back. Victoria Henderson was only a moment in his life. She had come, and gone, and now it was time for something different.

Victoria cried all the way back to the house. She slipped in the back door, and ran quietly up the back stairs, and prayed that no one had found out she was gone. In fact, Olivia had. She had come to bring her a cup of tea and see how she was, and what had happened with their father. And she had known instinctively what had happened when she saw that Victoria was gone, and she knew that Victoria had probably run off to see Toby. Olivia could feel in her own heart the agony that her sister was in. And without saying a word about Victoria having disappeared, Olivia silently closed the door, and went back to her work in the attic with Bertie.

The two sisters didn't meet again until late that afternoon when Olivia checked on her again, and this time found her in their room. Victoria was sitting in a chair, holding a handkerchief and staring out the window. She didn't turn when she heard Olivia come into the room, and just seeing her there that way almost killed Olivia as she watched her. She walked quietly up to her, and put a hand on her shoulder.

"Are you all right?" Olivia whispered to her. Any anger that had existed between them had vanished that morning. It was as though they had found each other again. And Olivia knew how badly her sister was going to need her.

There was a long silence in answer to her question, and then Victoria shrugged as fresh tears rolled down her cheeks, spilled onto her blouse and her fingers.

"I was so stupid," she finally whispered.

"How could I be so stupid?" She sounded tragic.

"You wanted to believe him, and he was very exciting. He wanted you to believe him. He's very good at it." But just listening to her sister made Victoria cry more, and finally Olivia just held her. "It'll be all right again, we'll go home, and you won't see him anymore . . . you'll forget, and so will everyone else eventually. Nothing like this lasts forever."

"How do you know?" Victoria sobbed in her sister's arms as she asked the question, and Olivia smiled at her. She loved her so much, and wished she could have taken the pain away, the disappointment, and the deception. She was furious with Toby Whitticomb on her sister's behalf, and relieved that Victoria was free of him, and she was also grateful that she and her twin were close to each other again. Toby had very definitely come between them.

"I'm older than you are," Olivia smiled down at her reassuringly, "I know about things. This won't hurt forever," she said, trying to sound hopeful.

"I never knew there were people like him . . . so deceitful . . . so evil . . . I hate men . . ."

"Don't," Olivia said, kissing the top of her

head wisely. "Just hate him." Victoria looked up at her then, and for an instant there was a familiar look between them. They knew each other so well, every look, every word, every joy, every moment of sorrow. It was frightening to realize that for the past few weeks they had almost lost each other. But Olivia knew, as she always had, that they could never lose each other. The bond between them was too tight, too strong, it ran too deep and was too important. It was like shared bone, or a common heart. It was something they owned as one, that neither of them could take from the other.

They held hands together the next day, in the back of the car, as they drove out of town. Olivia knew everything that her sister felt, the sorrow, the pain, the regret, the agony of never seeing him again. And as Victoria wept silently, holding her sister's hands tightly in her own, their father sat in the front seat in total silence.

Chapter 7

In some ways, it was a relief for all of them to return to Henderson Manor in Croton-on-Hudson. The two months in New York had been frantic, and the shock of the emotions of her affair had left Victoria completely shattered. It was good for the twins to be alone together again, and to talk, as they had before, of the things that mattered to them. It seemed as though Victoria had lost sight of everything in New York, except Toby. He had obscured all her goals, all her dreams, all her fervent beliefs that had once been so important to her. She had given up everything for him, in the end, even her reputation. In five brief weeks of loving him, she had destroyed everything, or so it seemed to Victoria now, and even their father.

He spoke very little of it, but it was easy to see how deeply upset he was over what had happened. Only Olivia remained somewhat philosophical, and she did everything possible to cheer them both up.

She pampered her father constantly, bringing him his favorite teas, ordering his favorite meals for him, planning menus, and cutting flowers that she knew would please him. But he had remained extremely stern in their first week back, and very silent with both his daughters. The sale of the mill was almost complete by then, but he seemed to have a great deal on his mind in the first week of November.

The leaves had completely turned, and Olivia loved that time of year on the Hudson. She urged Victoria to go out walking with her, and even to go riding with her whenever possible, although Victoria far preferred driving to riding horses.

"Oh don't be so spoiled," Olivia teased her late one afternoon, at the end of their first week home. Things had almost begun to seem normal by then. The house in New York had been completely closed, and Bertie had come back with the rest of their things, and the servants.

"Why don't we ride over to Kykuit?"

Olivia urged, but Victoria didn't look enthused about the venture.

"Because the Rockefellers have probably heard what a slut I am, and they'll throw rocks at me if we go near them," Victoria said, as Olivia chuckled at her sister.

"Stop feeling sorry for yourself. I'll throw rocks at you if you don't ride with me this afternoon. I'm tired of sitting here watching you and Father try to compete for who can be the most gloomy. I want to go riding, and I'm taking you with me." Victoria finally agreed and they didn't ride as far as Kykuit, but they had a lovely ride down by the river, and they were most of the way home, when a squirrel ran up a tree unexpectedly, and Victoria's horse bolted. She hadn't ridden him in a while, and she'd never been the enthusiastic equestrian her sister was, and before Olivia could even grab the bridle for her, Victoria had fallen right out of her saddle. She hit the ground with a thud, and looked surprised, as her horse galloped easily back to the stable.

"See what I mean?" Victoria picked herself up and dusted herself off as Olivia laughed at her. "That never happens to me when I steal Father's cars and go driving." She was smiling.

"You're hopeless. Come on up behind

me." Olivia gave Victoria a firm hand, and Victoria put a toe into her sister's stirrup and a moment later, she was sitting behind Olivia and they cantered home to the stable. It was a cold November day, and they were both freezing by the time they got home, and stood in front of the fire in the library, warming their hands, and laughing as they told their father about their adventure. He even smiled at them, and Victoria thought it was the first time he had talked to her normally since they got back to Croton. She commented on it to Olivia as they went back to their bedroom to change for dinner.

"Stop saying that," Olivia chided her. "He seems to be perfectly all right now."

"Not when he's alone with me. I don't think he'll ever forgive me," she said quietly, waiting for Olivia to pick their dress for dinner.

"That's nonsense," Olivia said firmly, but she had noticed that their father was much quieter than he had been, and Victoria herself was far more docile. She seemed to say very little these days and never went anywhere. She seemed far less interested in the suffragists and had stopped going to the meetings. In some ways, her heartbreak over Tobias Whitticomb seemed to have caused her to soften. She wasn't quite as sure of herself, or as adventuresome. It was as though she had ventured whole into the world, confident in herself, and she had returned two months later, broken. And all Olivia wanted now was to see her sister and her father become the people they had been. She knew it would happen eventually, but it was difficult being with either of them in the meantime. The only good thing that had come of the affair was that she had never felt as close to her twin sister. They were as inseparable now suddenly as they had been as children. It was as though in some unspoken way, Victoria needed her desperately and she knew it. And Olivia was happier than ever to be with her. They were never apart now for a single moment. And thus far, fortunately, news of Victoria's misadventure seemed not to have reached Croton.

They had dinner with their father that night, and as usual, everyone went to bed early. Olivia had gone to the library and gotten books for both of them. She was reading *O Pioneers* and fell asleep at midnight with the book in her hands. Victoria had long since turned her back on her and gone to sleep at ten-thirty. And eventually, at some point in the night, Olivia had woken up and turned their lamp off. There was still a fire in the grate and the room was warm, and as she drifted off to sleep, she thought she was dreaming when she heard a soft moaning beside her. She let the sound lull her to sleep again, but shortly after that, Olivia felt a pain knife through her in the darkness like none other she had ever known. It took her breath from her, and she woke gasping for air, and instinctively reaching for her sister. She instantly clutched Victoria's hand, but as she woke, she realized that the pain wasn't her own, but her twin's. She had felt it as her own, but as she came fully awake, the pain vanished, and what she saw was Victoria's face, contorted in pain, as she grabbed the bedpost. Her knees were pulled up to her chest, and she could barely speak as Olivia bent over her in terror.

"What is it? What's wrong?" They had felt pain for each other before, but Olivia had never before felt anything like this one. It had been like a knife ripping through her, and she could see easily now what agony Victoria was in. She had no idea what it was, but as she threw back the bedclothes on her side of the bed, she saw that there was blood all around them. "Oh my God . . . Victoria . . . speak to me . . ." She had no idea where it was coming from, but it was everywhere, and there seemed to be a lot of it. It was all over Olivia's nightgown, but she was sure that she herself wasn't bleeding.

Victoria's face was deathly pale as she turned to her and grabbed Olivia's hand fiercely in her own. She could hardly speak she was in so much pain, but she forced out the words very clearly. "Don't call a doctor."

"Why not?"

"Don't." She looked wild-eyed, as Olivia watched her, helpless in the face of her sister's agony. "Help me to the bathroom."

Olivia literally carried her, and there was blood everywhere in a trail behind them. Victoria was hemorrhaging, and Olivia didn't know what to do to stop it. She was doubled over in pain, and lay on the bathroom floor, suddenly in even greater agony as she cried, and Olivia cried with her. She was terrified that her twin was dying.

"Tell me what's wrong." She sensed that Victoria knew but wouldn't tell her. "If you don't, I'll call Bertie *and* the doctor."

"I'm pregnant." Victoria's face contorted in pain again, as random pains seemed to rip through her.

"Oh God . . . why didn't you tell me?"

"I couldn't face it," Victoria said honestly, crying in agony and sorrow.

"What do I do?" Olivia was kneeling beside her on the bathroom floor, praying her sister wouldn't bleed to death. It could have been from the fall from the horse that afternoon, or perhaps it even had something to do with their own mother's history. But that was too frightening to even think of, and there was no time now. Olivia was suddenly terrified that Victoria was going to die in the bathroom. "I have to call someone, Victoria. You *have* to let me."

"No . . . don't . . . stay . . . with . . . me . . . don't . . . leave me . . . ." She was crying horribly by then, and she seemed to be bleeding more than ever, and then just as Olivia began truly panicking, Victoria was seized by a viselike pain and the source of her misery slipped slowly from her. Neither of them had any idea what was happening at first, and then they both understood what had occurred. The pain seemed to grip her interminably, but as it receded eventually, the baby that might have been lay in a mass between Victoria's legs in her nightgown. She began to sob hysterically, and Olivia took it from her, and began cleaning her. And little by little the bleeding began to lessen. Olivia had wrapped her in blankets by then, and used towels and rags to clean everywhere, as Victoria continued to lie on their bathroom floor, racked by sobs, and despite the blanket Olivia had wrapped her in, convulsed by such terrible trembling that her teeth shook. It was six o'clock in the morning by the time Olivia had cleaned everything and changed both their nightgowns. And then, ever so gently, and with unusual strength, she carried her sister back to bed, and tucked her in like a baby.

"It's all right, Victoria, I'm right here. Nothing's going to happen to you now. You're safe, and I love you. It's all over." Neither of them had said a word about what had just happened, or the horror they'd seen, nor said a word about what could have happened if she hadn't lost the baby. Giving birth to Toby Whitticomb's illegitimate child would truly have destroyed her life forever, and killed their father. But there was no chance of that now. The baby had been formed but was still very early.

Olivia put a log on the fire then, and put another blanket over her twin, and she sat beside her as she watched her drift off to sleep at last, deathly pale, and wondering sadly if there was a curse upon them. Knowing what had happened to their mother when they had been born, she couldn't help wondering now if either of them would ever be able to have children.

She couldn't imagine herself marrying, let alone having a child, but it was intriguing wondering if it was even a possibility, or if they might die in childbirth. No one had ever told them.

Victoria was sleeping soundly by then, and Olivia put a coat over her nightgown, and went downstairs carrying the huge bundle of dirty linens. She was going to burn them. But much to her chagrin, the kitchen had come to life by then. It was nearly eight o'clock, and as she stepped outside, she was immediately met by Bertie.

"What's all that you've got there?" she asked pleasantly, and Olivia instinctively turned away from her.

"Nothing. I . . . I'll take care of it," Olivia said firmly, and the old woman caught a note in her voice that surprised her.

"What is it?"

"It's nothing, Bertie," she said, as the two women's eyes met and Olivia kept a firm grip on the bundle. "I'm going to burn it." There was an endless pause, as Bertie searched her eyes, and then with a slow step backwards, she nodded.

"I'll have Petrie build a fire for you outside. Perhaps we should bury some of it."

Olivia nodded. She had made a separate, smaller bundle with what might have been the baby, and that had been her intention.

Olivia and Bertie looked grim as they watched Petrie first dig a hole and then build a fire. The linens went onto it, the rest went into the hole and was quickly gone, and the two women stood side by side, shivering in the winter morning. It was a silent vigil that should never have been, and Bertie put a gentle arm around her shoulders.

"You're a good girl, Olivia," she said quietly. She had understood completely. "How is she?"

"She looks awful," Olivia said honestly. "But please don't tell her I told you. She'd kill me."

"I won't. But she must have the doctor today. She could die from an infection." Just hearing those words made Olivia's heart tremble in her chest and she nodded.

"Then get him. I'll deal with her," and then with worried eyes: "What'll we tell Father?"

"Influenza, I guess," Bertie said with a sigh. She had been afraid of that. Like everyone else in the house, she had heard whispers and stories. "It's not fair to worry him though. Perhaps you ought to say something."

"Oh Bertie, I can't." Olivia looked horrified. How could she possibly tell him Victoria had been pregnant? "I wouldn't know what to tell him." But she didn't want to worry him about influenza either.

"You'll think of something, dear." Bertie reassured her. But by later that morning, when Olivia checked on her, Victoria was hemorrhaging again, and she was barely coherent. By that afternoon, the doctor had been called, and he called for an ambulance and took Victoria to the hospital in Tarrytown for three transfusions. There had been no way of keeping it from their father by then, and Victoria was sobbing hysterically as bottles of blood went into her arm, and Olivia sat beside her trying to calm her down. But it was hopeless, she was consumed with guilt and misery, she was still in pain, she was weak and confused, and although Victoria swore it wasn't true, Olivia knew she was still in love with Toby, and longing for him.

Their father sat in the waiting room for hours, and he looked bleakly at Olivia when she finally came to tell him Victoria was sleeping. The doctor had assured them that she'd be all right eventually. They had decided not to do surgery, and he promised everyone concerned that he was sure she would still be able to have children. The baby she had conceived had apparently been larger than it should have been at that stage, she might even have conceived twins originally, and there had been an unusual amount of bleeding when she lost it. But there was certainly no way of pretending to anyone in the hospital or the family that Victoria had influenza. The doctor had promised Edward Henderson that everything would be handled as discreetly as possible, but Edward also knew that no matter what they did, eventually word would get out. And it would be all over New York that Victoria had lost Toby Whitticomb's baby. It would confirm every rumor they'd heard prior to that, and put the last nail in the coffin which contained her now-defunct reputation.

"He might as well have shot her in the head," Henderson said unhappily as he sat in the waiting room with Olivia before he left to go home again. Olivia had already said she would sleep in a cot at the end of her sister's bed for as long as she had to.

"Father, don't say that," Olivia gently chided. But she could see in his eyes how devastated he was by all this, and how gravely he feared for her reputation.

"It's true. The man destroyed her. And to put at least some of the blame where it belongs, she destroyed herself. She was incredibly foolish. I only wish someone could have stopped her," he said to no one in particular, and Olivia felt it a reproach which she instantly answered.

"I tried, Father," she said softly.

"I'm sure you did," he said through clenched teeth. His lips were so thin they were barely visible, as they always were when he was angry. And he was more than angry this time, he was worried about her too, and what she had done to herself, and the rest of them, through her brief, but stupid, alliance. And then he looked pensively down at his other daughter. "She really has to get married. That would clean it up a bit. The tongues might be less inclined to wag if the story had a proper ending."

"He can't marry her," Olivia said quietly. Her father was as deluded as Victoria if he thought Toby would do that. He was married to an Astor.

"He can't marry her," her father agreed with her, "but someone else can. If anyone is willing to, after all this. It would probably be the best thing for her."

"She doesn't *want* to marry anyone," Olivia explained as though her father wasn't understanding. "She says she never wants to marry anyone, or see another man again, and this time, I think she means it."

"That's understandable, after what she's been through." He hadn't been told the details, but he was sure that what had transpired the night before had been far from pleasant. Perhaps, in its own way, it served as an additional lesson for her. "I'm sure she'll feel differently about it later." And he was not sure he cared if she didn't. She had done something that would hurt all of them in the end, and now she had to make restitution. "Don't worry about it, my dear." He kissed Olivia absentmindedly, and he was frowning when he left to go back to the house, and left Olivia with her sister.

They gave Victoria another transfusion late that night, and for a while it looked as though she might have surgery after all, but in the morning, she seemed desperately weak, but slightly better. It was another two days before she sat up in bed, and two days after that before she walked, but by the end of the week she was home, in her own bed, with Olivia and Bertie fussing over her, and she looked more like herself when they propped her up in bed and fed her. But by the time she got home, their father had gone to New York, to attend to business. He had to meet with his attorneys about the mill, and it was all he could do to control himself when he ran into Toby Whitticomb at the University Club when he went there for lunch with John Watson and Charles Dawson. John Watson eyed Edward carefully and asked if he was all right, and Edward only nodded. But fortunately, Toby left with a group of friends a few minutes later. He had said nothing to Henderson, and he avoided making eye contact with John Watson.

Edward went back to Croton after two days, satisfied that he had taken care of everything he wanted to do in New York. He had stayed at the Waldorf-Astoria this time. He didn't even want to see the house again. Too much had happened there in the past, and recently, and in any case, he hadn't brought any of the servants. Just Donovan and his car, and the hotel provided everything else he needed.

It was ten days before Thanksgiving when he got back, and Victoria was walking slowly around the grounds on her sister's arm when he arrived. She looked a great deal healthier than she had when he left, and he was sure that in another day or two she'd be fine. He was going to wait until then to tell her.

He told them both at the same time. He had no secrets from Olivia, and he wanted her support. But whether she agreed with him or not, the arrangements had been made. And everything had been agreed to. On Sunday afternoon, he asked them both to step into the library with him, and Olivia sensed immediately that he had something to tell them. She had the odd feeling that he was going to send them somewhere, perhaps to Europe for a while, to get Victoria's mind off Toby, though she had said nothing about him since New York, and even in the hospital, she had refused to talk about him. Olivia knew she wasn't over him, but she still felt so betrayed, she couldn't bear to talk about it.

"Girls," her father began without ceremony, "I have something to tell you." He looked at them both somewhat ferociously, as Victoria wondered what he had to say to them, and Olivia nodded. Victoria could sense easily that this conversation had to do with her transgression.

And in confirmation of that, he looked straight at Victoria as he went further. "People are talking in New York, Victoria. There's very little we can do about it, except ignore it, or deny it. And right now, I think perhaps that silence is the only answer. People will be talking here soon, after your recent trip to the hospital. And unfortunately, both stories put together make an even uglier story. They're beginning to say, fueled by Mr. Whitticomb, that you're a very wanton girl, and in fact, not only badly behaved, but heartless. Apparently, he's telling some sort of tale of your attempting to seduce him. There are those who don't believe him of course, more than a few I hope, but no matter what he says, or people do or do not believe, even the truth is not a pretty story."

"I was foolish, Father," Victoria said, admitting her guilt again, and feeling weaker than she had in days, having to hear what he was saying. "I was wrong . . . I was wanton, if you will . . . but I believed he loved me."

"That only makes you stupid, rather than heartless," he said unkindly, which was unlike him. But he had not been pleased by her behavior in the past several weeks, and he was frustrated by the realization that there was very little he could do to fix it. He could do one thing at least, and that he was determined to do now. "We can't change the stories very much, I'm afraid, or silence Mr. Whitticomb. But we can make you respectable again, at least, and the rest of us by association. I think you owe us that much."

"What could I possibly do, Father? You know that I would do it." At that point, she would have done anything to please him. The force of his disappointment in her was a crushing weight she could hardly bear now.

"I'm glad to hear that. You can get married, Victoria, and you will. That will at least eventually stop the rumors. It will give people something else to think about, and although you may have been a foolish young girl, perhaps even the victim of a cad, it may be said one day, you will at last be a respectable married woman, above reproach. And eventually, people may well forget the other story. Without that respectability," he said, knitting his brows, and glaring at her frighteningly, "there is only one story to tell, and it won't be a nice one. It is the only story they'll hear or tell for years, and you will in fact become a social pariah, and be treated like a harlot." He made no bones about it, and both twins were staring at him in confusion, but it was Victoria who answered.

"But he won't marry me, Father. You

know that. He lied to me, he said so himself. He never had any intention of marrying me. It was all a game to him," she told them what Toby had said to her the last time she saw him, "and Evangeline is having another baby in the spring. He can't possibly leave her."

"I should hope not." Her father looked awesome. "No, Tobias Whitticomb will not marry you, Victoria. There is no doubt of that now. But Charles Dawson will. We have spoken of it at length. He's a reasonable, intelligent man. I believe him to be kind, and of good morals, and he understands the situation. He has no delusions about your feelings about him, and although he doesn't know the details, he realizes that there was some unfortunate event that took place during our recent stay in New York. He is a widower, he lost a wife he loved deeply, and he himself is not seeking to replace her in his heart, but he has a young son, and needs a mother for him."

Victoria was staring at him as he spoke, and she looked at him in total amazement. "Is that like a job I'm supposed to apply for? Mother to his son, but not wife of his heart? Father, how could you?"

"How could I? How could *I*?" Edward Henderson spoke in a booming, terrifying voice to the younger twin. It was a voice neither of them had ever heard from him in their entire lifetimes. This time their father was giving the orders. "How *dare* you ask me that question after disgracing us, carrying on with a married man in front of all of New York, and even coming home pregnant with his bastard! Victoria, how *dare you*?! And you will do exactly what I say now, without an instant's hesitation, or I shall either lock you up in a nunnery somewhere, or cut you off without a penny."

"Then do." She stood up and shouted at him, much to her sister's horror. What had their family suddenly come to? "I will not be forced to marry a man I barely know and don't love, who does not love me, sold into slavery like a piece of furniture, a thing, an object! You have no right to dispose of me this way, to make an arrangement with your attorney, to *order* him to marry me. Will you pay him for that too?" she asked, wounded and shocked to her very core. And besides, she didn't even like Charles Dawson. How could they do this to her?

"I am not paying anyone, Victoria. And he understands the situation very clearly. Perhaps better than you do. You're in no position to wait for Prince Charming to come along, or even to stay here with me in Croton, with your sister. None of us can dare set foot in New York again until you have set this ghastly situation to rights. It's up to you now to clean up your mess, and make restitution to us."

"Cut off my hair, cut off my head, lock me up, do what you want. But you cannot sell me to a man as 'restitution.' " To Victoria, of all people, it was the ultimate outrage. "This is 1913, Father, not 1812. You *cannot* do this."

"I can and you will, and that will be the end of it, Victoria. Or I will frankly disown and disinherit you from this day forward. I will not allow you to ruin yourself, or Olivia, simply because you are willful and stubborn. He is a good man, and you're very lucky he is willing to do this. Frankly, I think if it weren't for the boy, he might not do it at all, so you'd do well to count your blessings."

"Are you serious?" She stared at him, unable to believe what she was hearing. And in her chair, next to her, Olivia looked as shocked as she did, for different reasons. "You will truly disown me if I don't marry him?"

"I will. I mean this, Victoria. And you *will* do it. It's the price you must pay for your foolishness, and it's a fair one. You'll live very comfortably in New York. He's an honest man, with a good career, and a respectable future. And one day, you will share with Olivia whatever I have left you. That in itself will give you a great deal more freedom. Without that, you'll be scrubbing floors in boardinghouses somewhere, and I mean it. You *will* do this, for all of us, me, yourself, and your sister. If nothing else moves you to reason, do it for Olivia. She'll never be able to show her face in New York again if you don't do this. Victoria, you *must* marry Charles Dawson. It needn't be now, this week. You can wait a few months, even till spring if you wish, so no one thinks you were forced into it for . . . er . . . obvious reasons. But we will announce your engagement immediately after Thanksgiving." Victoria looked ill as she got out of her chair, and went to stand looking out the window. "Do you understand me?" he asked, indicating an end to their conversation.

Victoria didn't turn around when she answered him. "Yes, Father, perfectly," she said, hating him almost as much as she hated Toby, and now Charles. Men were all the same, slave buyers all of them, users of female flesh. To any of them, a woman meant no more than a chair as far as she was concerned. And she was surprised to see when she turned around again that Olivia was crying. She was sure that it was

223

because they would be separated now, forever. New York wasn't far, but it was far enough, and they would hardly see each other. She was sure that her father would never let Olivia come to see her.

"I'm sorry to drag you through this too," he said more gently to Olivia, as he patted her shoulder. He was deeply sorry to have upset her. "But I thought this might need your sensible touch to bring your sister to reason. I want to make sure she understands she has no choice here."

"I understand, Father," Olivia said quietly. "You have everyone's good in mind here." But it was odd that the cruel blow he had dealt Victoria was even crueler to her. It was she who was so taken with Charles Dawson, and Victoria who thought him a bore, and someone not even worth bothering to talk to. It seemed ironic that their father had wounded both of them so mortally with the same sword, and without even knowing. The blind goddess of justice.

"Perhaps you'd both like to go to your room and talk about this for a while," he suggested, feeling that they had gone far enough for the moment. He had made himself clear, and although he knew she hated him just then, he felt sure that Victoria would do it.

Both girls left the room feeling numb, and dazed as they walked slowly upstairs to their bedroom, and it was only when the door was closed that Victoria allowed herself to rage and scream and cry. She couldn't believe it.

"How can he have done this to me? How can he have gone to New York and sold me to that little worm? How dare he?"

"He's not a worm." Olivia smiled through her own tears at her. "He's decent and kind and intelligent. You'll like him."

"Oh stop it!" Victoria spat at her. "You sound just like Father."

"Maybe he's right, maybe you do have no choice in this after all. Maybe the only thing that will make you respectable again is marrying Charles Dawson."

"I don't give a fig about being respectable. I'd just as soon get on a ship tonight and sail to England. I can work there, and join the Pankhursts."

"Aren't they in jail for the next three years? Or one of them at least, if I recall what you said about it last summer. And how are you going to pay for passage on the ship? I think maybe Father is right, Victoria. You have no choice here."

"What man would want a wife he got like this? How can he do it?"

"You heard what Father said. He wants a mother for his son." It seemed odd to Olivia too, and she knew the man, or had spoken to him more than Victoria had anyway. Maybe he couldn't manage on his own. It seemed an odd thing to do, but perhaps it was for the best, for them at least. But it left Olivia with nothing. "Victoria, at least try to like him, for your own sake." She had never admitted to anyone, not even her twin, how much she liked Charles, and at least now Victoria had no idea how overwhelmed Olivia was with her own emotions. And Victoria was far too sorry for herself all afternoon to even notice how upset Olivia was, and that night she refused to go down to dinner with their father.

"How is she?" he asked Olivia quietly when she came down alone for dinner.

"Upset, shocked. She's had a hard time these last few weeks. She'll get used to it. Give her time." He nodded in answer, and as the meal drew to a close he patted Olivia's hand and looked at her sadly.

"That will leave just us here. Will you be very lonely?"

"I'll miss her terribly," she said, as tears filled her eyes again. The thought of not living with her twin anymore was almost more than she could bear, and losing Charles forever to her too was the final death blow to her own girlish dreams. "But I won't leave you, Father, I promise."

"Perhaps you should one day. Perhaps when all this settles down, after she marries Charles, we should brave New York again and see if you meet a handsome prince." He smiled gently at his daughter, and he had no idea of the pain he had just caused her.

"I don't want a handsome prince, Father. I have you. And I belong here. There is no one I would want to marry." She said it with absolute conviction. It seemed sad to him to let her remain an old maid, and yet there was a selfish side to him that wanted her to stay there with him. She handled his household so well, and she was such a comfort to him, far more than Victoria ever would have been. He wondered if this wasn't for the best then.

"I'll always take care of you. I promise you that too. And one day, this will all be yours. Henderson Manor will be yours, Olivia. You can spend the rest of your life here. I'll make it up to Victoria, but she'll have the house in New York to live in with Charles when I'm gone. You won't need it." He had disposed of both of them. It was all arranged. She would stay and take care of him for the rest of his life, and Victoria would have Charles. Olivia wondered which gods she had so offended that this should happen to her. She had never dreamed of having Charles, but she never expected him to be served on a platter to her sister, even more absurd as "punishment" for her transgressions.

"Will you let me go to New York to see her?" Olivia asked, holding her breath. That would be doubly cruel, losing both of them to each other, the one she'd never had but dreamed of, and the other she loved so intensely, and couldn't bear to be away from.

"Of course, my dear," her father agreed. "I have no desire to keep you two apart, only to help Victoria clean up the awful mess she's made." Listening to him, Olivia wished more than ever that she had been able to keep Victoria away from Toby. What rubble he had made of their lives in only moments. "You can visit her whenever you want to, as long as you don't abandon me completely." He smiled, and she put her arms around him, as her tears rolled silently down her cheeks and onto his shoulder. She had nothing left to wish for now, to want, or to dream of. She would always be his now. And to Olivia, it felt as though her life were over.

Chapter 8

Charles and Geoffrey Dawson arrived in Croton-on-Hudson on a bright autumn day in late November. It was crisp and cold, there were fires burning somewhere, and there was the smell of winter in the air. And just before they'd arrived, the cook had slaughtered the turkey. It was the day before Thanksgiving.

Their father had gone into Tarrytown on an errand, and Victoria had gone for a ride on her own, as she had been doing for days. It seemed as though no one was at home, as they drove up, and Olivia happened to see them as she glanced out a kitchen window. She wiped her hands on her apron, and ran quickly out to them, without putting her coat on, and without even thinking, she wanted to put her arms around Charles and kiss him, she was so happy to see him. She wondered if perhaps she could do that one day, when they were brother and sister. It was a very odd feeling. Instead, she smiled at him, shook his hand, and told him how pleased she was they had come, and then looked down at Geoffrey. And as she did, she felt something in her heart catch. It was as though he had already been a part of her life somewhere and she knew him. She felt as though it was meant to be, as she bent down slightly and shook his hand with great solemnity.

"Hello, Geoffrey. I'm Olivia. Victoria's sister." But as she glanced at Charles, she could see quickly that he had not yet told him. He wanted to speak to Victoria first, and see if they could really do this. "Victoria and I are twins," she explained, and she could see instantly that he was fascinated by what she had told him. "We look exactly alike, and I'll bet you won't be able to tell us apart when you meet her."

"Bet I can," he said bravely, all blonde hair and green eyes full of fun and mischief. He looked a lot like Charles, but there was someone else there too, and Olivia could only guess that it was Susan. The odd thing was that it was almost as if she felt her close to her, as she watched them, as though she had become their guardian angel, and was a peaceful spirit. It was an odd sensation she wouldn't have dared explain to anyone, perhaps not even her sister.

"I'll tell you a secret about us one day, if we get to be good friends, about how you can tell us apart for sure," she said conspiratorially as she led him through the back door into the kitchen, for some freshly baked cookies.

"I could have used that secret while you were in New York," Charles laughed at her. "Why didn't you tell me?"

"We've never told anyone, but Geoffrey's special," she said, looking down at the boy, and resting a gentle hand on his shoulder. She wasn't even sure what had made her do it. But she felt oddly close to him, as though he had come to her for a reason. Perhaps he was her consolation prize, the child who would light up her soul, since now she would never have one. By the time her father died, it would be too late for her to marry and have children. In a single week, she had lost both her sister, and her future. She had thought of staying here with him before, but that had only been idle talk, now it was certain.

"No one else knows?" The boy looked genuinely intrigued and somewhat honored.

"Bertie does," Olivia explained, and then introduced them as Mrs. Peabody walked through the kitchen. She was very pleased to meet Charles Dawson. And a few minutes later, she took them to their rooms, and unpacked their things for them. It was half an hour later when Charles wandered down again alone. Geoffrey was helping Bertie. "He's a wonderful little boy," Olivia said with a warm smile, and Charles stood there for a long moment, without saying anything to her, just looking at her, and then he turned away and looked sadly out the window. It was difficult to know what he was thinking. "He's a lot like his mother," Charles said quietly and then turned to Olivia again. "How have you been since you left New York?" He looked as though he really cared when he asked her, which only hurt more, and she wished the others would hurry and join them.

"Fine. We've been busy here." She didn't mention that Victoria had been ill, and wondered if he knew it.

"Keeping your sister out of jail these days?" he asked and they both laughed as Victoria strode into the room in her riding clothes, with muddy boots and her hair flying around her head like a dark halo.

"I don't find that comment amusing," she said, looking at both of them.

"Charles is here," Olivia said somewhat nervously, as Victoria looked at her in disgust.

"I can see that. I don't find that story about the demonstration in New York funny anymore," she informed them both, and Charles and Olivia exchanged a glance like two naughty children that had been scolded.

"I'm sorry, Victoria," he said kindly, and went to shake her hand. "How was your ride?" He was obviously making a sincere effort to get to know her, but her answer was curt and cool, before she went upstairs to change for dinner. "She doesn't seem very happy these days," Charles said bluntly after she left the room. It was an understatement that almost made Olivia laugh at the simplicity of it.

"I suppose you could say that. She's had rather a hard time since we left New York so quickly." She wasn't sure how much he knew, and she didn't want to be the one to tell him. "She's been ill recently too." She tried valiantly to make excuses for her sister.

"I suppose none of this is easy for her," he said openly, which surprised Olivia. "It's a bit of a shock for me too," he explained candidly, "but I think it will be good for Geoffrey."

"Is that why you're doing it?" She wanted to ask him if it was the only reason, but she didn't dare. She hardly knew him.

"I can't bring up a child properly without a mother," he said, looking restlessly around the room as he said it.

"My father did," she said quietly and Charles laughed.

"Are you telling me not to marry your sister?"

She wished she had the courage to do that.

"No." Olivia smiled at him. "I'm just saying there should be other reasons."

"I'm sure there will be when we get to know each other better."

The two nodded at each other, and they could hear voices on the stairs. It was Victoria coming downstairs with Geoffrey.

"You look just like her," he was saying, fascinated by the dark-haired girl, coming down the stairs just behind him.

"I know I do. And what's your name?"

"Geoffrey," he supplied, without a hint of shyness.

"How old are you?" She sounded as

though she didn't really care, and he knew it. He had an instinct about those things, and he suddenly wondered if she and Olivia were actually quite different.

"Nine." He answered her question, as they reached the bottom of the stairs, but she made no move to shake his hand or touch him.

"Are you short for your age?" She was surprised that he wasn't older.

"No, tall," he explained patiently.

"I don't know very much about children."

"Olivia does. I like her."

"So do I." The younger twin smiled as they walked into the library together, and she walked to Olivia's side and stood there, and suddenly the resemblance was beyond remarkable. They looked like two copies of the same person. Their hair, their eyes, their mouths, the way they wore their dresses, their shoes, their hands, their smiles. Geoffrey narrowed his eyes and stared at them both for a long time, and then he shook his head much to everyone's amazement.

"I don't think you look the same at all," he said seriously and all of the adults present laughed, including his father.

"I'm taking him to get glasses on Monday," he said, while the twins chuckled. But Geoffrey was insistent.

"They don't, Daddy. Look at them."

"I have. Several times. And I never fail to make a fool of myself every single time. If you can tell them apart, I congratulate you. I can't do it." Except that in an odd way he could too, at times, and he knew it. Not always, but sometimes. They affected him differently, if he let them. But if he just looked at them, without thinking about it, or "feeling" them, then he couldn't tell the difference. It was that quality that Geoffrey was referring to. It was something visceral and sexual for Charles, at least some of the time. But for Geoffrey, it was far more simple. He just knew them.

"That's Olivia," he said, pointing at the right one without hesitating, "and Victoria," he was correct again. And then they switched places, and he guessed again, and he was right again. And then Olivia teased him by dancing around holding Victoria's hands, and he got confused and was wrong. But the next time he got it right again, and all of them were startled, even Victoria who always insisted she hated children. Olivia had already suggested she not mention that this evening.

"Why not? Maybe he won't marry me," she had said, looking wicked.

"And then Father will send you to a nunnery in Siberia, or marry you to a fisherman in Alaska. Please, Victoria," she had begged, "don't offend them."

"All right, all right, I won't," she had agreed. And she didn't. She said almost nothing at all, even once their father came home, and when the four of them sat at dinner. It was Olivia and Charles who carried most of the conversation.

"Why don't you marry him?" Victoria said later that night when they went to bed. "You don't seem to have any trouble talking to him."

"I don't have a reputation to regain, and Father wants me to run his house," she said bluntly. He had made his position perfectly clear to both of them, of precisely what he expected, and Olivia marrying Charles was not part of the bargain, no matter how easy their conversations. "Geoffrey is adorable, isn't he?" Olivia said, as they lay side by side in bed, in matching nightgowns.

"I don't know. I didn't really notice. Children don't interest me, you know that."

"He's fascinated by us," Olivia smiled, remembering him trying to identify them, and most of the time he had done it correctly. Just as Olivia felt she had an unspoken bond with him, he seemed to feel the same for her, or perhaps for both of them. He seemed to like Victoria too, although she hadn't paid much attention to him.

Geoffrey had eaten in the breakfast room with Bertie that night, and she was enchanted to have a child in the house again, as was their father. He took him on a long walk the next day, before lunch, and Olivia eventually joined them. She had seen Victoria go outside with Charles, and she didn't want to interrupt them. They had a lot to say to each other now, and she hoped that her sister would make her peace with it, and wouldn't offend him. If she did, and he refused to marry her, their father would be even more upset than he was at the moment.

"It's a bit unusual, all this, isn't it?" Charles asked, as they walked slowly through the formal gardens. "I don't quite know what to say to you. I was a little startled when your father spoke to me. But actually, I like the idea. It makes a great deal of sense to me, with Geoffrey."

"Is that the only reason you're doing it?"

Victoria asked him bluntly. She couldn't imagine why a man would want a wife who didn't love him.

"Mostly," he said honestly. "It's not fair to him for me to be alone like this. Your sister even said as much to me when you were in New York, and she didn't even know us."

"I was very much in love with his mother," he said, obviously in pain when he said it. "There will never be anyone like her. We knew each other when we were very young. She was a bit wild, and very fey. She laughed all the time, and she was very strong willed." And then he smiled at Victoria. "Rather like you, in some ways," and then his eyes clouded over again. "In the end, that's what killed her. She was very stubborn, and she had a passion for children."

"Father said she died on the *Titanic*," Victoria said matter-of-factly. She was interested, but not nearly as sympathetic as her sister. But oddly enough, that made it easier for him to tell her. Talking to Olivia brought tears to his eyes sometimes. There was something so sensitive and caring about her.

"She did. She was about to get in the lifeboat with Geoff apparently, but there were a number of children around. She gave up her place for one of them. I can't believe somehow that there wouldn't have been room for her too, that she couldn't have gotten in with them. But she stayed to help get quite a lot of children in the last boat, and one or two rafts. She even gave one of them her life vest. The last person who saw her said she had a child in her arms. Thank God it wasn't Geoffrey." There was a long silence, and then, "She was an extraordinary woman."

"I'm sorry," Victoria said softly, and this time she meant it.

"I can imagine you doing something like that," he said generously, as he looked at her, but she shook her head. She knew herself better.

"Maybe Olivia. But I don't think I would. I'm far too selfish. And I'm not very good with children."

"You'll learn," he said gently. "What about you? What about this broken engagement? I gather it was still unofficial."

"You could say that." She'd been sleeping with a married man, it was certainly a nicer way to say it. "Is that what Father told you?"

"Not really," he smiled at her, not wanting to hurt her feelings. Her father had been as honest with him as he felt he could be. "I gather it got a bit rougher than that. But I don't have any delusions about this being a romance between us. I think we could be good friends. I need a mother for Geoff. You need a safe haven from the storm you're in right now." He had heard some of the rumors about her and Toby in New York, although he still didn't know exactly what had happened. He knew there had been a flirtation with a married man, and promises that weren't kept, and a broken heart. But he knew none of the details of her indiscretion, or the miscarriage that had nearly killed her. "We actually begin luckier than some, because we don't have any illusions. No broken dreams, or broken hearts. No promises that won't be kept. We could be very good friends, that's really all I want now." He couldn't imagine ever being in love again, and even the vague stirrings he felt for her were most unwelcome.

"Why don't you just hire a housekeeper for him?" she asked honestly. "Someone like Bertie." He laughed at the simplicity of the suggestion, and looked at her with open amusement.

"You must think I'm very strange, marrying a woman who doesn't love me. But I don't want to be in love again. I don't want to lose anyone I care about ever again. I couldn't bear it."

"What if we fall in love with each other eventually?" she asked, more to be contrary than because she thought it likely.

"Do you feel inclined that way?" he asked, totally aware of her indifference to him. "Do you find me irresistible? Do you think you'll fall in love with me very quickly?"

"Not in the least," Victoria said, laughing at him. She was surprised to find that she liked him. He wasn't attractive to her, but he was very pleasant. "You're in no danger."

"Excellent. And if I hire a housekeeper, you won't have a husband. Or at least not me at any rate, and then you'd have to go looking for someone else and that would be a lot of trouble. This would be much simpler. Only one thing," he said cautiously.

"What's that?" she asked, with obvious suspicion, but he had a twinkle in his eye when he addressed her.

"I would prefer it if you tried not to get arrested, or at least not too often. As an attorney, that could be awkward."

"I'll do my best," she said with a small smile, wondering what it would be like to live in New York again, and run into Toby. For the moment, she hated him, and would have liked to scratch his eyes out, or maybe rip out his throat the next time she saw him. He might as well have killed her. And then she looked at Charles seriously and spoke to him bluntly. "I'm not going to stop going to meetings. I'm a feminist, and a suffragist. And if that embarrasses you, I'm sorry."

"Not at all. I think it's very interesting. I see no reason to obstruct your political views. You're entitled to your own opinions."

"I don't know why you're doing this," she said, looking at him, unaware of how lovely he thought her. And he was foolish too. He knew precisely how wild she was, and there was a part of him that wanted to tame her. In a way, she was a kind of challenge, even more so because she didn't love him. Theirs would be an interesting union.

"I don't know why I'm doing this either," he said honestly. "Probably for a lot of very odd reasons, none of them dangerous, only stupid." And then, as they walked slowly back to the house again, he asked her the final question. It was like a business deal they had set up. Neither of them were enchanted with it, but they both thought it was worth trying. "When do you want to do it?" As late as possible, she wanted to say to him, but didn't.

"Not for a while. There's no rush." And that way, no one would think she was doing it because she was pregnant. "What about June?"

"That sounds reasonable. Geoff will be out of school by then. It would be a good time to get to know you. What about a honeymoon?" he asked matter-of-factly. It was the oddest conversation of both their lifetimes, almost to the point of being crazy. "Would you like a trip?"

"Yes, actually, I would," she said nonchalantly.

"What about California?" he proposed. It was the business deal again, but she declined his offer, and countered.

"Europe."

"I don't want to take a ship," he said, for obvious reasons, but she was far more stubborn than he was.

"I don't want to go to California."

"We'll have to talk about it later."

"Fine," she said, and they looked at each other. There was no emotion there, no romance, no sentiment, no love at all on her part, and only a vague sensual malaise on his. These

were the oddest reasons possible for two people to marry each other. They were building a
lifetime on less than nothing. But he needed a
mother for his child, and she needed a husband
to restore her reputation. And in effect, it was
all they had to offer each other. And they
walked back to the house in silence.

In spite of its odd beginning, the whole
Thanksgiving weekend went surprisingly
smoothly. Victoria appeared to be amenable,
and even Edward seemed surprised that it had
gone so easily, and Victoria was so willing. Victoria said very little to Charles, and she never
spoke to Geoff at all, but he fell in love with
Olivia, and Charles had gotten to know his future father-in-law and enjoyed his tales about
his business.

And although it was painful for Olivia to
spend time with Charles, she was completely
enchanted with Geoffrey. She took him riding
on Saturday, and he loved it. She gave him her
favorite horse, Sunny. And on Sunday morning,
as they sat on a rock in a field, while the care-
taker's dog played nearby, she showed him the
freckle. It was on her right palm, just creeping
between her fingers, and it was so tiny, you almost had to squint to see it. She made him
promise not to tell a soul, not even his father.

She made him hold up his hand and swear with an old Indian chant she and Victoria had learned when they were children.

"When we were your age, we used to play tricks on people sometimes, and trade places. I'd pretend to be Victoria, and she'd pretend to be me. It was fun, most of the time anyway, and no one ever knew we did it, except Bertie."

"Are you going to do that to my dad?" he asked with interest, and Olivia laughed at the idea.

"Of course not. That would be a mean thing to do to him. We just did it when we were children."

"And you've never done it since?" He looked surprised and as though he knew better. He was very wise for his age, and he was crazy about his new aunt by marriage. They had told him the day before that his father and Victoria were getting married. He seemed surprised, but not terribly worried about it.

"Actually, we've only switched a few times since we've been grown-up," Olivia confessed, "usually with people we don't like, or if one of us has something to do we really hate."

"Like the dentist?" he asked with interest.

"No, we don't switch for the dentist. But we might do it for a very dull dinner one of us has accepted and wishes they hadn't. But usually, we go to things like that together."

"Will you really miss Victoria when she comes to live with us?"

"Yes, I will," Olivia said sadly, unable to even think about it for the moment. "I'll miss her terribly. You'll all have to come here to see me, especially you," she smiled at him. "I'm glad you came here for Thanksgiving."

"So am I," he said, and then slipped a hand into hers. He really liked her. "And I won't tell anyone about the freckle."

"You better not," she said, and hugged him close to her. It was odd thinking about what it would be like to be his mother. She thought Victoria was doubly lucky.

They walked slowly back to the house, and late that afternoon Charles drove him back to New York. But they had promised to come back for Christmas. Geoffrey was all excited just talking about it, and Olivia had promised to give them a dinner. It would be their first dinner party after the announcement the following week of their engagement, and Olivia was going to invite everyone they knew all up and down the Hudson.

Their father looked satisfied when Charles left, and Victoria looked exhausted. It had been a strain for her, but not as bad as she had expected. She went to bed early that night. And Olivia sat for hours by the fire, thinking of Geoffrey and his father.

It was odd thinking of Victoria and Charles and Geoffrey. They had each other now. They were suddenly a family. And overnight, she had become a spinster.

Chapter 9

The engagement of Victoria Elizabeth Henderson and Charles Westerbrook Dawson was announced in the *New York Times* on the Wednesday after Thanksgiving. It said that the wedding would be in June, but no exact date had been set yet. And Edward Henderson looked pleased with himself as he folded the paper and set it on his desk. They had done it.

There was the usual mild furor after the news, some calls from New York, several letters came to her. And in the city, there were little ripples of gossip, but none of it as damaging as it might have been. Were it not for Charles, the outcome of Victoria's stupidity might have been disastrous. As it was, people were saying that she had had a serious flirtation with Toby

Whitticomb, and she had been seen in highly indiscreet places with him. But very little more could be said with total certainty. The only one who knew the truth was Toby, and for him to say it now would have made him look far worse than he wanted. She was safe. Almost. Or she would be, in her father's eyes, once she was Mrs. Charles Westerbrook Dawson.

But as Victoria sat reading the announcement later that afternoon, she stared at it in dull amazement. How could they have done this? And why? All because she had fallen so desperately in love with Toby, because she had believed him. Now she had to be sold into slavery to a man she didn't care about, to be punished. And she would have to do the same things with him that she had done with Toby. But instead of exciting her, this time she felt numb and disgusted. She wondered how she would ever do it. Charles had said they would be good friends, he said he didn't expect adoration from her. He didn't expect anything, except companionship, and a mother for Geoffrey. Even the thought of the child revolted her. She didn't want to be anyone's mother, and knew she never would again. Thinking of him reminded her of the lost baby, and that had been traumatic enough. She had every intention, once she married Charles, of doing whatever it was that women did to avoid having babies. She didn't know what it was, but she was sure there was something. And perhaps, she thought hopefully, he wouldn't expect that of her anyway. That wasn't part of being "friends," as he said they were. Perhaps he wouldn't expect anything of her at all, physically. She ardently hoped not. The thought of his touching her, in any of the ways Toby had, thoroughly chilled her.

"What are you looking so serious about?" Olivia asked as she came into the room, carrying an armload of fresh towels. One of the maids had been bringing them upstairs, but Olivia had offered to help her. But she saw now that Victoria was looking deeply grieved as she sat staring at the New York paper, and then she realized what it was, and she smiled at her gently. "You'll be happy with him, Victoria . . . he's a good man . . . and you'll be able to do whatever you want in New York . . . think of that . . ." It was something. Victoria looked up at her bleakly and nodded, so involved in her own despair that she didn't even sense Olivia's sorrow.

Victoria went on long walks after that in the afternoons, and Olivia never said anything anymore when her sister disappeared to Croton or Dobbs Ferry, or even Ossining. She knew she went to meetings with other women whenever she could, and she noticed easily that there was a sharper edge to Victoria now, a real anger against men which bordered on hatred. She kept her tongue in control most of the time, but when the opportunity arose, or anyone said something, Victoria was quick to lash out with her opinions. Most of them masqueraded as political, and they had been once, but Olivia knew only too well that her feelings against men now, and her championing of women as the victims of governments in general and men in particular, were spawned by Toby Whitticomb, and even Charles Dawson. She saw Charles as a kind of kidnapper, who was in league with her father, to punish her for having loved Toby.

Unfortunately, the party Olivia had planned for her was of no interest to Victoria, and she barely listened when Olivia read the guest list. She said she didn't care who came, and the fact that the Rockefellers and the Clarks had accepted was no victory to her. She was sorry that any of them were coming. There was nothing to celebrate. It was simply an arrangement.

"Don't call it that, Victoria," Olivia said unhappily when Victoria said as much to her the day before the Dawsons' return to Croton for Christmas. "It's well meant. You're both offering each other something important. Charles has saved you from the awful things people might have said otherwise, and think of little Geoffrey, and how happy he'll be to have you as his mother."

"I don't want to be a mother to him," Victoria said angrily. She had done nothing but think of how miserable she was since Thanksgiving. "I have no idea how to mother him. He doesn't even like me."

"Of course he does, don't be stupid."

"He likes you," Victoria said firmly. "And he's right. He knows the difference between us, and I think he senses that I don't like children." She was right about one thing, though Olivia wouldn't admit it to her, Geoffrey Dawson had an uncanny knack for telling them apart, even without seeing the famous freckle Olivia had shown him.

"He likes both of us. And I'm sure that in a very short time, you'll come to love him."

But Victoria felt forced into it, and she already resented the obligation. All she wanted now was a civilized arrangement with Charles, and the opportunity to see some friends in New York, and go to political rallies and meetings. She even dreamed of being in politics one day. She felt certain that it was her calling, as the religious life was to others. She saw herself as a kind of Joan of Arc, a purist who would lay down her life for her ideals.

Whenever Olivia listened to her, she was startled by the extremes toward which her twin was moving. "You need to think a bit more about ordinary things, Victoria. Like your husband, and your home, and your wedding." But calling Charles her sister's "husband" cut straight to her soul, and she almost recoiled from the shock of it as she said it. It was sinful for her to react this way, she knew, wicked of her to covet her sister's husband, and only because he was so kind, and she loved talking to him. She had no right to think of him that way now. She never had, but while they'd been in New York, it had been so easy to drift into girlish dreams about him. But for both of them, their girlish days were over. They would soon be twenty-one, and in different ways, for different purposes, they had both become women. Victoria had known carnal love, however illegitimately, and she would be married soon. And Olivia now belonged entirely to her father, and would spend the next decade or two, or perhaps even three if he lived long enough, in his service. Victoria's life would be one of compromise. Hers would be one of sacrifice and denial. And both had to come to terms with their futures, or thought so.

Olivia talked to her about the party again, and forced her to listen this time. She had ordered new dresses for them, heavy black velvet ones, with short trains. They were very modern and fashionable, and had been copied after designs by the Callot sisters in Paris.

"When I go to Paris," Victoria smiled at her lovingly, she appreciated all that Olivia had done for her of late, although she didn't always say it, "I shall buy you something 'real,' by one of the designers you love so much. What'll it be? A Beer? A Worth? A Poiret? You'll have to give me a list and I'll go shopping for you." It was agonizing for both of them now to think of a time when they would not be together, and there were times when Olivia flatly refused to do it. It was one thing thinking of her getting married and going away, but quite another letting herself feel the real pain of no longer having her sister with her, night and day, wherever they went. There hadn't been a day when they were separated for more than a few hours for their entire lifetimes. It would be like losing a limb, Olivia feared, or all of them. She could feel the air squeeze out of her with a dull pain whenever she allowed herself to think of it. She went and hugged Victoria then, and told her that she would miss her terribly when she was gone. Almost beyond bearing.

"You'll have to come and live with us," Victoria said matter-of-factly. She had already thought of that, and she wanted Olivia to do it.

"I'm sure Charles would be thrilled at that," Olivia laughed hollowly. It would have been agony for her to live under his roof with him and never have what she'd dreamed of.

"He'll get two for the price of one," Victoria said lightly. "And you can take care of Geoff." Victoria grinned and lit a cigarette in their bedroom, as Olivia made a face at her and opened a window. "It's perfect."

"Bertie's going to kill you if she catches you smoking," Olivia warned, and then locked the door of their bedroom so she wouldn't. "And what about Father if I come with you? Shall he come too?" She grinned ruefully at Victoria. They could pretend all they wanted to now, but eventually they both knew they'd have to face it. Starting with the honeymoon, their lives would be forever separate. "Father says he'll let me go to New York whenever I want to."

"That's not the same, Ollie, and you know it."

"No," she sighed, "but it's the best I can do for the moment." And then she had another thought, it would at least be some small consolation. "What about Geoff? Will you take him on your honeymoon?"

"God, I hope not." Victoria made a face as she took another drag on her cigarette, and Olivia waved the smoke in another direction.

"That is such a disgusting thing to do. I wish you wouldn't."

"Smoking is all the rage among women in Europe," Victoria said, laughing at her sister.

"So is milking cows. I wouldn't want to do that either, and that doesn't smell half as bad. Anyway, what about Geoff? Will you take him?"

"Charles and I haven't talked about it, but I can't imagine he'd want to. I want to go to Europe." Olivia felt her heart ache again at the mention of it. She would no longer be part of Victoria's life then.

"Maybe Geoff could stay here with me. It would be good for him, and I'd love it."

"What a great idea." Victoria grinned at

her. She liked nothing better than the thought of leaving the boy in Croton. The last thing she wanted to do was chase him all over the ship, worse yet all over Europe. Charles hadn't actually agreed to go to Europe on their honeymoon yet. He was still talking about California, but Victoria was adamant, and she was certain she could convince him. She was *not* going to California. From everything she had heard about it, it sounded uncivilized, uncomfortable, and dreadful.

"I'll suggest it to Charles while they're here. Or do you want to?" Olivia asked as she closed the window. It was freezing outside, and it had already snowed twice since Thanksgiving.

"You ask him. I'll work on Europe." She smiled, and a little while later, both sisters went downstairs arm in arm, feeling a little better. Victoria was thinking of her honeymoon, and the women she wanted to see in London. She had already written to them previously. In fact, unbeknownst to Olivia, she had sent a letter to Emmeline Pankhurst in prison. And Olivia was happy, thinking about having Geoffrey with them for the summer. It would be some small consolation for not being with her sister.

The Dawsons arrived from New York the

next day, in Charles' new Packard, and Geoffrey almost flew out of the car when they arrived, he was so excited. He raced right past Victoria who was standing outside waiting for them, and shouted at her. "Where's Ollie?"

"In the kitchen," she answered as he raced by, and around to the back door, as his father looked at her cautiously with a shy smile, feeling somewhat awkward. He wished he had his son's sure eye, but he didn't.

"Is he right? Are you Victoria?" It was ridiculous not knowing which one his fiancée was, but in truth he didn't. At first, he had thought he could sense who she was, but after his last visit with them, he was no longer as certain. There were times when Victoria was as shy with him as Olivia was, and other times when Olivia had relaxed, feeling that he was family now, and she was as bold as Victoria had been with him right from the beginning. It was becoming more confusing as he got to know them better, instead of less, and the differences between them seemed less distinct now. But as they became more at ease with him, he found that they had a similar sense of humor, and laughed at many of the same things. They had the same smile, the same laughter, the same mannerisms. They even had the same sneeze. If anything, he was even more confused now than he had been in the beginning.

And Victoria was laughing at him openly, as she nodded and confirmed that she was indeed his future wife, and Charles looked much relieved as he gave her a chaste kiss on the cheek and told her how happy he was to see her.

"I think I'm going to have to buy you each a pair of very handsome diamond pins with your initials, or I'll be making a fool of myself each time we come here." They both laughed as she tucked a hand into his arm and walked him into the front hall of Henderson Manor.

"That's a very nice idea," she said, and then looked up at him, aching to play with him a little bit. It was too hard to resist the temptation. Having reassured him about who she was, she suddenly thought it would be funny to turn the tables on him, and see how he reacted to it.

"How do you know I'm actually not Ollie?" she asked innocently, confusing him suddenly, and enjoying it more than she should have.

"Are you?" He stepped away from her quickly, looking mortified at having been so familiar with her. And Victoria nodded, pretending to be her sister. But just as she did, Geoffrey came bounding in, with pink cheeks and tousled hair, holding Olivia's hand as they came from the kitchen.

"Hello, Victoria," Geoff said nonchalantly, and his father looked somewhat exasperated at the trick Victoria had played on him. Or had the boy mistaken them too? Charles looked at both twins, unable to tell now, but Olivia began shaking a finger at her sister. She had instantly sensed what Victoria had been doing.

"Have you been torturing Charles?" she asked accusingly. She knew her sister too well. It had always been Victoria who genuinely loved switching.

"She has," he said, flushing darkly, with a grateful look at his future sister-in-law for ending the charade so quickly. "She was trying to make me think she was you," he explained, as Geoffrey laughed at him. "And she had me completely bewildered for a moment."

Geoffrey thought his father was pretty silly for not knowing the difference between the two women.

"Now, how did *you* know with such certainty?" Charles asked him in mild frustration. It amazed him that a child so young could discern the difference between the two, but he couldn't. Perhaps he was confused by his own emotions, he wondered.

"I don't know." Geoffrey shrugged. "They just look different to me."

"He's the only person I've ever met, other than Bertie, who knows the difference." Olivia smiled at the boy, and extended a hand to Charles and he shook it. He turned to his fiancée then, and she was still amused at what she'd done. She liked making him feel unsure of himself, and putting him off balance, and he sensed that about her.

"I won't ever trust you again, Victoria Henderson," he said to the right twin this time, and Olivia laughed at him.

"That's very wise of you, Charles. I suggest you remember that!"

"What's going on here?" Edward Henderson came into the front hall and he was pleased to see them.

They had a lively dinner that night, talking about New York, and Edward's business deals. The steel mill had finally been sold, and Edward was extremely pleased with the outcome, and the way Charles had handled it. He was a quiet man, but he was masterful in business.

And at last, after dinner, Edward and

Olivia left them alone. Olivia went upstairs to check on Geoff. And Edward said he was tired, and wanted to retire early. Olivia and her father walked slowly up the stairs arm in arm, and whispered about how smoothly things were going. He was very relieved about all of it, and Olivia nodded in agreement, but she had mixed emotions.

But she forgot all of them the moment she saw Geoff upstairs. Bertie had put him to bed, but he was not asleep, and he was lying in one of their enormous guest beds, with his arms around a frayed, tattered monkey.

"Who's that?" Olivia asked with interest, as she sat down beside him.

"That's Henry. He's very old. He's as old as I am. I take him everywhere, except to school," he said matter-of-factly, holding him in the crook of one arm, as he smiled at Olivia. The boy looked very little in the big bed, and she wanted to lean down and kiss him, but she didn't know him well enough yet to do that.

"He's very handsome," Olivia said seriously. "Does he bite? Monkeys do sometimes, you know."

"Of course not," he said, grinning at her. He thought she was pretty and funny. "I wish I had a twin. You could play tricks on people all the time, like Victoria did on Dad today. He really thought she was you. And he got all embarrassed." He thought that was particularly amusing.

"How can you tell the difference between us?" she asked curiously, wondering what it was he saw that others didn't. He had the innocence of a child, and as a result, somehow, a clearer vision.

"You think differently," he said simply. "I can see it."

"You can see how we think?" Olivia sounded startled. He was wise beyond his years, she wondered if he always had been, or if it had come to him when he lost his mother.

"Sometimes," he answered her question, and then startled her even more. "Victoria doesn't like me."

"Of course she does!" Olivia was quick to say, "she's just not very used to children."

"She's used to all the same things you are. She just doesn't like them. She doesn't talk to me like you do. Does she really like my father?" It was a painfully direct question for a child his age, and for an instant Olivia was not sure how to answer.

"I think she likes your father very much,

Geoff. I don't think they know each other very well yet, but they will in time."

"Then why are they getting married if they don't know each other? That's pretty stupid." He wasn't entirely wrong, but life was a lot more complicated than that, although she couldn't explain it to him.

"Sometimes people get married because they know it's a good thing to do, and they will grow to love each other in time. Sometimes those are the best marriages, the ones where you begin as friends, and become a great deal more over a lifetime." It sounded sensible to her, but Geoffrey looked doubtful.

"My mom used to say that she loved us more than the whole world and then some. She said she loved Daddy more than anyone in the world when she married him, even more than her mother and father. And then she had me, and she loved me just as much as him," he lowered his voice conspiratorially then, "actually she said she loved me more, but not to tell him, it would hurt his feelings."

"I believe that," Olivia said as her heart went out to him, for the mother he had lost, and the childhood that had nearly been shattered forever. "She must have loved you very, very much."

"She did," he said sadly and then fell silent as he thought about her. He thought about her often, and dreamed of her frequently. She was always wearing a white dress, and smiling at him as she walked toward him. But he always woke just before she reached him. "I loved her too," he said, holding tightly to Olivia's hand. "She was so pretty, and she laughed a lot . . . kind of like you do . . ." And then, without saying anything, she leaned down and kissed him on the cheek, and held him close to her for a minute. He was the child she would never have now, the gift that had been given to her unexpectedly, the child that had come to her in place of her sister.

"I love you, Geoffy," she said softly, and meant every word of it as she stroked his hair, and smiled down at him, and he smiled peacefully at her.

"My mom used to call me that . . . but it's okay . . . you can call me that too. I think she'd like it."

"Thank you."

She told him a story then about when she and Victoria were young and gave a tea party for all their friends from school, and teased everyone by changing places, and how confusing it got because everyone expected them to know things they didn't. And he loved hearing about it, and chuckled deeply. She sat with him for over an hour, and eventually he drifted off to sleep, holding her hand in his own, the monkey on the pillow next to him, and she kissed him again, and quietly left the room, thinking of him and his mother. Olivia felt a strange affinity with her, almost as though she knew her.

Victoria was already in their room. She was smoking a cigarette, and she hadn't even bothered to open the window.

"I can hardly wait till you leave." Olivia rolled her eyes and pretended to strangle on the smoke in the room, as Victoria laughed at her. They were such good friends, and so happy together. Olivia hated the thought of her leaving.

"Where were you?"

"With Geoff. Poor kid. I think he really misses his mother." Victoria nodded, but made no comment.

"Charles has agreed to go to Europe on our honeymoon." She looked pleased with herself, and Olivia smiled and shook her head.

"Poor man. You're a monster. Does he know you smoke?" Victoria shook her head and they both laughed. "Maybe you ought to tell him, or give it up, that's a better idea."

Danielle Steel

"Maybe he ought to start smoking."

"How charming," Olivia said, undressing slowly, and trying not to think of Charles in any way other than as a brother.

"I told him you'd like Geoffrey to stay here. He liked the idea. He doesn't want to take him to Europe. He's afraid the ship would upset him."

"I think it would," Olivia said, remembering what he had just said about his mother. It was obviously all still fresh in his mind. It hadn't even been two years, although it would be by the time they were married. "Have you set the date yet?"

Victoria nodded, but did not look pleased. They had just discussed it that evening. "June twentieth. The *Aquatania* sails from New York on the twenty-first. It will be the return leg of her maiden voyage." Victoria smiled with pleasure at that, but not the wedding, and Olivia looked concerned as she said it.

"You don't think that will be traumatic for him?" Olivia asked, and Victoria hesitated and then shrugged at the question.

"He wasn't on the ship with her. She was coming over from England with Geoff. He was never on it."

"But it must have worried him terribly.

You'll have to be very kind to him on the voyage," she said pensively, and Victoria looked annoyed.

"Maybe you should go with him instead. He'd never know the difference."

"Maybe not," Olivia said quietly, but Geoff would.

And the next day, Charles remedied the situation himself, when he took a walk with Victoria before lunch, and they sat quietly for a few minutes on a bench, looking out over the Hudson.

"It's so beautiful here, I don't know how you can leave it," Charles said, and Victoria forced herself not to point out to him that her father was forcing her to. But she was wise enough not to say it.

"Actually, I prefer New York anyway. This is incredibly boring. It's Olivia who loves it here. I like a bit more excitement."

"Do you?" he asked, teasing her. He knew her better than she thought, even if he couldn't always tell the difference between them. "I'd never have thought it." She laughed at him then. He was smart, and he had a good sense of humor. She liked that. And he had no illusions whatsoever about their union, or at least he appeared not to. "Actually, I came up

271

with a very good idea while I was in New York. It's a system for telling you apart from Olivia. I hope you like it." She imagined some kind of ridiculous ribbons like the ones they'd worn as little girls, and she was about to object when he took her hand in his and slipped his other hand out of his pocket, and without saying a word to her, he put a very handsome diamond ring on her finger. It was very delicate, the stone wasn't large, but it was fine, and it had been his mother's. She had died several years before, and he still had all her jewelry. Some of it had been Susan's before she died. But he had never given this ring to her, his mother had still been alive, and wearing it, when he was married the first time.

Victoria looked down at it in total surprise, startled into silence. It fit perfectly and her hand was shaking. And Charles only stood there, looking down at her from his considerable height, with something kind and warm and hopeful in his eyes. But unlike Toby, he didn't take her in his arms, or tell her how much he loved her. "It was my mother's," was all he said to her, wishing he had the courage to kiss her.

"It's lovely . . . thank you . . ." She turned to him then, wishing just for a moment, that things had been different.

"I hope we'll be happy one day," he said, taking her hand. "Marriage can be a great thing, between good friends."

"Doesn't it take more than that?" she asked sadly, remembering the brief but exquisite moments she had shared with Toby, the genuine love she had felt for him as well as the passion.

"Sometimes, if you're very lucky," Charles answered, remembering his own past, and wishing he didn't. This was going to be entirely different. But perhaps, if he conquered her, if she could be tamed, Victoria would be a good wife too. He was willing to try it, for Geoff's sake. "Love is a strange thing, isn't it?" he said, putting an arm around her. "Sometimes you find it where you least expect it. I won't hurt you, Victoria," he said very gently. "I'll be your friend . . . and I'll be there for you, if you let me." But they both knew that she was still holding him at a distance. He wasn't sure for how long she would, but for the moment, she was like a wild mare, and he knew he could not come any closer. "I won't frighten you," he said, and she nodded.

"I'm sorry, Charles." The sorrow in her eyes was real, for all of them. She wondered how long it would take her to forget the pain Toby had caused her, if ever.

"Don't be," Charles said quietly. They both knew the conditions under which their engagement had been entered into, and neither of them had any illusions. "You owe me nothing yet." But later? she wondered, Would it be different then? Would she suddenly want him as she had wanted Toby, just because she had worn a white dress and a priest would have said a jumble of words at them? What difference would that make?

"I suppose it's official then," she said cautiously, looking down at the ring on her finger. "We're engaged." She said it as though she didn't quite understand it, and he laughed softly at her.

"Yes, we are. And in June, you'll be Mrs. Charles Dawson. That gives you six months to get used to it," he said, and then he moved carefully toward her, and he very gently put his hands on her shoulders. "May I kiss the bride a little ahead of schedule?" he asked, and not knowing what else to do, she nodded.

He took her in his arms then, and ever so cautiously, he kissed her. And just feeling her there next to him, brought a surge of memories to his mind and body. He felt a rush of longing and desire for her, as he thought of Susan and of her, and he had to fight not to let himself be swept away by his own emotions. She was the first woman he had touched in almost two years, and he was almost overwhelmed by sorrow and tenderness as he held her, but she understood none of it. She felt only the lips of a man she didn't love, and was being forced to marry. He stood holding her afterwards for a long time, knowing she still felt nothing for him, and convinced that it would come in time. It was good that they would have the summer in Europe.

"Shall we go back?" he asked pleasantly, and he took her hand in his, feeling the diamond he had placed on her finger.

She said nothing of it when they returned, and it was at lunch when Olivia first saw it. The sight of the ring on Victoria's finger startled her. It was all suddenly real to her, the engagement, the wedding, the fact that Victoria would soon be gone, and she would be left alone with her father. Olivia's eyes filled with tears, and she looked away, deeply embarrassed. Victoria sensed instantly that something was wrong, and then looked down at her own hand, feeling remorseful and apologetic, and as soon as lunch ended she put her arms around her sister.

Charles didn't understand what was happening, as he watched the two hug each other close in painful silence.

"I shall miss you terribly," Olivia whispered when they finally left the dining room.

"You must come with me," Victoria answered fiercely.

"You know I can't," Olivia said as tears filled her eyes again, and Charles stood in the hallway, watching them from the distance, wondering what they spoke of.

"I shall never love anyone but you," Victoria said, and meant every word of it, but Olivia shook her head in answer.

"You must. You owe it to him. You must learn to love them," Olivia whispered, and then went to tell Charles how beautiful she thought the ring was. He seemed pleased, and the three of them walked arm in arm out into the winter sunshine.

Chapter 10

Christmas was more fun than usual with the Dawsons there, in spite of Victoria's hesitation. Olivia loved seeing Geoff's face as he opened his gifts, and they all went on a sleigh ride on Christmas morning. It had snowed heavily on Christmas Eve, and after they'd come home from church, the hills high above the Hudson had been blanketed with a thick mantle of white velvet.

Olivia let Geoff drive the sleigh, and together they made snowballs and pelted Victoria and Charles until they drove them indoors, and then Olivia helped him build a snowman. They didn't even come back into the house until nightfall. It was a perfect day for all of them, marred only by the fact that Edward caught a chill, and was in bed until almost New Year. But he managed to get up for the party Olivia had arranged for Victoria and Charles on New Year's Eve, and it was a delightful evening. Everyone ate well and drank lots of champagne, and looked very elegant for the party. And Olivia had even arranged for musicians. There was dancing in the front hall, and everyone was in high spirits.

They let Geoff come down to visit before dinner, and all the guests seemed happy to meet him. They generously congratulated Victoria, and there was not the faintest whisper of scandal. Her reputation had been saved. Her future was assured. All was well in Croton-on-Hudson. And by New Year's Day, Victoria and Charles seemed to be quite comfortable with each other. They chatted amiably from time to time, and if not deeply in love, at least they appeared to be fairly friendly. The only thing that seemed to make Victoria truly uneasy was Geoffrey. Olivia was well aware of it, and she took him away with her whenever possible, so Charles wouldn't notice. But she urged Victoria constantly to get to know him.

"He's just a child, for Heaven's sake. A nine-year-old boy. What harm can he possibly do? Don't be so stupid."

"He hates me," Victoria said simply.

"He does *not* hate you. He likes you." It was a lie, but Olivia was desperate for her twin to get to know him. "He's just more used to me. We could probably switch, if we really put our minds to it, and he'd never know it." But they both knew that was a lie, and on New Year's Day, as usual, Olivia took him out with her, to keep him away from her sister.

And in spite of some ice and snow still on the ground, she decided to take him riding.

"Be careful, miss," the stable man warned. "It's treacherous out there." Olivia could see for herself that there was another storm brewing.

"We won't go far, Robert. Thank you." She gave their tamest horse to Geoff, a sweet old nag she herself had ridden as a child, and she used her own horse to ride beside him. Her own mare was full of fun that afternoon, and more than a little feisty. She'd had too little exercise over the holidays, and the weather had been bad. But Olivia enjoyed a lively ride, and she took Geoffrey out over the hills, and showed him all the places she had loved as a child, even the tree house, and the secret glade where she had often hidden from Bertie with her sister.

She told him about the time they'd stayed out all night when they were twelve, because they'd gotten into so much mischief in school and were afraid their father would scold them. The sheriff had been called, with his dogs, and they had found them of course, and they had cried, but of course nothing serious had happened to them. Their father had always been kind, and even somewhat lenient. Until Victoria's last escapade in New York. There had been no leniency possible there, they were at the mercy of Victoria's own actions and the gossips of New York City. The only solution possible was for her to marry Charles Dawson, but Olivia didn't explain that to Geoffrey.

"Were you ever spanked?" Geoffrey asked with interest, as Olivia shook her head. Their father had never touched them. "Me neither," he confirmed, much to her satisfaction.

They played cowboys and Indians on horseback for a while then, and it was hard to believe that she was twenty and not ten, as they chased each other over ridges and across gullies and frozen streams. Olivia jumped a log now and then, but she was careful not to do anything to endanger Geoffrey. And as night fell, they rode slowly home, toward the stable. Olivia chased a few rabbits across the snow as

Geoff laughed at her, and they were almost home when there was a clap of thunder. There was a flash of lightning in the sky, and another roll of thunder, which seemed just above them, but before Olivia could say anything to him, Geoff's horse bolted. All she could see were Geoff's terrified eyes, as the horse raced across the icy ground, jumping all obstacles between him and the stables.

"Geoff, hang on!" she shouted in the wind, praying he could hear her. "Hang on tight! Don't let go! I'm coming!" The old nag that had barely moved in years fairly flew across the field as she followed, and she caught up with him very quickly. She leaned out as far as she could, with her graceful arms, hanging on to her own saddle with one hand, and grabbed the other horse's bridle. It was a neat move, and with a firm hand, she slowed the other horse to a trot just in time for another clap of thunder. She yanked hard this time, and took one of the reins from Geoff and held it tight, just as her own horse danced and bolted. She had to let Geoff's rein go not to take him with her, and her mare stood high on her hind legs, dancing beneath the lightning, while Olivia fought to control her. She could see that Geoff's horse was terrified, but this time his horse didn't move, she was exhausted. It was Olivia who had to fight this time, but yet another clap of thunder drove her skittish horse mad, and she danced first sideways then straight ahead, and jumped high in the air, unexpectedly, across a wall of hedges. The horse disappeared on the other side, but she left behind Olivia's crumpled mass, as she lay on the ground near Geoffrey. And he could see from a single glance that she was unconscious.

"Olivia! Ollie! . . ." He started to cry but he was afraid to dismount for fear that he wouldn't be able to get up again, and instead, sobbing hysterically as it began to rain, he headed for the stables.

His father and the stable man saw him come in, crying incoherently and waving, and before he could even explain, Olivia's mare galloped past him. She went straight to her stall, and it was easy to see that her rider was no longer in the saddle. Geoff was frantically trying to explain it to them . . . the thunder . . . the lightning . . . the horse . . . the fall . . . the hedges. Robert was already astride his own horse as he listened. "Can you ride?" he asked, and Charles nodded. He helped his son dismount, and took the tired horse from him. It was hard work getting her to leave the stable again, but they had no time to get out another horse and put on a saddle.

Robert had understood instantly where they had been, and Charles could feel his heart pound in his ears as they rode through the driving rain until they found her. They almost missed her at first. She was a thin mass of brown riding coat, with her long black hair spread out on the ground around her. The stable man was the first to dismount, and Charles was right behind him. She was dead white, and to both of them, she looked lifeless. Charles felt himself reel at the thought of it, and the terror of what he would tell Geoff and her father and sister if the fall had killed her.

"Is she . . . ?" he whispered, but in the fierce wind, Robert didn't hear him. He only turned to him, shook his head, and said he had to go back to get the carriage. "Stay with her. I'll be back in ten minutes. I'll call the doctor." Charles could see then, as he knelt beside her, that she was breathing, but deeply unconscious. He took his own coat off and tried to make a little tent for her, shielding her from the rain, and he was surprised to find, as he knelt beside her on the ground and looked at her, that he was crying. She was a fool to have gone out with ice on the ground, and it could have been

Geoff lying there, but he also knew she would never have let that happen. He knew from riding it just then, that the horse the child had ridden was practically dead it was so old, and it wouldn't have harmed him. And as Charles looked down at her, he felt something stir, something agonizing and warm that reminded him of Susan. It was what he had felt for her whenever he talked to her, that sweetness in her soul, that caring, the laughter in her eyes, it was that which hurt so much, which drove the stake through his heart and reminded him of what he'd lost nearly two years before. And looking at her now, he couldn't bear it. The boy was right, the twins were not the same. They were entirely different. Victoria, so wild, so free, so indifferent to him, so innately sensual, and yet uncaring. He wanted to tame her, own her, break her, yet he knew in his heart he would never love her. But this woman was entirely different. And what he felt as he looked at her made him want to flee to safety. Never again would he lose what he loved, never again would he give his heart, and then let Fate steal it from him. For him, Victoria was infinitely safer . . . Olivia excruciatingly dearer . . . and if she died now . . . if she died . . . if she went . . . he knew he couldn't bear it. Not again, not now. It wasn't fair . . . it wasn't right, what he felt for her. And yet, he knew that, whatever happened, he was going to marry her sister.

"Olivia . . ." He bent low next to her, calling her name, and gently stroking her hair, praying that her neck wasn't broken, he could see that she was still breathing. "Olivia . . . speak to me . . . Ollie, please . . ." he said, crying like a child, feeling a rush of love for her, and hating himself for it. "Olivia . . ." She stirred and opened her eyes, and he had to fight to regain his composure. She was looking up at him, dazed, as though she didn't know him. "Don't move, you've had a bad fall," he said in the fierce wind that blew around him. Her body was soaking wet by then, but her face was protected by the jacket he held above her. His own face was dripping wet, the dark brown hair matted to his head, his tears mingled with the rain on his face. And she could see nothing of what he'd been thinking. And then she remembered.

"Is Geoff all right?" She could still barely speak, she was so winded, and her vision was slightly blurred, which made it harder to see him. She wasn't sure who he was at first, and then she realized it was Charles. She tried to smile, but it was too painful.

"He's fine. He came to get us." She tried to nod, and winced, and then closed her eyes and lay there as he watched her. What he had just felt for her terrified him, and yet he knew he was doing the right thing marrying Victoria. It would be too dangerous to love a woman like this one. His whole heart and soul might give way like a seawall in a tidal wave. He had never felt what he did for her, for anyone, except Susan. Victoria was so much safer . . . dangerous in her own way, but not to him. She was only intriguing. It was this woman, with her gentle ways, who could destroy him.

"How are you feeling?" he asked again a minute later, still shielding her from the wind and rain, and aching to touch her.

"Terrific." She smiled blearily up at him, and he gently touched her face and kept his hand there, fighting everything he felt, reminding himself that this was only a mistake, a single brief moment of indulgence. "Will you help me up?" she asked, unsure if she could make it.

"I don't think you should. Robert's bringing the carriage around. He'll be here in a minute."

"I don't want to worry Father."

"You'd have worried all of us if you'd killed yourself, Olivia. I'd thank you to be more careful in the future." Geoffrey didn't need another tragedy in his life, nor did he. As he knelt looking down at her, he didn't know whether to scold her or kiss her.

"I'm all right."

"You look it." He grinned down at her, and the two exchanged a look that spoke volumes. She had forgotten everything but him, their past, their future, all of it, there was only this moment, with the rain beating down on them, and her on the ground, with his hand gently touching her cheek, and his eyes caressing her. She wondered briefly if she had gone crazy.

"Is my horse all right?"

"Your priorities disgust me," he said, as she tried to sit up. "Your horse is fine. A great deal better than you are." She lay down again, her head hurt so sharply, but as she moved, Robert came over the hill with the carriage, and for a crazed instant, Charles wanted to hide her from him. He wanted to keep her with him forever. They both knew this moment would never come again, never be referred to, or spoken of. It had to be forgotten. Their eyes reached hungrily into each other's souls and then the doors closed. Forever.

"How is she?" Robert asked, as he stepped down from the carriage.

"Better, I think." Charles nodded and then turned to look at her again. And then, with a single careful gesture he picked her up easily in his arms like a doll, and lifted her into the carriage. He set her down on the seat, and she leaned her head back with a groan, looking quite ill. Nothing seemed to be broken, but she obviously had a severe concussion. Charles got in with her, and sat across from her, as Robert tied the horse Charles had ridden to the back of the carriage, and drove them home, and he watched her in silence. There was so much he wanted to say to her, and knew he couldn't. There was no point saying any of it. It was far too dangerous for him. He had reached the fork in the road and gone beyond it. He had chosen his path when Susan died, and his marriage to Victoria was no threat to what he had felt for her. It was precisely what it was meant to be, an arrangement. This was different. This was fire that would sear his heart, and burn his fingers. Victoria was all sparks and sensuality. Olivia was something he longed for and knew he would never have again, nor dared to. He had had it once and knew how devastating it was to lose it. He would never pick the shiny penny up again, nor spend it.

She looked at him then as though she could hear his thoughts, and nodded. She held out a hand to him, and he took her icy fingers in his own and held them.

"I'm sorry," he said softly, as though she understood all that he hadn't said and was thinking. And she only smiled, and lay back again with her eyes closed. It all seemed like a dream to her. Charles next to her, the storm, the rain, the boy . . . his hand in hers. It was all so complicated, and so difficult to understand. There seemed to be reasons for things she hadn't understood, and then suddenly Victoria was there with him, as it should have been . . . and Bertie, and her father, and the doctor. Her head was reeling.

They put her to bed, and Victoria sat with her. And Olivia insisted on seeing Geoffrey, she didn't want him to be frightened. She told him that she had been silly to take him out in such bad weather, and he understood. He promised to come back and visit her soon, and then he kissed her, and he made her think of someone else, but she couldn't remember who, or when. It seemed only moments before, or

289

years. She wasn't sure which. They had given her something to sleep, although she didn't really want it. And Victoria sat with her while she went to sleep. Bertie had wanted to, but Victoria wouldn't let her. And Olivia had something to say to her. It was terribly important, she knew, and she had to say it.

"You must love him, Victoria, you *must* . . . he needs you." And then she drifted off to sleep, thinking of both of them. She saw them all standing there, on a ship. Victoria in her wedding dress, and Charles next to her, trying to say something to her, but Olivia couldn't hear him. Geoff was standing next to him, and he was holding his mother's hand. Susan was watching them, and Victoria didn't understand . . . she didn't understand any of it . . . none of them did. And then the ship went down in total silence.

Olivia woke at noon the next day with a crashing headache. She felt as though she'd been awake all night, battered by demons, but she knew she hadn't. Victoria told her the Dawsons were gone by then. Geoffrey had left a handful of flowers for her, and Charles had left her a brief note, telling her how sorry he was she'd had a fall, and hoping she felt better. She lay in bed and read the note again wondering if what she'd seen had been real or a dream. She'd seen something in his face that she'd never seen before, or had she? It was impossible now to distinguish truth from delirium.

"You got quite a knock on the head, old girl," Victoria said, pouring her a cup of tea, which she took with a pained expression.

"I must have. I've had the craziest dreams all night." She was still haunted by all of it, real and imagined.

"I'm not surprised. The doctor said you'd be better in a few days. Just close your eyes and sleep," she said. The person Victoria cared about most in the world was her twin sister. She sat beside her for hours that day, watching her, smoothing her hair, talking to her when she woke. And when Olivia got up somewhat shakily later that week, she knew that all the ghosts that had visited her for days in her dreams had been only that . . . figments of her imagination . . . and visions. Some of it was almost embarrassing. She actually thought she'd seen Charles in some of her dreams . . . he'd been looking down at her and holding her face . . . they had ridden in a carriage somewhere and he was crying . . .

"Feeling better?" Victoria asked as she

helped her down the stairs for the first time, to join their father at dinner.

"Much," Olivia said with wobbly conviction, but she was determined to be completely herself again. She had no time for this nonsense. "Now, we have to get busy and think about your wedding."

Victoria didn't answer her, and Olivia resolutely put everything from her mind except what she had to do now. The slight quavering she felt in her heart was entirely unimportant.

"You're looking very well," her father said, pleased to see her. And she was equally pleased to be with him, and far from the dreams that lingered in her bedroom. She had been trapped with them for days, and she couldn't stand it any longer.

"Thank you, Father," Olivia said quietly, and both sisters silently took their places on either side of their father, and sat down to dinner.

Chapter 11

As it turned out, Charles was too busy to come to Croton again in January or February, as he had an important trial to prepare, and matters to settle for his future father-in-law. But Olivia planned a trip to New York for the end of February, in order to look for a wedding gown for her sister. Victoria had agreed to it, but was far more interested in the news from London. Emmeline Pankhurst had apparently been released from prison after a year, and had organized an attack on the Home Secretary's London office where they'd broken all the windows, after which they had set fire to the Lawn Tennis Club, all in the name of women's freedom.

"Good for them!" Victoria said fervently

when she heard the news. She had become more feminist, rather than less, since her engagement.

"Victoria!" Olivia said, shocked at the violence of it. "I think it's perfectly disgusting. How can you condone acts like that?" Pankhurst's last incarceration had been for explosives.

"They're for a good cause, Olivia. It's like war, it's not pretty, but it's necessary sometimes. Women have a right to freedom."

"Don't be ridiculous." Olivia got seriously annoyed with her over it. "You make us sound like circus animals in cages, for Heaven's sake."

"Hasn't it ever occurred to you that that's precisely what we are? Animals, pets, for men to dispose of as they choose. *That's* what's disgusting."

"Don't, for God's sake, let anyone hear you say things like that in public." She gave her sister a quelling look, and dropped the subject. It was hopeless arguing with her, she knew. Victoria was rabid about women's rights and suffrage.

It was easier showing designs of wedding dresses to her, which aroused no emotion in her whatsoever. She had already told Olivia to pick whatever she liked, and she thought looked well on her. She had even suggested that Olivia shop for it alone, since she didn't really need her.

"That's bad luck, and no fun besides, and I won't do it." Olivia wanted to strangle her sometimes when she tried to talk to her about the wedding. As usual, Olivia was planning everything. She had dragged a handful of names out of Victoria for the list, and Charles had been very prompt in sending his. They had exchanged a brief, perfunctory, but polite correspondence, and there were about a hundred people he wanted to invite, if it was agreeable to them. He had no family, but a number of friends, and some acquaintances from business. Edward had two hundred or more, and the girls another fifty. In all there were four hundred people on the list, and Olivia felt certain about three hundred would come, some were just too old, or lived too far away, or were simply invited by courtesy. And the wedding itself was going to be in Croton-on-Hudson. The reception at Henderson Manor.

Olivia was going to be her maid of honor of course, and Geoffrey the ring bearer, and Victoria had stubbornly refused to have bridesmaids.

"There's no one I like as well as you," she said in a haze of cigarette smoke late one night when they discussed it for the ninetieth time. But Victoria wouldn't budge an inch on the subject.

"I wish you'd smoke somewhere else," Olivia growled at her. She seemed to smoke constantly these days, she was very nervous. "And besides, there were lots of nice girls we went to school with. They would love to be your bridesmaids."

"Well, I wouldn't like to have them. Besides, we haven't been in a school for eight years. And I can't imagine any of our tutors as bridesmaids." They both laughed at that, they had had a series of elderly, occasionally nearly bald, horse-faced maiden ladies as their tutors.

"All right, I give up, then your dress will have to be that much nicer."

"So will yours," Victoria said fairly, but still without much interest in the wedding. The only way she could actually tolerate the thought of it was to look beyond it, to their honeymoon, to Europe, to the things she wanted to do, and the people she wanted to see there, and then back to New York to a certain amount of independence. But the wedding itself was of no interest to her. "Why don't we both wear the same wedding dress?" She mused wickedly with a grin, "and confuse everyone? What do you think of that?"

"I think you've been drinking as well as smoking."

"Now there's an idea. Do you think Father would notice?"

"No, but Bertie would, so don't even consider it, and I'm not having you run a bar here as well as a smoking room." Olivia wagged a finger at her and then felt a stab of pain at the prospect of no longer having her there, smoking up her room, and complaining. The thought of Victoria leaving was unbearable, and it was only four months away now.

They went to New York, as planned, at the end of February, and stayed at the Plaza, so Olivia didn't have to open the house, and they didn't have to take a fleet of servants with them. Their father had suggested they take Mrs. Peabody with them, just for appearances, but Victoria had insisted they didn't need it. And she tossed her hat high in the air when they reached their hotel room. They were all alone in New York and could do anything they wanted. The first thing she did was order a drink from the restaurant, and light up a cigarette in front of her sister.

"I don't care what you do in this room," Olivia said sternly as she looked at her, "but if you do not behave in this hotel, or elsewhere in New York, I'm taking you right home, *after* I call Father. I'm not going to have people thinking I'm a drunk, or I smoke all day long, because you do. So behave yourself."

"Yes, Ollie," Victoria said with a mischievous grin, she was loving being there with her, particularly without a chaperone. She was having dinner with Charles that night. But that afternoon they were going to Bonwit Teller, to look at dresses. She not only needed a wedding gown, and a dress for Olivia for the wedding too, but she needed dresses for the honeymoon, both for the ship and for Europe. Olivia had already copied some designs and had some things made for her, but only simple things for her to wear on the trip. The grand gowns, and really stylish things, they were going to buy in New York. And Olivia had already told her where to go in Paris. But the oddest thing of all for them was buying things singly now. For the first time in their lives, they weren't buying double. Olivia had no need for stylish gowns, and they wouldn't be together to wear them. The first order she had made for one dress alone had almost broken Olivia's heart, but she knew she had to do it. It was almost time for Victoria to move on now.

They had a quick lunch at the hotel, and then took a cab to Saks, but everywhere they went, in the restaurant, in the lobby, stepping out of the cab, people looked at them. They were doubly beautiful, incredibly striking, and people couldn't stop themselves from staring. They caused an immediate stir the minute they set foot in B. Altman, and an army of salesgirls and a manager rushed forward to help them. Olivia had brought drawings with her, photographs from magazines, and a few sketches she'd done herself. At least for the wedding dress, she knew exactly what she wanted. She wanted tiers of white satin, done on a bias cut preferably, covered with miles of white lace, and a train the length of the entire church. And on her head, Victoria was going to wear her mother's antique diamond tiara. That would be covered with lace too. And Olivia knew she would look like a queen if they could find someone to do it. And at Bonwit Teller the manager said it would be absolutely no problem. They sat and talked about it for an hour, looking at fabric swatches, and discussing the kind of lace Olivia had in mind, while Victoria tried on hats and shoes and ignored them.

"They need your measurements," Olivia said finally, pleased with all she'd accomplished.

"Have them take yours, they're exactly the same as mine," Victoria said easily, and Olivia scolded her for it.

"No, they're not, and you know it." Victoria's bust was slightly larger, her waist just the smallest fraction smaller, but enough to make a hair of difference. "Come on, take your clothes off."

"All right, all right." Victoria put up with the measuring, and then the manager and Olivia got down to business about her own dress. Olivia had envisioned ice-blue satin, in a design similar to her sister's wedding dress, but not quite as long, without the train, and without the lace over it. Just ice-blue satin in tiers, bias cut, and perfectly simple. But as they sketched it, the manager insisted it was too plain in contrast to Victoria's wedding gown, which was going to be quite spectacular. They added a small train after all, and the pièce de résistance was a long pale blue lace coat over the gown, with a matching hat. It was in perfect harmony now with what her sister was wearing. Olivia smiled as she glanced at the sketches and showed them to her sister, who smiled amiably and then whispered irreverently to her.

"Why don't we switch on my wedding day? No one will ever know the difference."

"Behave yourself," Olivia said sternly. And they went on to look at designs for other gowns, and the countless dresses Victoria needed. It was going to be a long summer in Europe.

Olivia realized they'd have to come back again, to pick more things out, and also for fittings. She had just agreed to come back the next day without Victoria, and stood up to thank the manager for her help, when Olivia noticed her sister staring at some new arrivals. There was a tall dark-haired man talking to someone, she could hear him laughing, and all the salesgirls seemed to be flocking toward him and the woman with him. She was tall and blonde and swathed in a chinchilla cocoon, and as they turned, Olivia could see easily that it was Toby Whitticomb, and Evangeline, enormously pregnant. She couldn't imagine what she was doing out in public, looking like that, but she didn't seem to care, as she took off the chinchilla coat and exposed a vast expanse of well-rounded gray satin. She looked to be at least seven months pregnant. And as Olivia stared back at her, she glanced quickly at her sister. Victoria looked as though she had been struck by lightning. Olivia said good-bye to the manager as quickly as she could, and urged her sister toward the entrance.

"Let's go, Victoria, we're finished," she said gently, but it was as though she couldn't move. Victoria was riveted to the spot where she stood, staring at Toby. And as though he felt her eyes on him, he suddenly stared back at her, and then her sister, and it was obvious that he had no idea which one she was, but he looked more than a little unnerved by the double vision. He looked away from them as swiftly as he could, and led Evangeline to a far corner of the store, but she had seen them too, and she began arguing with him the moment she'd seen them. "Victoria, please . . ." Olivia said in a firm undervoice, embarrassed by the scene around them. Salesgirls were watching them, Toby had just said something sharp to his wife, and Evangeline had started crying and darting glances at the twin sisters.

With that, Olivia grabbed her sister's arm, and almost dragged her forcibly from the store, and back out into the street where she hailed a taxi. And mercifully, there had been one waiting. But as Olivia shoved her sister in ahead of her, and almost collapsed on the seat next to her, she could see that Victoria was crying. She gave the driver the name of their hotel, and sat in silence as Victoria sobbed uncontrollably. It was the first time she had seen him since that ghastly scene on the steps outside his office.

"I would have been five months pregnant by now," she wailed, mourning aloud for the first time the baby she'd lost in November in Croton.

"With your life smashed to bits around you. For God's sake, Victoria, look at what he did to you. He ruined you, and then he denied you. Please don't tell me you're still in love with him," she whispered in the back of the cab with horror, but Victoria only shook her head and cried harder.

"I hate him. I hate everything he stands for, everything he did to me," and yet when she thought of those afternoons in the cottage, it still made her heart ache. She had believed everything he said to her, about leaving his wife, and loving her, and now Evangeline was parading around, pointing at her like a floozie, and carrying his baby. It brought home the bitter realization of what her father had tried to protect her from when he forced her to promise herself to Charles Dawson. And it made her grateful to Charles for the first time, for his protection, but it would never make her love him.

She was still crying when they reached the hotel, and when they got back to their room, she lay on the bed and sobbed until Olivia thought her heart would break, and nothing she said or did stopped it. It had been a bitter lesson in the cruelty of men, and Olivia knew her sister would never forget it.

Victoria stopped crying finally at six o'clock, and she sat looking beaten and defeated as she glanced at her sister.

"You'll forget him one day. You will," Olivia promised softly.

"I'll never trust anyone again. You can't imagine the things he said, Ollie . . . I'd never have done it otherwise . . ." Or would she? She wasn't even sure she knew herself now. He had made her do things she never would have dreamt of. And how could she ever explain that to Charles? It was hard now, seeing Toby again, to believe that Charles would actually marry her, and she was even more grateful. "I was so stupid," she confessed to her sister again, and Olivia sat with her arms around her until Charles came, and he found both sisters unusually subdued, particularly his fiancée.

"Is anything wrong?" he asked worriedly. "Are you ill?" He glanced from one to the other, and Olivia smiled as Victoria shook her head dumbly.

"It was just a very long day, and somewhat emotional. Buying a wedding dress is one of the most important moments in a woman's life," Olivia explained, but did not entirely convince him. He wondered if they were both beginning to feel the pain of leaving each other, and he felt sorry for them as he thought of it, and a few minutes later, he invited Olivia to join them for dinner. They were going to the Ritz-Carlton, and then on to a concert. But she insisted that they go alone, she didn't want to intrude on them. They hadn't seen each other in two months, and she thought it was best if they spent some time together. She was going to have dinner alone at the hotel, in her room, and look over some more designs for gowns for her sister.

"You're sure?" Charles asked her quietly, while they were waiting for Victoria to finish dressing.

"Very much so," she said quietly, remembering something vague and elusive about the night she fell from the horse in Croton, but she couldn't remember what it was now. "This is hard for her sometimes," she tried to explain to him, wanting him to love her sister. She loved her sister so much that she couldn't bear to think of her with a man who didn't understand her. But she knew that Charles was decent and caring, and would be good to her, no matter what happened between them. "We're going to miss each other terribly," Olivia said with a wistful smile. "I'm glad Geoff will be with me this summer."

"He's ecstatic over it." And then his eyes searched hers, but could find no answers. He wondered who she was sometimes, and why she had been so willing to give up everything for her father. She was just as beautiful as her twin, why would she agree to give it all up for him? What was her lonely secret? She hadn't struck him as being quite so retiring when they met, the previous September. "We were thinking of coming to you for Easter," Charles said cautiously, to change the subject. "If it's not too much trouble. Your father mentioned it when I saw him."

"We'd love to have you for Easter," Olivia said with a look of pleasure, as Victoria joined them. She was wearing a dark blue satin dress Olivia had chosen for her, and she looked like the queen of midnight. Sapphires and diamonds their father had given them shimmered on her ears, and she wore the long rope of pearls that had been their mother's and they shared for important occasions.

"You look lovely," he said, as he looked at her proudly. She was a spectacular-looking young woman. And it was even more extraordinary to think that there were two of them. He was momentarily sorry again that Olivia wasn't coming out with them. He would have enjoyed it. But there was no convincing her, and Charles and Victoria left a few minutes later.

The restaurant was very elegant, and Victoria suddenly got nervous after they arrived. What if Toby came in with his wife? She felt completely unprepared to see him again, and extremely anxious.

"You're very quiet tonight," Charles said, as he took her hand in his own after they'd ordered. "Is anything wrong?" She shook her head, but he saw tears there and didn't want to press her further. They spoke of other things then, politics, their trip, their wedding, and problems in Europe. He liked the fact that she was interested in world events, and well informed, although her ideas were extremely liberal, almost to the point of being outrageous, but sometimes that pleased him.

He introduced her to a number of his acquaintances that night, and they sat in a box with friends at the concert, and Victoria looked more relaxed when he brought her back to the hotel. She even lit a cigarette as she shared a drink with him in the restaurant next to the lobby.

"Oh my," he said, and then laughed at his own reaction, as she smiled in amusement.

"Shocked, Charles?" She liked that. She looked more herself than she had all evening.

"Do you want me to be?" He sipped his Scotch and eyed her in admiration. She had lots of spirit and intelligence along with her looks. For the second time in his life, he'd been lucky, although this couldn't be more different from his courtship with Susan.

"Maybe. Maybe I like it when I shock you." She smiled and blew smoke in his direction.

"I suspect that's true," he said philosophically. "In which case, we should have a very interesting life, you and I, won't we?" And then with the Scotch loosening his tongue, he dared to ask her something he had wondered. "Were you very much in love with him? The man who broke your engagement." He watched her closely, and waited.

She hesitated, remembering the Toby she had known, the one she had loved so fiercely, and the one she had seen only that morning . . . the one on the steps of his office who had denied her . . . the one who had told her father that she had seduced him . . . "I was. Once. But I'm not anymore. Actually, there are times when I think I hate him."

"That's just the other side of love, isn't it?"

"I suppose so." It had almost killed her seeing him that morning. "We weren't engaged." She met his eyes squarely, not wanting to be deceitful. It was enough that he was saving her. She didn't have to lie to him as well, but he nodded.

"I knew that. It just seemed easier to put it that way. Your father gave me some vague idea of what happened. You were very young. You still are." He smiled gently at her, wishing that there were something more between them, and then relieved at the same time that there wasn't. She aroused him incredibly, but that was another matter entirely. "It was unfair of him to take advantage of you. That's easily done with young girls, and no gentleman should do it. Your father said he lied to you, and promised marriage." She nodded, unwilling to add to what he already knew. It seemed to be enough after all. And yet, he was willing to have her. It was hard to understand why. Perhaps it was just destined.

"It's hard to understand the things people do to each other," she said sadly. "It won't happen again," she said, eyeing him, as though with a warning.

"I should hope not," he smiled. But he had understood her meaning. She was telling him that she would never trust him. But it didn't matter. He would never hurt her. "I won't deceive you, Victoria. I won't lie to you. If that's what you're afraid of. I've never deceived anyone, not that I know of. I'm an honest man. Dull, perhaps . . . but truthful. That has its uses."

"I'm . . . I . . ." Having seen Toby that day, she understood full well what she owed him. "Thank you for doing this for me," she said, raising eyes full of tears to his. "You didn't have to."

"No, but you don't have to either," he said softly. "There are always other solutions. Perhaps we both want to, and we don't know how else to do it." He wanted to believe that. And he smiled at her, as he set down his drink, and she put down her cigarette and he kissed her gently. "Don't be afraid of me, Victoria. I swear I won't hurt you." She let him kiss her then, but her heart ached to realize she felt nothing, and she wondered if he knew it.

He took her upstairs shortly after that, and Olivia was waiting for her. She could see that Victoria was still sad, but she was more peaceful than she had been in a long time. In some ways it might have done her good to see Toby and his wife that afternoon. Olivia hoped that it had brought her closer to Charles. She seemed more at peace now about her future.

He had left very quickly that night, and he took them both to lunch the next day at the Della Robbia, in the midst of their shopping, and Olivia kept him amused with tales of their acquisitions. Victoria said very little, but she was pleasant to him when they left and he dropped them off at Bonwit's to continue. And that night, without seeing him again, they went back to Croton. Donovan picked them up at the hotel on schedule, and drove them back up the Hudson. Olivia was sorry not to see Geoff, but they didn't have time, and she promised to see him in March when they came back to town again to finish their shopping.

But all their plans changed when their father fell ill in late February, and spent an entire month in bed with influenza. Olivia was deathly afraid he would develop pneumonia, but he didn't. He was very ill, and she seldom left him for more than a few hours, but on the first of April, he finally emerged from his bedroom. And two weeks later, the Dawsons came for their promised visit for Easter. And Olivia had a wonderful surprise for Geoffrey. She had two little chicks that had recently hatched, and a tiny white bunny.

"Oh wow! Oh *wow*! Dad, did you see them?!" he said when Olivia presented him with them. She had tried to get Victoria to give them to him, but she insisted that she disliked animals even more than children. Olivia constantly felt as though she were coaching a reluctant schoolgirl to do her duty. But things were improving slightly. This time she seemed pleased to see Charles at least, so that was something.

There were several parties in the neighborhood for them, and a lovely concert at the Rockefellers', which everyone went to. And it was the perfect opportunity to introduce Charles to those who had not yet met him. He was always very polite to everyone, and extremely likable, and Olivia kept reminding her sister that this was not a funeral they were planning, but a wedding.

"Will you *please* get into the spirit!" She scolded her, going over the guest list with her again. It had taken three months to get her to discuss the menu. And now that the gifts had begun to arrive, Olivia had to open all of them for her, and catalog them, Victoria never even saw them. And in desperation, Olivia wrote the thank-you notes for her as well, for fear that she'd never do them.

"I think it's all stupid," Victoria said, sounding more like a spoiled child than a suffragette, according to her sister. "It's frivolous and unnecessary, and wasteful. They should send the money they spend on gifts to women in prison."

"Oh how lovely," Olivia said, rolling her eyes at her, "I'm sure they'd love that. We could send out little engraved notices explaining to people how to do it."

"Okay, okay." Victoria laughed at her sister, but all she could think of anymore was how much she was going to miss her. It made her hate the thought of the wedding more than ever. She didn't mind marrying Charles quite so much anymore, she could see the sense of it, and she knew it had been a necessary outcome of her own indiscretion, and she liked the freedom being married and living in New York would give her, but she still hated the thought of being so far from Ollie, and she was desperate to find a way around it. "You're much better with Geoff than I am," she said anxiously, thinking that was a compelling reason for her to come to New York and live with them.

"That's why he's marrying you, or supposedly anyway." Olivia was quite sure there were far more interesting reasons than that one. "He doesn't want me around to take care of his son if he's married to you. And besides, you know I can't leave Father. Look at the last month. Who would take care of him if I weren't here to do it?"

"Bertie," Victoria said blithely.

"That's not the same thing, and you know it," Olivia said firmly.

"What if you got married?" Victoria said practically. "Then he'd have to manage without you."

"I wouldn't," Olivia said quietly, "and he knows it. So that's that. Now what do you want for dessert at your wedding?"

Victoria pretended to scream and Charles rescued her for a walk along the river a few minutes later.

"My sister is going to drive me to distraction with our wedding," Victoria said, looking up at Charles with an easy smile before they left for their walk. They had managed to convince themselves in the past few months that this was the perfect solution for both their lives, and they both looked happier for it.

"She never wants to give me answers," Olivia complained. "You're going to have to beat her with a stick to do any work at all," Olivia warned him.

"I'll get a nice big one, or maybe a whip?" He smiled at his future wife and sister-in-law, and then took Victoria away and left Geoff with Ollie. He had long since begun calling her "Aunt Ollie."

And when Easter was over he took the bunnies and the chicks back to New York, but a few weeks later, Olivia gave him another present when she went to New York to do a few last errands. She had some odds and ends to buy, though all the gowns had already been sent. The wedding gown was already in a room of its own, waiting for the big day, in Croton-on-Hudson.

Charles was surprised when Olivia called from New York, and he was happy to see her when she came by with a birthday gift for Geoffrey. Their birthdays were almost the same. She and Victoria had just turned twenty-one. Charles had given his future bride a very handsome gold bracelet and Olivia a bottle of perfume. But Olivia had brought Geoff something much more exciting. She had asked Charles' permission some time before, and he had reluctantly agreed to it, though in the interim, he had forgotten all about it. She had brought him a speckled cocker spaniel puppy. And Geoffrey was beside himself over it. His eyes were the size of dinner plates when Olivia took the puppy out of the box and handed it to him gently. He clutched it close to him, and there were squeals of excitement from both dog and owner, and when Olivia glanced up at Charles, she saw tears of tenderness in his eyes, as he thanked her.

"You're so good to him. He needs that. He's had a hard two years without his mother." It had just been two years since the *Titanic* went down, in April.

"He's a wonderful boy. We're going to have a great summer," she said optimistically, trying not to think of losing her sister. They were both beginning to panic.

"We'll write to you from Europe," he said, as though he sensed what she was thinking. But that wasn't going to be the same thing, and they all knew that. Perhaps Victoria was right, and she should come to live with them in New York, she told herself, and then she laughed at her own terror.

"We'll be fine," she said to Charles, as Geoff came tearing back into the room with the puppy. "What are you going to call him?"

"I don't know yet," Geoff said breathlessly, all blonde hair and green eyes and excitement. "Maybe Jack . . . George . . . Harry . . . I don't know, he looks like chocolate chips, doesn't he?"

"What about Chip?" Olivia asked as she and Charles smiled broadly at his excitement.

"Chip!" He shouted with glee, "I like it!" And so did the puppy. He wagged his tail, what there was of it, and fell down and rolled over and barked the tiniest yip Olivia had ever heard, as everyone laughed, and Geoffrey took him to show the cook and the housemaid. They had a modest but attractive house, on the East Side, with a view of the river. It was certainly not glamorous, but it was respectable, and Victoria had said nothing so far about moving or making changes. Her interests were far less domestic than her sister's. Olivia would have been bustling everywhere buying plants and new fabrics, and footstools and new cushions and a piano. In some ways, it was easier this way. Victoria had no great interest in their domestic life, or in changing any of it. She wanted her own life, mainly in political circles.

Olivia only stayed for a little while, as she had a thousand errands to do, but Charles eventually convinced her to come back for dinner, which she did, and the three of them thoroughly enjoyed themselves playing charades, and laughing, and talking, and playing with the puppy.

"Victoria's right," Charles smiled, as the cook led Geoff off to bed with the new puppy. "Maybe you should come and live here."

"Has she bothered you with that nonsense?" Olivia looked blithe, and glanced out the window at a tugboat on the river. "You'll be tired enough of me when I come to visit. But I can't leave Father now, and she knows it."

"That's not much of a life for you, Olivia," he said sadly, feeling guilty for taking her sister away from her. What would she have in her life when Victoria was gone? The life of a sixty-year-old woman. What were they doing?

"It's the way things happen sometimes. We don't plan them the way we want them to be. They just are. Like you, for the past two years. That couldn't have been easy for you either," she said gently.

"It wasn't," he said, his eyes searching hers, and then shrinking instantly at the sorrow he saw there. Going anywhere near her was like reaching into a hot stove and burning your fingers. The emotions ran hot and high, and her heart was so warm he couldn't even bear to think of what she must be feeling. "I worry about taking Victoria away from you." She nodded at that, there was very little she could say in answer. He had begun to glimpse how painful it would be for both of them. She only hoped he would comfort Victoria adequately that summer on their honeymoon in Europe.

Olivia kissed Geoffrey in his bed that night, with Henry in one arm, and Chip nestled next to him, the boy was smiling from ear to ear, and she laughed when she saw him.

"Don't forget to bring him when you come to see me," she warned, and he swore he would never leave Chip for an instant to go anywhere, except school, and maybe his teacher would even let him bring the puppy with him. "I doubt it," she said, promising to see him again soon, and then she went back downstairs to his father.

Charles insisted on taking her back to the

hotel, and he walked her slowly across the lobby. "I don't suppose I'll see you again until the wedding," he said with an odd expression. It was so strange to think of marrying again, and in a way it felt like a terrible betrayal of Susan, but he knew he had to, for Geoff's sake. It was no life for the boy without a woman. Even Olivia's brief visits proved it. The boy blossomed like a little flower when he saw her. Victoria had not quite had the same effect on him, but he was sure she would in time. After all, they were identical twin sisters.

"I'll be the one in the blue dress," Olivia reminded him. "In case you get confused." She was smiling.

"It'll probably be the only time I know which is which without looking for my mother's engagement ring," he said, laughing at himself, and his constant confusion.

"Just ask Geoff," she teased, "he'll tell you." And then she looked at him, knowing that it would be different next time. They were just friends, but he would be a married man soon, and even more, her sister's husband. "I'll see you at the wedding," she whispered, and he nodded, with a look of sorrow.

He kissed her cheek then, turned, and walked quickly across the lobby.

Chapter 12

Victoria's last night in the familiar room was strange for both of them. They both knew she would never sleep there again. When she came back to her father's house again, she would sleep in another room with her husband. The sisters would never be together in quite the same way. And leaving each other was like peeling skin from skin, heart from soul, limb from body. Neither of them thought they would be able to bear it. Victoria slept finally, curled on her side, as she always did, and Olivia lay next to her and watched her. She touched the long silky black hair, identical to her own, and touched her sister's cheek. She held her hand, and lay clinging to her, praying that morning wouldn't come. But when it did, the day was glorious and sunny.

Olivia had never slept, she just lay there watching her, when at last Victoria stirred and turned to smile at her, and then she remembered. It would be a day of bittersweet glory. A price to be paid, a promise to be made, a life to be embarked on, a shore to sail away from. It made her heart ache just to think of all that would happen to them that morning.

"Today is your wedding day," Olivia said solemnly as they both got out of bed, in total harmony of movement. They often moved the same way at the same time, and seldom saw it. And it seemed so odd to say the words, to think of one of them getting married. And Olivia couldn't help thinking somewhat angrily that if Victoria hadn't been so foolish in New York nine months before, perhaps none of this would have happened.

They bathed, they dressed slowly, saying very little. They had no need to say the words. They felt them, they heard them in their heads, just as they had as children. They had had their own language when they were very young, and sometimes they didn't speak at all, their messages to each other were felt more than spoken.

And at last, their hair was done, they both wore it pulled back and in buns. They wore silk stockings, and satin underwear, and each of them had worn the smallest amount of eye makeup and lip rouge. Everything about them was exactly the same, identical, and absolutely no one could have told the difference between them that morning. Even Charles' mother's ring lay on their dressing table.

"It's not too late," Victoria smiled at her. "This could be your wedding." Olivia laughed at her, and for just a moment, they felt their private kinship, the world into which no one but them had ever entered. "We could dare them to guess which one is the bride. I doubt if even Charles would know the difference."

"He might. You would," Olivia said calmly. "This is your day, and his . . . and Geoffrey's . . . my darling Victoria, how I love you," her eyes filled with tears as she said the words, "I hope that you'll be very happy." They held each other tight, and Victoria's eyes filled with tears too, and then she pulled away and looked at her.

"And if I'm not?" It was a whisper of sheer terror.

"You will be. I know you will . . . give

him a fair chance. He loves you." Or at least she hoped so.

"If I'm not happy, Ollie," Victoria said as she sat down and looked up at her twin, "I'll divorce him. Toby may not have had the guts to do it, but I would . . . I won't stay with him if I'm not happy."

Olivia frowned as she listened to her. "That's no way to start a marriage. Give it your whole heart. I know he won't disappoint you."

"And if I disappoint him? We are both coming to it so strangely. He, with the ghost of his wife trailing behind him, and I with my terrible sin," she said somewhat sarcastically, ". . . Toby."

"He's gone, it's over," Olivia reminded her. "This is your life. And Charles'. It's been two years since he lost his wife . . . it's time. I know it's right for both of you. I feel it."

"Do you?" Victoria whispered unhappily. "Then why don't I? Ollie, when I'm with him I feel nothing." The tragedy of it was that when Olivia was with him, she felt far too much, and she was always afraid Charles saw that.

"You haven't given him a chance yet. Wait until you're alone for a while, with no one else around." Olivia looked at her wistfully. "It will be very romantic."

"But I'm not," Victoria said, and looked wearily at her sister. "Sometimes I think I just can't do this. And the worst part is we haven't even started."

"Give it a chance . . . please . . . for his sake . . . for yours . . . for Geoff's."

"You're trying to get rid of me, aren't you?" Victoria grinned at her ruefully. "You want my closet."

"I want your yellow hat with the green plume actually." It was a horror they had bought at the country fair years before and there had only been one of them, so Victoria bought it.

"I'll give it to you. You can wear it today! It might look nice with your dress at the wedding." They were stalling and they both knew it, and a few minutes later Bertie came to check on them, and scolded them for not being dressed yet.

"It's just our dresses, Bertie," Olivia explained, "everything else is done. We even have our shoes on."

"Well, you can't go to church looking like that. Hurry up . . . get your dresses on . . ." Olivia put hers on first, and it was spectacular, ice blue, and it molded her figure. She put her mother's necklace of aquamarines on, and then the bracelet and the earrings, and she suddenly looked very grown-up, as she put on the lace coat and the hat, as Victoria smiled at her, standing there in her white satin shoes and her white silk stockings.

"I wish you were getting married, Ollie," she said softly, and her sister nodded.

"So do I . . . but this is your day, baby." She hadn't called her that since they were tiny children, and then hand in hand they went into the next room, and put on Victoria's wedding gown, adjusted the endless train, pinned on the tiara, and settled the veil over it. Olivia thought she had never, ever seen anything like it, and when Bertie came in she burst into tears. The girls looked exactly like replicas of their mother.

"Oh my dears," was all she could say, adjusting their dresses, straightening Victoria's veil for the tenth time, and just staring at them. They were truly legendary beauties. She ran to get the flowers then. They were each carrying armloads of white orchids interspersed with lily of the valley. The fragrance was heavenly, and as Ollie followed Victoria out into the hall, they both saw their father. He stopped where he stood, and for a moment they were both afraid that he would faint when he saw them.

But he didn't, he just stood there and cried with pleasure. Bertie knew exactly what he was thinking then. They looked so exactly like her, and she had been just that age when she died. It was like seeing a double vision, as he walked slowly toward them.

"Well, at least today I know who's who," he said gruffly, and then wiped his eyes with his handkerchief, and then he smiled at them, trying not to think of their mother. "Or are you two playing tricks again. Is poor Charles getting the right one in church today?"

"Who's to say, Father," Victoria answered for them, and all three laughed, as they walked slowly downstairs and Olivia carried her train for her. They all agreed they had never seen a dress as nice as this one.

It took ten minutes just to get the train, the dress, and the veil into the car with them, but Donovan was extremely patient as Bertie helped them. And at last they took off for the church, and Bertie came in the Ford with Petrie. Olivia had offered to take Geoff with them as well, but Charles had wanted to have the boy at the hotel with him the night before, and they were going to the church together.

On the way to the church, the people they passed stopped and stared, cars honked, children waved, it was good luck to see a bride as pretty as this one. But Victoria only glanced at them, she was lost in thought, thinking of Charles, and all the foolishness and bad luck that had led them to this moment. It didn't seem providential to her at all, it seemed like a huge mistake, and all she could think of were the things she had said that morning to her sister. She was about to turn to her father as they reached the church, and tell him that she couldn't do it, that he'd have to send her to a nunnery in France after all, or Siberia, or worse, but before she could say anything, Olivia was helping her out of the car and straightening her veil again, and she had missed her moment.

They were rapidly escorted into the back of the church, and Victoria tried desperately to get a moment alone with her sister. It was another ten minutes before things had settled down again, and Victoria could already hear the music as she was engulfed with panic.

"I can't! . . ." she whispered, clutching Olivia's arm, just before they were to start down the aisle with their father. "I can't, Ollie . . . get me out of it."

"You *have* to!" Ollie whispered fiercely. She could see that Victoria was dead white, and seized by terror. "You have to do this. You can't stop it now. Go through with it, you'll never regret it."

"And if I do? There's no way out. What if he won't divorce me?"

"You can't think of that now, Victoria. You have to make it work, for his sake . . . for Geoff's . . . for your own . . . please, please, baby . . . do it."

Victoria's eyes were filled with tears and she was speechless with grief and terror, as a door opened, the organ played, and Olivia glided slowly down the aisle ahead of them, and before she could stop herself, Victoria was clutching her father's arm, and they were walking solemnly behind. She wanted to stop, to turn around and run away, to leave before it was too late, but it already was and she knew it. She felt as though she were marching to her death as she walked slowly to the altar behind her sister in front of four hundred people. And when they got there, her father squeezed her hand and left her there, tears streaming down his cheeks, and then she looked up and saw him. It was Charles, so tall, so proud, so decent, he was trying so hard, and cared so much, and wanted so to do the right thing, as he stood there in his morning coat and striped trousers.

He looked so handsome, and his eyes were so gentle as he looked at her that she almost believed that everything would be all right between them. She wanted it to be. They both did. And as he stood beside her and took her hand, he felt her trembling violently, and tried to reassure her. He stood very close to her and held her arm. He wanted her to know that she would always have his protection. It was less than he would have wanted to give her, less than he had once shared, but it was all he had to give now. And she looked up at him silently, and understood him. Theirs was not the union either of them would have wanted years before, but it was right for them now. It was an agreement, a solemn vow, an exchange of honor between two people who understood each other, and were willing to accept less than they had once dreamed of.

They exchanged rings, and vows, and promises, and Victoria stopped trembling. And she smiled as she walked solemnly back down the aisle beside Charles. Just behind them came Olivia on her father's arm, holding tightly to Geoff's hand. Olivia felt loss and grief and joy and love all at once, and along with her father, this small boy, this child who had lost so much, was all she had now.

Chapter 13

The wedding was a huge success, a total victory, as usual Olivia had attended to every detail. Her months of careful planning had paid off. The food was exquisite, the decor sublime, the flowers the most elaborate anyone had ever seen, the ice sculptures looked real, and actually stayed intact for most of the party. The orchestra had come from New York and played music everyone loved to dance to. The guests were beautifully dressed, and everyone agreed that no one had ever seen a bride quite as lovely as this one. There had been rumors, it was true, but it was difficult to believe any of that now, when one saw her looking so respectable, so demure, so much in love with her handsome husband. Four hundred people applauded at the first waltz, the "Blue Danube," which Charles danced with his bride, and her gown swept around her like a sea of lace with each graceful movement. And Olivia, of course, though less in evidence today, looked just as pretty. She danced with her father first, then Charles, then Geoffrey. And everyone agreed that she looked lovely.

It was late in the day by the time Olivia danced with Charles again, and she knew that Victoria was going to take off her wedding gown soon, put her honeymoon suit on, and leave for the city. They were going to spend a night at the Waldorf-Astoria, and then board the *Aquatania* in the morning. There had been some talk of her father and her and Geoff going to New York to see them off, but the child was terribly nervous about his father going on a ship, and Olivia had been the first to agree that he shouldn't see it. So they were going to say good-bye to the newlyweds here, in Croton.

"You did an incredible job, Olivia," Charles said handsomely. It had truly been the perfect wedding. "You're very good at this."

"I've been running Father's house for years," she smiled easily. "But I'm glad this went so well." She was pleased too. And then she leaned back and pretended to examine him through narrowed eyes that barely concealed all that she was feeling. "So, do you feel different now that you're a married man again?"

"Absolutely. Can't you tell the way I dance? That ball and chain around the leg really makes a difference."

"You're awful," she said, laughing at him, but it was nice to see him look so happy.

And Victoria looked relieved too. It was done, it was over. She had done it. She had almost run screaming from the church the moment before they went down the aisle, but now all that seemed to be over. She looked immensely pleased with herself, and totally relaxed as she greeted their guests, and danced with old friends of her father's, and new ones of her husband's. And as Olivia danced with Charles, Victoria signaled her. It was time to change from her wedding gown to the suit she would leave in, Olivia explained to him, and left him talking to some friends, with Geoffrey standing near him. The boy was uneasy about his father being away for so long, but Olivia had promised to take good care of him and keep him happy.

Victoria was waiting for her at the bottom of the stairs, laughing and smiling, and Olivia couldn't believe the change in her since that morning.

"What happened?" she whispered to her as they walked upstairs holding hands, looking more identical than ever, with the exception of their dresses. But their faces and hands and hair looked particularly identical that day, and all their gestures. "You look as though you're enjoying this all of a sudden." Olivia had been watching her in fascination.

"I don't know," Victoria said honestly. "I'm not sure. I just decided to go ahead and do it, and stop worrying about it. I guess we'll work the rest out later." She said it philosophically, and Olivia could see that she'd been drinking. Not too much, but just enough to take the edge off.

"Good girl. You'll be fine," she said reassuringly, as Victoria took the exquisite dress off. They laid it carefully across their bed, and Olivia went to get the white silk suit that had been made in New York just for this occasion. There was a white silk cloche to match, and Victoria's eyes looked huge as she put it on her head and glanced at her sister.

"What am I going to do without you?" Victoria asked in a whisper, and Olivia felt exactly the same way her twin had that morning, filled with panic.

"Don't think of that," she whispered, choking back tears. "I'll be here, waiting for you with Geoffrey."

"Oh God, Ollie," was all Victoria said and they flew into each other's arms and held each other tightly. "I can't leave you."

"I know . . . I know . . ." Ollie was trying to be brave for her, but for once, she just couldn't do it. "But I think you have to. Charles might be upset if you sent Geoffrey on your honeymoon instead, and stayed here with me in Croton."

"Let's try it, maybe he won't notice." They both laughed through their tears, but it was the worst moment of their lives, and it was half an hour later before they came downstairs again, looking suspiciously pink around the eyes, with carefully powdered noses.

"Where were you?" their father asked as he stood with Charles, but the girls only gave him vague excuses. It was time for Victoria to throw her bouquet, which she did from the top of the stone stairs outside, to a group of single women waiting anxiously for it in the garden. And out of duty, more than interest, Olivia was among them. Victoria aimed it carefully at her twin, and pitched it toward her. And she had to catch it, or it would have hit her. There were laughing shouts of "Foul," "Unfair," "Fixed," but no one really minded, and then suddenly Charles and Victoria were standing next to the car, and Olivia was alone beside her father, as a sob caught in her throat and she and Victoria flew into each other's arms and stood there, clinging to each other in silence. Charles' eyes filled with tears and he looked away, and then glanced at their father. He looked as unhappy as they did.

"I love you . . . take care of yourself . . ." Olivia whispered to her, unabashedly crying as the others first watched and then turned away. It was far too painful to see it.

Victoria could barely speak, and only nodded as she kissed her father and got into the car. She said nothing at all to Geoffrey. Charles held the boy tight for a long moment, with tears in his own eyes, then shook his father-in-law's hand and thanked him, and then for a single moment he hugged his new sister to him.

"Take good care of her," Olivia whispered to him, still crying. And he pulled away to look down at her with all the feelings that had so long been buried.

"I will . . . God bless you, Olivia . . . take care of my boy if anything happens to us."

"It won't," she said, smiling through her tears at him, and then watched him get into the car with her sister.

They waved as they drove away, and the others stood there, useless, alone, abandoned, like shipwrecked sailors on a desert island after the passengers have been rescued. Without saying a word, Olivia held Geoffrey close to her, and then hand in hand they went back to the others. There was nothing left to do now but wait for them to come home again. It was going to be a long, slow summer.

And as they rounded the first bend in the road, Charles handed his wife his handkerchief without a word to her. He could see how much pain she was in. And he knew there was very little he could do to soothe it. He knew from things they'd said before that they had never been apart for more than a few hours in their entire lifetimes. And he had come to understand over the past months, how rare and powerful that bond was.

"Are you all right?" he asked solicitously as she blew her nose for the third time, and continued crying.

"I think so." She looked at him and tried to smile, but it only made her cry harder. She had never been as miserable, even when she lost Toby.

"It'll be difficult for both of you at first," he said honestly, never one to lie about something painful, or unpleasant. "But you'll get used to it. Other twins must marry and move apart. Have you ever asked anyone about it?" She shook her head, and moved a little closer to him for comfort. It touched him more than anything ever had about her. Without Olivia, she seemed so vulnerable, so much smaller and less sure of herself. All of her brittle outrageousness seemed to have gone now. "You'll have fun on the ship," he said, for lack of something else to say. "Have you ever been on one?" She shook her head, and sighed. He was trying so hard, and she was so incredibly lonely for Ollie. It wasn't his fault.

"I'm sorry," she said, looking up at him, and noticing again how handsome he was. And yet, he was nothing like Toby, nor were her feelings for him. "I never thought it would be like this." She couldn't even imagine that leaving Olivia would be so painful.

"It's all right," he said gently. "It's all right, Victoria," he said, and put an arm around her. They spoke very little the rest of the way to New York, and when they got into bed that night at the hotel, she was so over-wrought and exhausted from the emotions of the afternoon, that she was asleep before he got out of the bathroom.

He had ordered champagne for them, and it was in the other room in an ice bucket, but he could only smile to himself when he saw her.

"Good night, little girl," he whispered and covered her. She was purring softly. "It's a long life . . . there will be lots of champagne an-other time . . ." He went into the other room, and helped himself to a glass, thinking about his son, and her sister, and wondering how they were doing.

Olivia was asleep by then too, as was Geoff, clinging to each other in Olivia's bed, with Henry the stuffed monkey in bed with them, and Chip, the sleeping puppy. It would have warmed Charles' heart if he could see them. Instead, he walked slowly into the bed-room, and looked at his new wife sleeping there, and wondered what it would be like be-ing married to her. In some ways, the prospect excited him, in others it terrified him. In truth, it was difficult to imagine.

Chapter 14

Charles was up and dressed when Victoria woke the next day. He had shaved, showered, and dressed by nine o'clock, and had ordered the newspaper and coffee.

"Good morning, Sleeping Beauty," he said with a smile, as she wandered into the room in her dressing gown, still looking very sleepy. She had had more to drink the day before than he knew, and it had caught up with her by the previous evening. "Did you sleep well?"

"Very," she said, and poured herself a cup of coffee. She looked for her handbag from the day before and took out a cigarette and lit it.

He glanced at her over the newspaper in surprise, and watched her do it. "Do you always do that at this hour of the day?" He looked amused, she was every bit the renegade he had always thought her.

"If I can get away with it," she smiled. "Can I?"

"I suppose so, if you don't blow it in my face before my first cup of coffee. I can't say I love the smell of it, but I suppose I can live with it, if I have to."

"Good." She smiled at him, pleased, their first hurdle had been successfully cleared. On to the next one. She glanced at the newspaper with him and commented on riots that had happened in Italy, and Mary Richardson's hunger strike in jail in England. The newspaper said they had had to force-feed her.

"You're fascinated by that sort of thing, aren't you?" he asked, intrigued. It was interesting being alone with her now. They could ask each other anything, or do whatever they wanted.

"I'm fascinated by freedom," she said honestly, "and what it takes to get it and keep it. Freedom of the underdog, whoever that may be at the time. And I believe very strongly in the freedom of women." She met his eyes openly, and he was struck again by the sensuousness she seemed to be so unaware of.

"Then why marriage?" he asked, amused at the conversation.

"Because that's a route to freedom too. I'll be much freer married to you than I was living with my father."

"How do you know that?" He laughed at her answer.

"Because now I'm a grown-up. I was a child until yesterday, and I had to do everything he wanted."

"And now you have to do everything I want," he said, sounding like a tyrant, and she watched his eyes to see if he meant it, but he was quick to reassure her. "No, Victoria, I am not a monster. You may do as you wish when we get back, as long as you don't embarrass me publicly, or endanger yourself in any way. I've already told you, I would prefer it if you refrained from getting arrested. But as for the rest, that's up to you. If you want to endorse hunger strikes, or attend meetings and lectures with your political groups, or spend time with other women talking about how evil men are, you have my full permission." She looked pleased by his answer. Her father had been right. He was an extremely reasonable person. And for the moment, he seemed to want nothing from her.

"Thank you," she said quietly, looking very young, and a little less daring than she had a moment before, with a cigarette between her fingers.

"I think you ought to get dressed now though, or we'll be late boarding the ship." He glanced at his watch. It was ten o'clock and they were meant to be there at eleven-thirty. "Would you like some breakfast?" he asked politely. It was like visiting with a very civilized friend. He was solicitous and courteous, and very well behaved. He had done nothing whatsoever to frighten or upset her.

"I'm not hungry," she said cautiously, wondering what it had been like to sleep with him the night before. He had come to bed after she was asleep, and left the bedroom before she woke up that morning. It was odd having spent the night with him, and being totally unaware of it. He didn't really feel like her husband. This was nothing at all like what she had shared with Toby. And she knew what would be expected of her here, but she couldn't even imagine it with Charles. In fact, she rather dreaded it, but so far, Charles had been a total gentleman, and shown no amorous interest in her whatsoever.

She went to dress, and an hour later stood

in the living room of their suite in the red dress Olivia had picked out for her with the matching jacket. She was wearing a bun again, and had a matching cloche, and in the startling red outfit, she made quite an impression. It was odd being by herself with him, and not automatically half of a pair, with an identical person standing right next to her, but it was very pleasant leaving the hotel with him, and having everyone greet him. Charles was respected and well liked, and she felt very well cared for as he shepherded her to the car waiting for them. Their trunks had already gone on ahead to the *Aquatania*, and would be waiting for them in their stateroom.

And when they reached the huge ship at Pier Fifty-four, there was a band playing, and confetti flying everywhere, and elegantly dressed people going up the gangplank, both to find their cabins, and to visit friends who were sailing. There was a huge crowd of people all around, and Victoria's eyes grew wide as she watched the excitement around her. She only wished that Olivia could be there with her to see it. And Charles saw the brief flash of sorrow cross her eyes and knew what she was thinking.

"Maybe she can come with us next time,"

he said gently, and she looked at him and smiled, grateful for his generosity of spirit.

Their stateroom on B Deck was handsome and large, and surprisingly sunny. It was near the Garden Lounge, which looked like an old English garden, and as they walked around the ship, Victoria was impressed by the marble chimneypiece in the Adam Drawing Room and the elegant style of the ship, and she was fascinated by what the other women were wearing. It was like looking at one of Olivia's fashion magazines, and she was glad Olivia had forced her to bring all the gowns that were carefully packed in her trunk, and that the stewardess was already unpacking.

"Oh this is such fun," she said to Charles, clapping her hands like a child, and he put an arm around her shoulders. He had been on ships before, and he had always liked them, but after what had happened to his wife he was sure he never would feel happy on one again. But Victoria had changed that.

They wandered down to look at the swimming pool, and then back to the main deck for the sailing. The music grew louder still and the boat horns blew, and the great ship began to move slowly away from the dock and out of the harbor. The visitors were waving frantically from the dock, and Victoria took off her hat, and her hair was instantly covered by confetti. This was the *Aquatania*'s first trip back, after her maiden voyage to New York the week before, and Charles only hoped that she was more fortunate than her earlier cousin, the *Titanic*. This was supposed to be a better ship, and she was meant to have the right number of lifeboats on board, but he nevertheless looked serious as they went back to their cabin. Inevitably, he was thinking of Susan.

"What was she like?" Victoria asked him boldly, as she lit a cigarette, but he didn't object. He wanted her to be comfortable with him.

"It wouldn't be fair if I said perfect," he said honestly. "Because she wasn't. But she was right for me, and I loved her very dearly. It's been a hard thing getting used to her being gone like this. Perhaps it'll be different now that we're married." He said it hopefully, like a long illness he was hoping was cured, but he wasn't sure yet.

"That was brave of you," Victoria said quietly. "You really don't know me."

"I think I do. And we both need help in bad situations."

"That's an odd reason to get married,

isn't it?" she asked, suddenly wanting more than that, as he poured a glass of champagne and handed it to her. She felt very grown-up now that she was married, and enjoying the privileges that went with it.

"Getting married is an odd thing anyway, isn't it? I mean two people together for life. It's a great risk to take, but I think it's worth it," he said, as he sat down near her and looked at her.

"And if the risk doesn't pan out?" She looked him in the eye and this time he was startled by her question.

"The risk does pan out if you want it to," he said firmly. "You just have to want it badly enough." And then he looked her in the eye and asked her a tough question. "Do you?" There was a long silence.

And then finally, "I think so. I was terrified yesterday. I almost ran away right before the wedding," she confessed, and then laughed at her own terror.

"That's understandable. If people were honest, most of them would tell you that they wanted to run away right before their wedding. So did I, for about half a minute."

"Mine lasted a little longer," she said softly.

"And now?" he asked, moving closer to

her, watching her with fascination. He could feel that sensual quality about her again, the thing Olivia didn't have, and it drove him crazy. "Do you still want to run away?" he asked, as he came very close to her. She looked into his eyes and shook her head. She didn't know what she wanted yet, but running away wasn't it. "You can't run very far on the ship," he said in a husky voice, as he set down his champagne glass and sat down next to her. And then without saying another thing, he put his arms around her and kissed her. For a moment, he took her breath away, and then she kissed him back, much harder and deeper than he had expected. She was exactly what he had suspected her to be, a wild horse he would never tame, but who would never ask for what he could never give her. "You're very beautiful, Victoria," he whispered to her, not entirely sure of the extent of her experience. He knew she wasn't entirely innocent, but her father had not supplied the details, nor had he wanted to know them.

Charles carefully took her crimson jacket off, and then pulled her into his arms again, as they sat on the couch in the living room of their cabin. The rooms were extremely luxurious, and Charles had spared no expense in order to spoil her.

She lit a cigarette again then, somewhat nervously, and this time he put it out, and kissed her. He could taste the cigarette smoke on her lips, but he didn't really mind it. Everything about her aroused him. And as she sat next to him, languidly, he kissed her and she kissed him back, it felt as though it went on for hours, and then finally, he picked her up and carried her into their bedroom.

They were at sea by then, but there were still seagulls flying past the portholes. There was no one nearby, they were totally alone with no one to disturb them, as he peeled off the red dress and dropped it next to the bed, as he admired her long legs and narrow hips, the tiny waist and full breasts, she took his breath away when he saw her, and then took his clothes off too. He drew the curtains before he took them off entirely, and slipped beneath the covers with her, and there he took off the rest of what she was wearing, and his own, and he felt the opulence of her flesh against his, the silkiness of her body that he had so longed for. His body was crying out for her, as it never had before. There had been no woman in his life since Susan. It had been two agonizingly long years, and as he reached for his wife now, he felt her suddenly shrink from him and begin to tremble.

"Don't be afraid," he whispered in her hair, as he touched her, aching to be inside her. "I won't hurt you, I promise." But she had turned away from him by then, and she was shaking so hard she couldn't stop as he held her. He held her that way for a long time, and then he turned her and forced her to face him.

"I won't force you to do anything you don't want, Victoria. You don't need to fear me, I know this is difficult for you." He remembered his first wedding night with Susan, and she had been so young and so innocent, and so shy with him, much more so than Victoria, who seemed so much bolder. But she wasn't. She was a twenty-one-year-old girl, and he imagined that despite her broken heart, she was still a virgin. He was sixteen years older than she, and he had time. Despite his hunger for her, he was willing to be patient.

"I can't," she said, burying her face against him, sounding every bit as panicked as she had before the wedding. All she could think of now were her raptures with a man she had loved, and the agony that had ended in the bathroom. "I can't do this with you. . . ."

351

"You don't have to . . . not now . . . we have a lifetime together." But at the sound of his words, she began to cry, and all she wanted was her sister.

"I'm sorry," she said miserably. "I'm so sorry . . . I can't do this . . ."

"Shhh . . ." he said, and held her for what seemed like hours, just as he would have Geoffrey if he had hurt his knee or been bitterly disappointed. And at last, she curled up and fell asleep in his arms. And while she slept, he got up and put on a dressing gown. He didn't want her to be frightened if she saw him naked. He ordered tea for both of them, and when she woke up late that afternoon, he was waiting for her, and he served her tea and cookies.

"I don't deserve this," she said unhappily, wishing that things were different. She didn't even want to take tea from him. She felt as though she had failed him. And she felt even worse when they got a telegram from home.

"We love you. Bon Voyage and Happy Honeymoon. Father, Olivia, and Geoffrey." It made her feel homesick just thinking of them, and she got up and sprinted like a doe across the cabin to their bathroom. He tried not to look at her, but she was so lovely he couldn't help it.

A little later she came back and sat with him, wrapped in the lavender silk dressing gown Olivia had bought her.

"Don't worry about it," he reassured her again, and kissed her gently. He would never have admitted it to her, but his desire for her was driving him crazy. But he made no attempt at seduction again, and a little while later they dressed for dinner.

She wore a white satin evening gown that clung to her figure outrageously, and was so low down her back that you could almost see her bottom.

"Well, that will certainly catch the boys' attention." He smiled at her happily and then followed her out of the cabin. They sat at Captain Turner's table that night, and as soon as the music struck up, Charles led his wife out onto the dance floor. They were playing a tango and he could feel her moving sensuously in his arms. It was all he could do not to rush her to their cabin.

"I don't think I can let you out again," he said as the music drew to a close. "You're driving all the men crazy." She laughed at him, and clearly didn't mind the stir she was making. But when it came to him . . . she was frightened. It was so odd, he just didn't understand it.

And when he lay next to her that night, he looked at her, and was almost afraid to touch her. But he just couldn't help it, and she knew she had to face it too. It couldn't go on this way forever. He slipped her nightgown off, and she lay in his arms, lifeless and exquisite. He knew how afraid she was, he could sense it, and he was determined not to force her. He wanted to drive her as mad as she drove him, and introduce her to all the avenues of pleasure.

He began very gently and very slowly, but as his desire for her mounted, he became more passionate, and he was in fact a kind and experienced lover. Far more so than Toby, who had actually used her far more roughly than Charles did. But the difference between them was that she had loved Toby, and her own desire for him had been so great, that she had minded nothing they had done, she had feared nothing at all. She had wanted all they'd shared. And she wanted to want it now, with Charles. She wanted to be the wife he expected of her, and yet as she felt him shudder in her arms, and lay spent finally, she felt nothing.

He was very quick to look at her, and to call her name and kiss her, and assure her that he cared about her deeply. He was terrified that he had frightened her again, and then he understood what had happened. He suddenly realized what she knew, and he hadn't.

"It wasn't the first time, was it?" he asked hoarsely, as he buried his face between her breasts, and then returned to face her as she shook her head sadly. "You might have told me, Victoria. I was terrified I'd hurt you."

"You didn't," she said quietly. She had gone nowhere at all while he was transported by passion. She felt closer to him, but only because she felt so sorry for him, and what she didn't have to give him. And she didn't believe what they said now. You didn't learn these things. You didn't "grow" to love someone. You either did, or you didn't. And she knew she had been cheated, and she had cheated him. They would not "grow" to anything. They would simply spend a lifetime together, as strangers.

"And you loved him, didn't you?" Charles wanted to know it all now.

"Yes," she said honestly. She didn't avert her eyes this time. It only seemed fair to tell him. "I loved him."

"How long did it go on?"

"Almost two months." Charles nodded, at

least it hadn't been a year or two, not that it really mattered. "He lied to me. About everything. He never really loved me. He told me he was trapped in a loveless marriage, that he was leaving her and getting divorced. And I believed him. I'd never have done it otherwise," and then she thought about it, "or maybe I would. I don't know now." She looked miserable, but at least she wasn't lying to him. That was something. "He started telling people, laughing about it. And when they asked him, he said I seduced him. He said I meant nothing to him, it was all a lark. He never intended to leave his wife, or marry me. In fact, she was expecting a baby all the time I loved him."

"What a bastard. And now you don't trust me, do you?"

"It's not that," she said miserably, touching his face with her fingers. "I don't know what it is. I just can't . . . it's like a wall between us . . . between me and everyone . . . any man . . . I don't want anyone to touch me." It certainly did not bode well for their future.

"Did anything else happen, Victoria, that you're not telling me?" He suspected it even before she told him. She started to shake her head, and then she looked at him, and shrugged. That was one thing she really didn't want to tell him.

"Nothing . . ."

But this time he knew she was lying. He cupped her breast with one hand, and wished that she wanted him, and she only looked at him sadly.

"I was pregnant," she said in the smallest of voices.

"I thought so."

"I fell off my horse and lost it almost as soon as we got back to Croton. Olivia was with me, but I hadn't told her. She saved me . . . I was hemorrhaging . . . it was awful . . . I think I almost died and they took me to the hospital in an ambulance." Tears rolled slowly down her cheeks as he held her hand, wishing that things had been different. "I never want to have children."

"It doesn't have to be like that. It doesn't have to be terrifying and awful and wrong . . . alone on a bathroom floor, with the baby of a man who didn't love you." But he couldn't tell her that he loved her, not honestly, and she knew that. And it wouldn't have mattered if he did, she didn't love him.

"My mother died when I was born. I

killed her," she said, as fresh tears rolled down her cheeks and he held her.

"I'm sure that's not true," he said, certain that there was more to the story.

"She was fine when Olivia was born, and I was so big that she died right after she had me. I was born eleven minutes after Ollie."

"But you didn't kill her," he explained, she was naive in some ways, even though she had lost a baby. "I don't mind if I never have another child," he explained, "but I don't want you to feel that you shouldn't. Having Geoff was the happiest moment of Susan's life, or . . . afterwards at least," he smiled. It hadn't been easy for her either, and Geoff had been a big baby. But he still remembered the look on her face the first time he saw her after Geoff was born, as the baby lay at her breast and suckled. He had never seen anything as sweet, and he had cried when he saw them. It was hard to forget that even now, ten years later. "You should have a baby one day, Victoria. Eventually, things will be different. We'll get used to each other. We'll both forget the people we once cared for, or put them away, along with the sorrows, and the things they did to hurt us."

"What did she ever do to hurt you?" Victoria asked, surprised, and wishing that she could believe that one day things would be different. But she didn't. They were too far apart. And the truth was, other than sympathy, she felt nothing for him.

"She died," he said bluntly, "she went down on that damn ship. That's what she did to hurt me. She gave her seat up to a child, to someone I don't know and don't care about, and she left me." There were tears in his eyes now, he had known pain and grief and loss and anger. He had known agony, but he had come back now. And he was willing to hold a hand out to Victoria and to let her join him. But the truth was, she didn't want to. "We can't give up," he said quietly, "we can't just look back at the people who've left our lives. Even if he hurt you terribly, if he betrayed you, you have to forget it."

"I can't yet."

"You will eventually. And I'll be there waiting."

"And in the meantime?" she asked, looking worried. It was by no means perfect between them at this point, but it was more than Charles had had in years and he was willing to settle for it for the moment.

"We do our best . . . we wait . . . we

become friends . . . I'll try not to upset you more than I have to." But she knew she had no right to refuse him. Yet she didn't want him, and he knew that. "We'll see . . . it's the best we can do, Victoria. We're married."

"You deserve more than I have to give you, Charles," she said and meant it.

"If that's true, then I'll find it someday. And so will you. Until then, this is all there is . . ." He smiled at her philosophically, willing to accept her as she was, a beautiful young woman who stirred him to his very soul, but didn't love him. But he knew she was young too. She would forget Toby eventually. She would come to want the man she had married. And when she did, he'd be waiting.

Chapter 15

Their honeymoon was definitely not what Charles had hoped it would be. Victoria's recalcitrance with him did not improve in the course of the trip. And then they arrived in Europe on the twenty-sixth of June, and two days later seven young Serbian nationalists attacked and killed the nephew of the Austrian emperor, Archduke Franz Ferdinand, and his wife, in the town of Sarajevo.

It appeared to be only an isolated incident, but within days it had caused considerable consternation in Europe. Victoria and Charles were in London then, staying at Claridge's, and seeing friends. And Victoria was more interested in the suffragettes' march on Washington, back in the States, and their demand for voting rights for women. Even among Charles' friends in London, she had met several suffragists, and she was fascinated by what was going on there. But her fervent wish to visit the Pankhursts in jail had been thwarted. There, Charles had put his foot down. He did not want his wife visiting anyone in prison. There had been a heated argument over it, but Victoria had not prevailed. Charles was willing to be tolerant, but not to be pushed beyond his limits.

"But I've corresponded with them, Charles," Victoria said, as though that would alter the way he viewed it.

"I don't care if you've seen them in religious visions. Visiting those women in jail is out of the question. You'll get yourself put on some kind of blacklist, and get us thrown out of England."

"That's absurd. They're far more open-minded here," she said naively.

"Somehow I doubt that." He was anything but amused, and he seemed testy these days, but they both knew why. All his attempts at getting their physical lives on track had been anything but successful.

And by the time they reached Paris, a week after they'd arrived, Victoria shuddered each time he touched her. She didn't know why she felt that way. It was visceral. She didn't want any man touching her again, she didn't want to feel any of the things she'd felt before, she didn't want to trust anyone, and she was adamant that she didn't want a baby. She had said as much to him, and he had assured her that there were precautions that could be taken. He had even availed himself of some of them, but they never got that far. She began to cry and shake now each time he touched her. And although he tried to be patient with her, he was beginning to get angry.

"Why didn't you say something before if you felt that way?" He reproached her late one night, after they had tried again in Paris. And it was beginning to affect him too. As badly as he wanted her, he didn't want to continue to make love to a woman who was either crying or shaking. He felt like a rapist, and he was rapidly becoming a very limp one.

"I didn't know it would be like this," she said between sobs at the Ritz Hotel. Their best suite was all but wasted. And the romance of Paris only seemed to make her more nervous. She didn't want to be trapped here alone with him. She wanted to be talking politics, and meeting suffragists, and going to meetings.

And it was beginning to seem to Charles that the last thing she wanted was a husband. "It wasn't like this with Toby," she blurted out unexpectedly, and finally pushed too far, and humiliated beyond words, Charles had stormed out of the suite and gone for a long, solitary walk around Paris. She apologized profusely to him when he returned, and she made a sincere effort later that night to make it up to him. She was young and sensual, and very exciting. He could feel her respond to him, but almost as quickly, he could feel her recoil in terror and revulsion.

"You won't get pregnant, Victoria," he reassured her almost in the heat of passion, but as he writhed and rolled, he could feel her in his arms, it was as though she weren't really there. There was something dead in her, and nothing he did revived her. "I'm not a doctor, or a magician," he said, almost in despair. He had never had an experience like this one, a woman who excited him so much, and seemed to feel absolutely nothing. It was torture, and by July it had done very little to improve his disposition.

They had heard from Olivia several times by then. And Victoria seemed to live only for news of her, or to read about the suffragettes in the papers. Very little else seemed to matter to her. And she seemed far more comfortable these days in the company of other women. He was beginning to wonder if she even liked men. Perhaps there was more of a problem here than anyone had ever dreamed of. And he could only wonder what nightmare Edward Henderson had foisted on him, and if he had known what he was doing. Charles didn't like to think so.

Olivia said that they were well. It had been unseasonably hot all along the Hudson River. Their father was enjoying good health these days, and Geoffrey was thriving at Croton-on-Hudson. He had learned to ride beautifully, and she reassured Charles that there had been no further mishaps. In fact, if he continued to ride as well as he had been, Olivia was thinking of buying a new horse for him, one that would suit him to perfection. They could leave it in Croton with her, and he could ride it whenever he came to visit.

She assured them, lest they were concerned, that Chip was doing very well too. He was gnawing on all the furniture, and had made excellent inroads on eating both carpets in her bedroom.

And most of all, she hoped that they were

well, that they were happy and prospering, and that the absurd incident in Sarajevo hadn't caused them any concern. They had heard news of it too, but there was no reason to think that the conflict would go any further. The Austrians were undoubtedly annoyed, but the rest of the world appeared to be unaffected.

Charles completely shared her view, even when in the last week of July, while they were in the south of France, they heard that Austria had declared war on Serbia. But it was hardly surprising. What surprised, and disturbed, them far more was when four days later, Germany declared war on Russia, and again two days later, when they declared war on France as well. Things appeared to be deteriorating rapidly in Europe.

They were in Nice then, at the Hotel d'Angleterre, and Charles wanted to return immediately to England.

"But this is ridiculous, Charles," Victoria objected vociferously. She loved France, and she didn't want to leave yet. They had been planning a trip to Italy a few days later. "I'm not going to change all my plans because some ridiculous European country has a temper tantrum." She looked at him with complete annoyance.

"That temper tantrum is called a war. We are now in a country that is at war, and Germany is not 'ridiculous,' and may very well attack at any moment. Pack your bags. We're leaving."

"I'm not going." She crossed her arms and sat down calmly on the couch in their suite at the hotel.

"You're crazy. And you'll leave here when I say so." She was anything but easy, and he was getting tired of it. It had been a long summer.

They were still arguing about it the next day when German troops invaded Belgium. And this time, Victoria got the message without any pressure from her husband. She packed their things, and they left Nice the following morning, the same day that Montenegro declared war on Austria. Europe was rapidly becoming a tangle of declarations and accusations.

They went back to Claridge's, and for the next week watched with fascination as the Serbians declared war on Germany, the Austrians on Russia, the Montenegrins on Germany as well. And then finally, on August twelfth, both Britain and France declared war on Aus-

tria, and in London, there were banner headlines.

Charles came hurrying back to the suite
as soon as he heard, and he had already exchanged their tickets at the Cunard office.
They had planned to stay another week in Europe, but that was over now. He wanted to get
Victoria back to the States as soon as he could.
And they were sailing on the *Aquatania* again
the next morning. By the time Victoria came
back from her shopping trip, their bags were
packed, their plans were made, and he had sent
a telegram to her sister. He explained all of it
to Victoria as she put her coat down.

"That's it? We're leaving?" She looked
shocked when he said it. "Without even asking
me what I thought of it?"

"That's right. Germany has just declared
war on Britain. I'm not going to wait around
here until bullets start flying, I am taking my
wife and going back to America, to safety."

"I am not a *thing* you can just pack up,
Charles, without any discussion."

"We seem to do a lot of discussing these
days, Victoria, and actually, I'm tired of it. I
find it a waste of time, and rather exhausting."

"I'm sorry to hear that," she said unhappily. She had been in a bad mood all day, and

she had a headache. They had had one of their unfortunate interludes, as she thought of them, the night before, and both of them had wound up frustrated and angry. She didn't know what was wrong with him, or with her, but her whole body seemed to convulse when he came near her, and his turned to jelly. She had very little experience to compare it to, but all she knew was that this had never happened with Toby. And Charles said he didn't want to ever hear her say that again and he assured her that it had never happened with Susan either. Which left both of them angry, isolated, frustrated, and very lonely, since neither Susan nor Toby were around, and all they had now was each other.

"We're leaving at ten o'clock tomorrow morning," Charles said coolly. As far as he was concerned, their honeymoon had been a nightmare.

"Maybe you are, Charles," Victoria said, daring to antagonize him again, but the worst of it was that she found she liked it. There was something about baiting him that excited her, and she couldn't stop it. "But I'm not. I'm staying."

"In Europe? At war? Over my dead body. You're coming with me."

"Maybe there's something to be learned here, Charles. Maybe there's a reason why we're here in this place, at this moment." Her eyes were alight with excitement, and she almost frightened him, but worse yet, just looking at her that way, made him want her. He wondered what demon had found his soul and had given him a wife who aroused him so much, and whom he could please so little. "This could be part of our destiny, to be here as war breaks out in Europe." She looked young and beautiful, and as far as Charles was concerned, maybe even a little crazy. She had a streak of rebellion and adventure in her that defied all reason. Perhaps that was why Edward Henderson had been so anxious to get her married. He had very sensibly kept the sane one. But even in his worst anger at her, Charles knew that Victoria wasn't crazy. She was just difficult to get along with. And he felt too old to argue with her over every point at every moment. The worst of it was that she loved it. He could see that. She loved torturing him, tormenting him, arguing with him, refusing to do the simplest thing, and then insisting on doing something dangerous and foolish, like staying in Europe.

"I know this will sound boring to you, Victoria," he said, trying to stay calm. She had taken to driving him to his limits. "But it's not sensible to stay in a country that has declared war, or which another country has declared war on. And if I leave you here, your father will kill me. So, like it or not, agree with me or don't, whether it is our destiny to be here at this time, or merely an accident, I am taking you back to New York tomorrow morning. And if you find it utterly unbearable, then I suggest you think about your sister. She will be worried sick if you stay here, as will your father. For myself, I am going to go home because I have a ten-year-old son, who has already lost his mother, and I don't intend to stay over here, and get killed needlessly by a random bullet. Does that explain the situation to you clearly enough?" This time, she nodded in silence. His mention of Olivia had finally brought it into perspective. And although she wouldn't have admitted it to him, she knew that Olivia would have said all the same things he did. But she still thought that going home now was incredibly dull of him. It would have been fascinating to stay in England to see what would develop.

She stayed up late that night after he went to bed, and thought about what had happened to them, the quirk of fate that had cast them together, and the bad luck that seemed to have marked her ever since her affair with Toby . . . the baby she had lost . . . the reputation she'd destroyed . . . the fact that she had been forced into marriage with Charles, and had to leave her sister . . . and now the physical obligations she was expected to fulfill and could no longer bear. It was difficult to imagine a happy future. For a strange moment, she thought of running away from him, and never going home again, but she knew she couldn't. If nothing else, she had to see Olivia, though she dreaded going back to New York now. And starting life with him, with his son, and all the responsibilities it would entail seemed painfully dreary. Europe had begun to give her a taste of what she wanted. She wanted excitement, and politics, and freedom. She had no real tie to this man, there was no bond of the flesh or the soul or the heart, and after two months with him, however kind or wise or patient he was, she knew there never would be. He knew it too. But she also knew that he was not prepared to admit it. Perhaps he never would. And then what would she do? She had bravely spoken to Olivia of divorce, when they were still back in Croton. But she knew that Charles would never agree to that either. She was trapped. Her destiny sealed to his. She was bound to him, and she knew that eventually they would drown together. If nothing else, this stifling life of being bound to a man she didn't love would kill her. She knew she had to talk to Olivia about it, but there didn't seem to be much to say. They had made their deal, and pledged their vows, they had gambled, and lost. In truth, they had known nothing about each other.

"Are you coming to bed tonight?" he asked, and she jumped when she heard his voice. He was standing in the doorway to their bedroom. She looked at him hesitantly, and then nodded, wondering if he wanted to try again, or if he just wanted her to do what he told her. In either case, she didn't like her options.

But when she went to bed a few moments later, she was surprised when he simply put his arms around her and held her.

"I don't know how to reach you, Victoria," he said sadly. "I know you're locked in there somewhere, but I can't find you." He knew he had a wife, but he hadn't met her yet, and he wondered if he ever would now. Like Victoria, he was beginning to lose hope. They had been married for two months, which wasn't long, but it had begun to feel like forever.

"I can't find me either, Charles," she said unhappily, and they clung to each other like flotsam in an ocean.

"Perhaps we will someday. If we wait long enough. I won't give up, you know. It took me months to believe that Susan was dead. I kept thinking they'd find her." She nodded, comforted in a way by what he said. It would have been so much easier to love him. She wanted to, but she didn't know how, and she seemed to have lost that kind of feeling. There was no love for him in her heart, and the worst part was he knew it.

"Don't give up on me, Charles," she said in a small voice. "Not yet." Without Olivia, she felt frightened.

"I won't," he whispered as he held her close. "I won't give up for a long, long time." He whispered into her neck, as he fell asleep, holding her, thinking that perhaps the honeymoon hadn't been quite so awful after all. Maybe eventually, things would get better. And as he held her, Victoria lay in his arms, dreaming of freedom.

Chapter 16

The return trip on the *Aquatania* seemed twice as long as the trip out, as Victoria and Charles sat side by side on deck chairs. He slept, she read, and she was intrigued to have met Andrea Hamilton on the ship, and they spent a lot of time discussing her latest theories on suffrage. Charles only wished that hearing about it still intrigued him. As it turned out, his wife appeared to be obsessed with women's causes and issues. This was not a passing fancy for her, or a slightly eccentric topic of conversation, it was what she lived and breathed for. And although he'd known of her interest before, he had not realized how advanced the disease was. It was all she read about, talked about, cared about, or pursued. And Charles was finding her passion for it excruciatingly boring.

"We're sitting at the captain's table tonight," he said sleepily, opening one eye, as she lay on the deck chair beside him. "I just thought I'd warn you."

"That's nice of him," she said without much interest. "Want to go for a swim?" Sometimes he felt the difference in their ages. He was happy lying there, soaking up the sun, and Victoria liked to keep busy. But he was willing to oblige her.

Half an hour later, they went down to the pool, and Charles had to force himself not to think about her body. She wore a black bathing suit, and as she swam laps the length of the pool, he couldn't help but admire her style and her long, lithe figure. He joined her then, and they swam side by side, and finally she stopped and smiled at him. She seemed to feel better.

"You're quite a girl," he said, admiringly. She had certainly run his legs off in the last two months, and challenged him in ways that were not always pleasant. Sometimes he wished he knew her better, at others he wished he'd never met her. And looking at her that way reminded him of her twin. And he wondered if now, after living with her for two months, he would find it easier to distinguish between them, or perhaps it would be harder. In some ways, he felt as though he had lost some of his sense of her in the past months. She had been none of the things he'd expected.

"Have you missed Olivia a lot?" he asked, as they dried off, and sat in chairs around the pool, watching the other swimmers.

"Terribly," she said honestly, with a wistful look. "I never thought I could live without her. When I was a little girl, I thought that if I were taken away from her, it would kill me." He didn't tell her that that was how he had once felt about Susan.

"And now?" he asked, genuinely curious. There was so much about them that intrigued him, the kind of communication they seemed to have, almost without words, the instinct they had for each other.

"I know that I can do it," she said. "But I don't really want to. I wish she'd come to New York to live with us, but I know she won't leave Father. And he doesn't want her to. He keeps her there to take care of him. It's not fair to her, but she doesn't see that." It was something Charles had thought too, and he had said as much to her sister, when Olivia brought Geoff the puppy.

"Perhaps we can talk her into it when we get home. Or long visits anyway. Geoff would love it."

"Would you mind her living with us?" Victoria asked, surprised by what he'd just said, as he was by her candor about their father. He was a selfish old man, and he got away with it, because his daughters were willing to let him do it. But Olivia was paying the price for it, and it irked him to see her do it.

"No, I wouldn't mind," Charles answered her question. "She's intelligent and polite, and incredibly kind, and she's always very helpful," he said thoughtfully, and then noticed the look on his wife's face. The odd thing was that he still didn't think of her that way, as his wife. Even after two months, they seemed like strangers.

"Maybe you should have married her," Victoria said tartly.

"She wasn't offered to me," he shot back at her, still angry at times that there was so much they hadn't told him. Victoria hadn't had a broken romance, she'd had an affair with a married man, she'd been well used, and even pregnant. That wasn't quite the same thing, although at this late date, he was willing to accept it.

"Maybe sometime we'll switch for you," Victoria snapped at him, but he didn't seem to like the idea as he frowned at her.

"That's not funny." The idea that he might be duped by them had always made him uncomfortable, or that he would say something he shouldn't to one or the other. In fact, he found it quite unnerving. "Shall we go back upstairs?" he asked finally, and she nodded. They always seemed to be arguing these days, even when they didn't mean to.

They dressed separately for dinner, and emerged in full dress for the captain's dinner. There was talk of nothing but the war in Europe that night, and Victoria found it fascinating, and had a great many radical, but interesting, opinions. Charles was proud as he listened to her. She was certainly very intelligent, it was only a shame that she wasn't easier to get along with.

Eventually, they strolled back to their cabin. They had danced for a while, but neither of them was in the mood, and it was a beautiful night on the North Atlantic. Victoria lit a cigarette, and she stood next to him, looking out to sea, smoking in silence.

"Well," he said, smiling at her ruefully. "Was it a good honeymoon, or not? Did you have fun?" At least that would have been something.

"To answer your questions, yes, at times, and I don't know yet. Was it good, or not? What do you think?"

"I think it was interesting, but not easy." And it was odd, coming home with war on their heels as they returned from Europe. "Maybe that's the way life is at this point. Maybe you only get one shot at the brass ring. I'm not sure yet." He was referring to Susan, and she knew it. She had Toby, who was certainly no dream, but she had loved him, madly. "Maybe it just takes time. 'We will grow to love each other,' as people say. It happens." But both of them were doubtful.

"What now then? I become a house-wife?"

"Do you have any other plans, Mrs. Dawson? Do you plan to become a doctor or a law-yer?"

"I think not. Politics." She was already fascinated by the war in Europe. "I'd like to go back and study what's happening over there, maybe get involved somehow. Make myself useful."

"Like what?" He looked horrified. "Drive an ambulance or something like that?"

"Maybe," she said thoughtfully.

"Don't you dare," he said, and meant it. "Suffragist demonstrations are bad enough, thank you very much. No wars please." But she wondered if he could stop her if she really wanted to go back to Europe. She knew Olivia would disapprove too so she certainly couldn't discuss it with her, or her father. But she had been thinking about it seriously, ever since they sailed from Southampton. She felt as though she were missing something going back to the States. They were leaving all the excitement behind them. "What about Geoff? How does he fit into your activities? Will you make time for him?" She knew how important that was to him, and he looked worried.

"I'll take care of him. Don't worry."

"Good." He smiled at her, satisfied that she meant it, and then they strolled back to their stateroom. It was so warm they left two of their portholes open, but that night Charles didn't touch her. He just didn't have the energy or the courage.

And the next morning, at nine o'clock they had a life-boat drill. It was unusually serious, since war had been declared, and Victoria wondered briefly if it would upset him and remind him of Susan. But he seemed all right afterwards, and when they went back to their room for breakfast, he smiled at her, and then without saying anything he kissed her.

"What was that for?" she asked in surprise, and he grinned at her.

"Being married to me. We haven't exactly been easy with each other. I'll try and do better when we get home. Maybe getting back to normal life will do us both good. Maybe honeymoons are too much pressure." He was referring cryptically to their unsuccessful sex life, and she nodded. But they tried it again that night, and although this time he entered her, and she made an effort for him, he knew that it had been no better for her than it had been before, and this time it worried him deeply. There had been a time in his life when sex was wonderful, Geoff had been born of that, and what he had now with Victoria left him feeling so lonely, and so empty. Afterwards when Victoria was asleep, he lay looking at her wondering if there was any hope for a real life between them. It remained to be seen when they got home, but he was no longer quite as optimistic.

When the ship passed the Statue of Liberty, Victoria and Charles were on deck, watching the sun come up, and it was the closest they had felt to each other in two months. They were both excited to be going home, she to see her twin, and he to see Geoff. Olivia had said they would meet them in New York. And as soon as the giant liner docked at ten o'clock, they began scouring the pier, and then Victoria let out a yell. She had seen them. They began waving frantically from the ship, and the next moment Olivia caught a glimpse of them, and she began crying as she jumped up and down, holding Geoff's hand. Her father had come too, and they had even brought the puppy with them. He was almost fully grown now.

Victoria could hardly contain herself as she hurried down to them, and it was easy to see who her first love was as she threw herself into her sister's arms, and the two girls spun around, holding each other, and laughing and crying. They were nothing more than a blur of legs and arms and smiles, and when they stopped and Charles looked at them, he realized that even after two months apart, they were still so much the same, that he could not tell them apart for a single instant. He remembered that Victoria had had on a red dress, but Olivia did too. It was the same one and they had done it without warning each other, and without plan. Olivia had simply worn it so they could see her. But Charles had to look for the ring on Victoria's hand to make sure which twin was his wife. It was eerie.

"Well, some things don't change, I guess," he said, laughing as the two girls spun around again, and hugged harder, as Olivia confessed she thought she would die without her twin sister.

"But Geoff took very good care of me," Olivia said, looking down at him proudly. He was a wonderful child, and they had had a good summer together.

"How was the honeymoon?" the girls' father asked, and Charles responded quickly.

"Marvelous. Except for the war in Europe, of course. We could have done without that at the end, but we got out very quickly."

"It looks like a terrible mess over there," Edward said, concerned, as the customs officials began going through their trunks. Their passports had already been checked on the ship that morning.

Olivia had opened the house on Fifth Avenue, and she and her father were going to stay there for a few days, to visit with the newlyweds, and in order for her father to catch up on business. But Geoff was torn about where he wanted to stay. He was aching to see his father again, but he hated to leave Olivia now. She was almost like a mother to him.

"She was so nice to me, Dad. We went riding every day, and swimming, and we had picnics. We went everywhere. She even bought me a horse," Geoff explained to Charles as he helped him load their trunks into the Ford. Their father had brought both cars, for them and their baggage, and when they got to Charles' house on the East Side, they could see Olivia's capable hand there too. She had opened the house for them, organized their maid and told her what to do. The house had been aired, the linens were all fresh, there were flowers everywhere. It didn't look like the same place. And there were small gifts for them, and some toys for Geoff waiting in his room, and a new bed for his puppy.

"Who did all this?" Charles looked stupefied as he looked around, but Victoria knew, and she wasn't entirely sure she liked it. This was her home now, and it was up to her what she wanted to do. She didn't want Olivia making her look bad, starting them off on the wrong foot, showing off all her domestic skills. Victoria had no intention of following in her footsteps.

"Olivia did, I'm sure," Victoria said quietly.

"Well, do have her come and visit more often," Charles said gratefully, with a playful look in his wife's direction.

"I don't do things this way, Charles. I do other things. We're very different."

"You wouldn't know it to look at you," he said jokingly. And when they went downstairs again, he illustrated the point without meaning to, by kissing his wife's cheek respectfully and thanking her for all that she'd done for their homecoming. He had thought she was Olivia, and they all laughed, as Victoria chuckled.

The maid had made lemonade for them, as Olivia had asked her to, and the men sat in the living room and discussed the war, and Geoff went out to the garden with his puppy. Olivia went upstairs with her twin to help her unpack, and there Victoria finally relaxed, and sat down with a smile as she stared at her sister.

"I never thought I could do it . . . leave you like that . . . it was terrible."

"I don't believe you." Olivia smiled, but it had been agony for her too. Every hour apart had seemed like a lifetime. "Did you have a wonderful time?" Olivia asked hesitantly. She didn't want to intrude, but she needed to know that her sister was happy. Victoria looked at her for a long time before she answered, and when she spoke, Olivia was shocked by her answer.

She spoke very softly so no one else could hear her. "I'm not sure I can do this, Ollie. I don't know. I'll try for as long as I can . . . but we never should have done it. I think he knows it too, and he wants to make the best of it. But it's so wrong . . . he's still in love with her . . . and I can't seem to forget Toby, neither the good, nor the bad of him. He constantly comes between us."

"You can't let a man like that ruin your marriage, Victoria." Her sister looked horrified, as she sat down next to her and took her hands in her own. "You have to put him out of your mind completely."

"And Susan? He's still in love with her. And Ollie," she looked sad but not heartbroken over what she was saying to her sister. "He's not in love with me. He never was, he never will be. All that nonsense about people growing to love each other is just that. How do you come to love a stranger?"

"You'll get used to each other. Give it time. And Geoffrey will help you."

"He hates me. They both do."

387

"Stop saying that." Olivia was near tears as she listened to her. She had never expected this. She had had some vague feelings of malaise about her once or twice, but nothing like this. She'd had no idea that Victoria would come home and say anything like this to her. "Give it time. Promise me. You mustn't do anything foolish."

"I can't even begin to imagine what I'd do," Victoria said honestly, and Olivia thought she suddenly looked more grown-up and more womanly, but perhaps it was only an illusion. To the untrained observer, they looked no different. In fact, it almost seemed as though they looked more identical than ever.

"I've never felt so helpless," Victoria went on. "Ollie, what shall I do?"

"Be a good wife to him, be patient, be kind to his son. At least try what you promised him you'd do on your wedding day."

"To love, honor, and obey him? It sounds so undignified, doesn't it? There's something degrading about all that," Victoria said irreverently and lit a cigarette. This was her home now.

"How can you say something like that?" Olivia looked shocked, and then she frowned at her. She was impossible, and even though she loved her, she could easily see how she would make a difficult wife. "Will Charles mind you smoking here?" Olivia asked with a look of concern, and her sister laughed at her.

"I hope not. I live here too now." Although it didn't feel that way yet. She was living in a strange house, among strangers. It was an odd homecoming for her, and all she wanted was to go home with her father and sister. But she knew without asking that Olivia wouldn't have let her, and neither would their father. "Will you stay in New York for a few days?" she asked worriedly, and was relieved when Olivia nodded. "I don't even know where to begin," she said frantically, and Olivia smiled at her.

"I'll come every day till you get settled."

"And then what?" Victoria almost wrung her hands in anguish. Now that she had her sister to lean on again, she could let out all her feelings, and they were coming out now in a rush of terror. "What do I do after that? I don't even know how to be a wife to him. What if I can't do it?"

"You can, you're just upset." Olivia put her arm around her, and Victoria immediately felt the effect of it. It was like coming home to a mother, and she began to sob as she put her head on her sister's shoulder.

"I can't do this, Ollie . . . I know it . . . It was terrible in Europe . . ." All her sophistication and grown-up poise had suddenly vanished, and she felt like a child again in her sister's arms, no older than Geoffrey.

"Shhh . . . you can do it," Olivia said soothingly. "Be a good girl and calm down, and stop worrying. We'll do it together." Victoria blew her nose after that, and when they went downstairs again, neither man could tell which was which, and when their father spoke to Olivia finally and said it was time to go back to their house on Fifth Avenue, both girls answered and everyone laughed. It was hopeless.

"I'm going to make them wear signs when they're in this house together," Charles said good-naturedly, pleased to be home, and happy to see his son again. It seemed like the old days suddenly, with a woman in the house, and flowers everywhere. The only thing he didn't fully understand was that the woman who had put the flowers there and made the house shine for him was not the woman he was getting.

As they left, Olivia kissed Victoria and promised to return early the next day to help her settle in, and she kissed Geoff and held him close to her.

"I'm going to miss you terribly," she said softly to him. "Take good care of Chip and Henry."

"Come back soon," he said mournfully as they waved from the front step, and one by one the Dawsons went inside and closed the door behind them, as they began their life together.

Chapter 17

Olivia spent a week in New York helping Victoria unpack and settle into the house on the East River. It was a bright, happy place, but Victoria thought it was uncomfortable and longed for the familiar surroundings she had shared with her sister. She and Charles shared a large sunny room, but she thought Geoffrey was too close to them. He was just across the hall, and he was always underfoot with his cannons, and his cars, and his dog, and his balls and marbles.

"My God, doesn't he ever go anywhere, except school?" Victoria complained. He had just started back that week, but he was anxious to come home and spend time with them. He had been away from home for two months, and he was happy to be back in his own house with his own belongings. And he waited on the front steps for his father every night. Victoria felt as though she had to stand in line to see her husband.

She had absolutely no idea what they liked to eat. The first dinner she ordered for them, they both detested although they tried to be polite, but they could barely eat it. She complained to Olivia about it the next day, and Olivia gave her a list of Geoff's favorites that they had been cooking for him all summer.

"Maybe you should stay here and do it," Victoria said petulantly, but she almost meant it.

"Stop saying that," Olivia chided her, she could see that Victoria felt unsure of herself, and she didn't like being so domestic. She seemed to feel it demeaned her, which seemed more than silly to her sister.

"He doesn't know the difference between us anyway, so why not switch with me for a while?" Victoria said jokingly, but there was something in her eyes Olivia didn't like when she said it. It was the birth of an idea that wasn't going anywhere, but Victoria didn't mention it again, which relieved her sister. And by the end of the week, things seemed to be going a little more smoothly.

Charles was in a fine mood, the dinners had been good, he was getting his work under control at the office again, and he had already started some new business for his father-in-law that week, and Geoff was behaving nicely. The only thing Victoria didn't like was that the business of running the house seemed to eat up her entire day, and she never got time to do anything else.

"Just do it for a week or two," Olivia suggested to her, "and when you get it under control, you can do other things you want to do as well, like shopping, or lunch with friends," or meetings, or demonstrations, or rallies. There were some informational meetings Victoria had read about at the press club too, and she wanted to go to those as soon as possible, to learn more about the war in Europe. Victoria devoured the news, but there was never enough information to help her understand all the complexities of what had happened. And by the time Charles came home from the office at night, he was too tired to tell her.

Olivia went back to Croton with their father finally. She had stayed as long as she could to help, and eventually he complained that he was tired and wanted to go home, so she had to take him. But she promised to come back soon, and Victoria and Charles said they would come to Croton in a few weeks for the weekend. But things piled up on them, as they always did in busy lives, Charles found he had a trial to prepare, Geoff was busy at school, and Victoria got engrossed in her meetings. She called Olivia once or twice, and they both wrote to each other almost daily, but it was late September by then, and the face of the world had already changed, not to mention their own lives.

Japan had declared war on Austria and Germany at the end of August. The Battle of the Marne had ended the German advance into France, but the Germans had begun air strikes on Paris. The Russians had suffered major defeats at the Masurian Lakes, and again in Prussia. Victoria could hardly keep up with it, but she was trying. In fact, the war was almost beginning to obscure her interest in women's suffrage. Somehow, for the moment, this seemed so much more pressing. So much so that she was almost never at home anymore. She had followed Olivia's advice for the first few weeks, running Charles' house for him, and then she had drifted back to her old ways, and spent all her time pursuing her own interests.

There were several very interesting lecturers speaking about politics these days, and Victoria went wherever she could to learn more about it. It made her far more interesting to talk to when Charles came home at night, when he had the energy to talk to her about the subjects she was interested in, which wasn't often. But what concerned Charles was that, once Olivia was gone, Victoria seemed to have no idea what the responsibilities of married life were. Without Olivia prompting her, or doing all her chores for her, Victoria left everything unattended. And within days, the house was uncared for, the place looked a mess, the garden was a shambles, and Charles had heard from their neighbors that Geoff was spending all his time playing in the streets because Victoria was never home to watch him.

"This was not our agreement," he reminded her, and she tried to listen to him, and do what was expected of her, but somehow she just couldn't do it. And the private situation between them had only worsened since they got home. They never made love at all anymore. She had an obvious aversion to it, and she seemed to be terrified that Geoff would hear them. Charles was drinking more than he had before they left, and she smoked constantly, and the smell of it drove him crazy. It was everything Charles didn't want in a house, a wife, or a marriage.

And when Olivia came back to visit them again six weeks after she had left, she found Victoria in a total state, and her husband in a worse one. Olivia had had a feeling of vague malaise before she came, and didn't know why. But she had been drawn to New York like a magnet. She was staying at a hotel, and when she visited them, the two of them barely appeared to be speaking.

Olivia took Geoff to the hotel to stay with her for a few days, with Henry, and the dog, and she suggested to her sister, in the strongest terms possible, that she do whatever she had to to make amends with her husband.

But when Olivia saw them again the next day, matters only seemed to have worsened.

"What's going on? What are you doing here?" Olivia ranted at her, and Victoria looked almost as angry as she did.

"This isn't a marriage, Olivia. It's an 'arrangement.' That's all it is, and all it ever was. He hired me to be the maid, the housekeeper, and a governess for Geoff. That's all I do here."

"That's ridiculous," Olivia argued with

her, as she paced around the sunny living room, scolding her "younger" sister. They were exactly the same age, but once again Olivia was far more responsible than she was. "You're behaving like a spoiled brat," she told her bluntly. "He offered you the protection of his name, and saved you from disaster with that mess you'd made, he's given you his home, his son, a very pleasant life, and you're furious that you have to run his house and see that the cook serves him a proper dinner. No, Victoria, he has not 'hired' you to be his maid. But you don't seem to be willing to be his wife either."

"You know *nothing* about it," Victoria raged at her, angry that Olivia had come so close to the truth in her accusations.

"I know how self-indulgent you can be," Olivia said to her more quietly, wanting to reach out to her and help her change it. She still missed her terribly, but not enough to want her to do something foolish, like walk out on Charles. Olivia knew how disastrous that would be, and how devastating not only for Charles, but for Geoffrey. "You have to make an effort, Victoria. You owe it to him . . . and to Geoff. Give it time, you'll get used to it. I'll help you run the house," she said, her eyes pleading with her sister not to do anything stupid.

"I don't want to run the house, his or anyone else's. I never did. This was all Father's idea, this was my punishment for what I did with Toby." But Olivia knew her real punishment had come long before, in their bathroom in Croton. This was simply an obligation she had to uphold, a life she had to become resigned to. But Victoria was like a bird thrashing about her cage, catching her wings in every corner. She could no longer fly, and she hated it. "I would rather die, Olivia, than be here," she finally said glumly as she sat down in a chair and looked miserably at her twin sister. But Olivia was not in any way amused by her performance.

"I don't ever want to hear you say that."

"I mean it. There's a war in Europe going on, men are dying by the thousands, innocent people are being killed. I would be better off doing something useful there, than wasting my life here, watching Geoffrey."

"He needs you, Victoria," Olivia said with tears in her eyes, wishing for a moment that she could change her sister. She always had some wild idea, some allegedly worthy cause that she was willing to live and die for. But she seemed to care nothing at all about her own world, and the people who needed her right on her own doorstep. "And Charles needs you too." Olivia's eyes implored her to listen, but Victoria shook her head, and walked across the room, to stare out the window at the unruly garden. She hadn't even spoken to the gardener since they'd returned from England.

"No," she turned to face her sister again, "he needs Susan and she's not here. She's never coming back. Perhaps she's lucky," Victoria said, and Olivia looked more upset than ever. Victoria had to settle down and adjust to her marriage. "We have no life at all, if you understand what I mean. We never did. It hasn't been right between us right from the first . . . I suppose he still dreams about her, and I . . . I just can't . . . after what happened with Toby." Her eyes filled with tears this time, and she bowed her head, looking completely defeated. And Olivia knew, as she looked at her, that this was most unlike her. It wasn't like Victoria to give up, or feel she couldn't do something, and it was so obvious to Olivia that with a little effort, her sister could set it all to rights again, if only that was what she wanted.

"Perhaps you need time alone with him," Olivia said softly, somewhat embarrassed by what she was saying. But this was no time to be shy with her. The situation was serious, and she knew it.

"We had two months in Europe," Victoria said hopelessly, and told her that, in all honesty, it had never worked there either.

"That was different," Olivia said, sounding like a mother now, "you scarcely knew each other. Perhaps you need some time here to get acquainted." She blushed faintly, and Victoria smiled at her. Olivia was so innocent, she had no idea about the complications of their situation, about how dismal it was to lie in his arms, and shudder every time he touched her, about what he expected of her, and she couldn't give, nor about what he could no longer do in the face of her scarcely concealed revulsion. "This house is new to you, so is he. Perhaps if you had a little time alone here, maybe without Geoff, you might grow more comfortable with each other."

"Maybe," Victoria said, unconvinced. But it didn't change any of the things she felt about him, the fact that she had felt forced to marry him, and that she sensed how lonely he was for his wife, and that although he desired her flesh, he really didn't love Victoria at all, in fact he loved no one. He was holding everything back from her, and she knew it. At least Toby had lied to her, he had made her feel she was adored, he had made her believe him. She had never doubted for a moment that he loved her. In Charles' case, no matter how considerate and polite he was to her or how well bred, she knew to the depths of her soul that he didn't. "It's all wrong, Olivia. Trust me. I know it."

"You can't say that yet. You've only been married to him for three months, and you scarcely knew him before that."

"And in a year, when I tell you the same thing? What will you say then?" Victoria asked her sister, her own eyes looked wise beyond their years and said that she already knew the outcome. They may have to spend a life at each other's side, but Victoria knew as sure as she breathed that they would never come to love each other. "Will you tell me then that I can divorce him?" They both knew that their father would never hear of it, and even Olivia looked shocked at the thought. But Victoria knew that she could not endure this forever. "I won't stay here till I rot, Olivia. I can't. It will kill me."

"You *have* to," Olivia said fiercely. "At least for long enough to truly know your heart, and his. You cannot make any decision now. It's way too early." In time, if she was truly miserable, perhaps she could come back to

Croton to live, and not divorce. But Olivia knew that that would destroy her too. Victoria needed so much more in her life, she needed ideas and politics and new horizons to look toward. She was not content to sit at home, and mend their father's socks as she did. But there was a part of her that almost hoped she would come home, so they could be together again. But a more generous side of Olivia truly wanted her to stay with Charles and be happy. "Why don't I take Geoff with me for a few days. He can miss a day or two of school, and I can take him up to Croton. It will give the two of you some time alone. It might do wonders."

"You're a dreamer, Ollie," Victoria said, knowing her twin didn't fully understand the hopelessness of the situation. Victoria already knew in her heart where her marriage was going. But she had to admit that it would be a relief to get rid of the boy for a few days. It wasn't that she hated him, as he had said, it was just that she didn't want to care for him, or worry about him, or pick up his toys, or chase the dog out of her bedroom. She didn't want to be responsible for another human being. She'd had no idea before that it would be as time-consuming as it was, or as annoying. "Maybe you could take Geoff with you for a day or two." At least then she could stay at her meetings. "I suppose if he were mine," she said thoughtfully, "it might be different. But he's not, and I just can't imagine what it would be like, having children." It was yet another thought that held no appeal for her. Although she had been forced into marriage, she had been adamant with Charles that there would be no children. And as Olivia listened to her, she was surprised to realize that she couldn't have loved Geoff more herself, if he had been her child, which she had often wished he were since she'd met him. He was going to replace, in her heart and mind, the children she would never have now.

"I'd be happy to take him back to Croton with me," she said calmly. "But I want you to spend some time with Charles, and not just meet with your suffragettes in old churches and dark hallways."

"You make it sound so sordid," Victoria laughed at her, but she was pleased to be relieved of Geoffrey for a few days. "I promise you, it's not. You'd see for yourself, if you ever came with me. But lately, I've been busy anyway, learning about the war in Europe."

"I suggest you learn about your husband

instead," Olivia said sternly and Victoria came to put her arms around her and kiss her.

"You always rescue me," she said, sounding like a little girl again as Olivia held her. Olivia missed her so terribly, particularly at night, lying in their too big bed, and now she didn't even have Geoff to keep her company, with his puppy.

"I'm not sure I can rescue you this time," Olivia said honestly. "You're going to have to work on this yourself."

"You know, it would be so much easier if we just switched," Victoria said, sounding flip, but Olivia did not look pleased. One did not "switch" in a marriage.

"Would it? How well would you like staying in Croton and caring for Father?" Victoria had had a taste of a bigger world now, and Olivia knew she wouldn't be satisfied in Croton either. Victoria hungered for far more than that. Olivia just hoped that Charles could give it to her. Perhaps if she did have children of her own, and settled down, it might solve the problem.

Olivia picked Geoff up at school that afternoon, with his suitcase, and his dog, and his tattered monkey in the car, and he was delighted to hear that they were going to Croton.

He was excited about being able to ride his horse again, and being with Olivia, and seeing her father whom he now called "Grampa."

But Charles was even more surprised when he came home and found the boy had gone to Croton. "What about school?" he asked Victoria, with a vague look of consternation.

"He can miss a few days. He's only ten years old, after all." She brushed it off. She'd had a very interesting afternoon, at a lecture about the Battle of Brussels in August. Olivia would have been less than pleased if she'd known it.

"You might have asked me," he said, looking tired and annoyed, but peripherally aware that he was alone with Victoria, and she was looking very lovely. Her eyes were excited and alive, and her exceptional figure was set off by a new dress her sister had brought her. It was long and sleek and black, and the latest style in Paris.

"I thought I was supposed to be his mother," Victoria snapped at Charles. He didn't like the way she spoke to him, but the fire in her eyes only made her more alluring.

"You are, but I'm older and wiser than you are," he said a little more gently. "It's all right. It'll do him good to be in the country for a few days. It might do us good as well, perhaps we should go up too this weekend." She didn't like Croton much, but she always loved visiting her sister.

But on the other hand, if they went to Croton now, it would defeat the whole purpose of Olivia taking Geoffrey with her.

"Maybe another time," she said vaguely. "We could leave him here, and go up ourselves to visit with Olivia and Father."

"Without Geoff?" Charles looked surprised. "He'd never forgive us." And then he looked at her sadly. "You don't like being with him, Victoria, do you?"

"I don't know how to," she said, as she lit a cigarette, and looked across the room at her husband. It was always a strain being with him. She wished she could see in him all the virtues her sister did. For Victoria, even now, it was like being with a stranger. "I'm not used to children."

"He's such an easy child," he said, thinking of the maternal love the boy deserved, and had had so much of from Susan. It was always hard for Charles not to compare Victoria to her. But she herself had never had any mothering, except from her twin. It had always been

Olivia who nurtured her, and Victoria who was treated like the baby. "I wish you two would get to know each other better." He had meant for the three of them to spend a summer together in Newport, and instead Victoria had insisted on a two-month honeymoon in Europe.

"Olivia says the same thing about us." His wife smiled at him through her cigarette smoke.

"Were you complaining to her?" he asked, somewhat unhappily. He liked keeping his family affairs private, but he had long since suspected that between the twins there were no secrets. And in the light of the awkwardness they still shared privately, he did not find that a comforting prospect. "Is that why she took Geoff away? To leave us together?"

"I just said I was having trouble getting used to all this," she said vaguely, but he knew from the look in her eyes that she had most probably told all to her sister.

"I wish you wouldn't discuss private matters with her, Victoria," he said, approaching her from across the room with a cautious frown, "it's somewhat indelicate." Victoria nodded, and said nothing, as the cook called them to dinner.

The hour they spent in the dining room

was somewhat strained, and after that Charles went to his study upstairs to look at some papers. Victoria was in their bedroom reading *Penrod,* and it was late when he finally came into their bedroom. He had been working very hard since they came home, and he looked tired and somewhat vulnerable when he glanced at her. She looked so sweet, sitting, reading there, and so young. It reminded him of why he'd agreed to marry her, and why at times he almost loved her. He never gave his heart full rein with her, and he felt sure he'd never do that again, but the way she looked tonight, with her long black hair cascading over her lace nightgown and her full breasts, she almost melted his defenses.

"You're up late," he said with a smile, and then went to undress, and she was still reading when he came back in his dressing gown and pajamas.

Although he hadn't with his late wife, he slept with Victoria fully clad, and nowadays he was cautious about keeping a careful distance. They had had a few more unsuccessful attempts, and she seemed to find physical contact with him at night extremely unpleasant.

When he got into bed, she put her book away dutifully and turned off the light, and they lay there for a while, side by side, awake, in silence.

"It's odd being here alone, isn't it? With Geoff gone, I mean." He always liked knowing that his son was near him. But he liked being with her too, and the thought of having the upper floors of the house to themselves had begun to arouse him. Victoria said nothing as she lay next to him. For some reason, she was thinking of her sister, and how much she missed her. She wished she were at home with her again, and not married to Charles, or worrying about Geoffrey. It was all so difficult and so tiresome, and so much harder and less bearable than she'd expected.

If she'd known what it would be like, she would never have married him, and she might have let her father send her to a convent. "What are you thinking about?" he asked in a whisper, as he lay on his side and looked at her.

"Religion," she smiled mischievously at him, embarrassed by her thoughts, and he didn't believe her.

"That is an awful lie. I'm surprised at you. It must have been something really wicked."

"It was," she said, all innocence. In some ways they were friends, in others they weren't.

He touched her cheek gently then, wishing that they'd gotten off to the right kind of start. So far it had been beyond ghastly between them, and it was painful and awkward for both of them. Particularly Victoria, who had no idea how to cope with her own feelings of recalcitrance, or his unexpected but totally understandable problem after her rejection.

"You're so beautiful," he whispered, moving slowly closer to her, as he watched her stiffen. "Victoria . . . don't . . . please . . . trust me . . ." But all she could think of as she looked at him was Toby . . . and then she could still feel the searing pain of the night she had lost his baby . . . "I don't want to hurt you."

"You don't love me," she said in words that surprised even her. She hadn't meant to say them.

"Let me learn . . . perhaps if we have this, it will bring us closer together." But it didn't work that way for her. She needed to feel close to him before they made love, in order to even want to. It was the primal difference between men and women. "We have to start loving each other somewhere . . . we have to trust each other . . ." But he was lying to her, and he knew it. He didn't trust any woman not to die and leave him. It was what he had felt for Olivia that night when she fell from her horse, she was so frail and vulnerable, and if she had died . . . He would never let himself feel that again for anyone, not even her sister. Susan had taken that part of him with her. "Let me learn to love you," he whispered, but Victoria knew instinctively that all he wanted from her was her body, and her life . . . to love, honor, and obey him. And she would obey no man, not even this one.

He made love to her that night, as gently as possible, and it wasn't quite as bad as it had been. But there were certainly no illusions about her feelings for him, or any bond that might have formed between them. There was none at all, and they both knew it. If anything, their repeated attempts, infrequent though they may have been, only seemed to drive them further apart. And even tonight, Charles realized that there was no magic between them, and they fell asleep at opposite ends of the bed in total silence.

The time Olivia had given them was spent in lectures and the library for her, and at the office for him. He had dinner at his club with John Watson and his partners the following night, and kept busy preparing for a trial all weekend. In fact, they scarcely saw each other, and never spoke when they did. They weren't angry at each other, just bereft, and unable to bridge the distance. And when Geoff came home with Donovan on Sunday night, it was actually a relief to hear voices in the house again, and for Charles to have someone to speak to.

Olivia had sent him home with some new toys, a thermos of hot chocolate for the ride, and a huge box of cookies that they had made together. It made Victoria's heart ache just to see the familiar signs so typical of her sister. He even had a handkerchief in his pocket with her perfume on it, and it brought a physical ache to her heart knowing that only hours before the boy had been with her. If anything, it made her jealous of him, and she snapped at him about why Olivia hadn't come home with him.

"She wanted to," he said, looking instantly wounded by the tone of accusation in Victoria's voice, as though he had kept Olivia away, which he hadn't. "But Grampa has a cough again, and she didn't think she should leave him. It's only bronchitis the doctor said, and not pneumonia, but we made him lots of soup, and Aunt Ollie wanted to make him some special poltergeists or something."

"Poultices," his father corrected him with

a grin, but Victoria looked bitterly disappointed. She had hoped to see her twin, and
now she had no idea when Olivia would come
again, particularly if their father wasn't well,
which seemed to be happening more and more
often.

In fact, the cough dragged on, and she
never felt right leaving him, and Olivia discouraged her from leaving Charles and coming to
Croton herself. The twins didn't see each other
again until Thanksgiving.

Their father was back on his feet again by
then, although thinner and pale, and delighted
to see the Dawsons. Victoria always felt as
though he were talking about someone else
when he said her name. She couldn't get used
to wearing a different name than her own, and
could never understand why a woman should
take a man's name just because they were married.

The weather was spectacular the whole
time they were there, and Geoff rode his horse
with Olivia every day, even on Thanksgiving
morning. She was very proud of him, he had
become quite a skilled little rider. He showed
Charles what he could do in the ring that day,
and announced that when he was bigger he was
going to play polo.

They were all in good spirits later that afternoon when they sat down to Thanksgiving dinner, except Victoria who seemed tense. She had spent most of that morning in the kitchen, talking to Bertie. There was always something soothing about being with her, and Victoria seemed to be starved for remnants of her old home life. It was all she could do to sleep in the guest room with Charles. All she wanted to do was climb into bed with Olivia and Geoffrey. But he had usurped her place. In fact, he seemed to be the object of everyone's attention, Olivia, Bertie, Charles, even her own father, and when everyone said later that night, after he had gone to bed, how good he had been, Victoria startled them all by lashing out about him.

"Oh for Heaven's sake, stop wailing about him like a bunch of old cats. He's almost eleven, and should be able to behave himself. What's so remarkable about that?" she snapped, and for a long moment there was absolute silence, and then even she looked embarrassed. "Sorry," she said, and swiftly left the table as her father stared at her, and Charles looked deeply grieved by what she had said about Geoffrey.

Olivia went to her as soon as she could,

and found her in their room, as Geoff slept peacefully in the bed, with his monkey and his dog, waiting for Olivia to join him.

"I'm sorry." Victoria looked up at her, mortified by her own performance. "I don't know what happened. I just get so tired of hearing how adorable he is." It startled Olivia to realize that her sister was jealous of him.

"You ought to apologize to Charles," Olivia said gently, sorry for both of them. They seemed to be in so much pain. Even Geoff had commented on it. He said that Victoria and his father fought every day at breakfast and every night at dinner. He didn't even seem amazed by it, he just said it like something they did, like saying grace at meals, or singing.

"I will." And then she sighed and lay her head back against the chair with a tired glance at her twin. "I suppose it will be like this forever. Angry strangers trapped in a small house with a rather irritating child, and absolutely nothing in common."

Olivia couldn't help but smile at what she had said. It sounded rather extreme to her, but that was obviously how Victoria saw it. "You certainly paint a pretty picture."

"It isn't, Ollie. Not for a minute. I have no

idea what we're doing together. And neither does he, if he's honest."

"Maybe you'd better give that some more thought," Olivia suggested, and then hand in hand, they both went back downstairs to Charles and their father. And as they walked into the room, Charles looked straight into Olivia's eyes and smiled ruefully at her. The directness of his gaze almost made her heart ache.

"Feeling better?" he asked when she stood closer to him.

"I . . . yes . . ." She didn't know what to say, and Victoria laughed at the confusion.

"She's feeling fine. I'm the dreadful one you're married to. And I apologize for my bad behavior." His confusing them had served to lighten the moment, and Olivia blushed, realizing what had happened. They had worn the same dress, as usual, and had done their hair exactly the same.

It was still far too easy to confuse them, and the newly characteristic sullenness of his wife, which would have identified her easily, disappeared the moment she was near her sister.

Everyone was in a better mood after that, and they all had a pleasant weekend. But Victoria looked particularly bleak when it was time to go home again. She had spent hours talking to her father about the Battle of Ypres in France, and it had been so comfortable being there with him and Ollie. She hated to go home now and leave them.

She and Charles got in the front of the Packard and Geoff in back with Chip, and Henry the monkey, and all their bags, and for a long moment Olivia stood looking at them, wishing that she could keep them there forever.

"Be a good girl," she whispered to her twin. "Or I shall come to town to beat you."

"Promise me you'll do that." Victoria smiled at her, looking so sad again, wishing she'd come with them. Every time they left each other, she felt a little part of her die, and so did Ollie. And as Charles watched them silently, he could see the bond between them that always fascinated him, it was a bond which he knew he would never have with her, if they lived a hundred years together. A bond no one else would ever have, with either of them. It was something that had formed between them long before birth, and would go on long after. They were made of one cloth, like two dresses made of one bolt of fabric, with no seams, no tears, no differences. There was no place where one began and the other stopped. In his eyes sometimes, even as different as they seemed to be, or said they were, they were almost one person. And yet, the woman who rode beside him to New York had none of the gentle softness of her sister. She had all the hard edges and bright ideas of someone very interesting but very different. Like two sides of the same coin perhaps. Heads you win . . . tails you lose . . . and he knew that for the moment, he had lost the flip of the coin. Victoria was never going to be easy.

"How do I know which twin I have in the car with me?" he said playfully as they drove home, in somewhat better spirits after a very pleasant Thanksgiving, Olivia had gone all out for them. The meal itself had been extraordinary, as had all their dinners, all the wines, their room had been perfectly set up for them, and the servants had attended to their every need from the moment they arrived till the moment they left. Olivia ran a perfect household.

"You don't know which twin. That's the fun of it." Victoria played with him, and they both laughed. He was still embarrassed at having confused them on Thanksgiving night, and he had always thought it would be truly embarrassing to make a mistake like that, or a worse one. It made him especially careful what he said around the two of them, whenever they were in Croton, or at his house in New York. He would have felt like a complete fool if he'd said something indiscreet, and he didn't want to embarrass Olivia. But Victoria liked the idea of causing people embarrassment, and she told him yet another outrageous story of their switching in school when they were children.

"I don't know why you think that's so funny," Charles chided her. "I think it would be very embarrassing, and really awful. What if someone said something you didn't want to hear?" The very thought of it unnerved him.

"Olivia and I have no secrets."

"I hope that's not still true." He eyed her carefully and she shrugged with a smile, and then Geoff piped up from the back and told his father all about his horse, and a horse show the following summer Olivia had said he could ride in.

The weeks after Thanksgiving fairly flew, with preparations for Christmas, and buying presents and making things, and a number of parties they went to. It was somewhat embarrassing when they went to a Christmas party at the Astors' and Toby and his wife were there, but with the exception of a few minutes alone in the garden with him, Victoria seemed to avoid him completely.

Toby had tried to speak to her, and she had been quietly smoking a cigarette when she turned and saw him. She began immediately walking away from him, but he grabbed her arm and pulled her back to him. And just his touch sent a long, slow thrill through her.

"Toby, don't . . . please . . ." Her eyes filled with tears and implored him. Without even knowing it, he had already ruined her marriage.

"I just want to talk to you . . ." He was more handsome than ever, and she could see that he'd been drinking. "Why did you marry him?" he asked, looking hurt, and she wanted to scream at the top of her lungs and hit him. It was all his fault, if he hadn't said anything, everything might have been different.

"You left me no choice," she said, trying to sound cold to him, but feeling things she hadn't felt in a year and didn't want to.

"What does that mean? You weren't . . ." He looked confused. He hadn't heard anything about a baby, and he knew she hadn't gotten married for several months afterwards . . . it was just too bad the way things happened . . . it had been fun . . . for him . . .

"You told everyone I'd seduced you," she said, looking hurt, and feeling the pain of it again as she looked into his eyes, wanting to hate him.

"That was just a joke."

"Not a very good one." She shrugged, and pulled away from him, and walked back into the living room where she saw Charles waiting for her. And he looked startled when he saw Toby walk in after her, but he asked her no questions on the ride home. He didn't want to know. And she had nothing to tell him. The joke had been on her. And now she had to live with what Toby had done to her soul and her reputation.

But Victoria had been surprised when she heard from Toby again. He had sent her flowers the day after he'd seen her at the Astors' party. Anonymously, of course, but she had known they were from him. Two dozen long-stemmed red roses. There was no one else in her life who could possibly have sent them. And despite the physical sensations she still seemed to feel for him, she had taken the roses and thrown them in the garbage. He had sent her a note after that, signed only T. and asking her to meet with him, and she hadn't answered that either. Whatever she still felt for him, she had no desire to resume her affair with him. Whatever it had been then, it was very definitely over.

As usual, she and Charles went their separate ways, and nothing was ever said of her running into Toby. And all of them were in high spirits when they left for Croton for Christmas. They packed their car with gifts and food and Victoria remembered her gift for Geoff. She had bought a complicated game for him, which the woman in the shop had assured her would be just what a ten-year-old boy would want for Christmas.

Victoria and Charles talked about the war almost all the way to Croton. Other than women's suffrage, it had become her greatest fascination, and she was extremely knowledgeable, which impressed Charles, but he did not enjoy talking about it as much as she did. By then, the Western Front, in Europe, had solidified into a four-hundred-mile trench from the North Sea to the Swiss Alps with the French, British, and Belgians fighting the Germans.

"We'll never get into it, Victoria, and it's profitable for us," he said practically. The Americans were selling munitions and guns to anyone who would buy them.

"I think that's disgusting," she said heatedly, "we might as well go over and kill people ourselves. Instead of staying home hypocritically and pretending to keep our hands clean."

"Don't be such a purist, for Heaven's sake," he said, surprised at how naive she was. "How do you think fortunes are made? What do you think your father's steel mill did?"

"It makes me sick to think about it," she said, looking out the window, thinking of the men spending Christmas in the trenches in Europe. It seemed wrong to even celebrate, knowing what the Germans were doing to them, but no one else here seemed to understand that. "Thank God he sold it," she said quietly, sad that Charles didn't share any of her passions. He was far more practical and down-to-earth, concerned with his legal work, and always worried about Geoffrey.

When they got to Croton, Victoria found that their father was sick again, and this time the cold he'd caught two weeks before had already turned to pneumonia. He looked weak and thin, and he only came down briefly on Christmas morning. They were opening their gifts, and he gave both his daughters identical, and very handsome, diamond necklaces. They were both thrilled, and they both put them on over identical dressing gowns, as Charles said, to confuse everyone further. He said he was afraid to give the right woman the wrong gift, or vice versa. But he gave his wife a lovely stomacher and a pair of diamond earrings, which went perfectly with the necklace from their father. And with a chaste kiss on the cheek, he gave Olivia a warm scarf and a book of poetry. Victoria was startled to notice afterwards that the book had been Susan's.

"Why would he give that to you?" Victoria looked puzzled.

"Maybe it upset him to keep it. And you hate poetry, he couldn't give it to you, could he?" She smiled, feeling faintly awkward. But it was a book she knew and loved, and she had been touched by his inscription. He had known exactly what she would like. Apparently, it had been a favorite of Susan's.

But the real fireworks came when Olivia gave Geoffrey two small guns and an antique cannon and a whole army of little soldiers. Their uniforms were actually accurate, and there were French and German ones, and British and Australian. She had ordered them months before, and he was ecstatic, as Victoria stared at her sister in outrage.

"How *could* you give him something like

that?" she said, far too loud for Christmas morning. But she was literally shaking. "How could you give him something so revolting? Why not cover them all in blood, for Heaven's sake? It would be far more honest, if you did that." There were tears in her eyes, and she was genuinely upset over her sister's gift. And it made matters even worse when it was obvious he found Victoria's complicated game impossible to understand and very boring.

"I had no idea you'd object . . ." Olivia looked crestfallen. "They're just toys, Victoria. And he likes them. He loves playing soldier."

"I don't know or care what he likes. There are men dying by the thousands out there, in trenches all over Europe. It's not a game, it's not fun. They're men that people love . . . and you're making little toys of them. I can't bear it." She turned away with tears in her eyes, and Geoffrey asked his father in a worried whisper if he had to give them back to Aunt Ollie. Charles shook his head reassuringly and a little while later, he and Victoria dressed and went for a walk to the place where her mother was buried.

"I don't think you should have been quite so upset," he said gently. "Your sister didn't mean any harm. I don't think she understood the violence of your feelings." Neither did he for that matter. In fact, he understood almost nothing about her, and they both knew it.

"I can't do this anymore," she said, looking at him miserably. "I can't be your wife. I'm not cut out for this, Charles. Everyone can see it but you. Even Geoff knows." She felt awful about the gift, and even about the book he had given her sister. It wasn't that she was jealous of her, it was just that she felt she was in the wrong shoes, constantly, and she was tired of it. "It was wrong of me to let Father push me into getting married. I should have let him send me away somewhere, and forget about me. I just can't do this," she started to sob, and he looked extremely unhappy, and then he decided to ask her what he had wondered ever since the party at the Astors'.

"Are you seeing him again? Is that it?" he asked bleakly as she stared at him, wondering how he knew Toby had even tried to get back into her life. It might have been simpler if she had let him, but she didn't want that now either.

"No, that's not it," she said coldly. "Is that what you think? That I'm cheating on you? I wish I were, it might be more entertaining." But she was sorry for saying that too. She was sorry for everything, but she just couldn't do it. And he didn't say anything to her as they stood there, next to her mother's grave, as Victoria cried and he felt totally helpless.

"I don't know what to say." He was sorry he had mentioned Toby, but he had wondered when the cook had told him about the roses she had thrown away. She thought it was a shocking waste, couldn't imagine who had done it, and wanted to tell him about it before someone else did. She had even rescued the card which said only "Please see me." But that had told him everything, or so he thought. But apparently, he'd been wrong. Not that that changed any of what Victoria was saying.

"Do you want me to leave?" She turned and looked at him in despair, and this time he came and put an arm around her.

"Of course not. I want you to stay. We'll work it out. It's only been six months. They say the first year is the hardest in any marriage." But it hadn't been that way for him before. The first year with Susan had been idyllic. "I'll try and be more reasonable, and you try and be more patient. What do you want to do about Geoffrey and his little army? I don't think he's anxious to give it up, but if you want me to, I'll discuss it with him."

"No." She blew her nose in his handkerchief and wished she had a cigarette. "He'd hate me for it, more than he already does. That was such a stupid game I bought him. I don't know what he likes, and the woman in the store said he'd love it. I can't even understand it."

"Neither can I," he laughed, "but I'll learn. I can learn anything," he said gently, "if you teach me." But she didn't want to teach him anything. She wanted to run away. That was all she could think of.

They walked slowly back to the house eventually, and they both seemed considerably calmer, but that afternoon she went to find Olivia who was sorting through some linens with Bertie.

"I'm sorry about the guns," Olivia said, looking genuinely remorseful as Bertie left them. "I had no idea they would upset you so much." They were wearing identical green dresses, and each of them had on identical emerald earrings. They both loved being together again, and they exchanged a silent smile that spoke volumes.

"It's all right. Maybe I'm just stupid. I've gotten all involved in what's happening over there, and it's so real to me. At times I forget that we're not part of it. I'm glad Father sold the steel mill at least, though I'll bet he's not. I'd probably be demonstrating outside and getting arrested." They both laughed at her honesty, and Victoria sat down in a chair next to her sister. And Olivia could see immediately, even before she spoke, that her twin wanted something. It took a minute, but then Victoria looked up at her mournfully and spoke in a conspiratorial whisper. "You've got to get me out of this, Ollie. For a little while at least. Before it drives me completely crazy. I just can't do this."

Olivia looked at her uncomfortably, worried about what she was going to ask her, but she could already see it coming, and she didn't want to hear it. "Should I say no before you ask, or let you ask and then tell you I don't want to hear it?"

Victoria lowered her voice still further. "Ollie . . . switch with me, please . . . just for a while . . . let me go somewhere, please, just to think . . . I don't know what I'm doing." Her eyes begged her twin to listen to her, and Olivia could see easily the pain she was in, but she was certain that switching was not the answer. Victoria just had to face it. She had made an arrangement, Charles was a good man, and she just had to adjust to it. Running away was not going to make anything better. But Olivia shook her head as she listened.

"You're right, you don't know what you're doing," she said in a whisper. "Switching would be disastrous. What if he found out? What am I supposed to do? I can't pretend to be his wife. He would know in five minutes. And even if he didn't, it's the wrong thing to do. Victoria, I won't do it," she said, and Victoria knew she meant it. Tears filled her eyes and she grabbed her sister's hand and begged her.

"I know it's wrong. But it was wrong when we cheated in school, and it was just as wrong whenever you lied for me, and pretended you were me and you weren't. We've done it a thousand times. And I swear, he'll never know . . . he can't tell us apart and you know it."

"He'll figure it out eventually. Or Geoff will. Besides, I won't even discuss this with you. *No!* Do you hear me?" She wasn't really angry at her, but she wanted to be sure that Victoria knew it wasn't an option. But Victoria didn't even argue about it, she just nodded and got up, and looked at Olivia in despair, which made it even worse. And then she walked slowly away from her sister.

Chapter 18

They didn't discuss switching again during her stay, but Victoria seemed unusually subdued when they left. And Olivia was worried about her. She wanted to go to the city to see how she was in a week or two, but their father took a turn for the worse again, and the pneumonia returned with a vengeance. It was a narrow scrape for him, and then Olivia came down with a nasty case of influenza. In the end, it was late February before Olivia was able to get back to the city. And nothing had changed between them. If anything, Victoria seemed a little more brittle about things. She seemed to snap at everyone more easily. And Charles looked even worse than she did. And on

Olivia's second day there, Geoff began running a fever.

Victoria was out when Olivia discovered it, and by late that afternoon, he was almost delirious and Olivia had called the doctor. She called Charles at work too, and he came straight home to see him.

"Where is she?" he asked about Victoria, and Olivia had to admit to him that she had no idea, though she hated to do it. And by then, spots had begun to appear, and he had a ghastly cough. The doctor said it was a bad case of the measles.

Victoria came home at seven o'clock that night, after a particularly interesting lecture at the British Consulate about the viciousness of German U-boats. They had just formed a blockade of Britain. There had been a high tea afterwards and Victoria had gotten drawn into lengthy discussions. She hadn't even thought of calling Charles and telling him she'd be late for dinner. She was hoping he'd be home late too, but bad luck for her he'd been home all afternoon with Geoffrey.

Olivia was quietly sponging the child's brow when she came in, and there was a hush in the house that only happens in the event of death or severe illness.

434

"What happened to him?" Victoria whispered to her from the doorway when she saw him, and Olivia tiptoed over to her, looking like her own image approaching in the mirror.

"He's got measles. Poor kid. He's really very sick. I wish I had him in Croton. I was thinking about sending for Bertie. He's going to be down for a couple of weeks, and he'll probably feel just awful. I can stay if you'd like." She glanced at Victoria, but she already knew the answer.

"Oh God . . . please . . . how's Charles?" She wanted to know if he was angry.

"I think he was worried about you." It was a polite way of saying that he was furious she was late, and suspicious of where she had gone, but he said it all to her that night, in their bedroom.

"And where did you say you were?" he asked nastily for the second time. The kind of tone he had taken with her was most unlike him.

"I told you. The British Consulate. At a talk about U-boats."

"How fascinating. My son has a fever of a hundred and five, and you're learning about U-boats. Fantastic."

"I'm not clairvoyant, Charles. I didn't

know he'd get sick today," she said calmly. More calmly than she felt. In the past eight months, they had become experts at fighting. Better undoubtedly than the captains of the U-boats, and surely just as deadly.

"You're supposed to be here for him," he shouted at her. "I'm not supposed to have to come from the office because no one can find his mother."

"His mother is dead, Charles. I'm just standing in," she said coldly.

"And not very well, I might add. Your sister pays more attention to him than you do."

"Then you should have married her. She'd make a much better wife. She has far better domestic skills than I do."

"Your father didn't offer her. He offered you," he said unhappily, hating himself for the kind of things he said to her. But their life together had been such a disappointment to both of them, and neither of them knew what to do about it. There was no way out. They just had to live with each other till it killed them. She had already mentioned divorce to him, but to Charles that was out of the question.

"Perhaps if you go back to Father he'll be willing to exchange us for each other. Like shoes that don't fit. Why don't you ask him?"

she snarled at him, feeling every bit as trapped as he did. And the fact that they had no physical relationship whatsoever anymore had virtually ended whatever they might have had between them. Their last futile attempt at making love had been in January, and they had each silently vowed never to try it again, and they hadn't. It was too disappointing, and much too depressing. It was just a mirror for all their ills, and all that had never been and never could be. Charles was determined never to lay a hand on her again, even if it meant being abstinent for the rest of his life. It just wasn't worth it. And Victoria felt the same. She had no desire at all to continue frustrating him and herself for no purpose.

"I don't find your suggestions amusing," he said to his wife darkly. "Or your behavior. And I expect to see you here every day, with our son . . . my son, if you prefer it that way . . . with your hand on his brow, or spooning broth into him until he recovers. Is that quite clear?"

"Yes, sir," she said, curtseying to him like a maid in a French farce on Broadway. And then, more seriously. "Do you mind if my sister stays to help me?"

"To take care of him for you, you mean,"

he said viciously but with truth, as Victoria knew. She had no idea how to care for sick children. "I don't care which one of you takes care of him. I can't tell the difference between you anyway," he said, looking distraught, "just so one of you does it."

"I'll take care of it," she said, and left the room to find her sister. She wished that she could sleep with her that night, but she knew that would enrage Charles even further. Although he had no intention of laying a hand on her, he didn't like other people knowing their business, especially her sister.

"How is he?" Olivia asked quietly about Charles, from the foot of Geoffrey's bed. He was sleeping, and the fever had not yet broken.

"Not pleased, to say the least." Victoria smiled at her. Even under these circumstances, it was good to be together. It was such a relief to be with her, to be able to talk to her, even to confide in her, as much as she dared to. It was actually embarrassing to admit to her how far their marriage had deteriorated, but she could sense that Olivia knew anyway, and she had heard him shouting.

In the end they were together for nearly a month, in the little house on the East River. Geoffrey was sick for three weeks, and Olivia never left him alone for a moment. Charles was aware of it, though he was under the impression that Victoria had done at least some of the nursing. He had seen her sitting by his bedside at times, and he was relieved to see that. What he didn't know was that it had always been Olivia, and she had let him think it was her sister. It was the only deception she would allow. But at least Victoria hadn't asked her to switch again, as she had over Christmas, and Olivia was relieved to think that she had come to her senses about it.

Relations between them did appear to be strained, but Olivia was still convinced that, with time, and love on both sides, they would make it. Maybe even if there was a child, Victoria hadn't told her that there was no chance of it, and never would be.

She also didn't tell her sister that Charles had recently repeated his accusation that she was seeing Toby. He found it hard to believe that a woman who had so far forgotten herself before, and been willing to risk so much for a man, would be willing to give it all up now, and live the life of a nun. Particularly since he never knew where she was, or where she was going. Her activities were all harmless actually, but she thought it was none of his business what she did, and particularly with the kind of people she had been meeting lately. She had met a general at the French Embassy, and several colonels at the British Club who had impressed on her how great the need was for people to come to Europe and do anything they could to help the people who were dying there. Their pleas had haunted her. But she didn't say anything about it to Olivia either.

When she finally went home again at the end of March, Olivia was absolutely exhausted. It was a strain being with them, in that small house, and nursing Geoffrey had taken all of her energy and attention. It was a relief to get out in the fresh air again, and ride her horse. And even as much as she loved her, it was a relief not to see her sister, or her family until Easter. They came to Croton then, and they were all more subdued this year. Victoria and Charles felt as though they'd been at war for ten months, and Geoffrey was still a little worn-out after the measles. But Olivia had nursed him well and he had made a complete recovery. Two little girls in his class had died in the epidemic.

Olivia was particularly grateful that he had done so well when she heard about them. And Charles had made a point of thanking her one afternoon as they walked the grounds, and her heart went out to him, as they looked out over the Hudson River in silence. She sensed a vast sorrow in him. He knew what he had done. He had once had love, and he had settled for something less in a foolish moment. He had thought he was doing it for his son, but in truth he had been protecting himself too from future pain, and he had been wrong to do it.

He looked down at Olivia for a long moment, and said nothing to her, and then they turned around and went back to the house. She tucked a hand into his arm, and just feeling her empathy for him stirred him, and he gently pulled away from her. It was painful being close to anyone now, particularly his wife's far more compassionate sister. He didn't want to be reminded of what was missing in his marriage. And although it hurt her when he pulled away, Olivia instinctively understood that.

Olivia was beginning to think that her sister had resigned herself to her fate too, when she suddenly slipped into their old room the day before they left and looked long and hard at her sister.

"I have to talk to you," Victoria said, looking tense, and for a mad moment Olivia hoped she was going to tell her she was pregnant. It might be the answer to everything, a bond which would finally join them. But she was not prepared for what Victoria said to her instead. She stood very close to her, looked into her eyes, and touched Olivia's face with her fingers.

"I'm leaving."

"What?"

"You heard me. Olivia, I have to. I can't bear it for a moment longer."

"But you can't do that to them. How can you be so selfish?" She hadn't even thought of herself yet, and what it meant to her if Victoria went, all she could think of now were Charles and Geoffrey.

"It'll kill me if I stay, I'm absolutely sure of it, Ollie." She paced the room then, glancing occasionally at her sister, and then she stopped and looked at her. "Switch with me, please. I will go either way . . . but at least then, you'll be there for them, if you're so worried about them."

"But where will you go?" Olivia was horrified by what she was hearing.

"Europe," she said confidently. "France, I think. I can work behind the lines. I can drive an ambulance if I have to, I'm a pretty good driver."

442

"Tell that to Father," Olivia said through tears, "and your French is terrible. I took all your exams for you," she said, starting to cry openly at the thought of losing her sister.

"I'll learn . . . oh Ollie, don't cry, please . . . just do this for me. One last time. Three months. That's all I want. I'll sail in three weeks, and I'll come back by the end of summer. I have to do this. All my life I've been reading about things, going to meetings, caring about causes, I've always been on the sidelines, I've never done anything important. I've never done anything for anyone . . . not like you, you do it in small ways, but you make a difference. I've done nothing." She sounded so determined that it frightened her sister. Olivia realized again that they were, in fact, very different.

"Stay here, and you can fold linens for me. You don't have to go anywhere. You can help me replant the garden . . . oh Victoria," she sobbed, "don't go . . . please . . . what if something happens to you?" She couldn't bear the thought of it, of losing her for a day or an hour, let alone forever. It was hard enough getting used to her living in New York, but at least it was only an hour away. And it took all of Olivia's self-control constantly not to be there with her.

"Nothing will happen to me, I swear." The two sisters held each other close in the room they had slept in together for twenty years until Victoria's wedding, and now without her, even the room seemed too empty. "I can't live like this anymore. We're all wrong for each other. We'll have to leave each other eventually, or maybe after I go away, things will be different."

"Why don't you tell him that," Olivia said sensibly, blowing her nose in her handkerchief, "why don't you explain it to him. He's an intelligent man, he might understand it."

"He'll never let me go," Victoria said with certainty, and Olivia couldn't honestly tell her she disagreed with her.

"And if I take your place?" Olivia looked at her pensively. "Then they'll think I've gone?" Olivia suddenly looked startled. It was so unlike her.

"We could say you've gone to California for a few months, just to think, because it's so hard for you without me."

"Everyone will think I'm a monster leaving Father. So do I. So will he," she said, shaking her head again. She just couldn't do it. But Victoria had actually made her think about it.

"I think Father would understand," Victoria said hopefully, amazed that the conversation had gone this far, and suddenly very excited. And then Olivia looked at her and shook her head. She had thought of something else. It was impossible. She was not going to do that for her sister. But Victoria already knew what she was thinking. "He won't touch you. There's nothing between us anymore. Not in months. And there won't be again. Neither of us want it." Olivia was shocked to hear it. All this time, she had been hoping there would be a baby.

"Why?" He seemed so vital and so alive and so warm, and he was still so young. She couldn't understand it, and wondered suddenly if it was her sister who had ordained it.

"I don't know why," Victoria said thoughtfully, "too many ghosts . . . Susan . . . Toby . . . something's wrong between us, we both knew it. I think it's just that we don't love each other."

"I don't believe that," Olivia said firmly.

"It's true," Victoria said, looking hard at her, "we don't. I don't love him, Ollie. I don't think I ever will. It's not there and it never will be."

"And when you come back? What will be different then?"

"Maybe I'll have the courage to really leave him." Olivia was devastated to hear it.

"And if I don't switch for you?"

"I'll leave anyway. I won't tell him where I've gone, I don't want him to find me. I'll come back when I'm ready. I'll write to you, at the house on Fifth Avenue. You can pick the letters up there easily and no one will know." She had given it a great deal of thought and Olivia was even more shocked as she listened. The biggest stumbling block for her was their father. She was afraid she'd break his heart, and yet the tie between the twins was stronger than the tie to him, and even she knew it. She always felt pulled by everything her sister wanted. And yet, this was utter madness and she knew it. She couldn't take her place with a husband and a child, it was an insane thing to do, and then she thought of Geoffrey.

"He would know, Victoria. He's the only one we can't fool, except for Bertie."

"You can if you want to, if you act more like me. Don't be so nice to him," she grinned, and Olivia wagged a finger at her.

"Shame on you. How can you say that?"

"Because I'm awful and I love you . . .

all right, I'll be nicer to him for the next three weeks, and to Charles, and then it won't be such a big change for them when you take my place. I'll stop smoking entirely . . . oh God, what a thought . . ." she grinned, "and I'll only have a little sherry, and only when Charles offers it to me." She was smiling from ear to ear and Olivia looked like a recalcitrant bride as she glared at her sister.

"Those are major sacrifices," she said sarcastically, and then looked seriously at her sister. "What makes you think I'm going to do it?" she said coyly.

"Are you?" Victoria held her breath as she waited.

"I don't know."

"Will you think about it?"

"Maybe." It was a chance to be with them, and more importantly an opportunity to keep Victoria from completely destroying her marriage. If Olivia took her place, she might be able to keep Charles from ever knowing she'd been gone, and then Victoria could come back and resume everything, having come to her senses. He might never know anything had ever happened. But if Olivia didn't take her place, Victoria would simply leave in three weeks, and slam the door carelessly behind her. Perhaps keeping her from doing that was even more important than caring for their father. And she'd be nearby. She would be in New York, she could come up any time he needed her. She knew it wouldn't be the same thing, but it was the best she could do if she was mending Victoria's fences.

"Will you?" Victoria was watching her, seeing everything she was thinking. "He'll be all right, and you won't be far."

"No, I won't, but he'll think I've gone running off without a care for him. That's a terrible thing to do," Olivia said sadly.

"Maybe you owe him that," Victoria said far more unkindly. "He thinks nothing of keeping you here for the rest of your life, taking care of him, so you can't find a husband." There was a certain truth to that but Olivia laughed at the way she said it.

"I don't want a husband, thank you very much," she said firmly. "I'm fine as I am." But if things had been different, and Victoria hadn't married Charles, she might have loved being with him. She would never know now. She couldn't even let herself think it. Even if she took her sister's place, it would only be for a short time, and to help all of them, not for her own gain, or just to be with him. She would never have done it for just that reason, she told herself, and tried desperately to believe it, fearing suddenly that the whole idea was far too attractive.

"You can have my husband," Victoria said happily, "for as long as you like. Three months or forever." She was teasing but not entirely and Olivia looked shocked. Victoria hadn't entirely forgotten that Olivia had once been somewhat taken with him, but that was long past, and she also knew that Olivia would never have tried to take her husband from her. She was far too decent, loyal, and honest. And Olivia's emotions were well in control now. She had never let herself think of Charles romantically since the day they'd been married, and she genuinely wanted him to be happy with her sister.

"You'd better come back at the end of the summer, or I'll tell everyone the truth and come over to get you myself," Olivia said emphatically, and Victoria laughed.

"They'd probably put us both in jail."

"And you'd probably like that." Olivia groaned at the thought.

"I might." Victoria laughed again and threw her arms around her sister, praying she would do it. It was the first glimpse of freedom she'd had ever since her disastrous affair with Toby. And she had paid a high price for her sins with him. Now she wanted her freedom. "Please say you'll do it, Olivia . . . please . . . I'll behave for the rest of my life, I swear. I'll knit doilies for you . . . shine your shoes . . . I'll never ask you to switch again. Just do it for me now, please . . ."

"Only if you promise to come back and be an exemplary wife and mother."

But Victoria's smile faded at that request and she looked pensive. "I can't promise you that. I don't know what will happen. Maybe he won't want me back," she said, thinking aloud.

"Then he must never know you were gone," Olivia said softly. "When do you leave?"

"On May first." It was three weeks away, almost time enough to prepare their father, and do anything else she had to do before stepping into Victoria's shoes. The two women exchanged a long hard glance, and then slowly Olivia nodded. Victoria let out a victorious whoop, and they embraced and for an insane moment, Olivia was startled to realize she actually felt elated. They talked about it excitedly for the next few minutes, like two extremely naughty children with an outrageous plan, as

Olivia wondered what she had gotten herself into. She was sure that in the next few weeks there would be doubts, but she was equally sure that Victoria would never let her back out now.

They walked downstairs arm in arm, and Geoffrey was in the front hall, playing with his cannon, and instinctively they both knew what they had to do, without saying a word to each other. Victoria slipped her left hand in her pocket so he wouldn't see her wedding ring, and smiled warmly down at him.

"That looks like a great game," she beamed, and then tousled his hair gently. "Can I interest you in some lemonade and cookies?" He beamed up at her adoringly and then shot twelve of his little soldiers with the cannon, and knocked them down as Olivia frowned at him.

"I wish you wouldn't play that game. It's so stupid," she said, walking coolly by him, waiting to see if he would believe her. But he cast an uninterested glance over his shoulder and went back to his game with a muttered apology.

"Sorry, Victoria, Dad said I could . . ." And then he winked at the woman he thought was Ollie and wasn't. They both went out to the kitchen then and Olivia was amazed. It was the first time they had ever fooled him.

"You'll be fine," Victoria whispered to her, as Olivia poured the glass of lemonade for Geoffrey, wondering if she would be just as lucky with his father.

Chapter 19

The hardest part of leaving, for Olivia, was figuring out what to say to her father. He was feeling better than he had in months these days, stronger too, and he was even thinking about going to New York to visit his daughter, but Olivia told him she didn't think he should yet. It would complicate everything if he did. She reminded him that Victoria and Geoff were both coming up in June, to spend the month with them, and it was only a little over a month away. He was far better off staying comfortably at home in Croton in the meantime.

That summer Charles was renting a house for them by the sea, and Geoff and Victoria would be in Newport for July and August. Charles had even invited her to join them. Little did he know now that she would be with them constantly. And by the time they got back, hopefully, the real Victoria would be home from Europe. Olivia had already gotten her passport out, and had it safely put away to give her sister.

"How do you suppose they're doing?" her father surprised her by asking her one day, just as she was thinking about the letter she would have to write to him, telling him she had gone off to California. She was going to tell him it was a religious retreat, and pray that he believed her. "I worry about her sometimes," he said honestly. "Charles is a fine man. But one senses at times that she isn't happy with him." Olivia was shocked by the observations of her father.

"I'm not sure that's true." It seemed safer to deny it now, in view of what they were going to do. "I think it's been a fairly normal adjustment. He was very fond of his wife, I'm sure that's difficult for him, and for Geoff . . ." But her father was right, and she knew it.

"I hope you're right. She seemed very restless when she was here, and very nervous." Oh God . . . Olivia had to turn away from him as her eyes filled with tears, hating the thought that in a few days she was going to hurt him. And then he startled her even more when she turned back to him again. "And you, my dear? You're not too lonely here with me, without your sister?"

"I miss her sometimes . . . terribly . . ." she said, her voice hoarse with emotion, "but I love you, Father . . . wherever I am, I'll always love you." He saw something strange in her eyes then, something he had seen there before, but thought was best left unspoken.

"You're a good girl," he patted her hand, "and I love you too," he said, as he walked out into the garden.

And that night, she echoed the same words to him in her letter. She was going to take the letter to New York with her, and bring it back when Victoria left, pretending to be her sister. It was absurdly complicated, but it was the only way she could think of to do it. She could hardly leave the letter here with Bertie now, and ask her to give it to him three days later.

In the end, all she could say was that, as he had guessed, it had been very hard for her without Victoria, and that now she must find her way alone, and find herself. And in order to do it she had gone away for a few months, to visit friends, and pursue a religious retreat in California. It sounded faintly mad, even to her, but she couldn't think of what else to tell him. She assured him that she would be safe, that she would write to them, and that she would be back at the end of the summer. She had said that a friend from school had invited her, but as she and Victoria hadn't been in school for the past ten years, it was a bit of an odd story, but she hoped he wouldn't notice. More than anything, she assured him of how much she loved him, that he had done nothing to drive her away, but that she needed this time for herself, and that she would come back better and stronger, and more devoted to him than ever. It was, in fact, exactly what she hoped for her sister. But her tears fell liberally on the page as she wrote it. Her eyes were so blurred she could hardly sign her name. And then she wrote another to Geoff, and sealed it too, and a short one to Bertie that said only, ". . . I'll be back soon . . . take care of Daddy . . . I love you . . . Ollie." It was enough, she could hardly breathe by then, and as she lay in bed the night before she left, she wondered at the madness that had seized them. Victoria was crazy to do what she was doing, and she was obviously crazier for switching places with her.

She only hoped that some good would come of it, that her father's health wouldn't fail, and that Charles didn't discover what Victoria had done, and divorce her. There was a lot resting on Olivia's shoulders, and when she woke up the next morning, she was determined to talk Victoria out of it, but she knew her twin well enough to know that Victoria would die first.

Olivia kissed her father good-bye before she left, and she stood with her arms around his neck and her cheek against his, wishing she could stay there with him forever. It was a good life for her, and though she might have once longed for other things, she accepted it now, and she was genuinely going to miss him.

"Have fun in New York, and buy some pretty things for both of you," he told her with a warm hug, and she felt the knife of guilt slice through her heart as she held him.

"I love you, Daddy," she whispered. She hadn't called him that in years, and he kissed her and went out to walk in the garden.

She was unusually silent on the ride to New York, even Donovan commented on it afterwards. But later it all made sense to them. She had been feeling guilty about running away to California. It would never occur to anyone that she was still in New York, openly living with Charles Dawson, and pretending to be her sister. That was beyond all their imaginations.

Olivia arrived at the house at three o'clock before Geoff came home from school, and Victoria was waiting. She was businesslike and cool, but Olivia could also tell she was very excited. She was sailing for Europe the next morning. Olivia had thought of coming down a few days before, but they had both agreed that they would be too nervous and it might arouse suspicion, and Olivia had wanted to spend as much time as possible with their father.

She handed Victoria her passport now. She would be traveling as Olivia Henderson, and not Victoria Dawson. The photograph obviously did not present a problem. There were some other papers, some keys, some notes about servants' names, things she had to know, like the name of Charles' secretary, and Geoff's teacher, but it was all surprisingly simple. There were so few details, so little to do. All Olivia had to do was step into her sister's shoes the next morning. It terrified her to think of it. And when Geoff came home from school, Olivia still looked shaken.

"Is something wrong, Aunt Ollie?" he asked, looking worried. "Is Grampa sick?"

"No, he's fine. Better than he's been in a

while. He loved your last visit." She smiled, thinking that she would have to be careful with him from the next day on, but she noticed that Victoria was being warmer to him these days too, in preparation for their switching. But it also showed Olivia that she could do it. And she said as much to Victoria when Geoff went upstairs to do his homework. "You see, you're just as good with him as I am."

"When I'm pretending to be you." She grinned. "The rest of the time I don't even think about it."

"Maybe you'll have to start when you get back," Olivia said pointedly. She was already planning for the future. In fact, she had a suspicion that this brief interlude might actually improve their marriage. In her fantasies, Victoria would come back, grateful for Charles, starving for him, and desperately grateful to have a child like Geoffrey. She would embrace them all, and Olivia would go back to Croton. No harm done. And they would all live happily ever after. She was sure now that Victoria could do it. Under Victoria's spell, she had already painted a thousand happy pictures. But it jarred her a little when Charles came home, and Victoria suddenly prodded her unexpectedly into switching. She was cool with him, which didn't seem to surprise him, asked him about his day, and mentioned something she'd read in the papers. And a few minutes later he went up to his study. He had no idea at all that he had been talking to Olivia for the past ten minutes, and not his wife.

"You see how easy it is," Victoria said to her, "it's just like it's always been, no different." In truth, it was, which surprised her. Olivia slept in Geoff's room that night, clinging to him in the narrow bed, revelling in the last opportunity to lavish affection on him. From the next day on, as Victoria she would have to be cooler, but perhaps in time, in the guise of Victoria, they could grow closer. She worried about the blow to him too, when he heard that she had gone to California for the summer without warning. She tried to say something to him that day, as she helped him dress to visit a friend. It was Saturday, and Victoria had long since arranged it. Olivia looked down at him with eyes filled with tears as she straightened his tie for him, and prayed he wouldn't notice.

"I love you very, very much," she said, "no matter what. You know, even if I ever went away for a while, I'd come back. Not . . ." She choked on the words, but went on. She had to say it. ". . . not like your mother." She wanted him to know that she would come back to him, she would not desert him.

"Are you going somewhere?" Geoff looked surprised as he glanced at her and then he saw the tears. "Are you crying, Aunt Ollie?"

"No, I have a cold. And I happen to love you very much, and I'm a stupid, sentimental old woman."

"Yeah," he grinned at her, and then took Chip downstairs for a walk, and they met again at the breakfast table. She had wanted to leave Victoria alone with them, in case she wanted her own silent good-byes with them, but Victoria seemed to need none of it. Olivia had never seen her as cheery. She was in tremendous spirits, chirping and laughing and talking about news of the war. She even gave Geoffrey a kiss when he left for his friend's house, which was most unlike her. She had really been making an effort, and she was so happy she wasn't going to see them for three months that she almost screamed with pleasure. And after three weeks of total restraint around them, by that afternoon she would be smoking.

When Charles left to go to the office, as he often did on Saturday, she was a little more cool, and he smiled and waved when he said good-bye to Ollie.

"Try to stay out of too much mischief, you two. I have a mountain of work to do this morning." Victoria had counted on that too, knowing that the ship was sailing on Saturday. She'd have been in trouble if he'd decided to stay home that day, but she knew him better than that, and if he had, Victoria would have found a way around it. She was determined.

"Have fun," Victoria said with gentle sarcasm, and he hurried down the steps and that was the last she saw of her husband. When he was gone, they went upstairs, and closed and locked the door to her bedroom. She handed Olivia her narrow wedding band, and his mother's engagement ring, and Olivia slowly slipped them on her finger. They fit perfectly, there was no difference. And then Victoria looked around the room, and then at her sister. "I guess this is it then."

"As simple as that? This is it?" Olivia looked wistful and Victoria nodded. She was too happy to conceal it. She was sad to leave her twin, as she always was, even for an afternoon, but she was so relieved to be leaving her life in New York, and with Charles, behind her. She knew now what she wished she had known eleven months before, that she never should have married him, no matter what her father did to force her.

"Take care of yourself," she said to Olivia, "I love you." She held her tight and then pulled away from her, as Olivia looked worried.

"Take care of yourself too. If anything ever happened to you . . ." She couldn't even finish her sentence as tears choked her.

"Nothing will. I'm going to spend the next three months rolling bandages and serving coffee to unwashed men well behind the lines," she said as Olivia made a face.

"It sounds charming. I can't imagine why you'd want to do that." Rather than be here, safe and comfortable, with Charles and Geoffrey. It made no sense to anyone but Victoria who was willing to risk her life to leave them and do something she thought was important and useful.

"Someone has to do it," Victoria said quietly as she changed into a plain black dress and then left her bedroom to go up to the attic, where she had concealed her one sensible suitcase. She brought it back downstairs, and took a somber-looking hat with a heavy black veil out of her closet.

"What's that for?" Olivia looked puzzled, and she thought it unlikely Victoria and surprisingly ugly. It was obviously meant for a widow, and the veil was so thick you couldn't see her face behind it. She was completely obscured by the thick veiling.

"There will be photographers at the ship. It's quite a nice ship, I hear. Even nicer than the *Aquatania*." And this would be better than a honeymoon for her. It was her trip to freedom. She had reserved a simple stateroom in first class, nothing like the one she had shared with Charles on the *Aquatania,* and she had carefully withdrawn some of the money her father had given her when she got married. Charles had suspected nothing. She had five hundred pounds on her in cash now, but she didn't imagine she'd need a great deal working behind the trenches. She had taken rough warm clothes, except for a few proper dresses for the ship. She was planning to stay in her stateroom for much of the trip, in case anyone recognized her, and talked about it later.

"You thought of everything, didn't you," Olivia said sadly. It broke her heart to see her go now, worse yet to see her so cheerful.

They took a cab to Pier Fifty-four on Fourteenth Street, and Olivia and Victoria held hands nervously in the taxi.

There was the usual furious hubbub of activity around the ship, music blared, people laughed, and shouted to friends, champagne flowed as the first-class passengers came aboard, and the widow in the heavy veil went quickly up the gangplank with her sister behind her. They found her cabin easily, and the porter had already put her bag there.

And for a long moment they stood looking at each other. There was nothing left to say now. It didn't need words. Victoria had left her life in her sister's hands, and she was going off to war now. And Olivia would take care of everything in her absence. But Olivia could hardly bear to leave her. She wanted to beg her not to go, but she knew her twin would never have listened.

"I'll know everything you do, you know, right here," she pointed to her stomach, "so don't make me crazy with worry, please."

"I'll try not to," Victoria laughed, knowing how true that was. They had always had an uncanny telepathy between them. "At least I know you'll be safe with Charles. Don't forget to fight with him night and day, otherwise he'll miss me," she teased, and Olivia hugged her.

"Swear to me you'll come back safe and sound."

"I swear," she said solemnly as the ship's

horn blew, and the warning sounded for visitors to go ashore, as Olivia felt her heart pound.

"I can't let you go," Olivia said, meaning it for the briefest second. She wanted to cling to her suddenly and keep her from going.

"Yes, you can," Victoria said quietly, "it's no different than when I went on my honeymoon." Olivia nodded, and Victoria walked her to the gangplank in the ridiculous black hat with the veil. It made Olivia smile again just before she left her.

"I love you, you stupid girl. I don't know why I'm letting you do this."

"Because you know I have to." And the truth was she did. Olivia knew she would have gone anyway. And it was better this way. They hugged each other one last time, harder than they ever had before, and Olivia could see her eyes through the thick veil. They were both crying. This was far from easy.

"I love you," Olivia said again, and Victoria crushed her to her.

"I love you . . . and oh God, Ollie, thank you for giving me my life back."

Olivia kissed her one last time, and whispered to her. "God be with you," and then walked slowly off the *Lusitania* and left her.

Chapter 20

Olivia spent the rest of the afternoon feeling numb. She didn't know what to do with herself, as she wandered aimlessly from room to room, thinking about her. She knew that the ship would be out to sea by then, and even though she was nervous about seeing them she wished Geoffrey and Charles would come home so she wouldn't feel so lonely. She felt so bereft without her twin, she had never gotten used to being without her for any length of time. It was so much easier for Victoria. Olivia would never have taken a trip far away, without her twin sister. But Victoria had already done it once before on her honeymoon, and now she had done it again. But Olivia felt lost without her.

And she knew that when they came home that afternoon she would have to give the greatest performance of her life. She had the letters for Geoff and her father ready for them, and even one to herself which pretended to explain everything, and why she had run off to California. She was supposed to have taken the train to Chicago that afternoon, instead of sailing for Liverpool on the *Lusitania*.

But by the time Charles got home, she was ready for him, and he was shocked when he saw her face as he entered their bedroom. He knew instantly that something terrible had happened to her, and forgetting all the arguments they'd had, he rushed instantly toward her.

"Are you ill?" She looked deathly pale, and she was reclining in a chair with a desolate expression. "What happened?"

"It's Ollie," she said softly. He knew she couldn't have had an accident, or his wife would have been at the hospital with her. As heartless as she seemed to be with everyone else at times, he knew how she adored her sister. "She left."

"She went home?" He looked surprised. "That's all?" Victoria, or the woman he thought was his wife, looked as though someone had died, not simply gone back to Croton. He knew something more must have happened. "Did you have an argument?" She was fighting with everyone these days, maybe even Ollie, but the real Olivia shook her head as she watched him. And she was feeling so lonely for Victoria by then that it was easy to look devastated. She was, so much so that she felt queasy, and she looked it. "Is your father ill?" Olivia shook her head again, and handed him the letter she had supposedly written to her sister. It was in fact in her own hand, allegedly to Victoria, although no one could tell their handwriting apart anyway, not even Bertie.

The letter explained simply that although it tore at her heart, she felt she had to get away for a few months, that her life was just too much for her at the moment. She was too lonely now that Victoria was gone, she realized that she was far too dependent on her, that she felt oppressed by the emptiness of her life in Croton, and she needed a few months to think about all of it, and get away from them. She said she was even thinking of joining a convent, since she knew she would never marry.

"Oh my God," he looked at her, horrified, "how awful." He began to check his pockets then, and looked quickly in his wallet. "I wanted to see how much money I brought home. I'll go to Chicago tonight, and stop her. She can't do this. It'll kill your father." Olivia was afraid of that too, and hoped he was wrong with his prediction.

"By the time you get to Chicago," she said practically, "she'll be on the train to California." She sounded a little cavalier about her twin, but she didn't want Charles running all over the country on a wild-goose chase while her sister sat comfortably in a first-class cabin on a ship to Europe. "You'll never find her." He could see the sense in what she said, and sat down heavily beside her. He was shocked at Olivia doing a thing like that, and couldn't imagine it, as he stared right into her eyes and didn't know it. And if he had known his wife better than he did, he would have seen her hand in all of it, but he didn't.

"Do you have any idea where she's gone? Who she might have gone to? What friend it could be?" He sounded as frantic as she would have felt if the story were true, and her heart went out to him for caring so much about his wife's sister.

"She's a very secretive person," Olivia said, and started to cry, thinking about her sister, steaming away from her for three months.

It was easy to cry when she thought of how much she hated her going, and already missed her.

"Oh my dear," he said, instantly putting an arm around her, and it surprised Olivia. This was not what she had expected. "I'm so sorry. Maybe she'll think better of it and come back in a few days. Maybe you shouldn't tell your father anything for a while and see what happens."

"You don't know how stubborn she is, Charles," Olivia complained convincingly. "She's not always what she seems."

"Apparently," he said, looking both worried and disapproving. "Do you suppose your father's been very hard on her since you've been gone? I've always thought it was unfair that she was trapped there with him, with no life of her own, no friends, no social life, no suitors. She never goes anywhere, and he doesn't seem to mind it, as long as she's there to take care of him. Maybe this is what it led to," he said sadly.

"Maybe." Olivia had never thought of it quite that way, but he wasn't wrong entirely. She wondered if her father would see it that way too, and feel guilty. She thought it unlikely. "But if she says a few months, I'm sure she means it. She left Father a letter. I thought I'd take it to him tomorrow." Tomorrow was Sunday.

"You don't think we should wait a few days?" He was very worried.

"Really, Charles, I know her, and I think it's only fair to tell Father."

"I'll drive you," he said solemnly and she nodded. "Did she say anything to you last night? No hint at all of what she was going to do?"

"Nothing," Olivia said, still looking bereft, and he didn't tell her that suicides behaved that way too. Maybe it was just as well she had only run away for a while and not done anything even more foolish. But for the first time in months, he felt sorry for his wife, she looked so gentle and so broken suddenly that she almost reminded him of her sister.

And when Geoff came home from his friend's, they were even more worried about him. He sobbed openly when they told him Olivia was gone, and it was even worse when he read the letter she'd left him.

"It's just like Mama," he said, as he sobbed in his father's arms, and tears rolled openly down Olivia's cheeks as she watched him. "She's never coming back, I know it."

"Yes, she is," Olivia said firmly through her own tears. "Remember what she told you . . . that no matter where she ever went she would always come back, and she would always love you." She had said it to him herself only that morning when he was dressing, and he didn't question how she knew it, but she instantly reminded herself to be more careful.

"She's not lying, Geoff," Olivia said softly, sounding as much like herself, as her sister. "She really loves you, you're like a son to her, the son she never had and never will have. We just have to wait for her to come back now." But he refused to believe she would, and later that night, Olivia pointed out to him that his own mother would have come back too, if she could have. Olivia was lying on his bed, playing with the dog, feeling the unfamiliar feeling of Victoria's rings on her fingers, as she said it.

"My mother could have come back, and she didn't," he said angrily. He was angry at Olivia too, for leaving him, and she didn't blame him. But she was surprised by what he had said about his mother.

"What do you mean, Geoff?" she asked in confusion. Susan had died. She hadn't left him.

"She didn't have to give her seat up, she could have gotten in the boat with me."

"She saved someone else's life, that's a very brave thing to do." He looked at her hesitantly and then he shrugged and two lonely tears slid down his cheeks.

"I still miss her," he whispered. It wasn't the sort of thing he would normally have confessed to Victoria, but he was so distraught over Olivia, he let himself go with her, and Olivia reached out and touched his fingers.

"I know you do," she said softly, "and I know you miss Ollie. I do too . . . but maybe we can be friends now." He looked at her strangely then, and there was a question in his eyes, but she turned away from him and reminded herself not to go too far, and a few minutes later she kissed him and left his room, and went back to his father in their bedroom. It had been an extremely difficult evening, and she didn't thank her sister for it.

"How is he?" Charles asked with troubled eyes. He was worried about his son losing yet another mother figure in his life. And so far over the past year, Victoria had been very little comfort to him, although she had been nicer tonight than she'd been in months and he was happy to see it. He would have been furious with her if she had left the boy grieving. At least there was some humanity to her.

"He's very upset," she said quietly. "I don't blame him. I don't know what got into her. It's as much a mystery to me as it is to him." She sat down on the bed, looking genuinely exhausted and hoping that at that moment Victoria was violently seasick. She deserved it. And Olivia realized again how crazy she had been to do this. And tomorrow she had to tell her father.

"Do you suppose she was in love with someone and no one knew it?" Olivia laughed at the idea he was proposing about her, it was certainly creative. The only man she had ever remotely liked was Charles, and he was married to her sister. She only hoped he didn't get that idea into his head, and no one else did, that she was secretly in love with Charles. That would be mortifying and disastrous.

"I don't see how she'd be in love with anyone. She's really not interested in that sort of thing. She's very shy," she said innocently, and he gave her an odd look.

"Like you, my dear," he said sarcastically, and she was startled.

"What does that mean?" It was the kind

of thing Victoria would have said to him, and Olivia knew it, so she went ahead and said it.

"You know what it means. We haven't exactly had a life filled with romance, have we?"

"I didn't know that was what you expected." Olivia tried sniping at him on for size hesitantly, and he seemed to think it was normal.

"Well, I certainly didn't expect what we ended up with. But I suppose you didn't either," he said sadly, and she looked at him sympathetically. He saw the look in her eyes and it surprised him. He decided to change the subject then. She'd been through enough for one day without their fighting too. And there was no point in it, and he knew it. From that standpoint, their marriage was over. "When do you want to go up and see your father tomorrow?"

"It's a long drive. We'll have to go up in the morning. Do you mind driving me?" She hoped he didn't, because she didn't know how to, and, of course, Victoria did. She would have to call Donovan in that case and say she was too upset to drive to Croton.

"I'm happy to drive you. Do you mind if we bring Geoff?" He felt he should ask her, he knew the boy made her nervous and she was already upset about her sister, but Olivia was quick to answer.

"Of course not."

He had noticed a subtle change in her all night, the shock of Olivia running away seemed to have softened her imperceptibly. She seemed more vulnerable, and he sensed something he had never felt in her before, though he wouldn't have known how to express it. She seemed tamer, and somehow smaller. Not physically, of course, but in some odd, intangible, spiritual way. She seemed just the merest trifle less daunting.

She lay awake for a long time that night, wearing Victoria's nightgown, and lying in her bed, huddled as far away from him as she could. It was the first time Olivia had ever slept with a man, and if it hadn't been so terrifying she would have thought it was funny. She was afraid that at any moment he would discover that they had switched places on him, and he would throw her out of his house in her sister's nightgown. But he did nothing of the sort. Instead, he lay looking at her in the darkness, wondering if he should reach out to her, but not daring to. She had her back to him, and he suspected she was crying. And finally, he settled for a gentle hand on her shoulder.

"Are you awake?" he whispered. She nodded but didn't answer. "Are you all right?" he whispered again, and she smiled, but he couldn't see it.

"More or less," she said softly. "I keep thinking about her." That was true. It was all she had thought about since that morning.

"She'll be all right. She's very capable," he said sensibly. "And she'll come back when she's ready. She's not going to disappear forever." He didn't realize that the woman he was talking about was his wife, which was just as well, Olivia thought sadly.

"What if she gets hurt?" Olivia shared her fears with him, and he dared to move a trifle closer.

"She won't. The Indians are all pretty tame out there now. In fact, I think most of them are in circuses and sideshows. And they haven't had an earthquake in nine years. I'd say she'll make it through the summer." He smiled at her back, but didn't touch her.

"What if they have another earthquake? Or a fire? Or a war . . ." It was all she could think of.

"In California? I don't think we're likely to go to war with California." He pulled her over to face him then, and as he had thought, she was crying. She looked like a lovely child in the moonlight. "Why don't you go to sleep and stop worrying. Perhaps your father will send investigators after her, and they'll bring her home in a few days." But she couldn't tell him they wouldn't find her. Victoria was going to be far, far from California. And Olivia wished she had never let her go there. She was thinking of sending a telegram to the ship telling her that she had changed her mind, and she had to come home now. Olivia knew she could still send the telegram before they reached Liverpool. Thinking about it reminded her of the German U-boats she had heard were outside the British harbors. She wondered what she had been thinking of when she agreed to let her sail to Europe. Just thinking about it made her cry harder, and without considering the danger of it, she let Charles pull her into his arms and hold her. She could smell the soap on his neck, and the aftershave he wore. He had obviously shaved before he'd come to bed, which Olivia thought was a surprising nicety and something she'd never thought of, and she was amazed at the strength and warmth of him as he held her, and then finally she pulled away and looked up at him in embarrassment. He was, after all, only her brother-in-law, and not her husband, although he didn't know it.

"I'm so sorry," she said awkwardly.

"It's all right." He looked surprised too, and he didn't tell her he had liked it. She went back to her side of the bed again, and a little while later, they both fell asleep until morning.

They got up and dressed separately, and Olivia was relieved to find that he was extremely polite and their arrangement very civilized. He was not overly personal with her, and she didn't see him again until he was fully dressed at breakfast. Victoria was right, in some ways this was easy. Geoffrey was still in a gloom understandably, and he didn't even want to go to Croton, but he had to. The maid and the cook were both off, and there was nowhere else they could leave him. But he said he didn't want to go to Croton without Ollie, not even to see Grampa.

It was a long, solemn drive, while Olivia thought about what to say to her father. She had rehearsed it a thousand times, but she still wasn't prepared for the look of grief he wore when she told him. If she had shot him he might have looked less pained and less stricken. And she was grateful that Charles was standing beside her. Together, they helped him into a chair, and Charles poured him a brandy. And as her father sipped it, he looked at them both in despair, and then directly at his daughter.

"Did I do this to her? I asked her just the other day," he mused, "I asked her if I had made her terribly unhappy. This isn't a life for a young girl, but she always said that this was all she wanted. And I let her do it because it's so easy for me . . . I would have missed her awfully if she'd left me . . . and now she's gone . . ." He was actually crying, and Olivia wanted to tear her heart out. And then he truly stunned her when he looked straight at Charles. "I think she might have fallen in love with you, if we'd let her. But we didn't of course." He looked away and they all knew what had happened, as the real Olivia stood there gasping.

"Father, I'm sure that's not true. She never said anything . . ." She was mortified, and sure she was blushing but no one seemed to notice.

"She didn't have to," he interrupted her, wiping his eyes and taking another sip of brandy. "It was easy to see. I'm a man. I know. But it was more important to save you at the time, so I chose to ignore it." Charles' lips were set in a thin line and he made no comment, and Olivia didn't have the courage to look at him again for several moments.

"I'm certain you're wrong. She would have told me," Olivia said, trying to save the last of her dignity in absentia.

"Did she tell you about this?" he boomed at her and she shook her head miserably. She truly was unhappy. "Then don't think you know it all, Victoria Dawson." She was aghast at the idea that Charles would think she had run away because she loved him. That was awful, and she knew she'd have to dispel that as soon as possible, for her own sake. But Charles seemed to share her opinion.

"I think it's impossible to know why people do things like this, sir. The mind is a secret place, and the heart even more so. And twins share an unusual bond, we both know that. We've all heard stories of how close they are, how much they know about each other, how they sense things other people can't even imagine. Maybe it was just too much for her that Victoria has her own life now. Maybe she's trying to find herself and become her own person."

"In a convent?" He looked appalled. It was not the fate he wanted for his daughter. "I threatened you with that," he said unhappily to the twin he thought was Victoria, but wasn't, "but I didn't really mean it."

"I thought you did," she said honestly. They both had.

"I couldn't have done that to you." But instead, he had forced Victoria into marriage, and that was why she had run away now. That was the truth of it. But Olivia couldn't tell him.

As Charles had said, Edward vowed to put investigators on it, and he asked Charles to see about it himself in the city on Monday morning. They gathered up all their letters from her, for Charles to give them, and Olivia promised to rack her brain over the names of the girls they'd gone to school with ten years before to see if anyone lived in California, but of course there wouldn't be any.

And when they left the library late that afternoon, Bertie was waiting with Geoffrey in the kitchen, and they were both crying. Bertie had gotten her letter too, and she was so distraught that she never looked carefully at the twin standing before her. And after a quick kiss on the cheek, Olivia hurried outside to wait for them. She didn't want to be around her longer than she had to. She never even went to her own room, she was afraid that if she did, she might give something away to one of them, and there was too much at stake now.

Edward Henderson offered to have them spend the night, but Charles said that they had to get back, or he did at any rate. He had to be in court the next morning. And he wanted to contact the investigators for them as soon as he could on Monday. But he told Victoria she could stay there with Geoff, but she didn't want to. Without her twin, being at Henderson Manor would depress her. And she was frankly afraid that Bertie would discern who she was, once she calmed down again, and Olivia needed more time to perfect her deception. So far neither of the Dawsons had suspected anything of what had happened.

Her father cried again when she kissed him good-bye, and she felt terrible. Bertie was standing next to him, and he waved as they drove away. Geoff hadn't even wanted to ride his horse. He had just gone to look at him in the stable.

"I wonder if she had any idea everyone would be so distraught over her," Charles said as they drove away, feeling sorry for her father. But he had taken the news better than Charles expected. Charles made no comment at all on the fact that Edward thought she was in love with him. He put it aside as an old man's delusion.

"I don't think she could have imagined how sad we'd all be, or she wouldn't have done it," Olivia said supposedly about herself, but thinking about her sister. She was missing her terribly, and felt the pain with each day they drifted further apart. The idea of sending a telegram and asking her to come straight home again was sounding better and better to her.

It was after nine o'clock that night when they got home again, and none of them had eaten dinner. Olivia told Geoff to put his pajamas on, and come back to the kitchen for soup. She put an apron on then, and went to see what they had in the larder, and ten minutes later she had chicken stock on the stove, with vegetables, and there were thick slabs of buttered toast, and a fresh salad.

"How did you do all that so fast?" Charles looked surprised. "You've been keeping secrets from me." He smiled cautiously, never sure of her humor or her temper.

"More secrets than you know," Olivia said with a smile, but Charles didn't look pleased by her remark, and he sat down to dinner in silence. Geoff came back downstairs then, and he livened up a little bit, as he ate the soup, and the toast, and had a second helping of the salad.

"This is good, Victoria," he said, sounding surprised, and then he glanced at her with a shy smile. But Olivia wouldn't let herself be too warm to him tonight, for fear that he would discover who she was. Instead she turned away from him, and then handed him a plate full of chocolate cookies.

"Did you make these?" He looked even more surprised, but this time she laughed and shook her head.

"No, the cook did," she said honestly.

"I like Ollie's better," Geoff said, munching one, and playing with his puppy.

Olivia cleaned up the kitchen while Charles took Geoff up to bed, and she joined them upstairs half an hour later. Geoff was already in bed by then, and as she stood in the doorway looking at him, she couldn't help thinking how lucky her sister was, and she didn't even know it. She was on a ship somewhere on the way to God knew where, when she could have been at home, in this cozy house, with her husband and stepson.

"Can I tuck you in?" she asked Geoff casually and he shrugged. He was still looking sad, but he was a little better. On the way home, he had talked about when Olivia came home, at the end of the summer. He was already looking ahead, and beginning to believe she would come back, as she had promised.

"Sure," he said, pushing his monkey aside, and holding on to Chip so he wouldn't jump off the bed. But he just wagged his tail and licked Olivia's hand. He liked her.

"Sleep tight," she whispered into his hair, and then walked back to her own bedroom. It had been a long day, and her back hurt after the long drive back and forth to Croton.

"You're in court tomorrow?" she asked casually, as she undid her hair, and Charles glanced at her in surprise. It was the first time she had ever asked about his work, and he nodded.

"It's nothing important," he said, and went back to reading his papers. And then he looked up at her again. "Thank you for dinner." She smiled, not sure what to say, it seemed so normal to her, but it was obviously something Victoria hadn't done often. "I thought your father did very well today, all things considered."

"So did I," she said sadly.

"I'll call some investigators for him tomorrow when I get back to the office. I still can't believe she did it. She's so responsible. It seems so unlike her to run away. She must have been terribly unhappy to do that."

"I know," Olivia said softly.

In fact, it was the longest conversation Charles had had with his wife in weeks, except when they argued with each other.

They changed in their dressing rooms separately, as usual, and that night when they went to bed, they each kept their backs turned. And as Olivia drifted off to sleep, she wondered how they had both lived this way. It was so lonely.

She got up and made them breakfast the next day. The maid usually did it for them, but Olivia said she didn't mind it. She knew she wasn't supposed to do anything Victoria wouldn't have done, but it seemed such a small thing to do for them, she hated not to. But Charles noticed the difference in her since her sister was gone. She seemed to have a need to take care of them suddenly, and he had to admit, he liked it. But Geoff looked at her very strangely. And she saw him instinctively look at her hand, but it was covered by the towel she had used so she wouldn't burn herself on their dishes. She knew what he was looking for, and she was determined that he was not going to find it. It was so small anyway, that she knew he wouldn't see it unless she was particularly careless.

"Have a good day at school," she said casually to him, and she purposely didn't offer to kiss him. Nor did she say anything at all to Charles when he left for the office. She knew she had to be careful. And she sensed that Victoria wouldn't have said much to them, if she saw them at all in the morning.

In fact, Charles seemed surprised to see her when he got home. And Geoff had been even more so when he got home from school and found her darning some of his father's socks in the kitchen.

"What are you doing?" He looked shocked, and she blushed as she answered.

"Ollie taught me how to do it."

"I've never seen you do that before."

"Well, if I don't, your father will be going to the office barefoot." She smiled and Geoff laughed and went to help himself to milk and cookies before going upstairs reluctantly to do his own homework. He only had another month of school, and he could hardly wait for summer vacation.

The rest of the week passed uneventfully, Olivia said very little to them. She was very careful about what she said or did. She wanted to be cautious until she knew them better. Living with them constantly was very different from visiting with them. And she wanted to be sure she didn't make some awful faux pas that would expose her. In fact, she was very relieved when on Friday, Geoff asked to stay at a friend's, and Charles said he had meetings all afternoon with out of town clients. In fact, he was planning to have dinner with them, and since he knew how much she hated that sort of thing, he didn't invite her.

She was happy to have the time to herself, to go through some of her sister's things. She wanted to take a closer look at the books Victoria had wanted to read, the articles she had cut out, the letters from a few acquaintances in New York, and the invitations she had accepted. There was something at the Ogden Mills' in two weeks, and Olivia worried about anything else Victoria might not have told her, but she seemed fairly familiar with most of it. Then shortly after nine o'clock that morning, she had the oddest sensation. It was a feeling of disequilibrium, almost as though she was going to lose her balance, in fact she felt quite ill, as she did all day, and by nightfall, she had a ferocious headache. She had no idea why she was ill, she had no fever, no cold, and she had been fine when she got up that morning. By the time Charles got home, she was in bed, and as she lay there, she had a rising feeling of panic, and he was surprised when he looked at her, to see how pale she looked. She looked genuinely awful.

"Is it something you ate?" he asked with mild concern. He'd had a long day, but the negotiations had gone well, and he had a new client.

"I don't know," Olivia said in a thin voice, feeling terribly dizzy. She felt as though the room were spinning around her. She had felt that way almost since lunchtime.

"At least we know you're not pregnant," he said sarcastically, and Olivia didn't answer. She felt too ill to respond to him by then, and she just lay in bed for hours that night, feeling grim, and when she fell asleep at last, she had the terrifying feeling that she was drowning. She sat up in bed, gasping for air, and she leapt out of bed when she couldn't get it. And as soon as she moved, he stirred, and he sat up and watched her.

"Are you all right?" he asked in a sleep-filled voice, and she shook her head still gasping for air. He came quickly toward her with a glass of water.

She took a sip and coughed, and he helped her into a chair. "I don't know what happened . . . I had a terrible nightmare." And then, just as suddenly, she was seized with a wave of panic, and she knew that something had happened to her sister. She looked up at him, and he read in her eyes what she was thinking.

"You're just overwrought," he said soothingly, amazed at the bond between the twins again. It was almost as though they should never have been separated at all, as though it were just too traumatic for them. "I'm sure she's fine, wherever she is," he said calmly.

But she was clutching his arm with a look of terror. "Charles, I know she isn't."

"You know nothing of the sort," he said in a quiet voice, and tried to get her to come back to bed with him, but she wouldn't.

"I can't breathe," she said, sounding frightened. It seemed impossible on a ship like that, but what if something had happened? What if . . . what if she were ill? . . . Olivia knew she could feel it. And Charles could see that something very strange was happening to her. She began to cry and she couldn't stop it.

He was afraid for her nerves, as he watched her.

"Shall I call a doctor, Victoria?" he asked, and she almost jumped at the sound of her sister's name.

"I don't know," she said, feeling strangled, and then she looked at him and began to cry again. "Oh Charles . . . I'm so afraid . . ." He came to kneel next to her then, he had never seen her this way before, and he didn't know what to do for her. He sat next to her and held her hand, and then finally he got her to come back to bed and lie beside him, but whenever she closed her eyes, she said she felt as though she were drowning. "I'm sorry," she said finally, "I didn't mean to be so much trouble," but she was still crying softly. "I just feel that something terrible has happened to her."

"I'm sure that's not true," he said, still holding her hand, wanting to comfort her, and surprised at how gentle and helpless she looked as she lay beside him. She never fell asleep again, but by morning she was calm. She lay very still, and she seemed almost as though she were in a trance when Charles spoke to her. "Would you like some tea, Victoria?" he asked. He still thought she looked ill, and he had decided that in a little while he would call the doctor. It was the first time in their eleven months together that she had been sick at all, and it somehow surprised him. She was normally very well balanced and very healthy. But he was beginning to think that the shock of her twin running away the week before had somehow unhinged her.

He went downstairs, and made tea for her, but before he could bring it back to her, she came downstairs, and puttered barefoot around the kitchen. She was looking a little stronger as she sat down and unfolded the newspaper, thinking that it might take her mind off worrying about her sister. But as soon as she opened it, she gasped and stared at the paper. There were four-inch headlines straight across the page, and it took her breath away as she read them. The *Lusitania* had been torpedoed thirteen miles off the coast of Ireland, and had sunk to the bottom in just under eighteen minutes. All that was known was what had been seen from shore, but great loss of life was feared, and no survivors had been listed yet, but according to the article there were bodies everywhere, and the entire ship had been destroyed by U-boats.

"Oh my God!" she said, staring at him.

"Oh my God . . . Charles . . ." And as he looked at her in total amazement, she slipped slowly to the floor, and he managed to catch her just as she fainted.

The kitchen maid had just come in, and Charles shouted to her to call the doctor and tell him to come quickly. Mrs. Dawson was very ill and had just fainted.

He carried her upstairs before she had regained consciousness, and laid her on their bed. And a moment later, she came around as he held smelling salts beneath her nose. There were some very old ones in his bathroom cabinet, which Susan had used when she was pregnant with Geoffrey.

"I . . . oh . . . what . . . oh my God . . . Charles . . ." The ship had gone down, and her sister was on it. She didn't know if she was dead or alive, and she had no way of finding out, or even telling him what had happened. All she could do was cry, and Charles was worried sick as they waited for the doctor.

"Don't speak, Victoria, just close your eyes." He tried to calm her but she was very agitated, and he was greatly relieved when he heard the doctor come up the stairs twenty minutes later. He was relieved that Geoffrey wasn't home, it would have been far too upsetting for a boy his age to see his stepmother in such a state of total chaos.

"What's happened here?" the doctor said in a cheerful tone, but he could see immediately that Mrs. Dawson was extremely upset and she'd been crying.

"I'm sorry, Doctor," she apologized and began to cry again, as Charles stared at her, thinking that there was something very odd about her. He had felt as though she'd been a completely different person ever since Olivia left and he was also beginning to think she was having a nervous breakdown. Olivia tried explaining her symptoms to the doctor, although they all sounded terribly foolish now. But she knew now what had caused them. She had begun to feel ill at the exact moment the ship had gone down, and she had been feeling wretched ever since then. What she didn't know was whether or not Victoria was alive, and all she wanted was that reassurance, and no one could give it to her.

The doctor conferred alone with Charles eventually, and he explained about her twin having run away just the week before, and they were in complete agreement about the conclusion. She was suffering from disturbed nerves, and the kind of hysteria that can happen when you separate one twin from another. He was, in fact, surprised it hadn't happened on their honeymoon, and he wasn't at all surprised it had happened now. In fact, he said there were instances when a remaining, or surviving, twin became confused and began to take on the identity, or personality, of the other. And to Charles, it explained his wife's recent almost imperceptible softness. She was suddenly ever so slightly more like Ollie.

The doctor suggested complete rest for her, and hoped that in time she would recover. But in the meantime, he wanted absolutely nothing to upset her. No disturbing news at all, nothing in the least unpleasant. Charles had explained to him what had happened to her when she read about the *Lusitania*.

"Dreadful, isn't it? A shocking thing to happen. Rotten Jerries." And then he suddenly remembered that Charles had lost his wife, and almost his son, on the *Titanic*, and suspected it was upsetting to him too and changed the subject. He suggested he keep Geoff away for another day or two, until she calmed down again, and he asked rather cautiously if it was also possible his wife was pregnant. Charles looked surprised at that, and said that he doubted it, but then suddenly, he began to wonder.

497

"I'll discuss it with her. I suppose she could be," he said expressionlessly. And the doctor promised to come back to see her on Monday. He suggested Charles keep her as calm as possible, and he left some barbital so she could sleep, but when she saw it, Olivia said she wouldn't use it.

"I'll be fine," she said weakly, embarrassed at the stir she'd caused. But all she wanted now was news of the *Lusitania*. She could barely contain herself as Charles sat down next to her with a pained expression. "Is something wrong?" she asked softly, wondering if something else had happened, if he knew or had guessed, or someone had called from Cunard. Her heart pounded as she watched him.

"Not really," he said quietly, "at least I hope not. The doctor asked me a question I realized I couldn't answer."

"What was that?" Who she was? What question? She began to feel hysterical with terror, but she tried not to show it.

"He asked me if you were pregnant." Olivia stared at him in horror. Her sister had told her that there was nothing physical between her and Charles anymore, what did he mean by asking her if she was pregnant?

"Of course not," Olivia said, barely audible as she wondered.

"I know you're not pregnant by me certainly, unless we have an immaculate conception here, which is rather less than likely. But I was wondering if you and Toby had struck things up again. I know he sent you flowers, but I have no idea how involved you are with him, although perhaps you still think it's none of my business." She had certainly stayed out late enough in the afternoon, and never told anyone where she'd been or where she was going. But Olivia looked horrified at the suggestion.

"How could you say a thing like that to me?" She looked incensed, but she was also shocked to hear that Toby Whitticomb had had the audacity to send her sister flowers. "How dare you accuse me of such a thing. I've never seen him again," she said, hoping she was telling him the truth, but she couldn't imagine her sister being stupid enough to fall into his trap again, and she felt sure she wouldn't do it. "No, Charles," she said, aghast. "I am not having an affair with him, and I am not pregnant." She was certain her sister wasn't either. She was too hurt by the past, too angry at all men now, and too hungry for her freedom. Olivia felt in her soul that Victoria would have died sooner than go back to Toby after his betrayal. That much she knew about her sister. And Olivia also knew that she herself was not pregnant, and could not be, she was a virgin.

"I apologize if I've insulted you, but you have to admit, it's not beyond the realm of possibility. You fell into his clutches once, you might have done so again," he said, looking mildly relieved. For some reason Charles didn't think she was lying to him and he believed her.

"I may have been naive," Olivia said coldly, thinking of how Victoria would answer him, and trying to stick to it. "But I'm not stupid."

"I hope not," he said, and left the room, hoping he hadn't upset her too much, but she looked a little brighter. But when he came back to check on her again later that morning, she was crying. She was beside herself over the *Lusitania*. And that afternoon, she snuck downstairs when he went out and read everything she could about the ill-fated ship. She even sent the maid out to buy an evening paper for her, and read the little they had added. They knew nothing yet, except that hundreds had drowned just off Queenstown, Ireland. Bodies had already begun washing up onshore, and Olivia felt her knees go weak again as she read it. But she also knew that all she could do now was wait until Monday, and then go to Cunard and hope they had a list of survivors. And all she could cling to now was the thin hope that her sister would be among them. And in the meantime, she had to keep Charles at bay, and pray he didn't think she was completely crazy.

Chapter 21

What Olivia had not seen, but her sister had, was the small notice the German Embassy put into both the Washington and the New York papers the day she sailed. It said simply that passengers intending to embark on Atlantic voyages were reminded that a state of war existed between Germany and Britain, and her allies. The zone of war included the waters adjacent to the British Isles, and that vessels flying the flag of Great Britain, or her allies, were liable to destruction in those waters, and that travelers in those areas, on British ships, sailed at their own risk. The notice was dated April 22, 1915, Imperial German Embassy, Washington, and sounded quite official.

But it was equally well known that the law

503

of nations dictated that a ship under any flag could not be sunk without warning and removal of its civilian passengers. Under those circumstances, the passengers on the *Lusitania* knew they were in no danger. Victoria also knew that she could have sailed on the American ship, *New York,* but it wasn't nearly as nice a ship, and she liked the idea of sailing on a Cunard ship better. The *Lusitania* was a much faster ship than the *New York,* and she had considered the possibility that it could outrun a submarine far better.

At the time, the *Lusitania* was making one trip a month from Liverpool to New York, and carried no national or even house flags, to keep it safe from the Germans. Even her name and port of registry had been painted out to be completely sure. Watertight doors were kept closed during the entire voyage, and once in the Irish Sea, lifeboats were swung out, and lookouts doubled. Everything was done to protect the ship, and passengers on the *Lusitania* knew they were about as safe as anyone could be from the Germans. Besides, it was an enormous ship, with four stacks painted red and black, a total of ten decks, seven above and three below the waterline. And she had proven herself more than reliable in the past eight years. When Victoria boarded her, she was embarking on her 202nd crossing. The *Lusitania* was no *Titanic*.

And to be absolutely sure no risks were taken at all, they observed full blackout, all staterooms were to draw their curtains at night, and gentlemen were asked not to smoke on deck. And in Victoria's case, nor ladies.

By the first night out, Victoria was completely at ease on the ship, and she was very excited to have seen Lady Mackworth, née Margaret Thomas. Victoria recognized her immediately and knew she was not only an active member of the Women's Social and Political Union, but a close friend of the Pankhursts. Margaret herself had set fire to a post office, and had spent time in jail, much to her respectable Liberal MP father's horror.

But she seemed in good form on the ship, after spending time in New York, and Victoria met her the first night out, as they stood on the deck together.

"It's brave of you to be journeying to Europe now," she said to Victoria, who explained that she was a young widow going to volunteer in France, to work behind the lines with the Allies. She had been given the names of a few contacts in the Red Cross, and some in the French army.

"We could use you in England too." She smiled at her, impressed by her spirit, and then Lady Mackworth had gone on to dinner with her father, while Victoria chose to dine alone in her stateroom.

But they talked her into coming out with them the following night. The first-class dining room was extraordinary, two stories high, with columns all around, and an ornate dome above it. There were also a library, smoking lounges, and a huge nursery for children. There were games for them, and as many entertainments for the young people on board as for the adults. And Victoria was surprised to find that, despite the war, everyone seemed to be in good spirits and spoke very little of it.

The men talked of the news certainly every day, particularly when they gathered to smoke, as Victoria and a few other women also did, but they didn't seem to dwell on it, and no one said anything whatsoever about U-boats.

Victoria had noticed Alfred Vanderbilt on board, but she was careful to avoid him, as he knew her husband. He was roughly the same age as Charles, and she remembered that they knew each other, and Charles had had lunch with him once that winter. And she didn't want anyone telling Charles where she'd gone, or destroying their story that "Olivia" had gone to California. Although she was traveling as Olivia Henderson, it was quite conceivable that someone who knew either of them might recognize her, and she might not even know them, if they were acquaintances of her sister's. So she was careful. She did less socializing than usual, and spent considerable time in the library, on deck, or in her cabin.

Charles Frohman, the theater magnate, was aboard too, he seemed to have brought along a coterie of friends with him, and he was considerably older. He was on his way to London to see James Barrie's new play, *The Rosy Rapture,* which Frohman wanted to bring to Broadway. Charles Klein, the playwright, spent a considerable amount of time talking to him, and had even brought his new play to work on. But although Victoria would have enjoyed meeting them, she kept to herself for much of the voyage, and even declined when she was invited to the captain's dinner. Captain Turner had seen her on deck and thought her stunningly attractive.

Actually, she felt surprisingly free on the ship, and after her year with Charles, it was a great relief to be alone now. The only one she missed terribly was her twin sister. She thought about Olivia constantly, and prayed that she hadn't given up their secret, but Victoria trusted her completely. And like her twin she felt the same agony over being apart now. It was almost haunting.

The weather was pleasant during the entire trip, they met no storms, and by the end of the week, everyone was looking forward to arriving. On Friday, Victoria had packed her bags in the morning, and was pleased to run into Lady Mackworth again at noon. She gave Victoria her address in Newport, and urged her to call her. Victoria was going to be traveling to Dover from Liverpool, and from there by ferry to Calais, and after that she had to make contact with the people whose names she had, and begin moving slowly toward the trenches.

Victoria had lunch alone that day, and it was unseasonably warm as they entered the Celtic Sea and the stewards opened every possible porthole in the dining room, and many of the first-class cabins. By the end of lunch, people were going to their cabins to get changed. Land had been sighted, and they were a mere dozen miles offshore, just south of the lighthouse at Old Kinsale, Ireland. There was an atmosphere of celebration and excitement. They'd made it.

Victoria went out on deck after lunch, and she was standing at the rail, looking out to sea as they headed toward Liverpool when a thin white trail raced just under the sea to starboard. She happened to look down at it as she listened to the animated strains of the "Blue Danube," and wondered if it was a fish of some kind coming at them. She was wearing a red dress Olivia had bought her ages before, and she had left her hat downstairs, as the sun shone down on her, and suddenly the entire ship jarred, and she was flung against the rail as a column of water shot up all the way to the bridge deck, and the whole bow lifted right out of the water. It was the most extraordinary thing she'd ever seen, and she stared at it as she clung to the rail, wondering vaguely if she'd be thrown overboard, but she wasn't. She was wearing high heels and she felt unsteady on her feet as the bow of the vast ship settled down into the sea again as a blinding cloud of steam shot up, and they headed straight toward the lighthouse in the distance.

But within minutes as people exclaimed about what they saw, the ship began listing severely to starboard. Victoria's cabin was on B deck, and all she could think of was getting back to it for her life vest and her money. But there were huge crowds of people everywhere suddenly, and as soon as she started downstairs the ship began listing even more severely to starboard. It was extremely difficult to walk now.

"We've been hit! . . ." she heard someone say. "Torpedo!" An alarm sounded somewhere and the noise was deafening, and beyond it she could still hear music, and all she could think of suddenly was Susan on the *Titanic*.

"Not now," she said to herself, as she hurried downstairs, fighting to keep her balance as she fell against the walls of the ship repeatedly. It was slowly turning sideways. But she reached her cabin in time to grab her life vest, her wallet, and her passport. She took nothing else. She had brought no jewels with her, and she had nothing of value, except her passport, and the funds she'd brought to sustain her.

She struggled to put her life vest on, as she left her cabin again and rushed upstairs, and in the distance she could hear people screaming. There were people panicking all around her, and when she reached the stairs, she almost collided with Alfred Vanderbilt, carrying his jewel case.

"Are you all right?" he asked, perfectly calm. She wasn't sure if he recognized her or not. As usual, he was smiling and courteous. He seemed completely unruffled and he had his manservant with him.

"I think so," she said in answer to his question. "What's happening?" She hadn't even had time to panic. It was all so confusing. But as she spoke to him, they both heard the sound of another explosion far below them.

"Torpedoes," he said pleasantly, "lots of them. You'd best get up on deck quickly." He urged her forward and she went ahead of him, and then lost sight of him. They had already swung the lifeboats out in their davits, but as the ship listed ever more heavily to the starboard side, the boats on the port side were useless. They dangled above the ship at a crazy angle, and those on the starboard side were dipping rapidly toward the water. The *Lusitania* looked like a child's toy, about to turn entirely on its side in the bathtub. But this was no toy, and they were just far enough out to sea for a real disaster. Victoria glanced toward the shore, suddenly wondering if she could swim it. They could see the shore from where they stood, and the people of Queenstown could see the bow of the *Lusitania* go down sharply, as the stern rose in the air. And the screaming on the ship sounded almost like seagulls.

And as the ship began to slide down, the many portholes that had been opened nullified the watertight doors, and took in the rushing water.

Victoria was watching the scene of utter chaos around her, her high heels cast aside by then, her stocking feet on the deck as soot and smoke enveloped them, and she suddenly had trouble breathing. She wasn't sure if it was smoke or panic, but the nose of the ship was well down, and she had to fight to keep her balance. People were literally falling into the sea as the radio antenna fell, nearly killing several people. People were leaping off the ship, and then shouting for help, children were crying and mothers were frantically trying to get them into lifeboats. And then she saw Alfred Vanderbilt again, helping children into the boats. She saw him take his own life vest off and give it to a little girl, and as she watched him she pushed her wallet deep into her dress, secured by her life vest.

And as Victoria watched the lifeboats lowered, she saw the first two overturn and heard people screaming, just as one of the giant funnels fell and engulfed a woman. It was like a scene from hell, as a little girl slid right past her legs on the deck and into the ocean. Victoria screamed, reaching for her, but it was too late, and the child tumbled down and drowned as Victoria watched her.

"Oh my God . . . oh my God . . ." she said, turning away from the horror of it as the blonde curls bobbed for only an instant and then the child lay facedown in the sea beneath her, and a voice behind Victoria told her to get into a lifeboat. Oddly enough, it sounded like her sister, but she never knew who it was, and there was a terrible roaring sound as she headed toward them. It had only been five minutes since they'd been hit, but the ship was going down rapidly, as Victoria reached the lifeboats. For a moment it looked as though there wouldn't be room for her. There were only two boats left and there seemed to be children all around them.

"Take them, not me," she shouted at the young officer helping them into the lifeboat, swinging crazily.

"Can you swim?" he called out, and she nodded and he called back to her again. "Grab a deck chair, we'll be down in a minute," he said, and with that, took off without her, and she followed his advice and grabbed a chair and literally slid off the ship as it went down only an instant later, and she suddenly found herself in a sea of bobbing mattresses, bits of wood, statues, deck chairs, and bodies. It was a hideous conglomeration of things that were literally shooting up from the ship as it hit the bottom, with a series of dull, terrifying explosions, and she screamed as two corpses bumped into her. Everywhere she looked were people screaming, dying, crying, children floating past her, women calling out, and she watched a woman drown as she clutched her dead baby. It was beyond unimaginable, and she went down beneath the surface more than once, but she always seemed to come up again to see one more horror, until finally her deck chair floated next to another one with a little boy in a blue velvet suit lying on it. He looked like a perfect little prince, sleeping there, except that he was dead, and so was his mother. It was the worst thing Victoria had ever seen or dreamt of. She kept closing her eyes and wanting the nightmare to end, but it wouldn't. And she couldn't believe it when she finally saw Captain Turner clinging to a chair, and Lady Mackworth, nearby, clinging to another. And in the distance there were a ship's officer and an old woman sitting on a grand piano.

But all around them people screamed, and everywhere they were drowning. Victoria couldn't bear it anymore after a while, it was just too horrible, her legs were cold, she couldn't breathe from the shock of it all, and people all around her were dying. She held on to her deck chair as long as she could and then, finally, mercifully, she slipped under the water.

Chapter 22

She could hear terrible scraping sounds, and people shouting, and birds screeching overhead, the sounds of hell, as she felt someone drag her along by her feet, her head bumping with each step. She wanted to scream but she couldn't. She knew she must be dead, but then she wasn't so sure, because every inch of her was hurting. She opened her eyes painfully to see who was pulling her, and found herself looking into the face of a man who was pulling her legs and about to drop her into a coffin.

"Oh my God, Sean, this one's alive . . . she's moving." She gave a horrible cough, and vomited what felt like gallons of water. Her hair was matted to her head and her lips were cracked. Her eyes ached, and her lungs felt as though they might explode, and as she looked around, it was nighttime and all around her were coffins, and the smell of death and the ocean. There were birds circling overhead, and Victoria didn't even have the strength to sit up as the man helped her. "We thought you were dead," he said apologetically. "You looked it."

"I feel like I am," she said and retched again, wondering what had happened to the others. But it was easier to see than she wanted. What looked like thousands of corpses were laid out all around them, mostly children. It broke her heart to see it. They looked so sweet, still so beautiful even in death, some of them with their eyes open, others closed, and here and there sobbing mothers.

"The Jerries got your ship," the man called Sean explained. "Fair blew out the bottom. She went down in eighteen minutes. That was five hours ago. We picked you up just outside the harbor, my brother and I. We've all gone out to get them. But there are damn few survivors," he said with a brogue that would have enchanted her at any other moment. "The subs have been out there for weeks, you know, rotten bastards. They hang around the mouth of the harbor." She couldn't help wondering if Captain Turner had known that.

"Come on," he said, "let me help you up, you're a lucky girl," he said, pulling her gently to her bare feet. Her silk stockings were completely gone, vanished, along with most of her dress. She was wearing only what looked like a slip and panties, and a red blouse under her life vest above her waistband, but when she felt for it, she still had her wallet. And she wasn't even embarrassed as the young seaman half dragged, half carried her into the local pub, where they were taking the survivors. They had opened the church too, and the Queen's Hotel, the Town Hall, and the Queenstown and Royal Naval Hospitals. And there was a hot tea stand at the station. They were doing everything they could for the survivors, and Cunard had ordered two thousand coffins.

As Victoria walked into the bar, assisted by Sean, she looked around and saw one or two familiar faces, among them the captain. He had come into Queenstown on a small steamer called the *Bluebell,* which had also picked up Margaret Mackworth.

"Nice dress," one woman said wryly, looking up at her. She was one of a few who still

had both her children with her, but all three of
them were naked. And in other corners of the
room, women sobbed for their lost husbands
and babies. They had seen them slip right out
of their arms on the deck, watched them fall, or
be hit by debris, or simply drown in the cold
water. It was beyond belief, beyond anything
Victoria had ever read about, or dreamt of.
And all she could think of now was sending a
telegram to her sister. She knew it was dangerous contacting her, but she also knew she had
absolutely no choice. She had to tell Olivia she
was alive, and had survived the disaster.

At midnight, the American consul, Wesley
Frost, made the rounds of all the locations
where the survivors were being brought and
asked what he could do for each of them. She
gave him Olivia's name and address and a cryp-
tic message. She knew she would understand
what it meant, and she asked him to confirm to
her when he had sent it, and he promised. He
had more than his hands full that night. There
had been 189 Americans on board, and there
was no way yet of telling how many of them
were dead, but he had hysterical people around
him everywhere, of all nationalities, many of
them severely injured. And all those who had

survived were desperate to contact their relatives and reassure them.

"I'll take care of it as soon as possible, Miss Henderson," he promised her, and handed her one of the blankets the local women had left them. There were people all around them in rags, some of them completely naked, and no one even noticed.

"Thank you, I appreciate it," she said, her teeth were chattering violently, and she still found it hard to breathe. She had taken in a lot of water. And as she sat leaning against the wall in the bar, sitting on the floor in her underwear, she thought about what had happened, all she had seen, the sheer horror of it, and wondered if Alfred Vanderbilt had made it. So far, she hadn't seen him. But it made her think too of Geoffrey who had survived a similar disaster on the *Titanic*, and watched his mother go down with her. Suddenly she had far more sympathy for what he'd been through and wished she could have put her arms around him at that moment, and her sister. She closed her eyes then, as though to shut out the images, especially of a woman, screaming, saying she was giving birth, just as she had become unconscious. But all she could see when she closed her eyes was Olivia sitting on the bed in her bedroom in New York and Victoria wished she could reach out and touch her. And with every ounce of her being she tried to concentrate and tell her she was all right, and prayed with all her soul that Olivia would know it.

Chapter 23

When Olivia watched Geoffrey and Charles eat breakfast on Monday, May tenth, she thought she would scream if they took a moment longer. She was still feeling ill, and she had had a fierce argument with Charles about reading the paper.

"The doctor said you weren't to upset yourself," he reminded her, taking the paper away from her, and she grabbed it from him.

"Give it to me, Charles!" she shouted at him in a voice she didn't recognize herself, and he looked at her in surprise and then handed it to her as she apologized. "I'm sorry, I'm not myself. I just want to read about something and get my mind off Olivia, that's all."

"I understand perfectly," he said curtly, and finally, mercifully, left for the office.

Even Geoff seemed to drag his feet going to school that day, but the moment he was gone, Olivia grabbed her hat and purse and ran out the door, hailed a cab and gave him the address of the Cunard office on State Street. But she was totally unprepared for what she found there. There was a veritable human sea of wild, shouting people, screaming, throwing things, calling names, crying, begging for information, and when they didn't get it, they got ugly. Officials from the shipping line did what they could to stave off the crowd, with the help of the police, but in the end, it was obvious that they had very little information. They had staggering numbers of losses by then, well over the thousand mark they feared, perhaps more, and Frohman's body had been found, floating near Queenstown, but other than that, there were only bits and pieces of information, and mostly terrifying rumors. There was also word that there had been celebration in Germany over the victory of the U-boat, which enraged the crowd even further.

But after seven hours of standing there, Olivia still did not have what she had come for, the list of survivors. They had promised it for the next day. And her heart felt like lead as she walked back outside at four-thirty. She had been on her feet all day, eaten nothing at all, and had done everything she could to grasp at every scrap of information. There were a few names, some lists of casualties. One young man had said the line was taking photographs of the bodies in Queenstown in order to identify them later. Just the thought of it made her shudder. And yet, when she stood very quietly, it was as though she could hear Victoria talking to her. She didn't feel as though she were dead, whatever that felt like. Perhaps she would die too then. Maybe that was how she would know. She was so tired she was numb, as she walked all the way back to the house on the East River.

And as she walked up the front steps, her body aching as much as her mind by then, she happened to see a young boy in uniform, approaching. He wore the uniform of Western Union, and as she looked at him, she felt her heart stop, and hurried back down the stairs to him. She grabbed his arm without thinking, and looked like a madwoman as she clutched him.

"Do you have a telegram for me? Victoria Dawson?" She knew that was the name it would come to if Victoria dared send it to her there, but she was sure Victoria wouldn't be cruel enough to leave her in silence if she were alive, and she was grateful she was right as he nodded.

"Yes . . . I . . . here," he said, and almost ran away from her. She felt like a witch as she snatched it from him and ripped it open. Her hands shook so terribly she could hardly read what it said, and she felt herself gulp great sobs of air as she read it. The girl was crazy. Absolutely nuts. But she was alive in Queenstown.

"Trip began with a bang. Stop," it said. "Thank God for Mr. Bridgeman. Stop. All well in Queenstown. Stop. I love you always. Stop." Mr. Bridgeman was their old swimming teacher in Croton. And Olivia stood whooping and crying on the steps as she read it, and she didn't care who heard her. There was no other information, no address, nowhere to reach her or find her. But Olivia knew her twin was alive and well and had survived the sinking of the *Lusitania*. It was all she needed to know now. And she crushed the message in her hand, and then hurried into the house, and burned the paper in the oven, although she suspected she probably should have saved it, but it was too dangerous to keep. Someone might have found it and figured out where she really was.

It had been the worst three days of Olivia's life, and she hoped she never had to go through anything like it again. She was so exhausted, she decided to take a bath, and filled her tub with hot water and bubbles. She didn't know what to do to celebrate, dance or sing or cry. Instead, she ran into Geoffrey's room and hugged him, which he found unusual. He thought Victoria was definitely going crazy. His father had said something to him about her nerves, but he was beginning to think it was her mind that was all messed up now. But he had never seen her in such good spirits.

"What happened to you today?" he asked as she pirouetted happily and grinned at him. I got my sister back, she wanted to say. She's alive. She's fine. She's in Queenstown. She didn't die on the *Lusitania*. "You sure look happy."

"I am. It was a lovely day," she said, beaming at him. "What about you? Good day at school?"

"No," he said matter-of-factly, "pretty boring. Where's Dad?"

"He's not home yet." She left him then to get into the tub, and she came down to dinner wearing a new dress and looking like a new person. Charles had just come in the door and he looked tired and grumpy. But he washed his hands and came straight in to dinner.

"What are you so happy about?" He looked at her unhappily, and glanced at Geoff, as though he expected an explanation.

"I just feel better, that's all."

"Have your intuitions calmed down?"

"Maybe," she said, embarrassed at the nightmare the weekend had been, and relieved beyond belief that it was over, but of course Charles didn't know that. "I just feel better, that's all." Looking at her, he wondered what she'd been up to, and if she really was having an affair, but she was very pleasant to him, and even sweet to Geoff that night, and he was somewhat mollified by the time the cook poured coffee after dinner.

"I spoke to an investigator today," he said quietly, when Geoff went upstairs to finish his homework. "He'll start looking for her in California next week. He says he has some very good contacts there," he reassured her, and she thanked him. But each time she looked at him, she could not stop smiling.

"What on earth did you do today, Victoria, to put you in such good spirits? I'm afraid you're making me very suspicious." But she looked so pretty and so young that night that he didn't have the heart to be angry at her, although he wondered if he should have been.

"I just feel better. I feel relieved," she tried to explain it to him to the extent that she dared. "It is as though I know she's all right now, although I can't explain it." But he had great respect for the telepathy they shared, although he didn't understand it.

"Maybe you're right," he said quietly, "I hope so." He was happy that she felt better at least. The weekend had been a nightmare, he had really begun to think she was having a nervous breakdown.

"I'm sorry I was so much trouble."

"Don't worry about it, you weren't. I was just worried about you," he said almost shyly, glancing at her. She seemed so much more open with him than she had before, he wondered if Olivia leaving so abruptly had changed her, or if the doctor was right, and she would take on more of Olivia's personality after her disappearance. In Victoria's case, it would have been a definite improvement. And in the time that Olivia had been gone, Victoria was more dependent on him than she ever had been, more willing to reach out to him than before her sister's disappearance. He remembered Friday night, when she had clung to him and told him she was frightened. It had made him look at her now a little differently, although he didn't want to be too optimistic. They had been married almost exactly eleven months by then, and he had all but given up on their marriage.

"I'll try not to be a nuisance again," she said quietly, and went upstairs to write some letters. She wished she could write to Victoria, but of course she couldn't. Not yet anyway, she would when her twin reached her final destination in the trenches. And she hoped that Victoria would write to her, soon preferably, at her father's house on Fifth Avenue, as they had agreed to. Olivia wanted to know all about what had happened on the *Lusitania*.

Charles read for a while before he went to bed that night. They had both kissed Geoff, and he came back into their bedroom and said something to her about the *Lusitania*. "It's a dreadful thing, the Germans sinking that ship. It sounds as though they've had a huge loss of life, worse than the *Titanic*. I didn't want Geoff to hear too much about it, I thought it might remind him of his mother." She looked at him for a long moment and then nodded.

"And you, Charles?" she asked quietly. "Are you all right . . . did it remind you of her too?" Her kindness struck him like a blow, and for a moment he couldn't answer. He hadn't expected that of her. Theirs was such an adversarial relationship, that it was odd to get a gentle touch from her, and not a tart word or an angry answer.

"It did," he said finally. "I had a hard time with it all weekend." While she was suffering, so was he, and she hadn't even known it.

"I'm sorry, Charles," she said, and he turned away and nodded. He didn't say anything to her again, and a little while later, they went to bed, both careful, as usual, to keep on their own sides, with a vast distance between them.

"That was nice of you," he said suddenly in the dark, and surprised her. "Asking about how I felt, I mean . . . about Susan . . . and the ship that went down. It's so odd how those things come back sometimes. It was so incredibly awful waiting to hear, desperate to know. I drove them absolutely mad at White Star, and they still didn't know, and then waiting on the dock in the rain for the *Carpathia* to come in . . . I didn't know till then if either of them were alive," he said, sounding choked. "I thought neither of them had survived . . . and then I saw him . . . one of the crew members was carrying Geoff . . . and I looked everywhere behind him for Susan. But she wasn't there. And I knew. I took the boy from him, and we went home. It took Geoff months to talk about it. I don't suppose you ever forget that." Just as Victoria would never forget what she had just been through.

"I'm so sorry you had to go through that," she said softly, and gently reached out and touched his shoulder. "It's not fair, for either of you. You didn't deserve that." She was so sorry for both of them, it tore at her heart, and as he looked at her in the dim light from the moon outside, he saw something in her that would have frightened him before, but suddenly it didn't.

"Maybe things happen in life for reasons. You wouldn't be here if that hadn't happened," he said kindly, and she smiled sadly at him, well aware of what they'd been through.

"And you'd be a lot happier if I weren't." She was still angry at her sister for leaving him and Geoffrey, particularly after all that had just happened. It certainly proved the trip was dangerous. And her flippant "off with a bang" was no exaggeration.

"Don't say that," he said generously. "Maybe Susan was taken from us for a reason.

I've thought that sometimes. It's impossible to know why some things happen."

"I feel very lucky to know you," she said kindly, and meant it, not realizing that it was an odd thing to say to her husband. Olivia was still so innocent, and he saw that in her as he looked into her eyes that night and it surprised him.

"That's a sweet thing to say," he said gently, wondering if he'd ever really known her, or only thought he did. She seemed suddenly so different. And without saying another word to her, he slid slowly closer to her and kissed her. He held her face carefully in his hands and kissed her ever so softly on the lips, afraid to scare her. He didn't want to start the old problems between them again, he just wanted to tell her that he was grateful for what she had said to him, and if nothing else, for her friendship. But when he kissed her, he felt something stir in him that she had never brought out in him before, though he didn't know why, and he kissed her again, and tried to tell himself that he shouldn't. "Should we be doing this?" he whispered hoarsely to her and she shook her head, but she didn't want to stop, although she told herself that she had to. But as he kissed her repeatedly, she forgot everything she knew about their relationship, and felt her arms go around his neck and her body press against his, and he sprang to life instantly as he held her. "Victoria, I don't want to do anything you don't want," he said huskily. They had been through this before, though not for months, and always regretted it. Their sex life had done nothing but make them both very unhappy.

"Charles, I don't know . . . I . . . ." She wanted to tell him to stop, she knew how wrong this was, he was her sister's husband, and yet Victoria had come back from the dead, and she had moved on to her own life, and Olivia was there in his arms with the man she had loved for so long. She couldn't stop now. "I love you," she whispered. She had never said that to him before, and he looked at her in tender amazement.

"Oh sweet girl," he said, feeling his heart go out to her, giving her everything he had tried to keep from her, and suddenly he knew what had been wrong between them. He had never dared to love her. "How I love you," he said almost in spite of himself, and then, as though for the first time, which it was for her, and he didn't realize, he made love to her ever so gently. In spite of the pain it caused her at first, she gave herself to him completely and without reserve, with total abandon, and as he looked down at her afterwards, he felt as though he had been reborn. For both of them, it was a new beginning, a new life, the honeymoon they'd never had and each of them had longed for.

He lay for hours in her arms, stroking her, caressing her, discovering her all over again, he thought, but in fact for the first time, and at last he slept, nestled next to her, as she held him, wondering what they would do when Victoria got home. Charles was the greatest joy she'd ever had in her life, and at the same time the worst betrayal. She had no idea what she would say to her sister when she got home, but she knew at that moment, that she couldn't leave him.

Chapter 24

After Wesley Frost, the American consul in Queenstown, found her a dress and a pair of shoes to wear, Victoria took a train from Queenstown to Dublin on Sunday. She was met by a Cunard representative there, and then took the boat train to the Lime Street Station in Liverpool. There were a number of other survivors on the train with her, and she was startled to see members of the press waiting to interview them at the Lime Street Station. Vance Pitney of the *New York Tribune* had already been to Queenstown by then, and then on to Liverpool after that, and from there he would go on to London. It was the biggest story any newspaper had had since the *Titanic*. And this one was even bigger because the giant ship had been torpedoed by the Germans. This was not only a tragedy, which had cost more than a thousand lives, it was war news. But Victoria was careful to avoid the press as she left the station and went to the Adelphi Hotel, where she tried to figure out what to do next. When she got there late Sunday afternoon, she was still very badly shaken.

And the dress she was wearing looked awful. As she checked into her room, she lit a cigarette, and as she sat down and looked around, she started to cry, wishing she were home in Croton. It wasn't too late to turn back, but it had been one hell of a beginning.

The hotel sent a tray to her room that night, they knew who she was, and why she was there. There had been whispers in the lobby when she arrived. She had explained her situation to the desk clerk, even her bank draft and her British currency was wet, as well as her letter of credit, and she was going to have to go to the bank on Monday to change them. But as much as possible, she tried to avoid any undue attention. But no matter what she did that night, she couldn't get the grisly images out of her head of the ship going down, bow first, and the faces of the people who had died all around her. She still remembered the face of the young crew member who had told her to grab a deck chair, fast, when she couldn't get into the lifeboats, and his advice had saved her.

She was awake all night, and she looked a mess when she got up the next morning. But after she'd had something to eat, and a big cup of hot coffee, she felt better. She went to the bank after that, and got her money sorted out, and then she went to the nearest shop, and bought a few dresses, some sweaters and a pair of slacks, and two pairs of shoes, and even a pair of boots she could wear when she got to the trenches. She didn't know if they'd give her a uniform or not, but this way she had something to wear when she got there. She needed underwear, stockings, nightgowns, cosmetics, a comb. She had absolutely nothing left, not even the shreds of her red dress which she had left in Queenstown.

"You running away from home?" the woman in the shop asked her with a giggle, but Victoria wasn't laughing at anything yet. She just looked at her and shook her head.

"I was on the *Lusitania* when it went down," Victoria said solemnly, and the woman gasped. Like the entire world by then, she had heard about it.

"You're lucky you're alive, dearie," the

woman whispered, and blessed her. And Victoria smiled sadly as she took her bundles and went back to the hotel, still haunted by the others. She wondered if she would see them all her life, especially the children with their sweet faces and unseeing eyes floating all around her. She kept thinking of the little boy floating dead on a deck chair in the blue velvet suit, with the commemorative *Lusitania* pin stuck on his collar. It was enough to make anyone hate the Germans forever.

But by late that afternoon, Victoria was slowly starting to revive, and she began thinking about how she was going to get to France. Her plans had changed to say the least, but the clerk at the hotel told her how to get to Dover, and what to do after that. She had to take a small ferry to Calais, and that was risky too, there were U-boats lurking in the English Channel between France and England, and the thought of them now made her shudder.

"Maybe I should have just bought myself a bathing costume and saved myself a lot of trouble," she said with a nervous grin and the desk clerk smiled at her spirit.

"You're a hell of a good sport, miss," he said, "I'm not sure I'd try it again after what you've just been through."

"I don't have much choice if I want to get to France, do I?" she said pensively, and knew she had to do it. It was why she had come here, and no one had said it was going to be easy.

The Germans had introduced chlorine gas at the Battle of Ypres two weeks before, and from everything Victoria had heard, the battle was still raging, and thus far it had been a slaughter. The question was how to get as close to it as she could, and reach the contacts she had been given. They were based in Reims, and the best she could do was try to reach them when she got to Calais, if the phones were working. That remained to be seen. It was all an adventure, a pilgrimage she had felt she had to make, and she hoped she hadn't been wrong in coming. The signs, so far, had certainly not been propitious.

She left Liverpool on Tuesday morning, and thanked everyone at the hotel. For the past two days, people had brought her little things, small gifts, cakes, fruit, little religious objects, just to let her know that they were glad she had survived the *Lusitania*.

She went back to the Lime Street Station by taxi, and from there took a train to Dover and then on to the ferry when they reached the docks. There were small ferry boats, and they looked harmless enough on a sunny day in May, but after the experience she'd just had in the Celtic Sea, she knew how treacherous the U-boats were and she wasn't anxious to encounter another.

She negotiated the fare with the captain of the ferry boat, and there were only a handful of other passengers when he took her over. It was a bright blue, cloudless afternoon, but she spent the entire voyage clutching the rail in total terror, prepared to die at any moment.

"Vous avez bien peur, mademoiselle." He smiled at her. He had rarely seen a girl as lovely or as frightened. He had commented on her being nervous on the trip over, and she only nodded and said one word to him, as she kept her eyes riveted to the water, watching for U-boats and the single white trail she had seen just before it hit the *Lusitania*.

"Lusitania," she said, knowing he would understand it. The whole world did, as she knew from reading the papers. And each time she read another article, she cringed, thinking of poor Olivia and what she must have been thinking.

But the sailor on the little ferry boat had completely understood her. He didn't say another word to her on the brief crossing to Calais, and when they got there, he carried her bags for her, and turned her over to a man with a car who drove her to the nearest hotel, and refused to take any money from her. There were several lengthy conversations, and then they gave her a pretty little room, looking out over the water.

She asked to use the telephone then, and called one of the names she'd been given in New York at the French Consulate. It was a woman who organized volunteers for the Red Cross in Paris, and she was going to be able to tell Victoria where to go from there, and where she would be needed. But as it turned out, she was out, and no one else spoke English.

"Rappellez demain, mademoiselle," and all she got was "tomorrow."

She sat alone in her room that night, smoking cigarettes and thinking of the journey she had made and what it had taken to come here. She had deceived a husband, abandoned a father and a twin, had a ship sunk under her and survived it, and now God only knew what waited for her here. She had to marvel at her own determination. Nothing seemed to stop her. Not even the unpleasant woman she reached in Paris the next day, who told her they were too busy to talk to her and to call back again the next day.

"No!" she shouted into the phone rapidly, determined not to be put off again. She was wasting her time here. "No, I need to talk to someone *now . . . maintenant . . .*" And then she threw in the magic words, just to see what would happen if she did. "I've just come off the *Lusitania*." There was a brief silence, and then she could hear muffled words at the other end. There was another pause and then a man took the phone and asked her what her name was. "Olivia Henderson. I got your name, or the lady's, from the French Consul in New York. I've come here to volunteer at the front. I'm American, and I'm in Calais right now."

"And you were on the *Lusitania*?" He sounded somewhat in awe and she was glad she had said it.

"Yes."

"My God . . . can you be in Reims at five o'clock tomorrow?"

"I don't know," she said honestly. "I think so. Where is it?"

"About a hundred and fifty miles southeast of you. If you can get someone to drive you there, they can come right through the back country behind it. There's fighting there, but it's not as bad as in Soissons nearby. But you'll still have to be pretty careful." And then he smiled into the phone, wondering why she had come so far to participate in a war that her government wanted no part of. President Wilson was still determined to stay out of it at all costs, and the costs were incredible so far. Five million men had died since war had been declared the previous summer. And seven million more had been wounded. "Find someone with a car," the voice at the other end went on, "and get there if you can. We have a delegation of volunteers coming down tomorrow. Are you a nurse?" he asked hopefully.

"No, I'm sorry," she apologized, wondering if they would still want her.

"Can you drive?"

"Yes."

"Good. You can drive an ambulance, or a truck, whatever they tell you to. Just be there tomorrow," he said, and was about to hang up when she stopped him.

"What's your name?" she asked, and he smiled at her naïveté. She was obviously very new at this, and he couldn't help wondering again why she had come here, to risk her life in a war that belonged to other countries. Others

545

had come too, but most of them were older, and had complicated stories. She sounded like a child to him over the telephone, and then he told her that his name was unimportant, he wouldn't be there. "Who do I look for then?"

He sounded irritated again. "Anyone who's bleeding. You'll find a lot of them, I'm afraid. You'll have your work cut out for you when you get there. Ask for the captain in charge of the area, he'll direct you to the hospital, or the Red Cross if we're there. You'll find us, don't worry. It's a small war, with a lot of people in it. You can't miss us." And he hung up then. She thanked them at the desk and went back to her hotel room.

She had a good dinner that night, and the owner of the hotel negotiated with a driver for her. He was a young boy with an old Renault, but he said he could get her where she was going, by the back roads. He said it would take all day, and he wanted to set out early in the morning. And she guessed as she looked at him that he was younger than she was. His name was Yves, and she paid him in advance just as he asked her. He told her to dress warmly and wear heavy shoes. It would be cold when they left, and if the car broke down he didn't want to have to carry her to Reims because she had

high heels on. She looked annoyed at the remark, but he laughed anyway, and she asked
him bluntly if the car broke down often.

"Not more often than it has to. Can you
drive?" he asked, and she nodded. And then he
left and told her he'd see her in the morning.

Victoria lay awake in her bed all that
night, she was so excited she couldn't sleep.
This was why she had come here. But it was
harder to remember the next morning. It was
cold, and it was damp, and she hadn't slept all
night. She was glad to find that the hotel had
packed a lunch for them, and the boy had
brought a thermos of coffee given him by his
mother.

"Why did you come here?" he asked as
she poured the first cup, on their way to their
first stop on the way to Doullens. It was going
to be a long journey.

"I came over because I thought I was
needed here," she said, wondering if she could
explain it to him. It was hard enough explaining
it to herself these days, let alone a boy from
Calais who barely spoke her language. "I felt
useless where I was, because I wasn't doing
anything for anyone. This seemed more important." He nodded. He had understood her. It

sounded noble, even to her, the way she expressed it.

"You have no family," he said, assuming she didn't. She didn't tell him she had a husband and a stepson that she had left behind, or he really would have thought she was crazy, or at least rotten.

"I am a twin," she said to him, *"jumelle,"* which seemed more interesting and it was a word she knew in almost every language. It was a word which always made people brighten. And it did him, as he glanced at her.

"Identique?" Yves asked her with interest.

"Oui." She nodded.

"Très amusant." He nodded his approval. "She did not wish to come with you?"

"No," Victoria said firmly, telling the lie that she had created in order to come here, "she's married, she couldn't." He nodded that he had understood, but in truth he had no idea how complicated it all was. He just thought he understood it.

And after that, they rode on for a long while in silence. They passed farms and churches, and the occasional country school, and fields that hadn't been planted that year. There were no young men to do it. He tried to explain that to her in pantomime, and she got it. And then they rode in silence again for a while and she lit a cigarette and had another cup of coffee.

"*Vous fumez?*" He looked impressed. French women of her ilk didn't do that. But she nodded. "*Très moderne.*" He nodded and laughed. She was "*très moderne*" even in New York, in fact a little too much so.

And then they drove through Montdidier, and after that Senlis, and it was long after nightfall when they finally got to Reims. She had long since missed her five o'clock rendez-vous with the Red Cross, and they had long since run out of coffee and food, and she and Yves could both hear guns in the distance. They sounded closer than they were, and there was the occasional rat-a-tat-tat of machine guns.

"It's not good for us to be here," he said nervously, glancing around him, but they were coming in to Châlons-sur-Marne exactly the way they'd been told to, and a few minutes later, they saw a field hospital and she told him to stop there. There were stretchers being carried in and out, and men in bloodied aprons standing in little knots conferring, and nurses rushing to help dying men, or wounded ones. Yves looked uncomfortable, and Victoria just stood there and stared at the action around her. She felt as though she had been awake for days, and her whole life had been turned upside down, and yet she felt a sudden surge of excitement just to be there.

She asked someone standing by if there was anyone from the Red Cross there, and they just smiled at her, and moved on, although she was sure they spoke English. And Yves said he had to go then. He was going to just leave her there and let her work it out for herself. But she hadn't hired him to be a guide for her for the rest of the war, her private chauffeur. He waved as he got back in the car again and she shouted *"Merci"* as he drove off, but he was obviously in a hurry to get out of Châlons-sur-Marne, and she didn't really blame him. But she had no idea what to do next as she stood there.

There were people hurrying in and out of the tent, and a few stared at her. She looked so clean and so untouched as she stood looking somewhat forlorn with her suitcase. And finally, not knowing what else to do, she asked an orderly for the nurses' station.

"In there," he said vaguely, motioning over his shoulder, as he hauled a huge bag of refuse away, and Victoria shuddered to think what was in it.

But the nurses were too busy to talk to her, a fresh group of wounded had just come in, and no one had time to waste on a greenhorn.

"Here," an orderly said suddenly, throwing an apron at her as the last nurse ran away to a man screaming in the corner. "I need you. Follow me." He moved hurriedly between two hundred stretchers lying on the ground, twelve inches apart, and she had to move as quickly and carefully as she could, not to step on them as she followed. There was a smaller tent beyond being used as an operating room. And there were men lying on the ground waiting to be carried in, some of them moaning softly, others shrieking piteously, some of them mercifully unconscious.

"I don't know what to do," Victoria said nervously. She had expected to meet someone, to have them explain things to her, to drive an ambulance, or do something she knew she could do, not be here with these men, so badly savaged by explosions and shells and shrapnel. There were hideous burns, and many of them had been poisoned by the phosgene and chlorine gases the Germans were pelting them with.

It was so new and so cruel that the Allies had no comparable weapon with which to fight it.

The orderly she was following was short and wiry, he had bright red hair, and she had heard someone call him Didier when they passed him. She was very grateful he spoke English. And she almost fainted when she realized he expected her to help him care for the men who had just been brought in from the trenches. All of them had been severely gassed, and many of them were incoherent. He pointed out a group of them to her, and spoke in an undervoice in English.

"Do what you can for them," he said quietly amidst the hellish din. She was suddenly reminded of the people she'd seen around her in the sea when the *Lusitania* went down. But this was so much worse, and they were still living. "They won't last the night. Too much gas. We can't help them." There was a man at her feet with green vomit oozing from his nose and mouth, and Victoria clutched Didier's arm as he moved to leave her.

"I'm not a nurse," she said, gagging on her own bile. This was too much for her. She couldn't do it. She knew she shouldn't have come here. "I can't . . ."

"I'm not a nurse either," he said sharply,

"I'm a musician . . . are you going to stay or not?" he asked her bluntly. This was her trial by fire. This was what she had said she wanted. "If you're not, go. I have no time for this . . ." He looked angry at her, as though she had come here for nothing, a dilettante, to show off to her friends. But the look in his eyes challenged her, and she nodded.

"I'll stay," she said hoarsely, and knelt slowly toward the man closest to her. Half his face had been shot off, and there were bloody bandages covering him, but the doctors in the surgery had decided not to waste their time on him. He was too far gone for them to spend hours on him. In a proper hospital perhaps, but not here. He'd never make it. He'd be dead within hours.

"Hello . . . what's your name?" he asked in a voice already tinged with death, "I'm Mark." He was English.

"I'm Olivia," she answered, giving him the name she had to use now. She felt helpless, as she took the boy's hand in her own, and held tightly to his fingers, trying not to look at him and see the wound, but something beyond it.

"You're American," he said softly in a Yorkshire accent. "I was there once . . ."

"I'm from New York." As though it mattered.

"When'd you get here?" He was clinging to life, holding on to her, feeling that if he talked to her, he would make it through the night, but they both knew he wouldn't.

"Tonight," she said, feeling very green again, as she smiled at him, and another boy yanked at her apron.

"From America, I mean . . . when did you come?" Mark asked her.

"Last weekend . . . on the *Lusitania,*" she said numbly. There were so many of them. All she could hear were their sobs and their screams. It was just like when the ship had been sinking.

"Bloody rotten thing of the Jerries to do . . . women and children . . . they're animals they are," he said, and she could see it from what they had done to him. And then she turned to the other one who was calling for her, he wanted his mother and he was thirsty. He was seventeen, from Hampshire, and he died holding her hand twenty minutes later. She talked to hundreds of men that night, and dozens of them died as she watched them. She did nothing in particular for them, held a hand, lit a cigarette, she gave all of her own away, gave them water though they shouldn't drink, but it didn't matter anyway, some of them had no stomachs left, or no lips, or lungs filled with gases. It was horrible beyond belief, and she wondered if she'd been of any use at all as she staggered out of the tent again in the morning. She was covered with vomit and blood and spit, and she had no idea where to go, or where her suitcase had gone the night before. She'd forgotten it and all else as she knelt beside the boys who called her name, held her hand, or just died in her arms as she watched them. She'd helped Didier carry them outside on stretchers and lay them on the ground until other men came to carry them away to be buried. There were thousands of them now, all so young, buried in the hillsides.

"There's food in the tent over there." Didier came by on his way to get fresh supplies, and he pointed to a larger tent just far enough away that she wondered if she'd make it. She hadn't slept all night, and every inch of her ached, but he looked tireless as he smiled at her. "Are you sorry you've come yet, Olivia?" he asked. She was so tired she almost slipped and told him Olivia was her sister. But while she was here, it was her name now.

"No," she lied with a tired smile, but he

knew she was lying. She'd worked hard the night before, she might actually be worth having around, if she stayed. Most volunteers didn't. They stayed for a few days, and then ran away, shocked by what they'd seen, and happy to go home again. Others, the hardy ones, the ones who could take it and they were rare, came and stayed forever. Some of the volunteers had been with them since the beginning. It had been nearly a year now. But he didn't think she'd be one of them. She was too young and too pretty. She had probably just come for the excitement, he figured.

"You'll get used to it. Wait till winter, you'll love it." They'd been up to their hips in mud for months. The rains had been relentless. But it was better than what had happened to the Russians, freezing in Galicia. But as she listened to him, she realized that by winter she wouldn't be there. She'd be back in New York again, with Charles and Geoffrey. They seemed so far away to her now, as though they didn't even exist anymore. The only one who still seemed real to her was Olivia, she seemed to live in her soul, and Victoria could almost hear her talking to her at night sometimes. It was uncanny.

She left Didier then, and staggered

toward the tent that he said was their mess hall, and as she approached it, she smelled coffee and food and unfamiliar smells, and she suddenly realized that despite the carnage she had seen, she was starving. She helped herself to powdered eggs and stew that was mostly gristle, and a thick slab of bread that turned out to be so stale it was like a block of wood, but she ate it anyway, softening it in her stew. And she drank two huge cups of strong black coffee. A few of the nurses and some of the orderlies said hello to her, but everyone was either busy, or exhausted. They seemed to have a whole city organized there, with tents as barracks, a hospital, supply depots, the mess hall. There was a small château well behind them where the senior officers were billeted, including the general who was their commanding officer, and there was a farmhouse too, for the rest of the senior men. The others all stayed in the barracks. And Victoria still had no idea where they would put her.

"Are you here with the Red Cross?" a pleasant, heavyset girl asked. She was wearing a nurse's uniform, and eating a huge breakfast although she was covered with bloodstains. Twelve hours before Victoria might have been horrified, but now it suddenly seemed normal.

"I was going to be," Victoria explained. The other girl had said her name was Rosie, and like many of the others here, she was English. "I think I missed them yesterday. I don't know what happened."

"I think I do," Rosie looked at her with an odd expression, as Victoria waited. "Their car was hit in Meaux. There were three of them. They were all killed yesterday afternoon on the way here." The horrifying thought was that she might have been with them, if she'd tried to join them in Paris. Thank God she hadn't. "What are you going to do?" she asked quietly, and Victoria thought about it for a long moment. She wasn't even sure she was going to stay yet. This was a lot rougher than she'd expected. While she was still in New York, and listening to lectures about the war at the consulates, it had seemed so clean and so definite, the ideology so pure, the problems so simple. She was going to drive for them. But drive what? Dying men? Corpses to their makeshift morgue? She had never really understood it till she got here. But she also knew now that if she wanted to be, she could be useful.

"I'm not sure," Victoria said hesitantly. "I'm not a trained nurse or anything. I'm not sure how useful I'd be to anyone." Victoria looked at Rosie shyly, which was unlike her. "Who should I talk to?"

"Sergeant Morrison," Rosie said with a smile, "she's in charge of the volunteers, and don't kid yourself, girl. We need all the help we can get, trained or not, if you can stand it." That was the question.

"How do I find her?" Victoria asked carefully, still trying to decide what to do about staying.

Rosie laughed at her question and poured herself another cup of coffee. "Wait about ten minutes, and she'll find you. Sergeant Morrison knows everything that goes on here. And that's a warning." She grinned. And she wasn't wrong. Not five minutes later, a gigantic woman in a uniform strode rapidly over to them and seemed to measure Victoria with her eyes. She had already heard from Didier about the new arrival. Sergeant Morrison was six feet tall, she had blonde hair and blue eyes, and she was Australian, from Melbourne. She'd been in France for nearly a year, and she'd even been wounded. She worked her volunteers like slaves, and according to Rosie, she put up with no nonsense.

"I understand they put you right to work last night," she said to Victoria pleasantly, and the young American felt herself quake as she looked up at her in amazement.

"Yes, they did," she said, sitting up very straight, and suddenly feeling like a private. It was odd being here, it was all so orderly and so civilized, in the midst of chaos. Everyone knew what they had to do, and what was expected.

"How did you like it?" Sergeant Morrison asked bluntly.

"I'm not sure 'like' is the right word," Victoria said cautiously as Rosie left them to go back to the operating room. She had another twelve hours of work to do. They worked on twenty-four-hour shifts there, or till they dropped, whichever came first. She had actually worked thirty hours straight once. "Most of the men I took care of last night were dead before morning," Victoria said softly, as Penny Morrison nodded briskly, but her eyes were not without emotion.

"It happens that way a lot here. How do you feel about that, Miss Henderson?" She had remembered her name, she knew who she was, and Victoria didn't know it yet, but she had already sent her suitcase to the barracks and assigned her a cot in the female section. "We can use your help here," she said honestly. "I don't know why you've come here, and I don't really care, but if you've got the stomach for it, we need you very badly. The men have been taking a terrible beating." Victoria had already seen that the night before, and she'd even been given a gas mask herself just in case everything went wrong, and the trenches broke, and the Germans overran them.

"I'd like to stay," Victoria said, surprising herself. She didn't even know what had made her say that, it almost sounded as though a voice other than hers had answered the question.

"Good." Sergeant Morrison stood up and looked at her watch. She had other matters to attend to. They were having a staff meeting at the château later that morning, and as the sergeant in charge of volunteers, they had asked her to join them. She assumed correctly she'd be the only woman at the meeting. "Oh." She turned as though she had forgotten to say anything. "You're in the women's barracks. I had your bag sent over last night. Someone will show you where it is. And you need to report back to duty in the medical tent in ten minutes."

"Now?" Victoria looked stunned. She'd been up all night, and she was ready to go to bed. But not according to the sergeant.

"You'll be off at eight o'clock tonight," she smiled. "I told you, Henderson, we need your help here. You can catch up on your beauty sleep later. And by the way," she looked at her somewhat sternly, but her eyes were warm and caring. But Victoria still couldn't believe she had to go back on duty. The woman was a tyrant. But she preferred to save her nurses and use her volunteers. They had to ration everything here, even people. "Tie your hair back," she said, and then disappeared as Victoria stared after her. She had another cup of coffee then, and contemplated another twelve hours on duty. She almost wondered if she could do it. But she had no choice now.

"Back so soon? You must have run into Sergeant Morrison," Didier teased when he saw her again. He was still on duty too, and Victoria helped herself to a fresh apron. She tied her hair back as Sergeant Morrison had told her to, and found a once-sterile cap to put over it. The Allied Forces sent them what supplies they could, but they were pathetically little compared to what their needs were. And then she went back to her duties.

The next twelve hours were more of the same, dying boys, screaming men, severed limbs, blinded eyes, and lungs filled with poison gases. This time, by the time she left the tent, she was almost reeling. She was so tired she thought she'd vomit as she asked someone for the women's tent, and when she got there, she didn't even look for her suitcase. She found the nearest cot, and lay down on it, and she felt as though she were dying as she fell asleep. She had never been so tired in her life, and this time, she didn't even dream of her sister. She didn't wake up again until late the next afternoon, and she showered in the makeshift tent set up for it, washed her hair, and went back to the mess tent for what should have been breakfast but was almost dinner. It was a glorious May afternoon, and she felt nearly human again, as she helped herself to some food, and more of the strong black coffee they all seemed to exist on. It was like fuel for their cars, they couldn't function without it.

As she ate, she wondered when she was due back in the hospital tent, she had no idea what her schedule was going to be, and no one had told her. And as she finished a plate of the familiar stew, she saw Didier and asked him. He was coming off thirty-six hours' straight duty, and he looked it.

"I don't think you're expected back until tonight. It should be posted in your barracks.

Morrison figured you needed some sleep, I guess."

"So do you," she said sympathetically, beginning to feel part of things. It was actually a very nice feeling. "Thanks, Didier, see you later."

"*Salut!*" he said, and walked off with a tin mug of coffee. He knew it wouldn't keep him awake, nothing would, not even bombs or men with hammers. He was beyond exhausted, but he smiled as he left. He liked her. He had no idea why she was here. Most people had their own reasons, and rarely told anyone why they had come, unless they became close friends. Many people were running away from unhappy lives, or had high ideals. Whatever brought them here, it was never the same as what kept them.

She went back to the barracks after that, and found her schedule. She was on again in two hours, and she lay on her cot for a while and rested, and then she walked around the camp and found out where things were. She thought of writing to Olivia, but she decided she didn't have time before she went back on duty. Instead, she reported to the medical tent a little early. There were no familiar faces there this time, except Sergeant Morrison who showed up a little while later to check on her. She looked satisfied by the hair, and gave her some uniforms. They looked like men's fatigues, except they had a long skirt. She wore a white apron over it, and a little cap with a red cross, and they gave her a red cape for when it was cold. It was an odd mishmash of garments, but it let people know who she was and what she did, if they needed her help anywhere. And then the sergeant asked her how things were going.

"Pretty well, I think," Victoria said cautiously. She wasn't sure how competent she was, but she was trying.

"I'm glad to hear it. You can pick up your identity card in the staff tent. Your stay was approved at the meeting yesterday," Morrison said matter-of-factly. "I think you'll do very well." Victoria was surprised by her praise, and a few minutes later the sergeant left her. And she had no time to even think after that. There was a battle in Berry au Bac that night, and waves of men were brought in on stretchers.

She worked fourteen straight hours, and was too tired and too sickened to even eat when she left, and she walked slowly back to her barracks. It was impossible not to think of the boys who'd died, and as tired as she was, she began thinking of the children she'd seen die on the *Lusitania*. It all seemed so senseless. The sun was high in the sky, it was May in France, the birds were singing, and people were dying all around her. Instead of going inside, she walked a little way past her tent, to a small clearing, sat down on the ground with her back against a tree, and lit a cigarette. She just needed to be alone with her own thoughts for a few minutes. She wasn't used to being surrounded by people all the time, never having a moment to herself, and having so many demands made on her, she hadn't realized it would be so draining. She leaned back against the tree, with the cigarette in her hand, and her eyes closed. The sun felt warm on her face, but she felt a thousand years old as she sat there.

"You might get a nice tan," she heard a voice say just in front of her, "but I can think of better spots for a vacation." The voice was French, and it was male, but he had said it in English. And when she opened her eyes, from her vantage point on the ground, he looked as tall as the tree she'd leaned back on. He had graying blonde hair, and in another place and time, she would have thought he was very handsome.

"How did you know I spoke English?" she asked, curious, but not smiling.

"I approved your papers yesterday," he said, his eyes meeting hers coolly. He wasn't smiling either. Each of them was appraising the other. "I recognized the uniform, and the description." Penny Morrison had said there was a very pretty young American who'd come over on the *Lusitania,* and would probably stay for about ten minutes. But he didn't say that to Victoria as he watched her.

"Am I supposed to stand up and salute you?" Victoria asked. She didn't know the protocol yet, but at this moment in time they appeared more to be a man and a woman, and not a captain and a medical assistant.

He smiled this time at her question. "Not unless you join the army, and I think you really shouldn't. You can do just as well with what you're doing, unless of course you feel a need for a rank, and you're not a nurse, I believe, so you'd only be a private. Frankly, I wouldn't bother." He spoke perfect English and had gone to Oxford and Harvard. He looked older than Charles to her, though she wasn't sure how much. In fact, he was thirty-nine, and very attractive. He looked extremely aristocratic. "I'm Captain Edouard de Bonneville, by the way." He was smiling at her now, and there was a light in her eyes that hadn't been there since she left New York. She had scarcely had anyone to talk to, except Lady Mackworth on the *Lusitania*. Ever since then, it had been purely perfunctory conversations. But this man seemed different.

"Are you the commanding officer here?" she asked. "I suppose I should stand up, but to tell you the truth, I'm not sure my legs would hold me." Her eyes looked tired and her smile rueful.

"That's another advantage of not being in the army. You don't need to stand up and salute, or stand at attention. I strongly suggest you don't enlist," he teased, and sat down on a log facing her. "And no, I'm not the commanding officer at all. I'm third or fourth in line, and of no consequence whatsoever."

"Somehow, if you signed my papers yesterday, I'm not sure I believe that."

"It's close enough to the truth." But not really. He had gone to Saumur, the cavalry school for nobles and gentlemen, and was career army. And eventually, if all went well, he would be a general. But he was far more interested in her than his own history. In the past two days, he had heard about her from several of the men, and Penny Morrison was intrigued by her. She was obviously well bred, and very young and beautiful, and no one could imagine why she'd come here. She looked like the sort of girl to be spending her summer dancing in satin gowns and going to parties. "I hear you came over on the *Lusitania*," he said, watching her eyes. He could see all the sorrow and the pain there. "That's not much of a start to your trip, I'm afraid . . . but then again," he grinned almost impishly, "this isn't much of a finish. Have you lost your way en route to somewhere rather more pleasant, or did you do this to yourself on purpose?" She laughed at him, and without even knowing him, she liked him. There was something very straightforward about him, and even a little bit sharp, and she liked it.

"No, I did this on purpose. It would be pretty awful if I hadn't." She laughed at him, and then met his gaze. Their eyes were almost exactly the same color, although her hair was so dark and his was fair. Anyone watching them would have thought they'd make an attractive couple, although the captain was obviously considerably older. Technically, though not easily at thirty-nine, he could have been her father. "Why is it you speak English so well?"

"I went to Oxford for a year after the Sorbonne, and then to adjust the accent perfectly," he grinned, and imitated a Boston twang perfectly, "I spent a year at Harvard. Then I went to Saumur, it's a rather silly French military school with a lot of horses." She loved the way he described it. Even she had heard of it, and knew it was very distinguished. It was the equivalent of West Point in the States, but with horses. "And now I'm here, and frankly," he lit a cigarette too, she had finished hers by then and she'd lit another, "I wish I weren't." She laughed at his honesty. Most of the men would have said the same thing. It was amazing to think she had come three thousand miles because she wanted to be here. "And if you had any sense at all, you'd get back on a ship, an *American* one this time, since your country is sensible enough to stay out of all this, and go back to where you came from. Where is that, by the way?" He knew she was American, but he didn't know more than that, except that her name was Olivia Henderson, or at least he thought so.

"New York," she answered cautiously.

"And you've run away from tyrannical parents?" He knew she was twenty-two from her passport, but she was still young enough to

live with them, or want to leave them, for whatever reasons. Or perhaps a broken heart had
brought her here. It was possible, but would
have been extremely foolish.

"No." She shook her head. "I have a very
kind father."

Edouard looked surprised by that. "And
he let you come here? What an odd man." But
Victoria shook her head in answer. She liked
talking to him, and the odd mixture of his accent, mostly French, somewhat British. "I don't
think I would allow my daughter to do that, I'm
sure I wouldn't, if I had one, which thank God,
I don't." She looked at his hand and there was
no wedding ring. But there was none on her
hand either, and she was married to Charles.
Olivia was wearing it for her.

"He doesn't know I'm here," Victoria said
honestly. "He thinks I'm in California."

"That is not a nice thing to do." He
looked at her with frank disapproval. What if
something happened to her? What about the
ship? "Does no one know you're here?" She
was very bold for a twenty-two-year-old girl,
very brave, and very foolish.

"My sister does," she answered him, leaning back against the tree again. She liked talking to him, but she was very tired. And yet

571

there was something about him that made her want to tell him things she wondered if she shouldn't. But he couldn't send her back now. She had her papers. And she was over twenty-one. What could he do to stop her? "We're twins," she said quietly.

"Identical?" He was totally intrigued by her as she nodded.

"Completely." She nodded. "We're mirror twins. Everything I have on the left side, she has on the right, and vice versa. Like this freckle." She held out her left hand to him and he could see only the tiniest of spots there, on her palm, just between her fingers. He glanced at it and nodded. He had no real need for this information and identifying process, since he was not seeing them together, but he could imagine it could be quite a problem. "No one can tell us apart, except the woman who took care of us when we were small. Not even our father." She grinned mischievously at him, and he could just imagine all the chaos she might have wrought, and had, with pleasure.

"That could be very complicated," he said, envisioning it, and then he smiled at her, "especially with men, no? Have you confused everyone of your acquaintance?" He was very clever, more than he knew, and she laughed at him. She didn't know it yet, but Edouard de Bonneville was dazzled by her beauty. He had heard of her, and the words hadn't been generous enough as far as he was concerned. She was gorgeous.

"We only confused some," she confessed, looking very innocent, which he did not believe for a single moment.

"The poor devils. How dreadful. I'm glad I have not met you together, though I must admit, I would like to have seen it. What is your sister's name?" he asked, and she hesitated, but only for a second.

"Victoria," she said simply.

"Olivia and Victoria. It's quite perfect. So Olivia," he went on, "you are here as a mystery, and only your sister knows. And how long will you stay with us? Till it ends?" He doubted it. Why should she? She was obviously wellborn, well educated, well spoken, intelligent, and very beautiful. She could go home anytime she wanted, and he was sure she would the moment she was tired of the dangers there, and the discomfort, and there were lots of both. He doubted that she'd be there much longer.

"I don't know." She looked at him honestly, and her eyes told him a tale he didn't understand yet. Perhaps she was running away from something. "I'll stay as long as I can. It depends on my sister."

"On your sister?" That did surprise him, as he raised an eyebrow and watched her. "Why on her?" She was a rare and curious being, and he would have loved to spend the day with her, talking, and getting to know her.

"She's taking care of things for me."

"It sounds complicated," he said discreetly.

"It is." She nodded, with an odd look in her eyes.

"Perhaps one day, you'll tell me about it." He vowed to follow her career while she was at Châlons-sur-Marne. It would be interesting, he was certain.

She stood up slowly then, and felt the ache in her bones she had felt when she left the medical tent. She didn't want to leave him, but she knew she could not stay awake much longer. But he surprised her by walking her slowly to the women's tent. She had been sure he wouldn't want to be seen talking to a lowly volunteer, and yet he didn't seem to mind it.

In fact, he turned up frequently over the next week, in the medical tent, watching her as she knelt beside someone vomiting their guts after they were gassed, or crying as she held them while they died. He turned up in the mess tent once or twice, and had coffee with her, and once he sat with her long enough for her to inhale dinner, on a ten-minute break before she went back on duty in the tent. They managed to talk, over the constant rumble of the guns that they were all used to now, and the occasional hissing sound that always reminded her of the sound when the first torpedo hit the *Lusitania*. They talked of the greenish yellow clouds of gas that had continued to hit near Dangemarck, and the thousands of men who were being maimed, killed, and crippled. And yet, interspersed with all that, they talked about foolish things, lawn tennis, summer yachts, his love of horses that had actually led him to the cavalry, and his time in Boston. They found that they even knew some of the same people in Newport. It was all so strange talking about it here, but most of the time, they spoke only about what they were doing day by day.

He dropped by to see her at the barracks now and then too. She'd been there for a month when he actually invited her to go somewhere. There was to be a small dinner at the château given by the general for the senior officers, and Edouard invited her to go with him.

"Here?" She looked shocked. She had

Danielle Steel

nothing at all to wear. She had lost everything on the ship, and what she had bought in Liverpool was functional and ugly. All she had were her uniforms and her starched aprons.

"I'm afraid Maxim's in Paris is out of the question." Edouard looked amused. After watching her wear bloodied aprons for a month, and drive ambulances to their makeshift morgue behind the lines, she suddenly sounded very much like a woman.

"I have nothing to wear but my uniform," she wailed, flattered that he asked her, but surprised too. They had become friends in the past month, but it never occurred to her that he might be attracted to her. He was older than she was, of high rank, and this hardly seemed the place for romance, although she knew others were romantically involved here. In some cases, the agony all around them brought people closer, in others it seemed more sensible to keep one's distance. And she had assumed that Edouard had chosen the latter tack.

"I have nothing to wear but my uniform either, Olivia." He looked amused. And it always made her smile when he said her sister's name. She answered to it easily now, but in his case, it really felt like switching. She had thought of telling him once or twice, but she

576

was afraid now of getting into trouble. She was traveling, after all, in a war zone, on someone else's passport. "That'll be fine," he reassured her again, and told her he would pick her up at seven, when she got off duty.

She knew she'd have to get special permission to get off duty then, but in the end, Didier agreed to cover for her. She told him why and he raised an eyebrow at her.

"I wondered when that would happen," he said approvingly. In the past month, he had really come to like her. She worked hard, she was always straight with him, and she did extra shifts, whenever she was needed, without a whisper of complaint. More often than not, she worked longer than her shift, and never said anything about it.

"We're just friends," she said, laughing at him and his insinuations.

"That's what you think. You don't know Frenchmen." Didier laughed at her.

"Don't be stupid," she said, and dashed back to her tent the night of the dinner, to at least change into a clean uniform for him. Her only concession to femininity that night was to let down her hair, and brush it quickly. She didn't even have any makeup. That had gone down on the *Lusitania* too, and she had never bothered to buy more after she lost it. At the time, it had seemed so unimportant. Now it seemed a shame.

Edouard picked her up in a truck at her tent, and only a few heads turned. Everyone else was either at dinner, in the trenches, or working.

"You look very nice, Olivia," he said warmly and she didn't even react to the name anymore as she laughed and thanked him.

"Do you like my gown?" She pretended to preen, "I had it made in Paris. And my hair?" She held it up like a model as she looked at him and grinned. "It took me hours to do it."

"You're a monster. No wonder your family sent you over here. I'm sure they were desperate to get rid of you."

"They were," she said, thinking sadly of Charles and Geoff. But the truth was she didn't really miss them. Never once since she'd been here.

"Have you heard from your sister since you've been here?"

"Yes. Twice. I've written to her too, but my letters sound so strange. It's so hard to explain all this to anyone who's not here. I've sent the letters, but they sound so artificial."

"It's difficult to understand a war, unless you're in it," he said, as they arrived at the château. She smoothed her hair again, and suddenly felt nervous as she walked in beside him. There were two other women there. The original chatelaine of the château, who was living on the grounds in a small cottage, was a countess, old enough to be Victoria's mother and very pleasant and polite. The other woman was the wife of one of the colonels visiting him from London. It was most unusual, but he hadn't been able to get away in months, and he had let her come to see him.

The dinner was a small, informal affair, and the conversation was mostly about the war at first, about the campaign in Galicia which had been so brutal. More than a million Poles had been killed in the past month, which seemed inconceivable to Victoria, though if she thought about it, she realized that she had probably seen a thousand men die since she got there.

Eventually, the conversation turned to other things. The general was extremely pleasant to her, they all spoke English perfectly to her, although Victoria's French was improving. And by ten o'clock, she and Edouard were on the way back to her barracks. He had been very proud of her, but he didn't say anything. He could see that both the general and the countess had been impressed, but Victoria was completely unaware of it as she chatted with Edouard all the way back. They could hear the rumble of the guns in the distance, and the familiar hissing around, and she prayed that that night at least the casualties wouldn't be too heavy.

"Where will it all end?" Victoria asked quietly, as Edouard pulled over just before they reached her barracks. There was nowhere else for them to go to talk, the mess hall was crowded with people at every hour, and there was no privacy for either of them anywhere. It was hard to find anyplace for quiet conversations, and most of the time they were surrounded by people. But just this once, he wanted to be alone with her, there were some things he wanted to tell her.

"Wars never take us to a better place," he said philosophically. "Looking back over history, all the way back to the Punic Wars, everyone loses in the end."

"Why don't we run out there and tell them that." She smiled over at him as he offered her a cigarette and she took it. She was

smoking Gitanes now. "We might save everyone an awful lot of trouble."

"Don't forget, they always shoot the mes-
senger," he said, as he lit her cigarette with a
gold lighter. "I had a wonderful time tonight,"
he said, looking at her, wondering what she had
left behind in New York. It was hard to believe
she hadn't left a trail of broken hearts, yet for
the past month, as he observed her carefully,
she always seemed so unencumbered. "You're
very good company, Olivia. I'd like to do this
again sometime," he said, wishing they were
back in Paris. Life would have been so different
there. He could have done so many things with
her, driven her to his château in Chinon, shooting in Dordogne, introduced her to all his
friends, a little time in the south of France. It
would have been Heaven. But all they had now
were the trenches between Streenstraat and
Poelcapelle, and men dying of phosgene. It
wasn't much of a courtship.

"I had a good time too," she said easily,
savoring the French cigarette, and his company. She enjoyed being with him. "The general is quite something." She smiled at
Edouard, and he took her hand and kissed it.

"So are you." And then he set her hand
down gently again, not sure how she'd react to

what he had to tell her. "There's something I want to say to you, Olivia. I don't want there to be any misunderstandings between us." But as he said the words, she felt a familiar ache in her heart where it had been wounded before, and she could feel her whole body stiffen.

She said it for him, without waiting for him to destroy her. She would never let this happen to her again. She knew she would be defended against all men forever. "You're married," she said, entirely without emotion, her eyes searching his, her heart completely hidden from him.

"What makes you say that?" He was totally startled. She was wiser than he realized, and he wondered what had happened to her. He could see the pain in her eyes now, it was brutal and still very much alive.

"I just knew. Not before . . . but when you said that. What else is there?"

"Oh . . . many things . . . people carry all kinds of baggage with them. This is mine. It's not a real marriage," he said, and she interrupted him harshly.

"No, of course not, it's a loveless one. You never should have married her, and you might leave her after the war, or then again you might not . . ." Her voice trailed off, and there was something very wounded in her eyes as she looked out the window, away from him.

"Not exactly. She left me five years ago. And yes, it was a loveless marriage. For both of us. I'm not even sure where she is right now. In Switzerland probably. She ran away with my best friend. But frankly, it was a relief. We were married for three years and we hated each other. But I cannot get divorced, this is a Catholic country. And I wanted you to know that. That presumes many things, all of them preposterous, I'm sure, but I didn't want to wait until any later time to tell you. As far as the law and the Church are concerned, I'm married. The rest is, unfortunately, a little more vague." She turned to look at him in surprise. The story was a little different than she'd expected. Or maybe it was all the same, and this was the French edition. She wasn't sure whether or not to believe him, and her uncertainty showed as she watched him.

"She left you?" She looked very young as she asked, and he smiled at her cautious expression.

He nodded, looking totally undisturbed. It had been a long time ago, and there had been one or two women of interest since, but nothing permanent, and no one lately. Not in a year. "Almost six years ago," he explained. "I should tell you that she broke my heart, to arouse your sympathy, but I'm afraid I can't. It was an enormous relief when she left. I owe Georges my life for it. One day, I'll have to thank him properly. The poor devil has probably always felt guilty." He was smiling at her, and she had to laugh at his expression.

"Why did you hate her so much?"

"Because she was spoiled, and difficult, and quite unbearable, and really profoundly very nasty. She was the most selfish woman who ever lived, and impossible to get along with."

"Why did you marry her? Is she very pretty?" Victoria was curious about him, more so than she would have admitted at that moment. But he was an intriguing man.

"Very pretty," he said honestly. He had always had a foible for beauty. "But it wasn't that. At least, I hope not. She was engaged to my brother, and he died in a hunting accident unfortunately. They were to be married in a few weeks, and he'd been stupid enough to get her pregnant," he looked at her apologetically, "I'm sorry, I've been at the front for too long, I shouldn't have said that," but she only waved a hand and took another of his cigarettes, as she listened to him with interest. It didn't sound entirely unlike her own story. "Anyway, I did what I thought was the noble thing. I stepped in for him, and married her. She miscarried three weeks later, or so she said. Actually, I'm not even convinced she was ever pregnant. I think she trapped him, and he was naive enough to believe her. And frankly, I think if he'd married her, he'd have killed her. He wasn't as patient as I am.

"Three years later, she left with Georges, after carrying on with him for nearly a year and assuring herself, and him, I didn't know it. I believe there were two or three others before him. And now they're gone, and my life is amazingly peaceful. The only problem is that unless Georges becomes very rich, which I doubt as he's not terribly bright, or she meets someone else, she will not divorce me. I could settle a large sum of money on her, and I've tried to, but for the moment, she prefers the title."

"Title?" Victoria raised an eyebrow, and he brushed his hand as though to sweep the word away like a cobweb.

"She's a baroness now, unfortunately. She'd have been nothing at all if she'd married my brother. He was the younger son. And I'm

afraid Heloise is rather fond of titles. What we
need now is a better one. Like a marquis or a
viscount." He was very funny about it, and she
was smiling at him. It was all a great deal less
frightening than when he'd first said it. But now
he looked at her in the darkness. Their eyes
had long since adjusted to it, and he had seen
everything in her face when he first told her.
"And now you must tell me about the man who
broke your heart, I believe I struck a nerve
when I said 'loveless' marriage. Do you want to
tell me about it?" he asked gently, and this
time he reached for her hand and held it. He
was relieved to have told her what he had to
say. He didn't want to give anyone the illusion
that he was free to marry them, because he
wasn't. He was free, but not for marriage. And
up until he met her, he had never minded. He
was only sorry not to have had children at some
point, but the thought of having them with
Heloise gave him nightmares.

"There's not much to say," Victoria lied
politely at first. "It's really not very important."

"Important enough to come here for?" he
asked gently, "or was it something else?"

"It was many things," she said honestly,
feeling obliged now to tell him something since
he had been so honest, or at least she thought

he was. But his story had the ring of truth, and the kind of stupidities she herself might have entered into. "Yes, there was someone," she said finally, "I was very young and very stupid, it was two years ago. I was twenty. And incredibly naive. Actually," she looked embarrassed briefly and he smiled encouragingly, "it sounds so unimportant now. Then it seemed so monumentally important. I fell in love with him, and he swept me off my feet. I did a lot of very foolish things in a very short time. We were visiting New York for a couple of months, and he was older, and very charming . . . and very married . . . he had three children. But he told me he hated his wife, that they had nothing more than an arrangement and not a marriage, and he was planning to leave her at any moment. They would get divorced, and if I would wait patiently, of course we would be married. And of course . . . it was all nonsense . . . I . . . I . . . ." She couldn't say the words to him, it was too embarrassing even after all he'd told her. "I believed what he said," and then she forced herself to say it, "and I fell very much in love with him. I . . . . I compromised my reputation, and someone told my father. My father confronted him and he said," her eyes hardened here as Edouard watched

her, "he said that I had seduced *him.* He denied me entirely, denied that he had ever made
any promises, he even told me that he never
intended to leave her at all, in fact she was
pregnant." And then she decided that if she
was going to shock him, now was the time. She
had nothing to lose yet, and if he told anyone,
she would hate him. But something deep inside
her told her to trust him. "His wife was having
a baby," she said softly, "but so was I. We went
back to Croton-on-Hudson where we live, and
I fell off my horse and lost it a few weeks later.
I had to go to the hospital, and I think I almost
died. I lost a lot of blood, but it was all over.
My father was in an uproar by then. He said
everyone in New York was talking about me.
The man I'd been in love with had been telling
people what I'd done. I suppose he thought it
was very funny, but my father said I had to do
something to regain my reputation, and his,
and my sister's. He said I had jeopardized everyone by what I'd done and we'd never be able
to set foot out of the house again. That sort of
thing," Victoria said, and sighed as she looked
out the window, remembering how awful it had
been then, and how desperate she had felt
when he said it. And then she turned to
Edouard with a sad smile. "So he forced me to

marry one of his lawyers. He said I had no choice. I *owed* it to them. And I believed him. I used to think I never wanted to get married. I just wanted to be a suffragette and go on hunger strikes and go to jail, and get arrested," she said, her eyes alight again and Edouard laughed with an interested expression.

"That's certainly an alternative, though not necessarily one I would recommend." He put her hand to his lips and kissed her fingers. "I don't imagine you were easy to control two years ago, or perhaps ever."

She smiled at him, acknowledging the possibility of that. "Maybe not. Anyway, I did it. I married him. He was a widower, with a son, his wife died on the *Titanic,* and he wanted a mother for his son."

"And were you?" he asked with even more interest. There was certainly a great deal more to her than he had expected. But she had not come here for no reason.

"No," she answered him honestly. "I was not a mother to him, or a wife to Charles. The boy hated me, and I believe the father does too. I was everything his wife wasn't. And he wasn't . . . the man I'd been in love with. I couldn't be who he wanted me to be, do what he wanted me to do. I hated all of it, and I hated him . . ." Her voice trailed off as Edouard watched her. "I felt nothing for him," she said sadly, "and he knew it."

"Is he a bad man too?"

"No." Her eyes filled with tears as she shook her head and looked at him. "No . . . he isn't. I just didn't love him." That was the whole of it, she never had, and she never would, and Edouard understood that.

"And where is he now?" Edouard asked softly. He wasn't the only one who was encumbered.

"In New York," she whispered.

"And you're still married to him, I assume?" He sounded disappointed. This was not what he had expected.

"Yes, I am." She looked at him, with wide, sad eyes.

"Perhaps he loves you more than you think if he let you come here." It was a generous thing for him to do, and Edouard admired him for it. He knew he couldn't have done it with a wife of his own, no matter how headstrong or independent.

But then she startled him even more. "He doesn't know I'm here," she said quietly, knowing she had to tell him all of it. There was no holding back now, whatever the dangers. She had to trust him. She wanted to. For the first time in two years, she trusted a man. And she knew that this man wouldn't hurt her.

"Where does he think you are?" he asked, horrified, and suddenly she grinned at him. It really was awful, but it suddenly struck her very funny. It was so funny she didn't know how to begin to explain it.

"He thinks I'm at home with him."

"What on earth do you mean?" He looked totally confused, and then he stared at her, his mouth opening in amazement. "Oh my God . . . your sister . . . is that it? Does he think . . ."

"I hope so."

"You changed places with your sister?" He looked appalled and she was suddenly frightened that he might expose her. He had her home address after all in her passport. What if he wrote to them and told them? "I can't believe you would do such a thing, but surely . . . but . . . a man and a woman . . . a husband and wife . . ."

"We stopped that right in the beginning. It was awful, everything we hated about each other was there between us like a boulder that kept us from ever getting closer. All she has to be is his housekeeper, and he'll never know the difference."

"Are you sure of that?" He looked at her, still amazed by the audacity of what she'd done in order to come here.

"Absolutely, or I'd never have asked her to do it. She is very sweet and very kind, and all the things I'm not, and the boy adores her."

"Will he know?"

"I don't think so. Not if she's careful."

He leaned back against the seat then, trying to absorb what she had told him. "You certainly left quite a tangle behind you, didn't you, Olivia?" She smiled at him again and shook her head, putting her finger on his lips.

"Victoria," she whispered.

"Victoria? But your passport . . ."

"It's my sister's."

"Oh you witch, of course . . . even your names must be switched . . . the poor man, how I pity him . . . how will he feel when you tell him, or will you?" Perhaps she was just going to slip back into his life again when she'd had enough of the war, but Edouard wanted to know that now too. And he hoped he had a right to.

"I'll have to tell him everything when I go back. I thought of telling him in a letter, but that seems so cowardly, and it's not fair to Olivia. I've thought about it ever since I left, and I know what I have to do. I can't go back to him again. I'll go home eventually, but not to him. I just can't, Edouard. I don't love him. It was the wrong thing to do in the first place. I never should have let my father force me to do it, but I thought he knew what was best. Maybe some people can live like that, but I can't. I'll go back and live with my sister. Or maybe I'll stay here. I just don't know yet. But I'm going to ask him to divorce me."

"And if he won't?" Edouard asked curiously.

"Then I'll live apart from him and remain legally married," she said philosophically. "I don't really care, just so I don't have to go back to him. And I won't do that. He deserves better than that too. He should have married Olivia, she would have been perfect for him."

"Perhaps he'll fall in love with her while you're here," he said, amused at the comic side of it, and there definitely was one. It was like Racine or Molière, a French farce at its best. The amazing thing was that she'd have done it. She was very brave and quite outrageous.

"I don't think they'll fall in love with each other. Olivia is far too proper. The poor thing, it can't be much fun for her, taking care of them and pretending to be me, she was an angel to do it. I told her I'd die if she didn't switch with me for a while. We used to do it as children. She was always getting me out of trouble." She smiled, thinking of Olivia, and Edouard could only laugh in amazement at the tale she'd told him.

"And you," he said pointedly, "are not an angel, but a devil, Miss Victoria Henderson. What a dreadful thing to do." But he was actually amused by it, it was so outrageous, and then he thought of something he had forgotten to ask and she hadn't told him. "How long did she give you?"

Victoria hesitated before she answered, her eyes wide as his blue eyes met hers filled with questions. "Three months," she said quietly.

"And you've been gone a month, haven't you?"

"Five weeks," she answered.

"That doesn't give us very long, does it?" But they both knew that nothing in life was sure, that they were in uncertain times in a place where nothing meant anything for an hour or a day, or a single moment. "How do you feel about spending time with a married man?" he asked her honestly.

She smiled at him then. "How do you feel about spending time with a married woman?"

"I'd say we deserve each other, my dear . . . wouldn't you?" In truth, they both deserved far more than they'd been given, and without saying anything more to her, he leaned across the seat, pulled her into his arms, and kissed her.

Chapter 25

Although Olivia had promised to stay with her father in Croton in June, she found that when it came time to go, she couldn't bring herself to leave Charles and Geoffrey. Their whole lives had been changed in the past few weeks. Ever since he had reached out to her the night that Olivia learned her sister was alive, he had hardly been able to keep himself from her. Their life had become the honeymoon they'd never had, and rather than shutting Geoffrey out, Olivia only felt closer to him. It was everything she had ever dreamed of. The only trouble with it was that everything she had now had been borrowed from her sister. Her husband, his son, even her wedding ring were really Victoria's, but all she could do now was

Danielle Steel

cherish them, and lavish all the love she had on her sister's husband and stepson. She told herself that whatever she was giving them would be credited to Victoria eventually, so it was in a sense the ultimate gift she could give her. But at other times, she knew how wrong it was, and she was consumed with guilt over it, until he turned to her and took her in his arms again, or reached across their bed to her at night and touched her. Their passion had reached heights he'd never known, and he had never for an instant suspected Victoria would have been capable of, even back in the beginning. Her sensuality was different than it first had seemed. She wasn't as wild or as uncontrollable as he first thought she was, instead her emotions seemed to run deep, and she bared her soul to him just as he had feared Olivia would do to him when they first met. In a way, it was a relief not to have to face her now. His feelings for her had always been confusing. But he was no longer confused about anything, except leaving for the office in the morning.

They laughed like children as they struggled to leave their bed, and hurried back to it at night, ready for fresh passion. In fact, lately they had been going to bed earlier and earlier,

598

until they had to force themselves to stay up at least as late as Geoffrey.

"We are terrible," Olivia giggled helplessly one morning, as Charles followed her into her bathroom and all the way into her bathtub. "This is obscene," she said, totally without conviction, as he took her slowly below the warm water. She moaned as she lay there with him, and she looked almost glassy-eyed half an hour later as she prepared their breakfast. And he patted her bottom playfully when he left. But when the house was silent again, Olivia stood quietly in the living room, wondering how she would ever leave him. They had two months left before Victoria came home again and reclaimed him. And the terrible part of it was that she knew without a doubt now that her sister didn't love him. The stories he had referred to, the comments he had made, and things she had gleaned from Geoff told her exactly what Victoria had said herself, that theirs had been a totally nonexistent marriage. The only trouble was that it was real and it was binding, and Charles had absolutely no idea she wasn't her sister. And eventually, Victoria would come back to him, and inevitably he would wonder what had happened. Olivia had no idea how to solve the problem. And all she could do in the meantime was stay with him, lavish attention on him and Geoff, and love them.

And Charles thought he had died and gone to Heaven. What he had with his wife now was what he had hoped to have when he married her, and more and even far more, than he had ever had with Susan, though he was still afraid to say that.

"It only took us a year to adjust," he said one night, teasing her after they'd made love, and lay in each other's arms together. "It wasn't long, was it?"

"It was far too long," Olivia said honestly, and he rolled over and looked at her.

"What do you suppose happened to change it?" As he looked into her eyes, he saw something there, but in a way it terrified him, it was too open, too dear, the doors of her heart stood wide open, and he rolled away from her again and looked at the ceiling. "I suppose I should just be grateful and not ask the Fates too many questions." But as he said it, Olivia had an odd sensation, almost as though he knew without knowing. But he fell asleep peacefully a short time later, and he never seemed to question anything, even when she didn't remember little details that she should have, like where he kept their bills, or his tools. Even Geoff lost patience with her at times over it. But she was in such a good mood these days that he didn't want to ask too many questions.

They left, as Olivia fought back tears, for Croton-on-Hudson as soon as Geoffrey finished school, at the end of the first week of June, and Charles promised to come up every weekend. He was true to his word, and stayed late on the night of their anniversary, which fell on a Sunday that year. He had decided to take the next day off from work, and stay in Croton overnight to celebrate their anniversary with her. Her father was pleased to see them so happy too. It was obvious to everyone, including Bertie, who more than once eyed Olivia with suspicion.

"You must want something from him, like a big new house," Bertie had teased her only that afternoon about being so kind to him, but they both knew Victoria was going to inherit the house in the city, since she lived in New York now. And Olivia would inherit Henderson Manor, though Olivia hated to think of it. But her father's health had been less than perfect for the past year, and since Victoria's disappearance, worse than ever. He seemed to be enjoying a lull for the past few days. His lungs were clear, his spirits were good, and he opened a bottle of champagne for their anniversary that night, and then, as he normally did anyway, he went to bed early.

Geoffrey was sleeping in Olivia's old room, as he always did now, and it still hurt Olivia to go in there. Just seeing the bed she'd shared with her twin for twenty-one years always made her miss her. She'd had two letters from her by then, she'd picked them up at the Fifth Avenue house as she'd said she would, and all she knew was that she was in Châlons-sur-Marne, working in a field hospital, and caring for dying soldiers. It sounded grim to Olivia. This was certainly not a vacation, particularly after the way it began, but it was obvious from everything she said that Victoria loved it. And whatever her reasons for being there, as much as Olivia missed her twin, she had to admit secretly to herself that she was glad she was gone, even if only briefly. It gave her these precious moments with Geoff and Charles, and that night on their anniversary, their lovemaking was especially tender.

He made reference afterwards to their time on the *Aquatania* the year before, and how lonely and disappointing it had been for both of them, and Olivia's heart went out to him, as she pretended to remember it, or at least know what he was talking about, which she didn't. All she could glean from everything he said was how unhappy they both had been, and in the end they made love again, and this time it seemed somehow different. She had felt a blending of their hearts and souls like no other she had ever known, even in the past weeks with him, and afterwards, as she lay beside him, wearing Victoria's rings, she felt truly married.

It was as though he felt something different for her too, he spoke to her differently now. Everything about them seemed more intimate now that they had entered a more physical union, and the next day when he left, he almost had to tear himself away. He couldn't take his eyes from her face, and he almost turned around and drove back as soon as he got to Newburg. He had to laugh at himself eventually, and he wrote to her that night, just to tell her what she had come to mean to him now, and how much he loved her. Olivia cried when she got his letter. Life was never meant to be this perfect.

Olivia rode with Geoff in Croton almost every day, his style had improved considerably, and she coached him over jumps that his father was afraid were too high for him, but she watched him carefully, and Geoff was capable of it. He was surprised that she rode with him so much now, he knew she didn't like horses as much as her sister. But she had changed a lot in the last two months, and he was willing to believe that Victoria was making an effort. She reminded him a lot more of Olivia these days, but she still had her moods too. And now and then, Olivia still made it a point of snapping at both of them, just so they would never suspect her deception. The only difference between her and her sister was that Olivia would be consumed with guilt the moment she'd done it. And she spent the rest of the day making it up to them, with kind gestures, and warm words. In fact, Geoff almost liked it. He liked spending time with his stepmother now, though he was still aching over the shock of Olivia's disappearance. He talked about it now and then, but it was obvious to her that the pain of it still ranked with the loss of his mother. And she felt terrible about it, but there was nothing she could do to change that, except love him, and she did, more than ever.

Charles was due to spend the last week in June with them, and the day before he arrived, Olivia and Geoff were riding as usual, they were on their way home when she jumped over a small brook, and her horse lost her footing. She stumbled, and Olivia didn't fall, but the horse seemed a little lame after that and Olivia dismounted and walked the mare home, with Geoff astride his own horse beside her. When they got back to the stable, she found a large rock wedged in the mare's shoe, and she grabbed a sharp pick to push it out, but a sudden movement from another mare startled her and the horse shied and moved away quickly, just as the pick dug instantly into Olivia's right hand between her fingers. There was blood everywhere, and a stable boy ran to get a towel as Robert, the old stable man, took the horse from her, and dealt with the rock himself. Geoff was nearly in tears as they walked outside rapidly, and Olivia held her hand under the pump to clean it.

"It might need a stitch or two, Miss Victoria," one of the stable hands said with concern, but she bravely insisted it didn't. She was feeling a little weak from the pain and the sight of so much blood and Geoff went to get a crate for her to sit on.

"Are you okay, Victoria?" he asked nervously. It made him feel a little sick too, and he looked away as the blood flowed freely into the cool water.

"I'm fine," she said, grateful for the box to sit on, as she put her head down and tried to clear it. Geoff was holding a clean towel for her, and when she finally thought she'd run enough water over it, she held her hand out to him and let him play doctor. "Tie it tightly please," she said, unable to do it herself one-handed, but as he stared down into her right hand, he gasped and looked at her. His whole world had suddenly gone topsy-turvy. She hadn't even thought of it. But he had seen the freckle, and he knew exactly now who she was, and who she wasn't.

"Aunt Ollie . . ." he whispered, unable to believe it, and staring at it again in disbelief. He had known there was something different about her, but he would never have thought they'd switched, not for so long. "Where's . . ." he started to ask as Robert, the stable man, approached them.

"How's it look?" he asked with concern. "Shall I call old Doc?"

"No, it's fine," she said, afraid now that he might see it too. Perhaps he knew the difference between them. And Bertie would for sure.

She couldn't show it to anyone now. She knew that. "I'll be all right. It just startled me."

"Good thing it didn't run right through your hand, Miss Victoria," he said, shaking his head. "Take good care of it now. Keep it clean. Wrap it up good," he told Geoffrey, who was tying it tightly at the time, as though anxious to hide something in his stepmother's hand, but as soon as they were alone again, he was smiling. She was back. He had never lost her after all. Olivia thought she had never seen a child beam as he did, and she took him in her arms and held him.

"I told you I'd never leave you," she whispered into his hair.

"Does Dad know?" He looked totally confused now as she shook her head and looked at him.

"No one does, Geoff. Except you now. You can't tell anyone. You have to swear. Not even your daddy."

"I promise." And she knew he meant it. The penalty might be his real stepmother coming back again, and he fervently didn't want that. It wasn't that she was particularly awful to him, he just didn't like her. And she wasn't Ollie. And then he thought of something. "Will Dad be mad when he finds out?"

"He might," she said honestly. She didn't want to lie to the boy any more than she had to.

"Will he send you away again?"

"I don't know. We're just going to have to be very quiet about this, you and I, and enjoy it while we can. And I mean it, Geoff, you can't tell a soul about this." Her eyes begged him to believe her.

"I won't." He looked insulted that she would repeat it, and with that, he put an arm around her waist, and they walked back to the house with her bandaged hand, and their secret.

Chapter 26

Charles spent the last week of June in Croton with her and Geoff as he'd said he would, her hand was fine again by then, and Geoff was as good as his word. He said not a whisper about what he'd seen in her hand that day, and nothing about his demeanor suggested that he had a secret. Olivia had been worried about it for a few days, but finally she relaxed, and by the time they left Croton, everything was fine again. Her father looked well, Bertie was sad to see them leave, and the three Dawsons were excited to be going to the seashore. Charles had rented a cottage for them in Newport, Rhode Island.

As usual, the Goelets were there that year, and the Vanderbilts, there were parties in the grand houses that were modestly called "cottages" almost every night, and the weather was exquisite. Geoff loved swimming with her, and Charles was happier than he'd ever been. He chased her down the beach more than once, and they laughed like children.

And on the Fourth of July, they stood and watched the fireworks from the beach club. The house they'd rented was very nice, and very comfortable, and after spending the whole month of July with them, Charles went back to the city on the first of August. And as he had done in Croton in June, he would come up on weekends. And by Friday afternoon, Olivia could hardly wait to see him. She was alone with Geoff during the week, and even when they were alone, he never called her Olivia or talked about their secret. He knew it was an unspoken thing that could never be said again, and he was old enough at eleven to understand it.

They went for long walks on the beach, had tea with friends, went to the Yacht Club frequently, and collected seashells. Together, Olivia and Geoff made collages for Charles, they even made a sailor's valentine for him with tiny shells, that looked like a real one. Olivia shared all her gentleness and love and talents with them. And when Charles arrived in Rhode Island late on Friday night, it was always worth the long trip it had taken him to come to see her.

"I don't know how I stand being without you all week," he said to her after dinner, and he meant it. His days without her now seemed colorless and empty. The house in New York was far too lonely without her, and the only time he felt himself come alive anymore was when he was with her.

"What did I ever do without you before we met?" he said, kissing her, holding her close, as they stood on the balcony outside their bedroom in the moonlight. It was a perfect night, and he was longing for her as he always did, though he hated to indulge himself quite so quickly. He liked talking to her, and holding her, and just being with her. But as soon as they strolled back into their bedroom, he couldn't resist her. It was a far cry from their first year when she had kept him at arm's length and shuddered each time he touched her. She was infinitely sensuous now, as he knew she had always been, but he simply hadn't been able to reach her before. It had all changed from the moment he had admitted to himself that he loved her.

And that night, as they lay together again afterwards, he held her close to him and stroked her cheek with his fingers. There was one more thing he wanted from her now, but he would never have dared ask her. He knew her sentiments on the subject. But perhaps if other things had changed, that would too eventually. She hadn't even mentioned suffragette meetings in two months, although she still avidly read the newspapers, and read everything she could about the war in Europe. And she had kept her word and never went back to smoking. He knew it had been an enormous sacrifice for her, but he thought it was worth it. It just wasn't ladylike or attractive, though he had to admit, at first, he had found it amusing. But after a while, he had tired of it, and he was glad she finally had as well. If nothing else, it smelled awful. He noticed now too, that as she curled next to him, she even slept differently than she had before. She had always shied away from any contact, sleeping as far away from him as she could, and now she couldn't get close enough to him as she purred beside him, and he loved that.

The day after he arrived, they all went to the beach as usual, and had a picnic on the sand, and on the way home, they stopped to do some shopping. Olivia said she needed a new parasol, the sun had been so strong lately, it had been making her dizzy. And Geoff needed a new pair of shoes. He had grown so much over the summer, he could barely fit in his old ones. And it was on their way home, that they were all chatting animatedly, when Olivia happened to glance into the road, and saw a little girl dart after a ball between two carriages, and she was instantly between the legs of the horses. One of the horses reared, and the mother screamed, but no one did anything to save her. Charles was about to lunge after her but before he could even move, Olivia had darted ahead of him, grabbed the child, and moved toward safety with her. The child couldn't have been more than two or three and her whole body was shielded by Olivia's, as the rearing horse returned his forelegs to earth again, and only slightly grazed Olivia. She still managed to get to the other side of the street, with the child safe from harm, but she was a little dazed, and people were shouting and darting all around her. The horses were being held, the mother of the child had burst into tears, the child's nurse was shouting at her, and the little girl was crying too, and Charles was oblivious to all of them as he dashed across the street to Olivia with Geoff right behind him.

"My God, are you trying to get yourself killed?" he shouted at her, only too aware of how close she'd come, far more aware than she was since she hadn't really seen it. She had just reacted to the situation and it was all over before she knew it.

"But Charles . . . the child . . . that little girl . . ." She looked up at him with wide eyes, and as she spoke to him, he seemed very far away, and the color seemed to be slowly draining from him. She could hear everything he said, and then she could see his lips move but he was making no sound at all and he became very small and turned quite gray. She looked at him with a puzzled expression, and he watched in horror, as she slid like melted molasses toward the sidewalk. He just caught her before she hit the pavement. And then suddenly he was shouting too, at anyone who would listen. He only thought she'd been grazed by the horse's hooves, but perhaps it had been far worse than he thought. He was terrified as he shouted to someone to get a doctor.

"What happened? . . . What happened? . . ." a woman asked. "What is it?"

"I don't know," he said, distracted by everything that was happening around them, and as he glanced over his shoulder he could see Geoff's eyes filled with tears, and he tried to calm himself enough to reassure him. But he was panicked about the woman he thought was his wife, and Geoff knew was Olivia. After all they'd been through, he couldn't lose her. "She'll be all right, son," he told Geoff, as someone went to fetch the doctor, and he laid her on the sidewalk, with Geoff's package under her head. But she hadn't regained consciousness. She had completely fainted.

"She's not, Dad, she's dead," Geoff said, crying openly, and more and more people were gathering around them, as Charles knelt next to her and asked people to give her air, and finally a man came who said he was a doctor. He had her carried into a nearby restaurant, and very sensibly laid on a banquette so he could examine her. There was no bruise, no obvious blow to her head, and from her eyes, he didn't think she had a concussion, but she was definitely unconscious. He chafed her wrists, put ice on the back of her neck and her temples, and then slowly she came around, saw Charles, and looked quite green as she asked what had happened.

"You rescued a little girl, you fool, and almost got stamped to death by two horses," he said, torn between terror, relief, and fury. "It would be nice if you left the heroism to someone else, my love," he said, kissing her hand, as Geoff wiped away his tears, embarrassed to have been crying.

"I'm sorry," she said weakly, and then glanced at the doctor. He had been listening to her heart and he was satisfied, there didn't seem to be much wrong with her, although he asked them if they'd like to take her to the hospital. Olivia said she wanted to go home, but as soon as she stood up, she almost fainted again, and she admitted to Charles in a weak voice that she felt dreadful. He could see she did, and he was near tears himself as he laid her down on the banquette again.

"I think perhaps if your wife went home and lay down for a little while, she might be all right. It's probably the heat, and the emotion. You can call me again this evening if she needs me," the doctor said pleasantly, and handed Charles a card. And a few minutes later, Charles left her with Geoff and went to get the car, and the boy looked down at her meekly.

"Ollie, are you okay?" he whispered.

"Geoff, no!" she said, although there was

no one around to hear them. "Remember what I told you."

"I know . . . I was just so scared . . . you looked like you were dead." His eyes filled with tears and she held his hand tightly in her own.

"Well, I'm not, and I'll beat you to within an inch of your life if you call me that again." She grinned at him, and they both laughed, as Charles came back to get her. He insisted on carrying her to the car, which embarrassed her, and she said she was fine now, but she was still very pale. And that night, she decided not to eat dinner. She was quite nauseous.

"I'm calling the doctor," Charles announced firmly when he checked on her after he and Geoff had eaten alone in the dining room. "I don't like the way you look."

"Charles, how unkind of you," she teased and he grinned at her. He loved her spirit of mischief. It was not as acute as it had once been, but with time it had gotten somewhat subtler. But she still had a wicked sense of humor.

"You know what I mean." He sighed as he sat down and looked at her. "I thought I would die when that damn horse nearly stomped on you. For God's sake, what a crazy thing to do."

"The little girl could have been killed," she said simply, with no regrets, since neither of them had been injured.

"So could you."

"I'm fine," she said, and kissed him gently on the lips. There was something she had to say to him. She didn't know what to do about it. It was not what she had meant to happen at all, and it was going to complicate everything. But she wanted it so desperately there was no way she could ever give it up now. "I'm very fine, actually," she said softly, looking at him, and he looked suddenly puzzled. She had a gentle way of saying things that sometimes confused him.

"What does that mean?"

"I'm not sure what to say to you," she said cautiously. She had no idea what his feelings about it might be, and she knew her sister had never wanted children. Perhaps he didn't either.

"Is something wrong?" he asked, looking worried, but she only shook her head and had to fight back tears of emotion. "Oh Victoria," he said, reminding her again that she had stolen him and had no right to this happiness, and yet she loved him so dearly. "Tell me what's worrying you . . ." He couldn't imagine anything that would make her look like that and he was anxious to reassure her.

"I . . . I'm . . . Charles . . ." But as he looked at her, and remembered what had happened that afternoon, he suddenly understood it.

"Are you expecting, Victoria?" he asked, looking stunned, as she nodded. He had been incredibly careless for the past two months, but she had never complained about it, so he had just let it happen. And knowing her feelings about that, he was suddenly terrified that she would be furious with him, and all the bad times would return again with a vengeance. But as he looked at her now, she looked anything but angry and she was crying.

"I am," she admitted to him. She thought it must have happened on their anniversary. She had already been to the doctor once, the baby was expected at the end of March, and she was two months pregnant. "Are you very angry?"

"Angry?" he said, staring at her, wondering how she could have forgotten all the things she'd said in the past about not wanting to have children. "How could I be angry? You're the one who never wanted to have a child. Are you angry at *me*?" he asked with worried eyes.

"I've never been happier," she whispered to him, as she closed her eyes and he kissed her, overwhelmed by how lucky they were, and how infinitely precious to him she was.

"I can't believe it . . . when will it be?" he asked her.

"In March," she said softly, wondering what she would do when her sister came home again and reclaimed him. What would happen to the baby then? Whose would it be? What would Victoria say to her about this? It was going to be a terrible scandal, but still all she could do was cling to him now, and pray that the future would never come. When it did, she would be the loser in all this. Particularly, if they demanded to keep the baby. She envisioned all kinds of terrifying scenarios, when she allowed herself to, but most of the time she just forced herself not to think of any of it, except Charles and the baby.

They told Geoff just before they went home, and he was a little startled too, but he didn't ask her any questions. They both took care of her like a piece of antique glass, and she laughed at them, but she loved it. Charles was even afraid to make love to her now, but much to his own chagrin, he found he couldn't stop himself, and he was as amorous as ever. The doctor in Newport told her there was nothing to worry about. She was healthy and young and the baby would be fine, as long as she didn't overdo it.

And the moment they got back to New York, Olivia raced to the house on Fifth Avenue. The letters had been gathering there for two months, and she hadn't dared ask anyone to send them to her. She prayed that Victoria was all right in France, and her hands shook as she sat in the doorway and opened each of her letters. She was still safe in France, in the same place, working in the hospital, and Olivia stared when she read the last letter from her. It was Providence. For a brief moment, it tore at her heart, longing to see her again, and then she knew it had to be, for her sake, and for Charles, and for their baby. Victoria said that it was too difficult to explain, but that she was needed there, and although her life was somewhat complicated, she had never been happier, and for reasons she would explain to Olivia later on, she wasn't coming home at the end of the summer as planned. For the moment, her life was there now and she begged her sister to forgive her. Olivia felt her heart pound as she read the letter again. She missed her sister terribly, but she knew it had to be this way now, for their sakes. She prayed that she would stay safe and well, and that one day, Victoria would forgive her for what she was doing.

Chapter 27

The summer in Châlons-sur-Marne had been hard for all of them. The heat of the battle had moved to Champagne, directed by General Pétain, and because the treeless meadows provided no cover and no natural defenses for the men, the *"poilus,"* as the French boys were called, dug themselves into trenches again and were slaughtered by the thousands. The goal of their mission in Champagne had been to cut the German rail lines, but as the Germans stood on the high ground watching them, the Allies made easy targets. The artillery barrage continued night and day, until the infantry went in and the boys were cut down like toy soldiers, knocked over one by one, until their remains or their broken bodies were brought in to the field hospitals for the doctors and women like Victoria to work on. But there was precious little left of them by the time they got them. It was a slaughter.

By the end of September, they were faced with blinding rains, and everywhere they went, they sloshed through mud and water. It was grotesque as some of the boys lay dying in the mud, literally drowning as they blew bubbles of blood in puddles of water. The horror and the shocking losses went on into October. And Edouard looked as tired as everyone else as he sat in his barracks late one night with Victoria when she came off duty. He had two rooms in the farmhouse that belonged to the château, one as his bedroom, and the other as his study, and Victoria was more or less living with him there, although everyone pretended not to know it, and she still kept some of her things at the barracks.

"It's not much fun, this war, is it, my love?" Edouard asked as he leaned over and kissed her. He was soaking wet and had just come from the hospital on foot in the pouring rain, but she was almost used to it by now. None of them had been dry in a month, their clothes, their tents, their sheets, everything was wet and moldy.

"Are you tired of it yet?" he asked. "Ready to go home?" Part of him wanted her to go so he knew she'd be safe, another side of him always wanted her near him. He had found in her something he'd never had anywhere before, a woman who was his equal, his friend, as strong as he, his lover, and at the same time his partner. They were perfect together.

"I'm not sure what home is anymore." She smiled tiredly at him and lay down on their bed after sixteen hours of duty. "Isn't it here, with you? I thought it was," she said softly and he lay down next to her and kissed her.

"I believe it is," he said, kissing her again, and then he looked at her with interest. "Have you told your sister about us yet?" He wondered if she would, they had talked about it repeatedly, but Victoria was still afraid to shock her. After all, they were both married.

"No, but I will. She knows. She knows everything about me."

"How strange to have someone like that. I was very close to my brother before he died, but we were always very different." He loved talking to her, about life, about the war, about politics and people, they shared so many of the same interests, and he was almost as liberal as she was. Almost, but not quite. He thought the suffragettes went too far, and he told her that if she ever grew a mustache or went on a hunger strike in order to get the vote, he would beat her.

"Olivia and I are different too," she said, lighting one of his Gitanes. They were getting harder and harder to get and now they had to share them. "But it's like two sides of the same coin. Sometimes it almost feels like the same person."

"Perhaps it is," he teased, rolling on top of her and taking a drag off the Gitane, "when do I get the other half?" He laughed.

"Never," she grinned at him, "you'll have to be satisfied with what you've got. We're all grown up now, no more switching."

He laughed at what she had just said and rolled off of her again. "I'm sure your husband will be happy to hear that," he said wickedly, "poor devil. After this mess here, you've got to go home and sort that out, for their sakes," he said kindly, and she had long since agreed to do that. When the right moment came to go home, she would go back and tell Charles herself. She owed that much to her sister.

"Maybe she won't want me to tell him by then."

"That could get complicated, I admit. At

least there's nothing physical between them, or so you say. But if she looks exactly like you, I'm not sure I believe that. I defy any man to resist either of you for more than a few weeks. God knows I couldn't do it."

"Did you try to resist?" she asked, looking intentionally evil and almost purring at him as he chuckled. Even in the ugly, wrinkled uniform, Victoria somehow managed to look sexy.

"Not for a minute, I'm afraid," he answered honestly. "I can never resist you, my love," he said, and moments later, he proved it.

Later that night he broke the news to her that he had to go to Artois in a few days, for the next Franco-British offensive. It had started the same day as the battle in Champagne, but it was not going well and the *poilus* hated the British commander, Sir John French, and wanted one of their own there. There was a movement afoot to replace Sir John with Sir Douglas Haig, but so far nothing had been done yet, and the French didn't want him anyway, so Edouard had promised to go to Artois and see what he could do to help morale, and help plan the battle.

"Be careful, my love," she said sleepily. There was something she wanted to say to him, but she was so tired she couldn't remember what it was, and in the morning he was gone, and she had to go back to the field hospital again. She didn't mind working fifteen- or even eighteen-hour days. This was her life now.

Life in New York was far more civilized than in Châlons-sur-Marne, to say the least, and October was bright and fair and sunny. It was unusually warm, and Olivia and Charles seemed to be unusually busy. They went to the Van Cortlandts several times, dinner parties with clients at Delmonico's, and at the end of October, planned to go to a large party at the Astors'. Olivia was four months pregnant by then, and it didn't show in the style of the dress she wore, but it had already begun to thicken her figure, and without clothes there was a small round bulge that he loved to hold. It was so sweet to see her that way, and it reminded him now and then of when Susan had been expecting Geoffrey. Somehow, older and having paid dearly for what he cared about, this seemed even dearer. Charles said he wanted a girl, and Olivia didn't care, she just wanted the baby to be healthy.

He made her go to the doctor regularly, and he had reminded her once, somewhat awkwardly, to tell the doctor about the miscarriage she had had before they were married.

"He doesn't need to know that," Olivia said, mortified. She hadn't had it anyway, but she couldn't say that to Charles, and she was terrified he might tell her doctor.

"Of course he does," Charles said soberly, "particularly if you almost died. You could hemorrhage again this time. Or worse yet, lose it." They were both afraid of that, and whenever she was too tired, or felt ill, she went home to rest, but it wasn't often. Olivia was in good health, and better spirits.

So far, despite the ugliness of the war, and the heavy losses in Champagne and Artois that fall, Victoria seemed to be safe and well, and as Olivia read what she said, she always had an odd feeling of peace from her, as though her sister had finally found what she wanted. She made no mention of Edouard and yet Olivia had a sense from her that she was not alone there. When she closed her eyes and thought of her, she had an uncanny sense of fulfillment and completeness, not unlike what she felt now, living with Charles, and waiting for their baby.

She wore a lavender silk gown the night they went to the Astors', and an ermine coat her father had had made for her when he'd heard she was having a baby. He was very proud of her, and pleased that things had worked out so well. It was easy to see how happy they were. The only sorrow they all shared was the fact that "Olivia" had not returned, as promised, at the end of the summer. The woman they all thought was Victoria, except Geoff, said that she had heard from her, that her sister was well, and that although she had given no address, she was in a convent in San Francisco and would be home eventually. But no amount of searching for her had turned up anything. The investigators had finally given up at the end of August. But Olivia had reassured her father again that her sister sounded well, and he shouldn't worry. This was what she wanted and they all had to respect that. He still reproached himself for Olivia's disappearance, and secretly admitted to the real Olivia again that he thought her sister was in love with Charles, and of course the real Olivia vehemently denied it.

But other than that, all was going well for them, and on the night they went to the Astors' ball, Olivia looked especially pretty. Charles stayed close to her, and it was only when he ran into an old friend, that he drifted away for a little while, and left Olivia to chat with an acquaintance of her sister's. She had never doubted for a moment that she wasn't talking to Victoria, no one ever did, Olivia was used to it by now, and they had a pleasant conversation. Olivia was a little surprised to learn that Victoria still owed her friend money from losing to her at bridge, which made her smile as she promised to pay up this time, since Victoria always swore to her she didn't gamble, because she thought it was stupid.

Olivia wandered out to the garden then, to get away from the heat and the noise of the room, and as she stood looking peacefully at the rosebushes, she was startled to hear a voice behind her.

"Cigarette?" he said, she didn't recognize the voice as she started to decline, and then saw it was Toby.

"No, thank you," she said coolly. He was as handsome as he had ever been, but she saw that he looked a little more used than he had two years before when she first met him.

"How have you been?" he asked rather pointedly, almost strutting as he came closer to her, and she could smell as well as see that he'd been drinking.

"Very well, thank you," she said, starting

to move away from him, and he grabbed her arm and pulled her close to him to stop her.

"Don't walk away from me like that, Victoria. You don't need to be afraid of me," he said boldly.

"I'm not afraid of you, Toby," she said in a clear voice that took him by surprise, as well as the man who was listening to her, unseen, a few steps behind them. "I just don't like you."

"That's not what I recall," he said, looking like a handsome snake, as she turned on him with eyes that glittered with anger.

"What exactly is it that you recall, Mr. Whitticomb? Was it deceiving me, or your wife, that you so enjoyed? Actually, what I recall most is your attempting to seduce an innocent young girl, and then lying to her father. Men like you belong in jail, not drawing rooms, Toby Whitticomb. And don't bother sending me flowers again, or love notes. Don't waste your time. I'm too old for that nonsense now from a man like you. I have a husband who loves me, and whom I love dearly. And if you come near me again, I'll not only tell him, but half the city you raped me."

"That was no rape, it was . . . ." he started to say, but before he could finish, Charles stepped out of the shadows, looking extremely pleased as he smiled at his wife. He had come looking for her, just in time to see Whitticomb follow her onto the terrace, and then he had gotten caught listening to them inadvertently, but he loved everything she'd told him, and it had warmed his heart to hear it. It had put an old ghost to rest. There were no specters left between them, except perhaps Susan, but even her memory had been laid to rest. The only one left, as Olivia knew only too well, was her sister.

"Shall we go, my dear?" Charles offered her his arm, and they swept back into the drawing room as he looked down at her with a small smile of pleasure. "That was very nice. Remind me not to tangle with you again. I'd forgotten how good you are at it, with words like daggers." The truth was, the real Victoria was far better at it than she was, but he didn't know that. And for once, Olivia rose to the occasion.

"Were you listening?" She looked both embarrassed and shocked.

"I didn't mean to, but I saw him follow you out there, and I went out to make sure he didn't annoy you."

"Are you sure you weren't jealous?" she teased and she thought he blushed faintly, and didn't answer. "You needn't be. He's a disgusting worm, and it's time someone told him."

"I think you did that quite successfully," he smiled, and kissed her cheek as he led her out onto the dance floor.

Chapter 28

It was a strange Thanksgiving in Croton-on-Hudson that year, with Olivia seemingly gone, although she was still in their midst and they didn't know it. And in Olivia's heart, she felt Victoria's absence terribly. It was the first time, on a holiday, that they hadn't all been together.

Their father said grace, but the atmosphere was subdued, as they each thought of years past, and missing loved ones. The only thing that really cheered them all now was the impending arrival of the baby. Geoff thought it was a little embarrassing, but he thought it might be fun too. Olivia was five months pregnant by then, and it had finally begun to show, in spite of the care with which she chose her outfits. And she knew that by January, she wouldn't be able to go out at all anymore, except to close friends', or very private dinners. The baby already seemed quite large, and she was secretly hoping for twins, but the doctor didn't seem to think so. She had said as much to Charles, and he had rolled his eyes and said he wasn't sure that he was up to that.

"Maybe next time?" he said, with his eyes full of questions. But so far, she'd had an easy pregnancy, unlike Susan's with Geoff, and despite all her supposed early dislike of having babies, she seemed completely at ease about it now. She had never even mentioned again the fear she had mentioned earlier generated by her mother having died in childbirth. She seemed quite unafraid, in fact, and very happy. But when he asked about having others after this, she only said it was up to him, and he knew he'd be satisfied with this one, if she chose not to have another. Twins would have quite undone him.

The winter in France was arduous in 1915, as both sides fortified themselves for future battles. New supplies were laid in, fresh troops arrived, and the old ones rested as best they could in the freezing trenches. The gas attacks continued. And by November, Edouard had returned from Artois and was back in Châlons-sur-Marne for the winter. He and Victoria were comfortably holed up in his two rooms at the farmhouse. There had been considerable talk about them of late, and it was no secret what was happening, but the camp seemed to regard their affair with warm affection. The officers who shared the farmhouse with him left them alone most of the time, and Victoria was laughing late one night as they cooked the smallest bird she'd ever seen in the old country kitchen.

"Don't be difficult. I'm sure it's a quail," Edouard said, trying to be optimistic.

"It's not," she laughed at him heartily, it was hardly bigger than a mouse when they took it out of the oven. "It's a sparrow."

"You don't know anything," he said, kissing her, and pressing her against him. He'd just gone to nearby Verdun for two days, and he'd missed her. He always did. He could no longer bear to be without her. And there was never any talk of going home now. In fact, he had talked to her seriously about moving to Paris with him, after she went home and faced Charles and her sister. Their situations were identical. Neither of them could get married, and he suggested that they shock the polite world, and live together in sin in his château, and live happily ever after. "And perhaps one day, when the witch dies, the current baroness, I can make you an honest woman."

"I'm an honest woman now," she said staunchly.

"Oh please . . . with your sister masquerading as you with your poor husband in New York, I don't think so." They both laughed mercilessly about that, and she at least had the grace to be embarrassed. No one in Châlons-sur-Marne could ever understand why everyone called her Olivia, and he called her Victoria. They thought it was a private joke, and Victoria never explained it.

That night with their tiny bird, Victoria informed Edouard that in the States, it was Thanksgiving.

"I remember that when I was at Harvard," he said nostalgically, smiling at her, "I liked it. Lots of food and good feelings. You know, I'd like to meet your father one day when we get through all this," he said wistfully, but neither of them, nor the rest of the world, knew when that would be. It seemed like it would be a long time before the *poilus* came out of the trenches.

"He'd like you," she said, eating an apple.

It was the smallest Thanksgiving dinner of her life, but perhaps the happiest, as she looked at Edouard, and tried not to think of her sister. It was so hard being away from her, and yet with him, she felt she had a life now. With Charles, she had had nothing. "Wait till you meet Olivia," she grinned at him.

"That frightens me. The thought of you two together is truly terrifying," he said, and then later, they lay together on his bed, and talked about their childhoods, their friends, the things they liked to eat and do and be as children. He talked about the brother he had lost, and Victoria could tell he'd loved him deeply, enough to marry the girl he had gotten pregnant, even though he didn't love her.

But as they lay together that night, and she began to drift off to sleep after they'd made love, she could feel his hands touching her gently, and she opened her eyes and turned to him. His eyes were filled with questions.

"Is there something we should talk about, Miss Henderson?"

"I'm not sure what you mean," she said, with a mysterious smile in her eyes.

"You're a terrible liar," he said huskily, moving closer to her, and lying right behind her as he held her stomach. "Why didn't you say something?" He sounded hurt, and she was truly sorry. She turned to face him then and kissed him gently on the lips as he held her.

"I only figured it out about three weeks ago . . . and I wasn't sure what you'd think . . ." He couldn't help but laugh at her, her stomach was already round with their baby. He assumed it was his, it certainly wasn't Charles', from everything she had told him.

"How long did you think you could keep that little *bonhomme* a secret?" He was smiling at her. It was the first child he'd ever had, and he had just turned forty. In spite of the circumstances, he was ecstatic, and then suddenly he looked at her, worried. "You should go home now, Victoria," he said softly, aching at the thought of losing her, but doubly wanting her safe now.

"That's why I didn't tell you," she said sadly. "I knew you'd say that. But I won't go. I'm staying."

"I'll tell them you're using a stolen passport," he said, wanting to sound firm with her, but not succeeding.

"You can't prove it," she said, smiling up at him. "Resign yourself, I'm not going anywhere."

"You can't have the baby here," he said,

horrified that she'd even think of it, but nothing in Europe was safe now, except Switzerland, and she might as well go home then. But he could tell from looking at her that she wasn't going to. And a part of him didn't want to argue with her.

"I'm going to have the baby right here," she said, looking very womanly and very beautiful, and a little too thin after all her hard work in the field hospital, but lately her appetite had been ferocious.

"I don't want you on your feet fifteen hours a day," he said adamantly. "I'm going to speak to the colonel."

"You'll do no such thing, Edouard de Bonneville." She looked furiously at him. "If you do, I'll say you raped me and you'll be court-martialed," she said, and rolled over in bed again with a look of satisfaction.

"My God, woman, you're a monster. I have a better idea. How would you like to be my driver?"

"Your driver?" She looked surprised. "What a good idea. I can do that till I can't squeeze behind the wheel anymore. Will they let me do it?"

"If I ask the colonel, they will. That would be a lot better for you right now, if I can stand your driving." He always complained that she drove too fast, and she told him he was a coward. This was France. And it was wartime. He suggested that neither of those were adequate reasons for suicide, but for the sake of their baby, he was willing to risk it. And then he looked at her seriously. This was no joking matter. "Are you serious about this, Victoria? You really want to stay here? It could be very rough on you." And he knew from things she'd said that she was afraid of childbirth. She'd had one bad experience and she could have another. And Châlons-sur-Marne was no place to have a baby, even without complications.

"I want to be here with you," she said softly, "I'm not leaving." He could tell from looking at her that the battle had been lost before he fought it. She was staying. And then he asked her a second important question.

"How do you feel about our not being married?" he asked seriously, and she grinned at him.

"We are married, *chéri*," she said lightly. "Just to other people."

"You have no morals," he said, kissing her from the bottom of his soul, and loving her more than any other being in his entire lifetime. "But a lot of courage," he said softly. And this time, when he made love to her, he knew he had no worry about getting her pregnant.

Chapter 29

Christmas at Croton was quieter than usual that year, but still surprisingly happy. Geoff loved everything he got, and Charles was extremely generous with all of them, as was her father. But it was also obvious that he was not well. He'd had a bad cough for months, and flirted with pneumonia several times that year. And it worried Olivia to note that he was looking considerably older. She wasn't sure if her sister's disappearance had even done it to him, he just seemed to be running out of steam, and the doctor said his heart was getting weaker. But they still spent a happy holiday with him, and they drove back to New York shortly after New Year.

They'd been home for two days, when

Bertie called Olivia and said that she thought she should come back. Her father was suddenly failing. Apparently, he'd caught another bad cold right after they left, and he had an enormous fever. He'd been delirious all that afternoon, and the doctor wasn't sure his heart was strong enough to sustain him. She wanted to send Donovan down for her, but Charles insisted he would drive her back himself in the morning. He didn't like the idea of her going anywhere without him anymore. She was more than six months pregnant, and she was huge, or so she thought, for a woman carrying a single baby. But the doctor was absolutely sure. He could only hear one heartbeat, and each time he said it, Olivia foolishly felt a stab of disappointment.

They kept Geoff out of school, and he went back to Croton with them, and as soon as Olivia got there, she was glad she had come. Her father looked as though he'd aged twenty years in the three days since they'd been there.

"I don't know what happened to him." Bertie wrung her hands, in tears, and then looked at Olivia strangely. But she didn't say anything. She just blew her nose and went back to the kitchen, she knew he was in good hands now. She just wished Olivia could be there, she knew how much it would have meant to him, but at least he had one of his daughters.

Olivia sat with him all that afternoon, and Charles went out riding with Geoff. There was very little else he could do. The estate was well run, and there was nothing for him to do there, except keep Olivia company whenever she came out of the sickroom. He had told his office he'd be back in a few days, and he waited patiently as Olivia came and went, making broth, making teas, and using herbs which she was convinced would help him. It made Bertie watch her all the more closely. But she could never quite believe what she was seeing. It wasn't possible, they wouldn't do a thing like that. She was imagining things, and she knew it.

But Edward Henderson only got worse in the next day or two, and by the end of the third day they were there, he was having a very hard time breathing. The doctor wanted to take him to the hospital, but he flatly refused, and told Olivia he wanted to die at home. He belonged here.

"You're not dying, Father," she said, fighting back tears. "You're just sick again. You'll be fine in a few days." But this time he shook his head and the fever got worse, and that night she sat with him all night, holding his hand, and watching him, and putting a glass of fresh water to his lips whenever he would take it. Her hands were gentle and firm and loving. And she wouldn't let anyone else nurse him. Charles was upset over it, but as he had always known, his wife was very stubborn.

And it was early the next morning, when Olivia suddenly knew that the end had come, he was gasping for breath and looking wild-eyed, as he begged her to get her sister and bring her to him.

"Victoria, bring your sister upstairs . . . I have to see her now . . ." he said, gripping her hand so hard it hurt her to hold it, and for a moment, she didn't know what to say, and then she nodded and left the room, and came back only an instant later. "Olivia, is that you?" he asked, and she nodded as tears streamed from her eyes. She hated to deceive him.

"It's me, Daddy . . . it's me . . . I'm home now."

"Where were you?"

"Away," she said, as she sat next to him, holding his hand. He didn't even see that she was pregnant. "I needed to think for a while, but now I'm back, and I love you very much," she whispered, overcome by her own emotions.

"You have to get well now," she said firmly but he shook his head, fighting to stay conscious.

"I'm going . . . it's time now . . . your mother wants me."

"We want you too," Olivia said, sobbing as she sat next to him.

And then in a small, anguished voice, he asked her the question that had tormented him for eight months. "Were you angry at me for making her marry him?"

"Of course not, Father. I love you," she said again, and soothed his brow. He was so hot and so agitated and so worried.

"You love him, don't you?" She smiled at him then, and nodded. Maybe it was better for him to know the truth. Maybe in the end, that would calm him.

"Can you forgive me for making her marry him?"

"There's nothing to forgive. I'm happy now. That's why I went away. I have everything I want now," and he could see in her eyes that she meant it. He closed his eyes for a while then, and drifted off to sleep, and then he opened his eyes again and looked at her with a smile.

"I'm glad you're happy, Olivia. Your mother and I are very happy too. We're going out together this evening, to a concert." He was delirious again, and he drifted in and out of sleep all day, unsure of who she was, sometimes he thought she was Olivia, and at other times, her sister. And by nightfall, she looked almost as bad as he did.

"I'm not letting you stay in that room another hour, Victoria," Charles said to her fiercely in a whisper, when he saw her in the hallway, speaking to Bertie.

"I have to. He needs me," she said with equal conviction, and then she went back into the room again. The fever broke mysteriously that night, and she sat next to him, holding his hand, convinced that he was going to be better in the morning. She only drifted off to sleep once, briefly before dawn, sitting in a chair beside him. While she dozed she could see Victoria's face so clearly she thought she was next to her, and her mother, and when Olivia awoke again, she put her hand on her father's brow, and then she looked at him, and saw that he was gone. He had gone peacefully to join his wife, convinced that he had said good-bye to both his daughters.

Olivia was crying when she came out of the room, and Bertie saw her and put her arms around her. The two women stood crying for a long time and then Olivia went back to Charles. He was sound asleep, and she lay down next to him, and thought of her sister. Olivia wanted her to know somehow, that their father had gone, and she wondered if she did. Olivia would write to her that day, but she was sorry Victoria couldn't be there with them. At least he had thought she was. Olivia knew that was something. It had been the only gift she could finally give him.

"Are you all right?" Charles was awake and looking at her. She was lying there, so pale and still that he had been worried.

"Daddy's gone," she said softly. They hadn't called him that since they were children, but she felt like a child again, losing him. She suddenly felt as though she had lost everyone, with Victoria gone, and now her father dying. And yet she had this man, whom she loved so much, his son, and their baby. But all she had now were gifts she had borrowed from her sister. But Charles knew none of it as he put his arms around her gently and held her.

It was two o'clock in the morning when Victoria woke up, with a very odd feeling. At first she thought it was the child, but when she put a hand on her stomach and felt it moving, she knew that it wasn't. It was something else. She closed her eyes and saw Olivia sitting in a chair, deathly serious. She wasn't sick, she wasn't saying anything, she was just sitting there. And yet Victoria knew that something had happened to her.

"Are you all right?" Edouard asked her, rolling over on his side to look at her. She was driving him now, and he was always worried that jiggling around on the bumpy roads was going to send her into labor and she was only six and a half months pregnant.

"I don't know," she said honestly. "Something's wrong."

"With the baby?" He sat up, looking worried, but she shook her head.

"I think the baby's fine . . . I don't know what . . ." It was as though Olivia were sitting right next to her bed, saying something to her and she couldn't hear it.

"Go back to sleep," he said with a tired yawn. He had to get up in two hours to arrange for special movements in the trenches. "It's probably something you ate," or didn't. They never had enough to eat these days, and most of them were always hungry. He put an arm around her, and she lay next to him, but she never slept again that night, and for days, she had the oddest feeling.

It was the beginning of February before Olivia's letter reached her in France, and then she knew what she had felt that night. Their father had died. She felt terrible about it, and about not seeing him again before he did, but she was infinitely glad and relieved it wasn't her sister.

"It must be very strange," Edouard said when she explained it to him. He had a great respect for what they shared, and never belittled what she told him. "I can't imagine being that close to anyone, except you," he smiled. "Or him." He pointed to her stomach. But the relationship the twins shared was entirely beyond him.

Chapter 30

On the first day of spring in New York, Olivia looked as though she were going to explode as she came down the stairs in the morning to have breakfast. And Charles couldn't resist grinning at her. She looked adorable, but unbelievably enormous. They both enjoyed her pregnancy, and were excited about the baby being born, but in the past few weeks she had looked almost comical, and had given up going out completely. The farthest she ventured now was their garden. Her belly literally hung out ahead of her like a huge, round, independent structure. And it was so big and hard and tight that she hardly even felt the baby move now. It was a far cry from a month before when it seemed to jump up and down night and day, as she put it "with roller skates and a hat on." There was no denying that this was going to be a big baby. Charles was faintly worried about it, but he hadn't wanted to frighten her, particularly not after her stories about her mother.

"I think you're extremely rude," she said, grinning at him and Geoff, who was chuckling too. She had begun to look really funny. But she seemed to feel well, and the baby appeared to be in no hurry. As closely as she could figure it, it was due that week, but the doctor said one never knew. She'd know when the time came, and she was going to have the baby at home, in their little house on the East River. It was what she wanted to do. There was no reason to go to a hospital, she said that was for sick people. And having a baby was hardly an illness.

"What are you doing today?" Charles asked casually, as she poured him a cup of coffee. Bertie had come down from Croton that week to help her, and she was in the guest room, but Olivia had insisted that she wanted to make her husband's breakfast. It was the only thing she could still do unassisted. Even getting her into the bathtub now took Charles' help, and getting her out of it almost took a crane. But Bertie had come to town so that she could be there when Olivia had the baby. She had insisted on it. And with her father gone, Bertie had virtually nothing to do in Croton. She had agreed to spend the entire spring with them, and Olivia was happy to have her to help with the baby.

"I thought I'd walk out to the garden and back again," Olivia said with a grin. "I might sit on a chair for a while, and then the couch." Lying down was dangerous, it was like having a piece of furniture dropped on her. She couldn't get up again unless someone helped her.

"Do you want me to bring you a book?" he asked.

"I'd love that," she said with pleasure. H.D.'s new book of poetry, *Seagarden*, had just come out and she was dying to read it. "I'd love some pickled radishes too if you happen to see any somewhere."

"I'll be sure to look," he said, when he kissed her good-bye that morning, and patted her tummy. "Make sure he doesn't come out while I'm gone."

"Don't be so sure it's a boy," she said, not wanting him to be disappointed with a "mere" girl, although he claimed that was what he wanted.

"If it's a girl that size, we have a serious problem," he said laughing as he hurried down the stairs. He had a lot to do that day and he wanted to come home early. He liked spending time with her, particularly now, when she was so close to delivering. He knew she was a little more nervous than she admitted, or so he thought. But much to Olivia's own surprise, she actually wasn't nervous at all. She was surprised herself at how calm she was. She had a strange conviction that the birth was going to be very easy. And she had said as much to Bertie, who in turn said very little.

And as soon as they'd left, Bertie came down and did the dishes for her, and Olivia went upstairs to what had become the baby's room, and began cleaning and tidying and sorting. Bertie smiled when she came upstairs again. Olivia looked happy and busy. In fact, she stayed in there most of the afternoon, and then she went out to the garden. But as she came back in, she saw how dirty the living room windows were, and she began cleaning them, and despite all of Bertie's exhortations, she insisted on doing them herself. She was scrubbing and washing, and when Charles came home, she was tidying up the kitchen and talking about starting dinner.

"I don't know what's wrong with her," Bertie complained as the cook smiled at them.

"She's been cleaning this whole house all day, from top to bottom."

"She's getting ready," the cook said knowingly as Bertie shook her head, and Olivia laughed and went to the sewing basket to get socks to mend. She had never felt better. And she had more energy than she'd had in weeks. Charles was happy to see it.

She had dinner with him and Geoff, and after Geoff went to bed, they played cards, and Charles beat her.

"You cheated," she accused, and laughed as she went out to the kitchen for a glass of milk, and as she stood there, she heard a large splash at her feet, and thought she had dropped the milk without realizing it, but as she looked down, she saw water everywhere and it took her a moment to realize what had happened. She put down the milk bottle, and looked for some rags to clean it up, as Charles came in and saw what she was doing.

"What happened? . . . What are you doing? . . . Victoria!" She was actually used to the name now, and answered to it as easily as she did her own, possibly more so since no one had called her Olivia in eleven months now. "Will you stop . . . here . . . let me help you." He mopped up the floor for her, she could hardly bend over, and she was laughing at both of them, and he didn't understand what she had done, or what had spilled, and as she stood there, she suddenly felt the first pain and grabbed his arm. It was much harder than she had expected. "What's wrong?" he asked, still not understanding.

"That was my water on the floor . . . ." She sat down on a kitchen chair, and was no longer smiling. "I think I'm having the baby."

"Now?" He looked startled, as though no one had told him it was coming this month, and she smiled at him again.

"Maybe not this very instant, but soon. Give me a few minutes." But as she said it, she frowned again. She had another pain and this one was worse. No one had told her it would be anything like this. She wondered if something was wrong, all she knew of this was what she had seen of her sister on the bathroom floor two and a half years before. She didn't have a mother to tell her what to expect, and the doctor had told her everything would be fine, and he was sure it was going to be very easy. The real Victoria would have been a lot more realistic. But somehow Olivia had never expected it to be this painful.

"Let's get you upstairs," Charles said quietly, and helped her out of her chair, but it took them nearly ten minutes to get her up the stairs and into their bedroom. He sat her down in the bathroom and helped her get undressed, and she was having a lot of trouble moving. He left her for a few minutes to knock on Bertie's door, told her what was happening and asked her to call the doctor, and she rapidly moved into action. But by the time Charles got back to her, Olivia was gasping for air and panicking, and the pains were awful.

"Don't leave me again," she said, sounding desperate, and clutching at him, just as Bertie came in, and they helped her to the bed, and spread out old sheets and towels all around her. Bertie was experienced at this, but Charles wasn't. Susan had given birth to Geoff eleven years before, with female relatives all around her. He had gone out to get drunk with his brother-in-law, and when he'd come back, he'd had a baby. Olivia seemed to have no intention of letting him go anywhere, and by the time the doctor came, she was grabbing his arms with each pain, and fighting not to scream aloud, for fear that Geoffrey would hear her.

"This is awful," she informed the doctor, and he and Bertie exchanged a smile, but Charles looked very worried about her.

Danielle Steel

"How long will this take?" he asked innocently. Geoff had seemed like only an hour or two, or maybe he had just had a lot to drink, he couldn't remember.

"Probably all night," the doctor said calmly and Olivia burst into tears as soon as he said it.

"I can't do this. I want to go back to Croton." She was crying like a child, and all she could think of suddenly was her sister. It was as though she were right there again, but she was sharing the same pain, and neither of them could get away from it. It was like the worst nightmare she'd ever had, except for when Victoria had been on the *Lusitania*. But in some ways this was worse, because Olivia was in so much pain, she couldn't think straight. She couldn't control herself, she couldn't stop screaming after a while, and eventually she saw Bertie lead Charles away. He looked as though he was going to cry, and Olivia begged her to bring him back, but she wouldn't.

"You'll only upset him," she said soothingly, "you don't want him to see you now . . . like this . . ."

"Yes, I do," she said frantically, "I want him now . . . get him . . ." But Bertie wouldn't, and Olivia just lay there and cried as

662

the pains grew worse and worse and closer together, and then she couldn't take it anymore, and from a great distance somewhere Bertie and the doctor were holding her legs and telling her to push the baby out, but she couldn't. "I want Victoria," she said between gasps, and suddenly Bertie looked up at her, and there was a moment of silence and then another pain came and swept Olivia away again, and it was a long time before she could listen to them again, it was just too painful. "Victoria," she whispered her sister's name again, and in the distance, she could hear her sister calling.

"Be careful what you say," Bertie whispered to her softly. "Be careful," she said again, and squeezed Olivia's hand hard, but she was too far gone to know what she meant, as she lay there screaming and pushing. It was dawn and nothing had happened yet. Olivia couldn't believe the pain of it, and still she had no baby. Even Bertie was beginning to look tired, and Charles had made coffee for her and the doctor. And then Charles knocked softly and came into the room again, asking how his wife was.

"Terrible," she moaned, answering for them. "Oh Charles . . ." she said and started to sob, and he wondered if her earlier terrors had been well founded after all. Maybe she had some congenital malformity like her mother, something that might kill her before she had their baby.

"Oh sweetheart," he said looking over-wrought, and the doctor told him he might be more comfortable if he waited downstairs in the parlor. He was beginning to worry about her himself, but he didn't show it. And then before Charles could say anything else to her, the pains began again, and they told her to continue pushing. Charles stayed unobserved by any of them. But an hour later, the situation genuinely seemed to be hopeless.

"I do wish you'd leave," he snapped at Charles. And Charles snapped right back at him, much to everyone's surprise. "I'm not going. She's my wife, and I'm staying right here," and despite the pain, her spirits seemed to rise, having him near her. He held her hand, and told her to push when the others did, but still nothing happened. And finally, after forcing his hand into her, the doctor announced that the baby was in the wrong position.

"I'm going to have to turn it," he said, and Charles almost cried as she screamed this time, but slowly, slowly, the baby began moving. But it had been just as Charles had feared.

The baby must have been too large. It was easy enough to see that. He didn't know why they hadn't made her go to the hospital, or at least warned them. But the doctor had been so intent on pacifying her all these months, telling her it would be easy.

"I can't do this anymore," she said miserably to Charles, between pains, and then she threw up, and cried more. He wanted to take her in his arms, and run away from there. He was sorry he had ever made love to her, and then suddenly, as they both cried, she made a terrible face and pushed again, and this time there was a small wailing sound, and out of the huge ball that had been her belly for the past several months came the tiniest of babies. She was small and sweet and pink, and a perfectly formed little girl as the doctor held her up and they both looked at her in astonishment. "Oh she's so beautiful," Olivia said as Bertie held her.

"Now, that wasn't so bad," the doctor said, and Olivia made a terrible face, and then looked at Charles with a smile, but the smile turned instantly to pain, as he watched her in horror.

"What's happening?" he asked, suddenly

frightened, she was convulsed with pains again and she had already had the baby.

"That happens sometimes," the doctor explained, "it's the afterbirth, sometimes it can be even more painful," he said in an undervoice as Olivia started screaming again, and Bertie watched her.

"Not again . . . please . . ." Olivia begged, "no more . . ." She looked at Charles again as though she were being swept away from him on merciless tides, and all he could think of was no more children, this was awful.

"I don't think," Bertie started to say knowingly, but the doctor cut her off.

"In a minute, she'll deliver the placenta," but she suddenly began bleeding very heavily instead, and she was racked with pain, and without anyone telling her to, she began pushing as Charles held her.

"Doctor, is this normal?" Charles asked in a strangled voice, as suddenly a small head appeared where the first one had been, this one even a little larger, and a small face was suddenly looking at all of them and waiting, as Charles looked down again between her legs in complete amazement. "Victoria," he said, she was lying on the bed, with her eyes closed, clutching at him, and gasping for air, as he smiled at her. "Come on, sweetheart, push, we're having another baby." He was laughing and crying at the same time and so was Bertie.

"What? Oh my God . . ." she said, and then understood and pushed harder, and a second baby girl came out, and a moment after her, a single placenta. They were identical, just as she and Victoria were. Olivia stared at the baby in disbelief and then at Charles, and then started to laugh. It was just after ten o'clock in the morning. "I don't believe this. Not again." They were all laughing suddenly, and even Olivia didn't feel so bad. The bleeding had almost stopped and she was holding both babies in her arms, as Bertie draped her in clean sheets and towels. She was more than a little shocked that Charles had been there, but in fact she had found him a greater help than the doctor.

"I love you so much," Charles whispered to her, as he bent over her, and then with both their babies in his arms, he took them to see Geoff, who couldn't believe them either. They were so perfect and so beautiful, and there were two of them. And in their bedroom the doctor was explaining why he had thought he had heard a single heartbeat.

He stitched Olivia up a little bit, and Bertie bathed her body and her face in cool scented water. And when the doctor left, and they were alone again, she looked at Olivia and smiled at her.

"What have you done, you foolish girl?" she said, and Olivia knew exactly what she meant. She was surprised she had gotten away with it for so long. It was almost a year now.

"She made me do it."

Bertie nodded and laughed. "What, this too?"

"Well, not exactly," she laughed, happy, even after so much pain. It seemed such a small thing now.

"Where is she?" Bertie whispered softly.

"In Europe." But before she could say anything else, Charles came into the room with Geoff, who wanted to see her.

"They're so cute, Aunt . . . Victoria . . ." He had almost slipped and looked at her in panic, but she was smiling when she kissed him.

"They look just like you when you were little, your dad said," Olivia said gently. Geoff looked embarrassed then, and left the room to go and tell their neighbors. And finally, Charles was alone with her again, Bertie had taken the babies to the next room to bathe them.

"I'm sorry I put you through all that," he said, looking proud, but guilty.

"I'd do it all again," she said honestly, "it wasn't so bad." He looked at her in utter amazement.

"How can you say that?" he said, kissing her, remembering just how bad it had been, better than she did.

"It was worth it," she said softly, kissing him, and thinking of the two little girls that had been born, just like her and her sister.

"I'm not sure I'll survive all their tricks," Charles said wanly as he sat beside her on the bed, thinking about how confusing it had been to be around her and her sister. "Your father said he could never tell you two apart."

"I'll teach you," she said and kissed him. And a few minutes later, Bertie came in with both their babies, and as she settled them into their mother's arms, she couldn't help wondering what Olivia was going to do when Victoria returned from Europe.

In Châlons-sur-Marne that night, Victoria had been sleeping peacefully, when she felt Edouard stab her with what felt like a hot knife, over and over again until she screamed, and then as she began to wake from the ugly dream she realized that it was Olivia that they were stabbing and she was screaming. She kept screaming over and over again, and never stopped, until Victoria put her hands over her ears, but then she felt the pains herself again, and she was writhing on their bed, confused, and wet and in agony, crying for her sister, as Edouard woke her.

"*Eh . . . petite . . . arrête . . .* it's a nightmare . . . *ce n'est qu'un cauchemar, ma chérie.*" But it was so real she couldn't stop dreaming, and as she clung to him, gasping for air, she realized their bed was wet and the pains were real. She could hardly catch her breath, as she felt a huge pain bearing down on her, pressure that seemed to press right through her.

"I don't know what's happening . . ." she whispered in the dark, as he turned on the light, still confused himself, and then he saw her. She was lying in a pool of water and blood, and she was holding her belly as he watched her.

"*Ça vient maintenant?* . . . Is it coming now?" When he was half asleep, he often spoke to her in French, but now she could understand it. She nodded, looking terrified, and he got out of bed quickly and grabbed his trousers. "I'll get the doctor."

"No . . . don't . . . don't leave me," she begged, she was in too much pain and far too frightened. Unlike Olivia, Victoria was deathly afraid of childbirth, and all she wanted now was Edouard beside her.

"I have to get him, Olivia . . . I have no idea how to deliver a baby. I've only seen horses."

"Please don't go," she cried, and then gasped horribly as she felt another pain and clutched her belly. "It's coming now . . . I know it is . . . Edouard, don't go . . ." She was in total panic, and her eyes were wild as he watched her.

"Please darling, let me go and get someone to help you . . . Chouinard," their best surgeon at the field hospital, "will come back with me, and I'll bring one of the nurses."

"I don't want them," she gasped, clutching at him again. Her fingers were like claws as she grabbed him. "I want you . . ." And then as she caught her breath for a moment between pains, "I was dreaming that Olivia was having the baby." He smiled this time at the convenient transference of her dream.

"This is one thing she can't do for you, my

love. Nor can I," he said gently. "I wish I could take all the pain from you," he said, as he knelt beside her and held her. She was obviously in agony, but he knew it could go on for hours, and he was determined to get someone to help her. He tried to put his shirt on then, but she wouldn't let him.

"It's coming now, Edouard . . . I can feel it . . . it's coming . . ." She felt terrible pressure and pain, and he was frightened when he saw the blood all around her, but in a moment she screamed, and unluckily, there was no one in the house with them all night. The others were all on duty. And he couldn't use his field telephone to call the doctor.

"I'll be back soon," he tried telling her again, but she wouldn't let him go. She was frantic and too frightened for him to leave her. All he could do was sit there with her and hold her. And at that exact moment, in New York, Olivia began having pains again, only mild ones this time, she said something to Charles and he pretended to look faint, and said please, not triplets. But when Bertie came into the room, she said having pains afterwards was normal. Olivia lay her head back against the pillows then, and slept for a little while. But when she slept, she dreamt only of her sister.

"Edouard, please . . ." It was another pitiful scream, and she sat up suddenly and moved to the edge of the bed. He had no idea what she was doing. "I have to push," she said, panting as she clung to him. She didn't know what to do, or where to go, but she was driven by a force she couldn't stop now.

"Hold on to me," he said, and she clung to his hands, as she pushed against the force she felt, sitting there, and then fell back against the bed. She didn't know what to do to get it out of her, but still she could feel it coming. He got the idea then to push against her legs, and told her to lie back and push against him. And when she tried it, although she made terrible sounds, she felt better. She did it again, and then fell back against the bed again, and the next time she pushed he could see a little tuft of blonde hair appearing.

"Oh my God," he said, utterly amazed by what he saw. "Oh my God . . . Victoria, it's coming . . . keep pushing." She did it again and again and again, and he kept holding her legs and letting her brace herself against him, and in a matter of minutes, there was a little face between her legs, squalling mightily at his mother. "Victoria!" he said, almost shouting at her as they both laughed and cried and she

673

pushed, and two pushes later, their son squirmed out of Victoria's soul and lay on the bed crying. Edouard picked him up as carefully as he could, and held him up so he could see his mother.

"Oh . . . look at him . . ." Victoria cried, unable to believe what had happened to them, and so quickly. He was so perfect, and he looked just like his father. "He's so beautiful . . . oh I love you," she said and kissed Edouard. There were tears rolling down his cheeks. They had truly been blessed. In this place of anguish and death, they had been visited by an angel.

"He is the most beautiful thing I've ever seen," he said to her in French, crying with unabashed tears of joy, "except for his mother. *Je t'aime*, Victoria, more than you'll ever know." He lay the baby gently on her chest then, and went to get towels and water to clean them. It was the most extraordinary thing he'd ever seen. And the little boy had been born in less than an hour from the moment his mother had woken.

"What do we name him?" he asked, after he had ministered to both of them. He was proving to be an excellent amateur doctor, and midwife.

"You did that very well," she smiled, and then she looked somewhat embarrassed. "I'm sorry I got so scared . . . I was so surprised and it went so fast," and quick as it had been, it had been very painful. He was a very big baby, but even she had to admit, it had been much easier than she'd expected. She'd been afraid of a long agonizing delivery, like their mother's, that may have ended in tragedy. "Thank God we didn't have twins," Victoria said, looking relieved.

"I think I'd like that," he said, looking very much the proud father, as he lit a cigarette and offered her one, but for once she didn't want it. She was feeling a little shaken up still, and more than a little queasy. But the baby was already nursing. And looking at her, Edouard was reminded again that she should go home soon. This was no place for a baby. And then he smiled at her again, and smoothed the long dark hair back from her face, as she lay there naked, with their son, covered only by an army blanket. "And the future baron's name?" he asked formally and she looked from her son to his father with a thoughtful expression.

"How about Olivier Edouard, after my sister, and you and my father? That seems to wrap it up. The only one it leaves out is

Charles," she grinned, "and under the circumstances, I don't think he'll mind that."

"Are we sending him an announcement, or are you going to write to the poor man one of these days?" They had finally decided that that would be the best way to do it, otherwise Charles might not know for years, and Olivia would be trapped forever playing the role of her sister. Victoria had been planning to write to Olivia and tell her. She was sure it would be a relief to her, although Charles was undoubtedly going to be very angry. She hated leaving Olivia to face the music alone, but she just couldn't see herself going back to the States now. But as always, whenever she thought about her, Olivia was heavy on her mind for the next few days, and she wished more than anything that she could show her the baby. She would have given anything to put her arms around her just then and hold her. She actually lay in bed and cried for two days, in spite of her joy over little Olivier, but for the first time in ten months, Victoria was deathly homesick.

Chapter 31

The solution Edouard and Victoria came to eventually was to leave the baby with the chatelaine, the countess Victoria had met months before, who was now the mistress of the general. But her house was safe, it was well back from the front lines, and she lived there under the protection of the Allies. Although Edouard said he would have been happier knowing that Victoria and the baby were safe in Switzerland, he was willing to agree to leave them there, at least for a few months, while she was nursing. Victoria stayed home with her son for several weeks, until she got on her feet again, but she felt surprisingly well very quickly. Several of the nurses came to visit her, and Olivier became the mascot of the camp, even to those who didn't know him. The soldiers sent presents for him, and carved little toys. Didier knitted him a tiny pair of socks, and from God only knew where one of the men found him a stuffed bear, that someone else had gotten from their girlfriend. And as he lay on his mother's breast, with his adoring father watching him, Olivier Edouard de Bonneville looked like a very happy baby. For all of them, he was the flower of life in the midst of a field of death and ashes.

By June, Victoria was herself again. She had regained her figure, much to her husband's delight, and was driving Edouard's jeep again, only nursing the baby now at night and in the morning. They left him with the countess when they were gone, and Victoria would pick him up on the way home, anxious to see him, and sometimes dripping with milk as she waited to nurse him. But he was very good-natured, and made do with goat's milk whenever he had to, particularly if they ventured too far away, or Edouard had to go somewhere overnight and took Victoria with him. For them, it was the perfect arrangement. And given the demands of the war, it was amazing they pulled it off. But fortunately for Edouard, the general liked him. Edouard had recently been making runs to rendezvous with the Escadrille Américain, a flying force with seven U.S. volunteers, and he had taken Victoria with him to meet them. It had been exciting for her, and they were thrilled to see another Yankee. Two of them were from New York, so they had that in common too, but the war was enough bond for all. They were all in it together.

And in June, while Victoria was driving for Edouard, the Dawsons were christening their babies. Olivia had insisted on naming them Elizabeth and Victoria for her mother and her sister. The Victoria had been harder to explain to Charles, but he had thought she wanted a namesake. But Elizabeth's middle name was Charlotte, for her father. Victoria's was Susan.

Geoff was enchanted with both of them, and Bertie had her hands full, dressing and feeding and washing, and changing, there were never enough hands to help her. Olivia had tried nursing them, but they had been too much for her, and after the difficult delivery she'd had, the doctor thought she was too weak to continue, so they'd switched them to bottles, and now everyone could help feed them.

But by June, Olivia was feeling wonderful. It was as though nothing had ever happened.

And as they stood in Saint Thomas Church, the day before their second anniversary, Olivia felt like the luckiest woman alive, except for the knowledge that she had borrowed it all from her sister. She had no idea what they would do when Victoria returned. Maybe they'd have to continue the masquerade forever. She just hoped that Victoria hadn't decided that she was madly in love with Charles, but nothing in her letters to Olivia had indicated that, or mentioned anyone else for that matter. Olivia had the impression that something was going on, but she had never figured out what. Victoria mostly confined herself to war news, to the extent that the censors would let her, but at least Olivia knew her sister was happy.

In June, during the Battle of Verdun, after Fort Vaux fell, Edouard and Victoria were coming home from a top secret meeting with the Allies in Anscourt. All of the high-ranking officers had been there, including Churchill, representing his new battalion. Everyone had been depressed about how the Battle of Verdun was going, the carnage seemed endless. And the meeting had been top secret. Victoria had had to wait outside with the other drivers. And he said very little to her on the way back. He seemed to be thinking, and he paid very little attention to the road, it was familiar to both of them. Victoria knew it like the back of her hand, she had been over it a hundred times. And she was in a hurry that night to get back to her baby. As usual, her breasts were dripping with milk for him, and she wanted to get back to the château quickly to pick him up and nurse him. The discomfort she felt increased hourly, and made her just a little bit careless.

"What was that?" Edouard glanced at something by the side of the road, when they were more than halfway back, and she smiled at him. He was tired and looked strained. The war was not going well for the Allies. She wished the Americans would get into it, but President Wilson was still resisting. If only they would come over and see for themselves how badly the French and English needed them, maybe things would be different. She was thinking about that when they hit a small bump in the road, and swerved and almost hit a tree. They were both tired and jumpy.

They were almost back to Châlons-sur-Marne, and had just come through Epernay, when Edouard said he thought he saw something again. He wanted to slow down, and she wanted to go more quickly. They argued about it for a minute, and he pulled rank on her, and was only half joking.

"Slow down, Victoria, I want to see this." He was sure he could see movement in the bushes, and he wanted to warn them in Château-Thierry if the Germans were somehow encroaching from the rear, which would be disastrous. But after they stopped for a minute, which Victoria thought was suicide, it turned out to be nothing and they started moving. She had finally just started to pick up speed, when a dog ran into the road in front of them, and she swerved to avoid it and almost hit a tree, and as she was calming her nerves down again, she heard a strange whizzing sound, and was reminded for no reason in particular of the *Lusitania*. It was a long low whine, and she glanced at Edouard, her whole body tense, and his eyes were suddenly wide as he shouted at her.

"Duck! *Baisse-toi* . . ." he shouted, and they both dove as low as they could while she kept moving, but as she turned to look at him, he had an odd expression in his eyes, and she saw suddenly that he was bleeding. She started to pull over and he shook his head frantically, telling her not to stop, but another shell hit them in a single moment. They had been hit by snipers. She drove as fast and as far as she could, reaching a hand out to him, not sure what to do. He had his field telephone with him, but they were still too far to use it. He was starting to spit blood, and she could see he was losing consciousness. She was torn between trying to get him to the field hospital, or stopping to care for him there. But there was no decision to make now, he pitched forward onto the floor, and she could see that he was dying. She had no choice but to pull over.

"Edouard," she said, pulling him back and laying him against her. She had seen faces like that a thousand times in the past thirteen months, but never his, or even anyone she knew. This could not be happening, not to him, not today, not now. It wasn't possible . . . she was shouting his name and shaking him to keep him from becoming unconscious, but she could see then that the whole side of his head had been shot away, and he was almost gone as she held him. She couldn't believe he was still breathing. "Edouard!" she shouted at him, half crying, half sobbing. "Listen to me . . . listen to me . . ." She was shouting and she wondered if the snipers could hear her. The snipers were still far enough from the camp, to be fairly typical, and not a real danger to their field camp. "Edouard, please . . ."

He opened his eyes and looked at her with a smile, squeezing her hand as hard as he could, which was very little. ". . . *je t'aime* . . . always be . . . with you . . ." And then he looked at her again, and his eyes opened a little wider, as though he were very surprised, and then suddenly he was staring, and he had stopped breathing. It was all over much too quickly.

"Edouard," she whispered in the darkness, alone . . . "don't . . . go . . . please . . . don't leave me . . ." And as she looked at him in horror and disbelief, his blood smeared all over her, she barely felt the bullet that entered her back just below her neck, though she heard the one that whizzed past her helmet. She laid him gently on the seat next to her, and feeling something very cold trickle down her neck, she pressed her foot onto the gas and hurtled down the road at full speed. She had to get him back to the hospital to see if they could help him. The doctors would do something . . . they would wake him up again . . . he was just sleeping, she told herself. She was in shock. All she knew was that she had to take him back. He was her captain, and she was his driver, and he was her captain . . . and . . . She hit a tree as she crashed into camp, barely missing two nurses on their way to the mess tent. They shouted at her, and one of them said something rude, and then stared at her.

"He's wounded," Victoria said, staring blankly at them. And the nurses looked at her very strangely, as their faces reeled around her. "Do something, he's wounded," she shouted, and they could see without looking twice that Captain de Bonneville was dead. But then they saw the blood dripping down her shirt from her neck, and they understood what had happened.

"So are you," one of them said gently, and reached into the truck to touch her, just as Victoria slipped slowly into the darkness all around her. They caught her as she fell forward against the steering wheel, and saw that her whole back was covered with blood.

"Get a stretcher!" one of them shouted to anyone behind her, as she held Victoria's chin gently in her hands to support her. "Orderly!" . . . she called, and two men came running. One of them recognized Victoria and shook his head when he saw Edouard.

"The captain?" he asked, and the nurse shook her head. It was hopeless. "They were shelled . . . take her to surgery. See if Chouinard is there . . . or Dorsay . . . anyone . . ." If it had touched her spine, anything could happen. If nothing else, the infection could kill her.

The orderlies ran with her to the surgery, and then came back more slowly for Edouard. Two soldiers carried his body to the morgue, as another drove the truck away, and went to report to headquarters about Captain de Bonneville.

There was nothing more they could do for her, except operate to remove the bullet. She might never walk again if she survived it, which was less than likely. The damage the sniper's bullet had done had been tremendous, as it ricocheted through her body. And later that night, the nurses and orderlies she had worked with were talking about her and Edouard. Sergeant Morrison came to look for her papers. They knew her as Olivia Henderson, American, from New York, and Morrison had long since recorded the home address and next of kin. It was a woman called Victoria Dawson. Morrison wrote the telegram herself, and there were tears in her eyes when she did it.

Chapter 32

The carriage Olivia had to use for the twins was the most unwieldy antiquated thing she had ever seen, but Bertie had insisted on bringing it from Croton. She'd had Donovan drive it down specially, and it was huge, and had been hers and Victoria's, but despite their mother's complaints, the twins looked very happy in it. The house had become too small for them overnight too. The twins were sharing a room with Bertie, and she and Charles had talked more than once about moving into her father's home on lower Fifth Avenue. As far as Charles knew, it was hers now. But Olivia knew it was her sister's, and didn't feel right moving into it until she discussed it with Victoria when she got back from Europe. The house she had inherited was in Croton, which was magnificent, but far less useful. So for the moment, they were staying where they were, and living in very tight quarters. She and Charles could hear the babies cry at night, and Geoff was on top of them constantly, usually with Chip, or even one of the neighbors' children. It was beginning to drive Charles crazy.

And lately Olivia was having trouble sleeping and was very tired and seemed to ache all over and she hoped she wasn't getting sick.

And as Olivia struggled with the huge pram on the front steps, she was beginning to think Charles was right and they should move, and she'd explain it to Victoria later.

"Can I help you with that?" a man in uniform said, and as she thanked him and glanced up at him, she realized that he was holding a telegram with her name on it, and she suddenly felt her heart stop. She had had an odd feeling for days, and had finally convinced herself she was just nervous from lack of sleep, trying to take care of two babies.

"Is that for me?" she asked hoarsely.

"Victoria Dawson?" he asked pleasantly, and she nodded. "Yes it is." He handed it to her and had her sign for it, and then helped her get the pram into the house, as her hands shook. She pushed the pram into the front hall, with the babies still asleep in it, and ripped the telegram open without waiting another minute, and she felt her heart seize as though a steel vise had clamped around it. The words blurred the moment she saw them. It was an official notice from a Sergeant Morrison in France, attached to the Allied Forces. "Regret to inform you, your sister, Olivia Henderson, has been injured in the line of duty. Stop. Cannot be transferred. Stop. Gravely ill. Stop. Will advise you further developments. Stop." And it was signed by a Sergeant Penelope Morrison of the French Fourth Army, in charge of volunteers. Victoria had never mentioned her before, but that was beside the point now. She had been injured. Olivia stood crying in the front hall, holding the telegram, unable to believe it. And yet she had sensed it. The malaise she had felt had been far too easily explained by fatigue from the babies. But now she suddenly understood what she'd been feeling. Victoria had been ill or injured.

Olivia was looking around her frantically, as Bertie came into the hall from the kitchen, and knew instantly that something terrible had happened.

"What is it?" She rushed toward the pram immediately, thinking it was one of the babies.

"It's Victoria . . . she's hurt . . ."

"Oh my God . . . what'll you tell Charles?" She dared to use his first name in his absence, although she never would have in his presence.

"I don't know," Olivia said frantically, as they both took the sleeping babies upstairs and laid them down in their cribs without waking them, as Geoff came rushing up the stairs to do his homework. But Olivia didn't say anything to him. She had to tell his father first, and she had no idea where to begin, whether to tell him the whole truth, or only half of it. But whatever she did, she had to do something. She was going to go to her immediately, and whether or not he joined her was up to him. But she was going. Nothing on this earth would have kept her from it.

She was waiting for him in the living room when he came home late that afternoon. She had been pacing there for more than two hours, and she was beside herself with fear and worry.

He knew the moment he saw her face that something terrible had happened that afternoon. She was deathly pale, and her hands were shaking as she folded the dreaded telegram again and again, but like Bertie, he thought it was one of his babies.

"Victoria, what is it?"

She took a quick breath, and decided to only tell him some of it. She had been agonizing all afternoon about the decision. "It's my sister."

"Olivia? Where is she? What happened?" He didn't understand what his wife was saying.

"She's in Europe. And she's injured." It was actually easier than she thought, now that she had started. But the whole truth never would be. There would be no way to dress that one up in clean linens, and her worst fear was that he'd divorce her. He didn't even have to. All he had to do was throw her out. She wasn't even sure that, under the circumstances, he'd have to give her the babies, or even let her visit them. But this was not about them right now, not yet, this was about her sister.

"She's in Europe?" He looked totally lost as he sat down and stared at her. "What's she doing there?"

"She's been driving for the Allied Forces, and she's been wounded," Olivia said, sitting down across from him, and looking at him with terror. He was beginning to realize that there had been some deception here, and suddenly he knew it.

"Did you know about this?" he asked, searching her eyes, wondering if she had lied to him, and her father, and when he asked her, she nodded. "How could she do a thing like that? Was she there all this time?" Olivia nodded again, terrified at what else he would guess, but the rest was so outrageous there was no way he could divine it. It had all gone much too far in the past thirteen months and she knew it. She wondered if Victoria knew it too now, and was sorry about it. Thirteen months was a long time to carry on a deception and switch lives. It far exceeded their bargain. But she had far exceeded hers too, and she knew it. "Why didn't you say anything, Victoria?" Suddenly her sister's name rang in her ears like an accusation, but it was too late to change it, and she answered him without flinching.

"She didn't want anyone to know. She wanted to do this desperately, Charles. I didn't think it was fair to stop her."

"Fair? Do you think it was fair of her to run out on your father like that? For God's sake, it killed him."

Olivia's eyes filled with tears when he said it. "That wasn't the only thing, and we don't

know that. He'd had a weak heart for years."
She tried to defend herself but he looked unim-
pressed and angry.

"I'm sure that didn't help it," he said
sternly, appalled at "Olivia's" wanton deception.

"Probably not," the real Olivia said
weakly, feeling like a murderess, although her
charade had convinced her father he'd seen her
at his deathbed, but it was small comfort.

"I could have understood you doing
something crazy like that, in the old days, when
you were all involved in politics and radical
ideas, but Olivia . . . I just can't understand
it."

"And if I'd gone?" she asked gently, as he
smiled ruefully.

"I'd have killed you. I'd have dragged you
back by the hair, and locked you in the attic."
Perhaps he should have. But it would have
taken that to get her back there. And then he
looked at her more seriously. "What are you
going to do now?" he asked, expecting her to
go to the French Consulate or the Red Cross,
and see what could be done to help her. "Is she
badly hurt?"

"I don't know. I'm not sure. The telegram
says 'gravely ill.' " She looked at him very hard

then, and told him the truth this time. But he couldn't stop her. "Charles, I'm going."

"You're *what*?" He was outraged. "There's a war in Europe and you have three children to take care of."

"She's my sister," she said, and to her it spoke volumes, but he was livid.

"No, she's not, she's your *twin* and I know what that means. It means you drop everything for her every time you have a headache and think she's sending you a message. Well, I'm not putting up with it. She may be your twin, but I'm forbidding you to go to her, do you hear me? You're staying right here where you belong and not running halfway around the world to rescue a woman who dumped her entire family a year ago to run off to do God knows what in Europe. You're *not* going," he said in a voice she had never heard before, as he stood in their living room and shouted. But she looked at him with eyes he'd never seen before either.

"*Nothing* you do will stop me, Charles. I am getting on a ship the first day I can this week, and I am going to her, whether you like it or not. My children will be safe here. I am going to my sister."

"I've lost one wife on the high seas," he

shouted at her as the rest of the household pretended not to hear them, but it was impossible not to, "and goddamn it, Victoria, I'm not going to lose another." There were tears in his eyes and on his cheeks as he shouted at her, both in rage and terror.

"I'm sorry, Charles." Olivia said quietly this time, "I'm going to her. And if you want to, I'd like you to come with me."

"And what if we both die? What if we both get torpedoed on the way there? Who will take care of our children? We have three of them to think of now. Have you even thought of that?"

"Then stay here," she said sadly, "they'll have you." They probably wouldn't have her anyway once he threw her out and wouldn't let her see them. It was all she could imagine now, and as she held them in her arms that night, she ached at the thought of never holding them again, but she knew she had to go to Victoria. Every ounce of her being and intuition said so.

She put Geoff to bed that night, and he had heard the argument and looked very worried. "It's Victoria, isn't it?" he whispered and she nodded. "Does Dad know now?"

"No," she whispered, "and you mustn't

tell him. I have to see her first, and then we'll tell him together. But I want to talk to her."

"Do you think she'll be mad about the babies?" he asked wistfully and she kissed him again.

"Of course not, she'll love them." She tried to sound calmer than she felt. Inside, she was frantic with terror for her sister.

"But will you stay with us when she comes back? You belong here now," he said insistently and she smiled at him. She only hoped that Victoria would be coming back, whether to this house or not, no one knew now.

"That's why I have to go to Europe, to talk to her and make sure she's all right, and work all these things out with her."

"Will she die?" He looked suddenly surprised and a little frightened.

"Of course not," she said, wishing she believed it. Oh God . . . please, please don't let her die, she said to herself that night over and over as she lay in bed, next to Charles. For a long time, he said nothing to her, and then he rolled over in their bed and looked at her. Olivia couldn't read what he was thinking.

"I always knew you were stubborn, even when I married you. But if you insist on going, Victoria, I'll go with you." She was stunned, but relieved. Going to war-torn Europe without him would have been terrifying, and she was grateful that he'd do it.

"Can you get away?"

"I'll have to. It's an emergency. I'll tell them I have a crazy sister-in-law and an impossible wife, and I have to run off to Europe to help them." He smiled and Olivia kissed him, grateful beyond words for what he was doing, and sorrier still for what she'd have to tell him once they got there. She wasn't going to tell him anything more now until she saw her sister. "But let me tell you, if those two brats in the next room ever pull the kind of stuff on me that you two do, I'm turning them in now for two totally unrelated children of different sexes, or two puppies." She laughed at him, and as she clung to him in fear that night, he held her and kissed her.

Olivia prepared frantically for the trip for the next two days, and on the third day they boarded the French ship *Espagne,* bound for Bordeaux in seven days. It was the only ship sailing, other than the *Carpathia* which had set sail the week before, and four years before had rescued Geoffrey from the *Titanic.*

They had a small, outside cabin, on B Deck, and although it wasn't luxurious, it was comfortable, and they carefully observed black-outs, and spent most of their time in their cabin. All Olivia could think of by then was her twin, and Charles tried hard to distract her and raise her spirits.

"It isn't exactly the *Aquatania*," he said one night, jokingly, remembering their honeymoon and she smiled at him, and he astounded her with his comment, "what a miserable trip that was."

"Why?" she asked in surprise, and he looked at her very strangely.

"Maybe I just have a better memory than you do, but I can tell you now, that first year almost killed me. If things hadn't changed a year ago, I think I might have shot myself, or gone to a monastery. I might as well have." She knew he was referring to the celibacy her sister had promised her, and that made her feel guilty toward her all over again. They all had so much explaining to do to each other. Just thinking about it made her quiet.

They docked in Bordeaux two days before their anniversary, oddly enough, and the local consul gave them all the advice he could on how to get to Châlons-sur-Marne. They hired a car, which looked as though it wouldn't have made it around the block, and they were to pick up a Red Cross representative in Troyes, to go the rest of the way with them. The trip was expected to take them fourteen hours. Normally, it would have been less, but with battles going on all around them, they had to take a more circuitous route, and they had already been warned of potential dangers. They had been given gas masks, and minor medical supplies, and water. It reminded them both that they were in a war zone. Olivia tried on the gas mask and she couldn't imagine how anyone could breathe through it, but the warden who gave it to her assured her that if they ran into chlorine gas, which the Jerries were using that week, she'd be very grateful. Seeing that made Charles thankful that he had opted to come with her. She could have never done this alone, or so he thought. He wouldn't have wanted her to anyway. And as they drove farther into the interior, and saw the ravages of war, he was even more relieved that he'd had the wisdom to join her.

They picked up the woman from the Red Cross in Troyes and she directed them to Châlons-sur-Marne. They had a flat tire halfway there, and soldiers stopped them several times, and forced them to make detours. It was long after midnight when they reached the camp that night, and all three of them were exhausted. But all Olivia wanted, no matter what the hour was, was to see her sister. Charles tried to get her to wait till the next day, but there was no stopping her, and as soon as they got out of the tiny Renault, she asked an orderly where the hospital was and they pointed her in the right direction. She found a nurse just coming out and asked her if she knew Olivia Henderson. It was like asking for herself, but she knew who she was looking for, and she had come a long way to do it.

Charles was right behind her by then, and he heard the young nurse tell her where to find her sister. And then he followed her slowly into the tent, and gasped at the evil smell, and almost gagged at the terrible sights there. There were men who were maimed, and injured, and vomiting green from the chlorine gas. They were all the familiar things Victoria had seen for a year, and neither of them had ever imagined. Olivia started to turn away and then a boy on the floor reached a hand out to her, and she gently took it. He had reminded her of Geoff, and she realized that she would have wanted someone to hold his hand if this ever happened.

"Where you from?" he asked in an Australian accent. He had been in the Battle of Verdun and had lost a leg, but he was going to make it.

"I'm from New York," she whispered, not wanting to wake anyone, but no one seemed to be sleeping. Everything around them was moving.

"I'm from Sydney." He smiled at her, and saluted Charles, who saluted back with tears in his eyes, and then they moved on to find her sister.

She was on a cot in the far corner of the room, and her head and neck were swathed in bandages, so much so that Olivia didn't even recognize her at first, or realize she was a woman. And then a homing instinct directed her right to her, and suddenly she was looking at her and touching her and holding her. Victoria was very weak, but she smiled and they could see she was happy to see them. But mainly she had eyes for Olivia, and the two barely spoke in finished words or complete sentences, it was all sounds and half words and little murmurs of excitement as Olivia put her arms around her and held her. This was the moment she had waited a year for. There was so much they had to tell each other and so little they could say here. But they were each over-whelmed by a maelstrom of feelings.

There were tears pouring down Olivia's face as Victoria held her hand and smiled over at Charles, and then spoke in a weak, strained voice. It was hard for her to talk still. She had an infection of the spinal column, and they were still afraid it might go to her brain and kill her. The lucky thing for her was that it hadn't been severed. If she survived, she would most probably walk again. Lots of others were not as lucky. This was the cruellest of all wars, and it had already destroyed millions.

"Thank you for coming," she whispered to Charles, and he reached out and touched her hand, but as he looked at her there was something in her eyes which jarred him. It was as though she had grown harder here, and tougher in some ways. There was a brittleness to her that Olivia had never had before, at least he didn't think so. But inevitably, she had grown up here.

"I'm glad we found you," he answered, and then, "Geoff sends his love. We've all missed you. Especially Victoria."

Victoria looked at her sister then, and im-perceptibly, Olivia nodded. He still didn't know. Not even now, as she lay dying. And she wanted to ask Olivia now if they were going to tell him. She hoped so. She wanted to make a clean breast of it to both of them and ask Olivia to take her baby if she died. But there was no time to ask them anything that night. Olivia only stayed for a little while, and then the nurse told them to go, and they were taken to separate billets. There were no accommodations for married couples here. What she and Edouard had had was rare, and his rooms had already been given to another captain. The waters closed over them quickly. He had been buried in the hills behind them, with other men just like him. It was only to Victoria that he had been different, and to his son, but not to the Allies, or the Germans. Victoria was still reeling from the pain of losing him. It was all she thought of in her moments of consciousness, that and Olivia. But at least now she could see her sister.

Charles and Olivia met in the mess hall again the next day, they had both slept miserably and all Olivia wanted now was to go back and see her sister. Charles agreed to wait outside so they could be alone for a while, and he talked to some of the men, feeling guilty suddenly that his country wasn't in it. They were impressed that he had come this far, and crossed the Atlantic to visit his sister-in-law, and he was touched to realize that several of them knew her and thought highly of her. They all said how much they hoped she'd survive it.

And as Olivia sat at her side, Victoria was smiling at her, as though she had seen a little piece of Heaven.

"I can't believe you're really here. What made you come?" She knew they would probably notify her, but she'd figured they'd write her a letter that would take forever. She had even wondered more than once if she'd be dead by the time it got there.

"I got a telegram from a Sergeant Morrison. I'll have to see her later and thank her," Olivia said gently, overwhelmed by her feelings. It was so incredible to be with her sister.

"Good old Penny Morrison." Victoria smiled and then kissed Olivia's fingers. "Oh God, how I've missed you, Ollie . . . I have so much to tell you," and she felt as though she had so little time. The nurses had said she was better that day, but she had such a terrible headache. And then she looked seriously at her twin, amazed that she had been able to keep up the charade for this long. "I don't know how you did it."

"I always was a better liar than you were."

Olivia grinned and Victoria tried to laugh but it hurt too much, she felt as though her head would fall off if she moved it.

"That's a nice thing to brag about," Victoria said, wishing she could laugh, but too tired to do it. They had both turned twenty-three the month before, and for different reasons, they both felt ancient. "I'm sorry about Father," she said then, trying to touch on all the important things that had happened since she left them. "I'm sorry I wasn't there with him."

"He thought you were," Olivia smiled lovingly, "that was good enough. He died peacefully. I was with him."

"Sweet Ollie, you're there for everyone . . . even poor Charles, because I was too rotten to stay and be his wife."

"Victoria, I have something to tell you," she said awkwardly. "Things didn't work out the way we'd planned . . ." She wondered if her sister would ever speak to her again, but she had to tell her. This was why she had come here. "We had twins three months ago," she bit the bullet and just spat it out, as Victoria stared at her in total amazement.

"Twins?" She almost choked on the word, and Olivia had to give her a sip of water, but she assured the nurse that they were all right, and prayed that no one would disturb them. Victoria was looking tired, but they were far from through yet. "You did say twins, didn't you?"

"Yes, identical, like us, girls . . . they're beautiful . . ." She smiled wistfully, but for the moment Victoria didn't look like she was going to kill her. "Elizabeth and Victoria, after you and Mother."

"I figured that part out." Victoria smiled at her weakly. "What I haven't figured out yet is how you had them," she was smiling wickedly at her older sister, "am I to believe that you have stolen my husband?" She was actually grinning, but Olivia was looking down at her hands, crying, and didn't see it.

"Victoria, please . . . no . . . I'll go back to Croton when you come back . . . I just want to see them when I can . . . please . . . don't."

"Oh shut up," Victoria was smiling at her, as best she could in spite of the pain, when Olivia looked up again, "you're a bad girl, aren't you? But I think it's very funny. Olivia, I don't love him. I never did. I don't want him back. He's yours, if you want him." He was like a doll they had shared, and now Victoria was giving it to her, and Olivia stared at her in amazement. "That's why I never came back last summer . . . I didn't want to . . . I couldn't . . ." And then she smiled again, "when actually did this happen? When did . . . er . . . things change between you, I mean?"

"After I found out you'd survived the sinking of the *Lusitania,*" she said meekly. She was so happy being back with Victoria, it was like a miracle being there with her. Even with the bandages, she was still the same as she'd always been, there was that raw, sharp edge to her that Charles had sensed the night before and suddenly remembered.

"I take it that was your idea of a little celebration?" Victoria grinned, even near death, still full of mischief.

"You're disgusting," Olivia whispered, trying not to smile at her, but smiling anyway. She was so happy to be here, and so relieved that her sister wasn't furious at her.

"No, you are disgusting," Victoria continued. "I give you a nice chaste relationship with a man who hates me and wouldn't sleep with me if you paid him to, and what do you do with him? You seduce him. You're the one. *You're* the seductress in the family. You deserve to be married to him. Personally, I can't think of a worse fate, but actually, you both look very happy together. He's very lucky."

"So am I," she whispered. And as Victoria looked at Olivia, her heart filled with love for her, she thought of how fortunate she herself had been, for a while, with Edouard and their baby.

"So what do we do now?" Victoria asked her seriously. "We have to tell him."

"He's going to hate me," Olivia said, looking pale, but also aware that they had to do it.

"He'll get over it," Victoria reassured her. "He's a decent man. He'll have a fit for a while, but what's he going to do, leave a woman he loves, because I'm sure he must, and two babies? Don't be stupid. Speaking of which," she looked sheepishly at her older sister, "I have a confession to make."

"Yes." Olivia pretended to make the sign of the cross over her and they both giggled. "After everything I've done, I hope it's a good one." The two still had the most remarkable bond and understanding between them. It was suddenly as though they'd been apart not for a year, but for only minutes.

"I had a baby three months ago too. Not twins, thank God, but a beautiful little boy named Olivier," she said proudly, wishing she had a picture to show Olivia, but she didn't. "Maybe you can guess who I named him after." For some odd reason, although Olivia knew she should have been shocked, it did not surprise her. It was almost as though she knew it before Victoria told her.

"So that's why you didn't come home last summer," Olivia said pensively but Victoria shook her head as gently as possible.

"No, it isn't. I just didn't want to. I don't think I even knew yet that I was pregnant. His father was a very special man." She told her about Edouard then, all he had been to her, all she had thought of him, what they had planned, she cried as she talked about it, she had never met anyone like him. She told her sister everything about him, and about how he'd been killed. She knew now that life would never again be the same without him. And Olivia knew as she listened to her, that her sister had found the right man, here in Châlons-sur-Marne, with all the agony of the war happening around them.

"Where is the baby now?" She told her about leaving him with the countess at the cottage near the château. But one of the nurses had come to give her the message two days before that the countess had gone to her sister's house because there had been more snipers.

"I want you to take him home with you. I put him on my passport. Yours actually. You won't have any trouble traveling with him, for obvious reasons, as long as Charles doesn't mind you traveling on your old passport."

"I think there's a lot Charles is going to mind after we talk to him, but some of it he'll have to live with." He didn't have to stay married to her, since they weren't anyway, but he couldn't stop her from taking Victoria's baby home to New York, to safety. "What about you?" she asked her then, sure she would get better now that they were together. "When are you coming home?" With the man she loved gone, and after her injury, there was no point in staying here, but Victoria only looked wistful.

"Maybe I won't have to, Ollie," she said sadly, and a shiver ran down her spine. More than anything, without Edouard, she felt as though she had no home now. Olivia would stay with Charles, and she couldn't see herself living in her father's house in New York she'd inherited, and even less at Henderson Manor. The only place she wanted to be was with Edouard, and she said as much to her sister.

"Don't say things like that," Olivia said, looking frightened and hurt, but it was almost as though Victoria didn't want to live without Edouard now, even for her baby.

"He left Olivier his château, and his house in Paris. As soon as he was born, he contacted his lawyers and redid his will. He wanted to be sure his wife didn't get everything, but according to French law, Olivier is protected anyway. And he has Edouard's name. When you get home, you should get him his own passport in his own name." She was very concerned about the baby, but Olivia was deeply worried about her.

"Why don't you come home with us?"

"We'll see," she said vaguely, looking restless, and Charles came to join them a little while later. But everything had been said by then, and Victoria was getting very sleepy. He watched her for a few minutes again, and then they left. He thought she looked terrible, but he didn't say that to Olivia. Instead, they went to the mess hall for coffee. And when they went back again afterwards, she was sleeping.

It was late that afternoon when they returned to see her again. The nurse said she had a fever and they shouldn't stay long, but she didn't say anything about what it meant, or

711

there being any graver danger. Victoria had said that she wanted to see Charles that afternoon, she wanted to tell him herself, she thought it was only fair, and when he came in and stood next to her, she looked very pale, but strangely peaceful.

"Charles, we have something to tell you," she said softly. Olivia couldn't imagine hearing it, let alone saying it, and her heart was pounding. But Victoria had always been braver than she had. "We did something terrible to you a year ago. It's not her fault," she glanced at Olivia but didn't say her name at first. "I want you to know that I forced her to do it. I felt I had to." An odd chill ran down his spine, as he looked at her. There was something frighteningly familiar about her, those eyes, the coldness there, and yet there was still a strange kind of excitement about her.

"I don't want to hear this now," he said, wanting to run out of the tent like a child running away from a punishment, but Victoria held him firm with her gaze as she lay there.

"You have to, there is no other time," she said almost coldly. She wanted to get this over with, for all of their sakes. It was time now. She knew she had to do it. "I'm not who you think I am. I'm not even who my passport says I am,

Charles." She looked at him long and hard and he knew as she lay there. He stared at Olivia openmouthed, and then back at his wife again, the real one, who lay injured in the hospital tent in Châlons-sur-Marne, not the woman he had lain with for a year, and who had given birth to his children.

"Are you telling me . . . are you saying to me . . ." He knew, but he couldn't bear to say it.

"I'm telling you something that you already know and may not want to hear," she said, still strong, even at death's door. But she knew him well, despite her disdain for him. She had sensed his instinctive intuition when he looked at her that she was the woman he had married, and not the woman he had come from New York with.

Olivia felt tears in her eyes as she listened to her twin continue, however painful it was for all three of them. "I'm telling you we hated each other, and you know it. We would have destroyed each other, if I stayed. It was an arrangement neither of us could live up to . . . she loves you, you know . . . Olivia has been kind to you for a year. I haven't been there, but I can see it in her eyes, and yours . . . you love her too. Charles, you never loved me, and

713

you know it." She was right but that only made her words sting more. If she had been whole, he thought he would have slapped her, but now he couldn't. He could only stare at her in horror, suddenly forced to face something he hadn't ever allowed himself to even think of. And forced by her hand to face it now, he looked at his real wife in fury.

"How dare you tell me this now . . . how dare you . . . both of you . . ." He was raging at them, in as soft a voice as he could muster, with hundreds of men around them. "You're not children, playing games . . . this switching you were always so proud of . . . you were my wife, you owed me something, Victoria, more than this . . ." He was almost speechless with outrage.

"I owed you a lot more than I gave you. All I ever would have given you is pain. And you would never have let yourself love me. You were too afraid . . . you were too hurt by what you'd lost, but maybe Olivia . . . maybe she gave you what you wanted. You're not afraid of her, Charles. If you were honest about it, you'd admit you love her. You don't love me, you hate me." For Olivia's sake, if nothing else, she wanted him to see that.

"I hate both of you, and I'm not going to

stand here and let you tell me what I did or didn't do, should or shouldn't have done, or who I love, because it's convenient for you. I don't give a damn if you are sick, or wounded, or God knows what. I think you're both sick, you play with people like toys. Well, I'm not a toy for either of you. Do you hear me?" he said, raising his voice finally, staring at both of them in total rage, and then he strode out of the tent as fast as he could, fighting back tears, unable to believe it. Olivia was crying softly by then, and Victoria was holding her hand as tightly as she could, which wasn't very.

"He'll get over it, Olivia . . . believe me, he doesn't hate you . . ." But she was getting agitated and the nurse came to ask Olivia to leave. She kissed her sister's cheek gently then, and promised to come back later. They were all too overwrought to talk any longer.

Olivia looked for Charles outside, but she couldn't find him anywhere, and then finally, she found him pacing outside the men's barracks.

"Don't talk to me," he said angrily as she approached, and he held a hand out as though to stop her. "I don't even know you. You're a stranger. I don't know any decent human being who could do a thing like that to anyone. Not for a day, or a year, or thirteen months, and certainly not in order to have two babies. It's obscene, you're immoral, both of you. You're sick. You should be married to each other." He was so enraged he was shaking.

"I'm sorry . . . I don't know what else to say . . . I did it for her at first . . . and for you and Geoff. I didn't just want her to leave you. It's true." She was sobbing almost beyond control as she said it. She couldn't bear the thought of losing him, but she knew she had to pay the price of their lie now.

"I don't believe you," he said coldly. "I don't want to hear anything more from you, or your sister."

"And then I did it for me," she said sadly. "Father was right." She decided to throw all her chips in. She had nothing to lose now. "I was always in love with you, right from the beginning, and when he asked you to marry her, I had nothing left, except a lifetime with him. It was my one chance to be with you, to be yours." Tears were streaming down her face as she looked at him, but he wouldn't look at her now. "Charles, I love you," she said in utter agony, but he looked at her with equal fury.

"Don't tell me that. You made a fool of me. You seduced me, you lied to me, you fooled me. But you're nothing to me," he said cruelly, "everything you did and had and got was a lie. We're not even married. You mean nothing to me," he said, as she felt her heart break in a thousand pieces.

"Our children are not lies," she said gently, pleading with him silently to forgive her, if it took a lifetime.

"No," he said, with tears choking him, "but thanks to you, they're bastards." He turned away from her then, into the men's barracks, where she couldn't follow him. And she went back to sit next to her sister. Victoria was asleep by then, and a nurse put a finger to her lips and asked Olivia not to wake her. She was exhausted, and the fever was higher.

Olivia didn't see Charles again that day. She didn't know where he went, but he never came back to the hospital tent, and she wondered if he was planning to leave now without her. If he did, she'd have to deal with it. She was planning to stay until she could bring Victoria home with her baby. Olivia slept in a chair beside her all night, trying to block out the noise of the men who were suffering and dying. Her sister woke once or twice, and whenever Olivia walked around to stretch, people spoke to her, thinking she was her sister. It was particularly unnerving since they called her by her right name, as Victoria had been known as Olivia here, to everyone but Edouard.

Charles appeared at Victoria's bedside again finally the next morning. She was awake, and Olivia had just left to get some coffee.

"That was quite a performance yesterday," she said to him, looking tired, but still mean enough to fight him. And he smiled at her, some things don't change. He could see now what she had said, that they could never have been married. He had done a lot of thinking during the night.

"You took me by surprise. That was quite a revelation," he said and she narrowed her eyes at him. She didn't believe him.

"I don't think so, Charles, not really. Are you telling me you never knew, never even suspected, that she was never any different than I am? Look at us, she's gentle and soft and loving and would lay down her life for you even now. You and I would kill each other, given half a chance. We're like the French and the Germans." They both smiled. It was true and they knew it. "Don't tell me you never knew, never wondered, never thought it. You must have, at least once . . . maybe twice . . . or more . . . but you chose not to know it."

"You may be right," he admitted, which surprised her. "Maybe I didn't want to know. It was so easy and so comfortable, and so good. I wanted it so much to work between us, and maybe Olivia was the answer."

"Don't forget that now. Don't destroy her because you're angry." She was very firm with him. She didn't want him to hurt her sister.

"You're amazing, you two," he said with a sigh, admiring her in a way. She was so strong, so willing to do anything for her sister, just as Olivia was for her. "I'm not sure it's a relationship I'll ever understand. It's like two souls, and one person. Or maybe it's the other way around," he smiled. "I don't think outsiders ever understand it."

"You could be right. I feel her in my heart sometimes. I know when she needs me." As she did now. Olivia was in a terrible state over the things Charles had said to her the previous morning.

"She says the same thing," he said quietly. And then he remembered something and it all came clear now. It was right after Olivia had supposedly left for California. "Were you on the *Lusitania,* by any chance?" he asked with a strange look, and she nodded.

"I don't have much luck with ocean voyages," she said ruefully, and he smiled.

"She kept dreaming she was drowning. I had to call a doctor for her."

"It took me three days to send her a telegram, things were crazy in Queenstown. I could never tell you what all that was like. Compared to that," she remembered the woman giving birth in the water next to her, before she passed out, "this is nothing. The children were what made it so awful." She closed her eyes then to block it out, and he touched her hand. He could sense that she was fading.

"What about you now? What do you want me to do?" He had come here to make peace with her. For him, despite his shock initially, the war with her was over.

"I have a child. I want Ollie to take him home with her," she said clearly, her eyes filling with tears as she thought of him and his father. She hadn't seen her baby in two weeks now, and she ached to see him.

"How did that happen?" He looked surprised, and she laughed through her tears at the man who had once been her husband.

"Same way it happened to you and Ollie. I wish I could see your little girls," she said wistfully.

"You will," he said, forgiving her for all she'd done, though he wasn't sure why, but it didn't seem to matter anymore. It was over. He had come here to tell her that, that it didn't matter. And if she wanted, he'd divorce her. "You'll see the girls when you come home," he said, willing her to believe it, but she shook her head with a look that said she knew better.

"No, I won't Charles . . . I know it . . ." She didn't look frightened, only wistful.

"Don't be silly. That's why we're here. To take you home . . . and your baby." Life was never simple. "Where's his father?" Charles asked gently, wondering if he'd ever known her.

"He died . . . that's when I got wounded."

"Well, get better, so I can take you home and divorce you." He smiled and bent to kiss her, and she looked up at him strangely.

"You know . . . in my own crazy way, I suppose I did love you. It just wasn't right for either of us . . . but I meant to do it right in the beginning."

"So did I," he said wistfully, "I don't think I'd gotten over Susan."

"Go find your wife . . . or your sister-in-law . . . or whatever she is . . .'' She tried to laugh but it hurt too much and she was getting woozy.

"Good-bye, crazy girl . . . I'll see you later," he said and left her then, with a very odd feeling. He didn't know what it was, but he was beginning to feel like Olivia, with all her premonitions.

He went back to the mess tent then, to look for her, but he couldn't find her. And she wasn't at the women's barracks either. He managed to miss her all that afternoon, and he realized as he walked around that it was his wedding anniversary that day. Their second. The question was with which woman? He had to smile at the absurdity of it all, and when he went back to check on Victoria again, he saw Olivia sound asleep in a chair beside her, and Victoria was sleeping too. The two were holding hands as they slept and looked almost like children.

"How is she?" he asked the nurse, and she only shrugged and shook her head. The infection was moving slowly upward. It was hard to believe. She was so coherent at times, so outrageous and still so feisty, and so fuzzy at others. Olivia had seen both sides of her as she sat there. Charles disappeared without waking either of them, and at midnight, Olivia called the nurse. She herself was having pains in her chest, and she could see that Victoria was having trouble breathing.

"She can't breathe," Olivia explained for her, but her twin looked mostly sleepy.

"Yes, she can," the nurse insisted, "she's all right." As all right as she could be under the circumstances, but Olivia knew better. She put a damp cloth on her brow, and propped her up a little bit, and when Victoria woke up again, she smiled at her sister.

"It's okay, Ollie . . . don't . . . Edouard's waiting."

"No," Olivia said furiously, suddenly panicked at the look on her face. She was slipping away, and no one was doing anything to stop it. "No . . . you can't do that, dammit. You can't quit." Olivia was crying as she held her.

"I'm so tired," she said sleepily, "let me go, Ollie."

"I won't." She felt as though she were wrestling with the devil.

"Okay, okay . . . I'll be good . . . go to sleep," she said to her older sister. And Olivia held her for a long time, watching her, and then finally Victoria slipped into a peaceful sleep, and Olivia felt easier about her. Victoria opened her eyes and looked at her once, and smiled at her, and Olivia leaned down and kissed her. Victoria kissed her back, and whispered something to her, and when Olivia listened to her she heard her say she loved her.

"I love you too." She lay her head down on the pillow with her and slept for a while, and dreamed that they were children.

They were playing in a field in Croton, near their mother's grave, and their father was watching them and he was laughing. Everyone looked so happy.

And in the morning, when she woke, Olivia looked down at her, and she was gone. There was a small, sweet smile on her lips, and she held her sister's hand. But there had been no holding her back from it. Olivia had tried everything she could, but Victoria had gone to play with the others.

Chapter 33

When Olivia came out of the hospital tent that day, she was reeling. It was the twenty-first of June, 1916, and her twin was dead, half of her life, half of her soul, half of her being. She couldn't imagine being alone without her. Even though they had been apart for the past year, Olivia always knew she was there somewhere and she would see her. Now she would never see her again. She was gone. It was over. Finished. She had lost Charles, would have to give her children up, and now she had lost her twin sister. She couldn't imagine a worse fate than hers, and she wanted to scream at Victoria to take her with her. She didn't want to live another day without her. And then, as though she could hear her sister's voice in her head, Olivia remembered her promise to take her baby.

She walked into one of the office tents, and asked if it was possible to get a driver to take her to the château. She explained what she wanted, and a young French boy smiled at her and offered to take her. He had known Edouard and Olivia, as he called her, though he didn't know yet that she was dead. And Olivia couldn't bring herself to tell him. He said it was only a short drive away, and she thought of telling Charles, but she knew she couldn't tell him anything anymore. She had lost her right to. He had told her she meant nothing to him now, she was nothing to him. And he didn't even know it yet, but at that moment, he had been widowed.

Olivia was already on her way to the château when Charles went back to the medical tent to see Victoria. And when he got there, the nurse shook her head and pointed at the empty bed, and he stood there gaping. He didn't even feel sad for her suddenly, he had known that she wanted to be released, he had sensed it easily, but all he wanted now was to find Olivia and console her. Despite how he felt about her deception, he could only begin to imagine her grief that morning. It was unthinkable, and he knew he had to find her quickly.

"Have you seen my wife . . . my . . . er . . . her sister?" he asked the nurse. It was still all too confusing, but she shook her head, and told him she had left, after her sister had died, sometime around seven. He looked for her in the mess tent, but couldn't find her anywhere. By then Olivia had been to the château, and been told where the chatelaine was. She was in Toul, which was a two-hour journey, and Marcel, the boy who had driven her there, had agreed to take her.

She said very little to him on the trip east, he glanced at her once or twice, and saw that she was crying softly. He offered her a cigarette, and she shook her head, and finally looked at him. He was so young, barely eighteen. They talked about the war for a while, and then finally they were in Toul. Olivia met the countess, at the little house they'd been sent to, and then, as the countess offered her sympathy, she showed Olivia the baby. He was beautiful and round and blonde and happy. There was a feeling of Victoria about him, even more than his looks. In fact, her own children looked more like her sister than he did, but he was very lovely, and he cooed happily when she held him. It was almost as though he knew she had come to take him, and he made her lonely not only for Victoria, but for her own children.

The countess was sad to say good-bye to him, but she was glad he was going home to safety with his aunt, and then she urged Marcel to be careful. The lines had been shifting for weeks and there had been snipers in the hills daily, as Olivia knew only too well. She held the baby on her lap on the way back, and he slept most of the way, and then, halfway back, Marcel saw something he didn't like on his left, and swerved away, as bullets narrowly missed them.

"Merde!" he said without hesitation. "Get down," he told her, and she crouched on the floor of the car, holding the baby. The snipers shot at him again and he sped away, but then he heard gunfire again, and shells up ahead, and he drove down an old country road, into an old, deserted farm, and hid the car in the stable. He pointed to the loft, and they hurried up the ladder leaning there, as she carried the baby. This was not what they had planned, Olivia thought to herself, trying to assess the situation. Things did not look good, as she sat in the hay with an eighteen-year-old French boy with his gun drawn, and her dead sister's baby.

No one came after them, and they sat there all day, unable to go anywhere, as little knots of Germans moved all around them. They never came as close as the barn, but the barn was in an open field and there was no cover for them to leave it. There was no way they could go anywhere, and they had neither food nor water for themselves or the baby.

"What are we going to do?" she asked nervously. The baby was beginning to cry, and she was not nearly as brave as her sister. She had only come here to get her. She had never expected to do anything like this, but for Victoria and her child, she had been willing to be somewhat heroic.

"We'll have to try it again after nightfall," Marcel said with a worried expression. There was nothing else they could do. By that night, they could hear heavy shelling closer to them, and the whistle of mortars. She just prayed there wouldn't be a gas attack, she hadn't even brought her gas mask. In the shock of leaving Victoria at the hospital when she died, Olivia had lost it somewhere.

"We have to feed him," Olivia said finally about the baby. He hadn't been fed for hours and by then little Olivier was screaming. He wanted his mother, or someone he knew, or at the very least some dinner. But at least in one way, Olivia had an advantage. He looked at her, and thought he knew her. But familiar or not, she had nothing to give him. She had stopped nursing months before, and she never even thought of trying.

It was nightfall when they came out of the loft at last, and Marcel suggested she stay there and wait, and he would go back to the camp on foot through the bushes. He wanted to get help, but he didn't want her to take the risk of coming with him. He insisted it wouldn't take him more than two hours, and then he could send help for her. It sounded reasonable, but terrifying to her anyway. She knew that if the Germans captured him, they might come back looking for her and shoot her. Or she and Olivier might never be found at all, and they might just simply stay there and starve. But even if they killed her, she hoped that at least the Germans would spare the baby. But Olivia had no other choice, and twelve hours after they'd set out from camp, Marcel left her in the farmhouse, and she watched as he sprinted away toward safety. He was almost to the trees at the end of the field when she saw them shoot him in the head and the back. She saw him go down, and lie facedown at the edge of the field.

There was no hope of his being alive, he lay completely motionless, and the snipers never even bothered to check him. They knew he was dead, just as Olivia did, and they moved on to other pastures, leaving Marcel dead in a field somewhere in France, and Olivia trapped in a farmhouse with her sister's starving baby. This was not how it was meant to be, and she had no idea what to do now. The only thing she could do was wait and see if anyone ever came by, Allies preferably, or even farmers, or get in the car and drive hell for leather. But she had only driven once or twice before, and she wasn't at all sure she could even start the car, let alone drive it.

"So what do we do now?" she asked Olivier, who had finally cried himself to sleep in her arms, even without dinner.

But he was awake again at six o'clock the next morning. He was desperate for food or drink, and Olivia cried as she listened to his angry wailing. She had nothing to give him, and felt as though she were failing her sister. He hadn't seen food in eighteen hours, and neither had she, and she was afraid he would get dehydrated if she didn't get him some milk or water quickly. She thought about walking back to camp with him in her arms, or even telling the

Germans she was American if they stopped her, but she was afraid they might shoot first and ask questions later. In the end, she did absolutely nothing, she just sat there praying the baby would fall asleep again at last. And finally in desperation, she lifted her shirt and nursed him. She had no milk, but at least it seemed to offer him some small comfort, and she no longer had to worry that passing snipers might hear him.

At last at four o'clock in the afternoon, she heard two trucks roar by, and when she looked out the tiny window in the loft, she could see that they were Allies. She let out a shout and waved a hand through the broken panes and they stopped and circled back, as she came quickly down the ladder, holding the baby, and she was surprised that Sergeant Morrison was in one truck, with a driver, and Charles was being driven in the other. When she and Marcel did not return, at Charles' insistence, they had sent a convoy for her.

"Thank God," she said, looking at all of them at once, relieved beyond belief that they had found her. She had been sure they never would and she and Olivier would die. She had just about given up hope when they found her. But Charles said not a word to her, as he sat in

732

the truck, staring at her. And to Olivia he still looked extremely angry.

"You could have gotten killed," he said icily, his voice and hands shaking. This whole experience had been beyond the worst of anything he could have imagined. Their revelations to him, Victoria's death, the war itself, the wounded boys, and Olivia nearly getting killed now, trapped in a farmhouse, trying to save her sister's baby. It was all too much for him to stomach, and he could barely speak as he watched her.

"I'm sorry," she said quietly to him, trying to brace herself against the force of his hatred. But oddly enough, to him it made her sound like her sister. He didn't even get a chance to tell her how sorry he was about that, before Sergeant Morrison whisked her into the truck with the baby, and they went back to camp as quickly as possible before nightfall. Olivia had told them about Marcel, but they'd had men in the area the night before, and already knew it. They were going to come back with a detail later, for his body, and five others. It was awful. "I'm so sorry," she said to Sergeant Morrison, about Marcel, about the war, about Victoria, about the look in Charles' eyes when he looked at her now. She knew now that he would never forgive her. And as soon as they got back, she went to the mess hall to feed the child, and he went to the office to try to arrange passage on a ship out of Bordeaux. They were burying Victoria in the morning, and Olivia felt almost numb. It was all too much to absorb now.

Her burial, such as it was, was small and strange. A priest intoned a few words over her, and a dozen others. They buried her in a plain pine box with no name and no marking on her grave. She was just a small white cross on a hillside in France. Olivia just hoped they had put her somewhere near Edouard. But she was so shocked, she could barely cry. She was too dazed to feel anything as she stood there. She felt as though they were burying part of her, her heart, her soul, her mind. Olivia felt like loose parts with no mind at all, as she watched them lower her sister into the ground, and held her sleeping baby. He had eaten and drunk his fill again, but in order to comfort him, Olivia had continued to nurse him.

Charles watched her face at the graveside, aghast at what she must feel, but out of sheer pride, she didn't let him anywhere near her. They stood like two strangers, watching Victoria's body lowered into the ground so far from home, and Olivia put a small white flower on the grave, and cried as she walked away, holding the baby. She could hardly breathe it was so terrible. It was as though they had buried her, and maybe they had. She had lost everything she loved in the last week, even her children. But the loss of her twin was much more than that, it was something physical that hurt so much she thought she would go mad from the pain of it. It was almost beyond bearing.

They walked slowly back to the heart of the camp crying and not speaking, both of them trying to absorb that Victoria had just been buried. And before he could say anything to her, Olivia disappeared into the women's barracks and didn't come out until morning. Charles asked for her several times, but the people he asked were busy, tired, and didn't seem to know her. There had been a recent influx of volunteers and the women didn't know Olivia or her sister.

The nurses in the women's tent took the baby from Olivia when she came in, and she just lay on her cot and cried all day. There was no one she wanted to see or talk to, not even Charles, who she knew was still so angry at her. All she could think of were the things he'd said to her after she and Victoria had told him the truth, and the way he had looked when he came to find her at the farmhouse.

They left for Bordeaux again the next morning at six o'clock, and before they left, Olivia thanked Sergeant Morrison again, and all the nurses. Didier came up to her with tears in his eyes, and kissed the baby good-bye, saying he would never forget him, or his mother. There were a handful of people waving good-bye as they left and Olivia didn't know who most of them were, but the sad truth of it was that it no longer mattered.

They were in Bordeaux late that afternoon and waited in the lobby of a small hotel to board the ship at midnight. They had hardly any luggage with them, and Olivia bought only a few things for the baby. All she wanted now was to get him home safely. Nursing him, and loving him in her sister's place, had begun to create a strong bond between them. And little by little, even three months after her babies' birth, as she nursed him, her milk started coming. But more than anything, nephew or son, she felt as though he were the final gift from her sister. And he was even more precious to her for that reason.

"What are you going to do with him?" Charles asked her quietly as they waited in the hotel to board the *Espagne* again. They had only been gone from New York for two weeks, but it felt like forever.

"I'll take him to Croton with me," she said quietly, as Charles watched her.

"Is that where you're going?" he asked politely, and she nodded.

"I assume so," she answered and he didn't say anything after that, until they boarded.

They had two cabins on the return trip. He had requested them, assuming she'd want them. The proprieties had to be observed now as Mr. Charles Dawson, and Miss Olivia Henderson, and baby. Things were a little different than on the way over. And Charles literally never saw her while they were on board. He was still licking his wounds, thinking of Victoria, and the mess they'd previously made, and keeping his distance. And sensing all of it, Olivia never came out of her cabin, or if she did, he never saw her.

He spent most of his time alone, thinking of the last time he'd seen Victoria, and the things she'd said. She'd been right about all of it. And he felt as though he'd made his peace with her, and she with him, and he thought too about the things she'd said about her sister. He could only imagine what a blow it must have

737

been to Olivia to lose her, the tearing of flesh from flesh, soul from soul, the peeling of their hearts away, or maybe just the breaking of one heart. He couldn't even imagine how Olivia was going to live without her. Nor could he imagine that they had been crazy enough to switch places and have Olivia live with him, as man and wife, for an entire year, and not tell him. He thought of what Victoria had said then, that he must have known, and didn't want to. He wondered if there was some truth in that, and thought of the times when he'd almost suspected and then forced the thoughts out of his mind because it was easier not to have them. He realized too that Victoria must have promised Olivia a loveless relationship with no physical demands involved, and then everything had changed . . . but everything had changed because . . . she'd been so gentle . . . and so kind . . . and he had wanted her so badly. And married or not, he had had something with her that he had never had with any other woman. He remembered too the night the twins had been born. Stranger yet, he had realized, as had Victoria and Olivia, that if you took the time difference between the two places away, their babies had been born within a few hours of each other. It was all so strange and so incredible, and so difficult to sort out where one began and another ended, where the lie was, or the truth, or merely the discreet intention, it was difficult to know what had been love, or desire, and she had been right about that too, he had been afraid to love her, and he hadn't let her love him. But with Olivia it had all been so different. He had lived a year with each of them, as insane as that was, and it was clear to him now, who was his wife and the woman he loved, and who wasn't.

It was their third day out, halfway to New York from France, when he finally couldn't stand it any longer, and knocked on the door of her cabin. Hers was smaller than his, but she had insisted on it, and she had told him she would reimburse him as soon as they got home, which he found insulting. He did not expect, or want, to be paid for her passage.

Olivia opened the door about two inches, and she looked terrible. Thin and pale and tired, and it was obvious she had been crying.

"May I come in?" he asked politely. She hesitated, and then opened the door a trifle wider.

"The baby's sleeping," she said, as though to discourage him, and he smiled.

"I'll try to keep my voice down. I've

wanted to talk to you for days. Since before your sister died, in fact. But I couldn't get near you. I saw her the morning before . . . we had a good talk."

"She told me. She said you weren't angry at her anymore."

"I wasn't. I think she was right about a lot of things. I was just too stupid to know it. She was smarter and braver than I was. I'd have stuck around till the ship went down, as it were. She got out. I should have."

"That's not always easy," Olivia said softly, knowing it only too well now. But in her case, there was nothing to be out of. They weren't married. It was all delusion.

"I wanted to apologize to you," Olivia said then formally. "You were right about what you said too. We had no right to do that to you. It was wrong . . . I don't know what made us think it was all right, that we had a right to . . . I just thought . . . I don't know, it seemed my only chance at a life with you, which was really crazy."

"Not really." He smiled at her, still a bit stunned at what they'd done, but in some ways, he could see their reasoning, though it still scared him a little. "There really was no other way we could have gotten together. And you were both right. We were good together."

"Were we?" she asked sadly.

"We are," he said softly. "We're very good together, Olivia. It would be wrong to give that up now. That's not what she wanted," he said very gently, afraid to even go near her, she looked so upset and so frightened.

"And what do you want?" Olivia asked him, remembering the things he'd said and the look of hatred, both outside the mess tent and at the farmhouse, where he had looked as though he wanted to kill her. She had never seen him as angry. What she didn't know was that he'd never been as afraid. He was sure, by then, that she had been murdered by the Germans, with or without the baby. And all he wanted to do was to bring her back from the dead and shake her.

"I want you," Charles said softly, "just like we've had for the last year, like we could have been from the beginning, if I'd told your father to go fly a kite with his crazy wild daughter, with all due respect to your sister, and if I'd been brave enough to go after you in the first place. I knew then I could have fallen in love with you, and she was right, I was afraid of you, and of her. I was so damn afraid of loving you that I ran right into her arms, because she was wild and exciting and safe, and I knew there was no chance on earth I'd ever love her."

"You were almost as crazy as we were." Olivia smiled at him as the baby stirred in the crib behind her. "That's a really stupid reason to get married."

"Then maybe we deserve each other." He smiled shyly, and then she tried to explain something to him which made him smile more broadly.

"You know I never intended to . . . Victoria said . . ." He knew exactly what she meant and she was blushing darkly as she said it.

"I don't believe a word of it, you had every intention of seducing me . . . I know you did . . ." He argued with her, and took her in his arms as he did so, wishing she would do it again, but he wasn't at all sure what she'd do now. He had been incredibly cruel to her, and she had every right not to forgive him. And then he thought of something else, and asked her another question. "Did Geoff know, or suspect? He always knew you so well, and could tell you apart when no one else could."

"I fooled him for a while," she said. "I think he suspected a little bit, but I made a point of being nasty to both of you from time to time, so you wouldn't. But when I cut my hand in Croton last June, he saw the freckle before I could stop him."

"And he's known all this time?" She nodded apologetically. "Amazing." He reached for her hand then, and looked down at it. The freckle was in her right palm, but tears filled her eyes as she looked at it. It didn't matter anymore. She was gone, there would be no more games or laughter or deceptions.

She turned away from him then and bowed her head in pain. "I miss her so much," she whispered.

"So do I," he said softly. "I miss knowing that she's someone special in your life, that she's there for you, that you're happy," he said sadly. "I miss seeing you smile . . . and loving you . . . and being with you . . . I'm sorry for all the terrible things I said . . . I'm sorry I took it so badly at first." And then he cried just as she did, "I'm sorry you lost her."

She nodded and stood crying in his arms for a long time as he held her, and then finally she looked at the man who had almost been her husband. "I loved you, Charles . . . I'm really sorry."

"And now? Could you still love me?"

743

She smiled at him, it was a foolish question. She would always love him. "Of course I could. I still do. You can't change that."

"Will you marry me then?" he asked her solemnly, and meant it.

"Wouldn't that be a little embarrassing for you, or a little odd at the very least? And certainly scandalous if anyone knew why you were doing it."

"I'm not in the least embarrassed. I think it's far more embarrassing to be surrounded by children, none of them legal, or far too few at least. I was thinking that the captain could marry us here, on the ship, before we even get home." He smiled at her, and she smiled back at him. She loved the idea of marrying him on the way home, and then staying with him. And everything would at last be legal. He got down on one knee then and held her hand in his and asked her to marry him and she giggled. "Well, do you accept?" he asked formally.

"I do."

"Thank you," he said and stood up and kissed her. "I'll talk to the captain." And as he said the words, the baby started to scream, and Olivia looked at him with a smile and glanced at her future husband.

"You know, with Olivier, it will be like triplets."

"Maybe he'll put a little balance in their lives," he said pointedly at her, and she looked sheepish, and he kissed her again and left her cabin to make the arrangements, as she picked the baby up to nurse him.

They were married the next day at noon in the captain's cabin, and she wore the only decent dress she had, a green one, and carried the only flowers the ship's florist had, white carnations. This was wartime. Charles kissed the bride when the captain declared them man and wife, and the next day as they steamed toward New York, they radioed Geoff and Bertie and told them they were on their way home to New York, due to arrive on Friday. And they signed the radiogram Dad and Ollie. They were standing on deck, at the rail of the ship as the *Espagne* pulled slowly and safely into New York Harbor at last, and Bertie was on the dock with Geoff, and both babies. They were each carrying one, and as Geoff waved at them, he looked puzzled as he saw the child in his father's arms, and Olivia knew they'd have to explain it all to him, as best they could, and save the rest till he was older. But she saw him staring at her as the ship drew near, and she held Charles' hand. He was trying to see which one she was, who had come home, and then she saw him nod and say something to Bertie, and then he waved frantically at her. He had recognized her. She had come home to him again. He hadn't lost his beloved Ollie. It was Olivia who had lost the dearest person in her life this time, the sister who had been her partner, her confidante, her friend, her cohort in all mischief. She couldn't imagine being without her now, not having her to argue with, or laugh with. It was going to be a different world for Olivia without her, and she knew that she would always feel a part of her missing, but at the same time she knew she would always be there, in her head, and heart, and soul, and she could not forget her. For her, Victoria had been the person she had loved most until Charles and her children. She was the other side of her life, her heart . . . the other side of the mirror.